CAVERNS

PENGUIN BOOKS

LYNN JEFFRESS   KEN KESEY   NEIL LIDSTROM

H. HIGHWATER POWERS

JANE SATHER

O.U. LEVON

MEREDITH WADLEY   CHARLES VARANI

PENGUIN BOOKS

Published by the Penguin Group

Viking Penguin, a division of Penguin Books USA Inc.,

40 West 23rd Street, New York, New York 10010, U.S.A.

Penguin Books Ltd, 27 Wrights Lane, London W8 5TZ, England

Penguin Books Australia Ltd, Ringwood, Victoria, Australia

Penguin Books Canada Ltd, 2801 John Street,

Markham, Ontario, Canada L3R 1B4

Penguin Books (N.Z.) Ltd, 182–190 Wairau Road,

Auckland 10, New Zealand

Penguin Books Ltd, Registered Offices:

Harmondsworth, Middlesex, England

First published in Penguin Books 1990

1 3 5 7 9 10 8 6 4 2

Library of Congress Cataloging in Publication Data

Levon, O. U.

Caverns: a novel / by O. U. Levon.

p.   cm.

ISBN 0 14 01.2208 7

I. Title.

PS3562.E924C38   1990

813'.54—dc20   89-16307

Printed in the United States of America

Set in Meridien

Designed by Michael Ian Kaye

to Barbara Platz
who took the time

—*San Francisco Chronicle*

All that is visible must grow beyond itself into the invisible.

—*The I Ching*

"Don't try to find the answer; try to find the mystery!"

—*Grandpa Loach*

You Can't Mistake

Those Burning Eyes

An Introduction by Ken Kesey

Before the Reagan administration cut off liberal money to the arts and humanities I traveled around to a lot of posh little writing-teaching gigs. They'd fly you in, you'd get a pile of manuscripts to look over, and a bunch of students. After some seminars and receptions you'd take your check and fly home.

The money was good, the hours short, the limelight sweet; but when I look back and try to figure out "what exactly did I *teach* those people?" the only thing that stands out occurred, I think, at a weekend fiction workshop somewhere in Texas. Thirty students had been picked by the regents—not on their ability, I gradually found out, but according to how much money their family had donated to the university.

One of this chosen thirty was a nervous old lady, blue-haired, about sixty-five; donated a lot of money to the history wing of the library, one of the regents confided before he introduced her. She was famous locally for her letters to the editor. She was known throughout the state as a philanthropist, activist, and amateur anthropologist. But I discerned at once that what she wanted to be known as, above all, was a writer. You can't mistake those burning eyes. . . .

When her turn came she pitty-patted primly to the front of the class with a gay bouquet of pink-inked pages, and began reading—a tale dealing with her youth in an orchard where she was trying to pick peaches, and her mature life in a nursing home where she was trying to teach people who could barely speak the English language something about English literature. And about her husband and his near rise to the Senate, poor man. Chopped in among all this was a goodly selection of whatever non-sequitur oil-widow opinions she happened across in the old ice box. The result was schizoid stir-fry. "My daddy's jackknife was never sharp enough for him, and if the Communists had got around to it, they might have built better, but, the truth is, the best book in the world is *Gone With the Wind* and my daddy knew that by the time we got to the airport we were never going to find our way home."

I listened to her sing-song this sort of stuff for forty-five minutes. I was amazed, impressed, appalled, touched, embarrassed. Most of all, I was pissed. Nobody'd screened this story at all! Or, worse, *had* screened it but felt that telling the old dame that her story was unseemly gibberish might be fiscally imprudent.

By the time she'd been reading about half an hour, she didn't have to be told. She knew. Everyone who has ever read in front of an audience knows—"Eek! This is hideous bloody awful and I'm only halfway through!" The gleam started going out of those old eyes but she sing-songed bravely on. The manuscript began to shiver in her hand like dead weeds; the preppies at the back of the room started sniggering, finally laughing out loud. When she finished and sank back into her seat there was blood in the water of that Texas classroom. Twenty-nine sharks were ready to show off their literary chops, and our old dowager knew she deserved devouring.

Luckily, I remembered something that Malcolm Cowley had taught us at Stanford—perhaps the most important lesson a writing class (not a writer, understand, but a class) can ever learn. "Be gentle," he often admonished us, "with each other's efforts. Be kind and considerate with your criticism. Always remember that it's just as hard to write a bad book as it is to write a good book."

I was able to pass this lesson on to that Texas workshop, and it worked. It was oil on bloody waters. We were all grateful.

Every writer I know teaches. At some point you have to, even if you don't have to. It's like having to yell instructions during a high school wrestling match if you used to be a collegiate grappler. You may not have been any world beater but you had your own little specialty—two or three good moves that you could pull out of your pocket, a few simple tricks, like "Look away from the half-nelson!" or "Swing out on that bar-arm!" For some reason you *have* to yell these things, *have* to teach what you were taught—especially if you were taught by a great coach.

It's been my good fortune to have a number of such coaches. Bill Hammer taught me the bar-arm series—the basis of most pinning-hold combinations. In Speech 101 Robert C. Clark taught me the three secrets of good diction, "Lips, tongue and teeth! Lips, tongue and teeth!" And a great writer-teacher named James B. Hall revealed for me one of the keyholes of literature.

I n t r o d u c t i o n

I was a junior at the University of Oregon, majoring in Speech and Drama. One of the requirements toward a degree was a term of TV writing. My screenplay instructor told me, "You need to learn something about *story*. I'm transferring you to J. B. Hall's fiction class."

Fine with me; I loved fiction, especially the science sort. Ray Bradbury was my favorite. "They don't get any better than Bradbury," I was fond of explaining. Then, Professor Hall had me read a story by Ernest Hemingway, called "Soldier's Home," and asked me to explain to the class what the story was about.

"Well"—I shrugged—"all I can see is it's about this guy Krebs sitting in his mother's kitchen eating breakfast. She's hollering on him about getting out of the house and getting a job and developing some interests now that the war is over but all he wants to do is go watch his sister play baseball someplace—"

"No!" Professor Hall said. "Here's what it's about—here!" He strode over in his white shoes and stabbed a finger on a paragraph in the middle of my textbook. "Right after his mother has served him his bacon and eggs and is telling him how she carried him next to her heart . . . what does Krebs *do*? What does he *look at*? Read it again—aloud."

The paragraph was only one line long. "Krebs looked at the bacon fat hardening on his plate."

"That's what the story is about! That one line is the key. That line sounds the note for all the rest of the story. The whole composition would be in disharmony without that key to tune it. See?"

Damned if I didn't. That key unlocked for me the great resounding hall of real literature, and eventually got me in the door. A couple of short stories won me a Woodrow Wilson to the famous Wallace Stegner writing class at Stanford.

Professor Stegner mistook me, I fear, for an anti-intellectual, not understanding that I was in fact something far less presumptuous—a near-illiterate, especially compared to the rest of his blue-chip roster. There was C. J. Koch from Australia (*Year of Living Dangerously*), Ernest Gaines (*The Autobiography of Miss Jane Pittman*), Tillie Olsen (*Tell Me a Riddle*), Peter Beagle (*A Fine and Private Place, The Last Unicorn*), Robert Stone (*A Hall of Mirrors, Dog Soldiers, A Flag for Sunrise, Children of Light*), Ken Babbs (*Cassady in the Backhouse*), a trio called the Kentucky Mafia—Wendell Berry, Ed McClanahan, and Gurney Norman—all with numerous and notable novels and collections in print, and Larry McMurtry, with a pile of work that should stretch—if all the pages are ever laid end-to-end—from Texas to Stockholm.

xiii

There were others but you get the idea: a hell of a team, like Green Bay under Lombardi. And when you include the assistant coaches—Richard Scowcroft, Malcolm Cowley, Frank O'Connor—you've got a hell of a program. Maybe we weren't entirely aware of this at the time (this was in the wild young years of the early sixties, remember; there was a lot to be aware of), but we have all surely looked back on those seasons together with something like awe.

There is a binding tie about being part of a good, tight team, a bond that never fully unravels when the season ends and the members go their different directions. Most of us still keep in touch and many of us are lifetime friends. Family. My kids, Ed's kids, Wendell's kids, and Bob Stone's kids all have known each other all their lives. Ken Babbs' kids have all gone to the same school as mine, kindergarten to graduation.

Moreover, Cowley's lesson has kept us all available to each other as kind and considerate critics. We can send each other unfinished drafts without fear of getting cleverly gutted by some green-eyed literary demon with a grudge to grind. When *A Flag for Sunrise* wins Bob Stone the National Book Award, or Larry gets the Pulitzer for *Lonesome Dove*, I feel nothing but joy for their glory. Does us all proud. Another of Cowley's teachings: "Good writing glories all writers. You aren't in competition."

So, okay. All well and good to say but after doing enough of those posh little weekend workshops I learned it isn't so easy to bring off. Competition is often in full swing before the visiting coach gets there. If young Mr. Melonhead comes down hard on Ms. Melancholia's tender tale of troubled teenage girls in the bougainvillea, you can bet your best thesaurus that Ms. Melancholia is going to thump Melonhead roundly for his roisterous romp in the ROTC camp. After years of refereeing this cruel and futile give-and-take I hit upon a plan: Have everybody work on the same project. Even better than walking a mile in the other writer's moccasins, mix them up till nobody can be sure whose are whose.

After talking this plan over with a number of people at the University of Oregon for a number of years, I eventually got a crack at it. I had the writing department pick me out a baker's dozen from the Creative Writing program—second-year grad students ranging from ages twenty-two to forty-two. Our house was the classroom. My wife and I own this two-story place near campus—are making payments on it anyway—but we had never lived there. It's about two blocks from the U of O library. The living room in it is big enough to hold thirteen people around a long table. This table is important. The table in the Jones Room at Stanford was as important as the books on the shelves. It was long and oval-shape with an indentation at one end where the teacher sat, like a captain at the helm. Our living room table wasn't as classy but it served.

The first day of class I headed in from the farm, nervous and late. My palms were moist and my mouth was dry. I was driving my 1973 Eldorado convertible, white with red trim, hoping to make an impressive entrance. I swing into the drive and there they all are, waiting. But the house is locked and Faye gone and I don't have the key to get in. Farm boy. I get through a little window into the basement but the door is locked at the top of the basement steps. I crawl back out. I find one rear window that I can see isn't locked, but it is painted so tight I can't get it open. I get the tire iron out of the car, pry it into the sill, push the window open. I get a good grip, make a jump, hit my head on the bottom of the window frame I've just pried up, knock myself clean out. I fall in with my legs sticking up and as I'm coming to I hear somebody outside say, "Well, that's Curly . . . wonder when Larry and Moe get here?"

The first assignment was that they write a character sketch about themselves. In the third person. Doesn't take very long, an assignment like that. As I collected the papers I told them the goals and the rules of the class. The goals were to conceive, rough-out, write, rewrite, and submit a finished novel in the three terms allotted us. The rules were even simpler and fewer, only two. The first rule being that we cannot tell anybody outside the class the plot of the novel we are working on; the second was that I make up half the class. In a critical dispute I wanted to be able to call gee or haw and keep plowing. A crop like we were going to try to bring in didn't have time to luxuriate in literary debate; the season was too short.

After reading the character sketches that came back I said, "Okay, it's clear to me you guys can write. We can all write. Now; *what* will we write?"

It took several sessions of this before they all gradually came to the grudging realization that I really *didn't* have a cold idea in hell what we were going to write—no plot, no characters, nothing. I did come up with some suggestions about what to avoid:

"Don't let's set it in a university. The university novel is Saul Bellow's corner, or Philip Roth's corner. I also suggest that we don't set it in current time, that way we avoid having to compete with the hip 'Miami Vice' kind of current-time dialogue. And just as I suggest we arbitrarily *do not* write about this place, or this time, I suggest as well that we *do not* write about what we know. One of the dumbest things you were ever taught was write what you know. Because what you know is usually dull. Remember when you first wanted to be a writer? Eight or ten years old, reading about thin-lipped heroes flying over mysterious viney jungles towards untold wonders? That's what you wanted to write about, about what you *didn't* know. So. What mysterious time and place *don't we know* . . . ?"

We gnawed this bony problem for a week or so before we realized something—that it's hard to create any sort of righteous plot without some character. Character comes first. Medea doesn't start in a soap writers' meeting—"I got it! Let's do a thing about a wife that gets beaked at her old man and kills the kids." No. Medea starts with the character of Medea. This prompted another assignment. "Let's arbitrarily pick a time before any of us were here. I was born in 1935. Let's go back to 1934 and each design a character that fits into that tme, then we'll let them go somewhere."

I n t r o d u c t i o n

They came back with a collection that would have made Chaucer grin. This pack of pilgrims had integrity. Independence. Some of them were as independent, as my Grandmother used to say, as a hog on ice. They wouldn't be manipulated. We tried to set up love affairs between Such and So, only to find that So wouldn't have any of it, and neither would Such. The best we could get them all to agree to was that they were all going someplace together.

"What place? The road to Canterbury is long ago loaded, the Mississippi choked with rafts and runaway slaves. Hunting whales on the high seas is out of vogue and Lost Horizons on Tibetan mountaintops out of focus. Let's find a place where people haven't been. Let's go down a hole! Good, at least we know where we're going. Whew! Now all we have to do is find out *why* these people are going down this hole, and *what happens* to them on the way, and *what it means* to everybody, and we got us a novel.

"On second thought let's not step on that what-it-means-to-everybody step; that plank is always a little squeaky."

I didn't go over to the University much. It wasn't that I avoided the academic scene so much as the book began to push everything else out of my life. We met twice a week, 2:30 on Monday and 2:30 on Friday. As these encounters approached I would find myself spinning around in my skin the way I used to before I went on the mat. It wasn't as though the class was my opponent. My opponent was some kind of indistinct inertia. The class was my team.

A few months into the first term we had the plot blocked out and I began assigning sections—write 'em at home then read 'em aloud to the class. The trouble was, I quickly saw, that the prose being brought in was going rapidly purple, like bothered bruises. Segments were becoming involuted—worked and reworked. Personal! When we tried to sew these pieces together we came up with a monstrosity that only Mary Shelley could love. That's when we came up with our third rule: that we would henceforth not write any of this novel *apart* from each other. We would sit down at the table, design the section that we were going to write, divide it into segments enough to go around, and draw lots. We'd look up on the board, see what our task was ("Dr. Jo gets up, goes outside, looks at the sky, thinks about what happened the night before, gets ready for the trip"), then bend down and write. No talking, thirty minutes, then read it aloud. An immediate presentation before your peers . . . not of your ability to rewrite, but to *write*. There's a difference.

When the thirty minutes was up we refilled the coffeepot, opened another bottle of Cabernet, took this little tape recorder that I'm talking into right now, passed it to number one, and he started reading aloud our new chapter. Number two came after that and all the way through until the chapter had run its course and the wine bottle was empty and the tape was ready for Barbara.

Barbara Platz is an old ally of mine from a number of projects. She'd take the type, run it through a transcriber she played with her foot and feed it into the computer in our computer room. We'd print it out and when the class came back next meeting there was the section we'd just written, ready for rewriting.

As they say of circus fires—it was intense. But nobody missed much class. You couldn't afford to. One afternoon H. Highwater Powers had to leave early, for his job as organist. He read his section first, out of turn, then split for the church. No sooner was he out the door than Jim Finley passed around a note: "Let's kill Highwater's character."

Cold as this sounded it did in fact suggest a solution to a problem we were having at that point in the plot. You see, the mysterious lake that we had discovered in the grotto had to have some kind of outlet flowing out of it because of the underground river flowing in, and Highwater's character just might be the very—

But that's getting ahead of the story.

—Ken Kesey, 1989

CAVERNS

Prologue

America is halfway out of the Depression, beginning to hope again. The evidence of the change is clear. It can be seen everywhere—in the color of next year's models in the automobile ads; in the spiffy cut of the latest women's fashions; in the very look of the new season itself. It's the first fall in recent memory that the nation seems able to find once more a little of that bright old glory in the turning autumn leaves.

The summer has been filled with news of dark happenings in Europe—anti-Semitism and pro-fascism; the last of the League of Nations and the first meeting between the ominous blue-eyed Fuehrer of Germany and his rock-jawed Italian counterpart. But Europe seems far away, across an awful lot of water, and in the United States folks have had enough of a lot of water. They are still enjoying the recent repeal of Prohibition. Still celebrating. The news shows it. The *San Francisco Chronicle* headlines boast GOLDEN GATE PROGRESS "GREAT"! at the top of the front page. Farther down it declares DOLLAR ON

O. U. L E V O N

THE RISE and UNEMPLOYMENT DECLINING and COMMUNIST CLUB CLUBBED BY COPS.

In the movie section Gary Cooper, Cary Grant, James Cagney and Shirley Temple are being held over by overflow audiences. In the comics Joe Palooka bops Bully Billy Bologna, Dick Tracy closes in on Creampuff and the Katzenjammer Kids keep the Captain and the Inspector hopping.

The sports page touts the upcoming Big Game down at the Leland Stanford Junior Farm. The writers see it as a battle classically divided into perfect halves: BIG BUCKS AGAINST BEAR BRAVERY. Stanford, of course, being endowed with the first half, California having to make do with the second.

The rooms of the fancy Frisco hotels are once more half full or, according to the less optimistic in the hotel trade, still half empty.

The October fog is half lifted from the streets, the morning households half awake.

A block and a half from Stockton on the outskirts of Chinatown, one Victorian house appears to be actually halved horizontally. The top story is painted in conventional San Francisco pastel blue with white trim. The bottom half is flat black all the way to the foundation. A black pike iron fence encloses the yard. A black chain across the drive supports a metal sign: KEEP OUT BY ORDER OF SFPD in raised red letters on the stamped black metal.

Behind the gate a weedy flagstone walkway crosses the yard to the stone steps. The front door that once waited at the top of the steps has been completely bricked over, the bricks painted the same flat black as the bottom half of the house. But the pathway turns right at the steps, runs along the overgrown porch front to the driveway fence, then turns left through the unclipped laurel hedge and ends at a side door. The door is heavily hinged and made of riveted metal plate, the seams gone green with age. The door handle has been removed and a massive padlock installed in its place.

A small stained-glass window is set in the metal door, no bigger than a porthole. Its faceted pattern describes the looping cross of an Egyptian ankh, and a shaft of morning sunlight has poked its way through the hanging fog and into the beveled glass of the symbol's center. The shaft zigzags down carpeted steps to a room located below the house, a subterranean hall—vast and still.

The room is elliptical, its length impossible to assess as the coved stucco walls recede into darkness. The air hangs thick. A layer of dust covers everything like a protective drape. On the tables and tile floor the dust is crisscrossed with the busy trails of tiny feet.

One of the circular tables has been painted with the alphabet, and inlaid with large ivory words: YES and NO and ASK AGAIN. In the center of the circle of letters is a golden sun with outbeaming hands for rays. This symbol is repeated in the arrangement of the floor tiles.

Bookcases have been built into the sidewalls. Tiffany lamps sit near the shelves on walnut reading tables. Some of the tables are still casually cluttered with prints and sketches, some in inks, some in pencil, all depicting the same scene. This scene also appears in various newspaper clippings and magazine covers framed and hung about the room. It is a black-and-white photograph of a tall man in jodhpurs and safari boots, standing in firelight before a limestone wall. The wall is decorated with savage paintings, primitive figures of animals and men, intertwined with symbols and characters.

3

These images swirl like wings from the man's ballooning shadow, up into dim distances, out of frame. Near the top of the photograph two ambiguous shadows flutter, face-to-face, unfocused in movement. They might be bats, they might have been a blemish of mud on the camera lens. This distracting blur has been left out of the prints and sketches.

Suddenly there is a thump along the wall outside, jarring the stillness, and skittering out of a crack in the stucco comes a mouse. It darts along the baseboard then onto the floor, bound for the opposite wall. But it stops in the center of the room, skewered by the odd shaft of light through the door's circular window. It stands blinking about in confusion. Light rarely penetrates this domain, only on a certain few fall days when the October sun aligns with the little porthole.

4

As its vision adjusts, the animal is able to see to the end of the room. It stands as though transfixed in pebble-eyed awe by what it sees. An elaborate fresco dominates the curved wall, like a painting inside an eggshell. It is a rendering of the wall in the photograph, except that the fluttering blurs have been deleted and the man with jodhpurs has been replaced with the ankh symbol.

Another sound penetrates from the street. It is the morning's first cable car, the bell clanging syncopated rhythms. Startled into action, the mouse completes its crossing and disappears into another crack.

The **bell clangs** again and, outside, a pile of blankets heaves apart beneath the laurel, revealing an unkempt head and a crumpled face. The hair is white, the face is blue. The man rises slowly to his hands and knees and painfully rotates his head. His shoulder creaks and his neck pops. He begins to shudder and cough. He coughs for a long time, then spits through the gate toward the street.

He waits on his knees until the shuddering passes, then he gingerly reaches back beneath the hedge and draws out a battered instrument case. He unbuckles a belt holding the ancient leather together, and peeks in.

"Good morning," he whispers. The voice sounds like wind through hot weeds, but the tortured face seems soothed. He is speaking to a cornet. "Good morning," he says again, rubbing the silver bell. The discovery of a half-full package of cigarettes alongside the instrument makes him feel even better. He belts the case shut and lights one of the bent smokes.

He draws carefully on the cigarette, trying to clear his head. A jagged thought nags at him through the haze. It seems there was something he'd been told yesterday, about something he was supposed to do today. He concentrates hard. Something he was supposed to find. But the effort threatens to set off the coughing again, and he lets it go. Instead, he allows the pleasant fragments of the night to slide back into his mind, soothing him further. The Sugarfoot Stomp, Benny Goodman, Gene Krupa—at the Colonial Ballroom. Was that last night? No matter; what a hell of a band whenever it was. Who'd have thought white boys could blow like that? Blow, blow, blow. That Krupa, he's become a wild man, pounding those tom-toms like jungle drums. Of course, Goodman's still the best clarinet ever, white or colored. And the trombone section—tight. Tight and on tour. All they need is one hot trumpet. Or better yet, a cornet. If Ol' Juke woodshedded for a month or so, betcha he could catch them at the Palomar. But first—he ran two fingers down the bell of the horn and withdrew a dirty bag made of Oriental silk and tied with a gold drawstring; the bag felt limp and empty—first he'd better go get a fresh charge from Old Mao Tsu to mix with his

5

Asthmador. Then to the Palomar. They got some good bands in L.A. A Chinatown, too. Bet Juke could do that, he tells himself, hoping. Yeah, Old Juke could do that.

If Old Juke could just remember that other thing he was supposed to do first.

6

1

Coming out
and getting together . . .

Blocks away, in a narrow cloister, Father Paul D'Angelo was hoping he'd be able to repair his damaged chalice. It was pretty badly bent. The strap barely reached across the now-asymmetrical curve of the chalice's bowl when he strapped it in his mess kit.

"Bent six ways from Sunday," he muttered under his breath. The new boy had caught the corner of the altar cloth in the Book this morning and when he turned to leave he had pulled the whole shebang with him. The chalice smashed to the floor.

Father Paul sighed and touched his vestments to feel the lump of stone that had broken loose. He wouldn't have time to fix it right away. The next few days were just going to be too busy. They would all be leaving for the cave before next Sunday. Forlornly, he regarded the mutilated cup. His mother had given it to him on the day he was ordained. She must have spent a small fortune on it. It was 18-carat Florentine gold, not plated but cast. That was the reason it bent so easily; it was malleable and pure, like a human soul. Father Paul smiled, thinking of the will of God and the notion that nothing ever happens by chance. Perhaps the morning's accident was a sign, the starting gunshot indicating the journey had begun. When the chalice hit the floor Paul had experienced a shiver down his back. He hoped the chalice would be the only casualty of the affair.

He began to remove his vestments, slowly, one at a time. He hung the heavy gilt and silk carefully in the closet. Then the sashes. Finally he lifted off the amice, a narrow shawl with a cross embroidered in the upper edge. This is the only special garment a priest must wear to perform the sacraments. The amice did not belong to the church like the rest of the vestments. It had been another gift from his mother, at his ordination. He raised the heavy damask cross to his lips and kissed it, praying, "Place upon my head O Lord the helmet of salvation for repelling the attacks of the Evil One, Amen."

He folded the amice and placed it in a small traveling case. Next he went to the sink. Reaching through the curtain beneath it, he pulled out a burlap folder filled with unblessed host and a bottle of the good Brothers' finest. The Benedictines always claimed it to be the best fortification against the ardors of travel. He strapped the bottle down in the case and carefully laid the host between it and the chalice. He put the chalice shroud in, folded it neatly across the bottle and placed his daily missal on top. He closed the case, locked the three small hasps and straightened. Slowly, he looked once more around the sacristy.

He felt a wicked excitement, like a good kid about to play hooky. Of course, he would certainly be coming back as soon as the trip with Loach was done, and when he returned to the church he'd pay for the bottle. Then fix the chalice. The

8

chalice could not remain mutilated. He would take it to the metalsmith to be repaired the moment he got back. First thing, absolutely.

He felt sure of all this. Still, somehow, he felt quite odd. A tinge of guilt perhaps, of sin. He knew that somehow this feeling had to do with Dr. Loach. Was he forsaking the Lord's word for Loach's? No. Loach was one of God's children in distress. Paul had done nothing more than bring him books during his incarceration, bring him word from the outside and play a few hands of poker with him and the guards. And even then, not for money; for cigarettes, though neither he nor the prisoner smoked. Still, there was this feeling. It had been building as these final days of Loach's confinement ticked off, and it had been dramatically enhanced this morning by the racket of the ringing chalice in the vast acoustics of the cathedral, heightened, like a moment in a movie.

9

He looked once more about the sacristy, decided to grab another bottle. Better take along a peace offering for Warden Duffy. At last he turned decisively and walked through the small portal that opened out onto the altar. He pushed open the massive bronze door of the cathedral and stepped outside into the clean San Francisco air, smiling. The gold rims of his glasses flashed in the sun and his smooth face gleamed like the rump of a cherub in an icon.

His old Plymouth was ready and packed. Fumbling in his pocket he came across the stone from his chalice before he found the keys. He swung himself in behind the wheel, started the car, adjusted the choke. While the car warmed up he checked the briefcase on the seat next to him. The papers were there, all in perfect order, all that was needed was Warden Duffy's signature. He pulled out of the parking lot without looking back at the cathedral. Behind him, back up the hill, he could hear the bells beginning to peal vespers.

"I hope there are no hitches at the pen," he said, turning down Guerrero toward the ferry landing. "I hope the release is all in order."

◇

On the third tier in San Quentin, Warden Duffy was pacing his office and hoping just the opposite. But his hopes were in vain. The wire from Sacramento confirmed that. He read the message twice before he sighed and thumbed down the toggle on his intercom box—

"Go wake Loach. Tell him his conditional kick-out came through. From the goddamn Governor himself. Take him his streets and have records send up his goody box. I'll have to muster the bastard out as soon as the priest gets here."

The warden peeled off his shirt and stepped behind the filing cabinets where his tiny washbasin was hidden in a corner. He had already shaved once that morning—at dawn, in his bedroom in Larkspur—but he felt compelled to repeat the chore. Maybe even get a fresh shirt up from laundry. Maybe even a goddamn necktie, he thought wryly as he stropped the razor.

For all the publicity the warden of San Quentin had garnered in his campaign for modern prison reform, Duffy did not consider himself a vain man. For all the praise and the pillory and the journalistic name-calling—from "the Saint of San Quentin" to "Egomaniacal Genius" to "Duffy the Demigod"—he still considered himself nothing more than a simple turnkey who had made it to the top. The theories for prison reform were not even his own; they were the logical conclusions of a score of astute penologists from across the nation, prompted more by the times than any manifestation of genius. Prohibition had jammed the pens with a new kind of criminal, a vulnerable soft-skinned speakeasy amateur, thrown in with the hide-hardened veteran thug. It did not take a genius to see that the casualties of the Roaring Twenties were going to need little modern consideration. In fact, he had met but one man in all his years of penitentiary work whom he felt might be vain enough to consider himself such—and that man would be marching free in a matter of minutes.

The warden dried his face and returned to his desk in his undershirt, his suspenders dangling down his thin thighs. On the cluttered desk was the manila folder, unopened. Duffy leaned across to the intercom again, pushed down one of the toggles with a wet thumb—

"Laundry? This is the warden. Send me up a fresh shirt and tie, dark blue. And get Loach a new kick-out suit if he needs one. I can't remember what he checked in with . . ."

11

Twenty minutes later, washed and shaved and wearing a fresh white shirt, Duffy felt better. Maybe clothes didn't completely make the man but, all things considered, he'd seen plenty of evidence how the lack of nice duds could *un*make one. Better for the state to pay up front the ten bucks for a Monkey Ward worsted than down the line to pay the ten times ten—plus that it costs to slam the miserable bastard in again. Just as the free tobacco had taken a lot of the starch out of the stiff old in-prison custom of trading smokes for souls and assholes, so had the free suit program significantly reduced early recidivism. Most of the big pens in the country were now following Quentin's lead. And if Duffy had been hung with a jacket as a liberal pussy warden, it was a reputation of which he had grown increasingly proud.

The order from the Governor still waited, topmost of the

pile, but he still wasn't ready to sign it. Why not? What did he have against Loach? Not a damn thing, really. Still, he didn't want to sign it. Not yet.

Groaning, he put the paper aside and opened the manila folder instead. The contents were remarkably sparse for six years of records. No beefs, no formal bitches, no carbons of written requests for the special privilege most cons found they had to have after a few months—different diet; medications; cell changes. In all of Loach's records not so much as an application for a cell switch. And, except for the Hole, of course, Loach was in the worst slot in the whole place.

It was a cell both guards and inmates had named the Cracker Box. It was so small because the room had been intended as a utility space, built beneath a stairwell, and the ceiling slanted so low a normal-sized man could not stand without cracking his head. It had always been uncomfortable enough that bad eggs could be stashed there as punishment for minor infractions—food hoarding and cold-deck dealing— beefs not bad enough to get them the complete Hole. And after a month or so in the Cracker Box they would usually be promising to mend their wayward ways, just let them live someplace where they could stand up *straight* again.

But Loach, six-six at least in his stocking feet, had never sniveled so much as a peep. Duffy had stuck him in the Cracker Box the day he checked in. It wasn't for any specific infraction, but neither was the act completely without malice. The warden didn't like what he'd read about this Loach character even before the murder, and he hadn't liked the stuff he read from all the bleeding-hearted old biddies afterwards— letters to the editors to hell and back. He simply did not *like* the guy! He didn't like his way of standing or his fancy way of speaking. He didn't like his famous riveting eyes and he didn't

12

like the way photographs of the bastard had appeared in every gossip column before the trial. None of it. This was a *murderer*, out on bail, awaiting sentencing, not Peck's Bad Boy coming off a scandalous weekend. The bird had broken some dude's neck with his bare hands and the gossipmongers were treating it like he was some mischievous hero. And all those editorials about the nobility of the deed? Crap!

So Loach had been a gall on the warden's ass long before he ever encountered Charlatan Charlie face to face. And when they did meet—here in this office, six years ago—Duffy was disappointed to discover that the man he had come to loathe through the newspaper accounts did not seem like a charlatan in the slightest. Quite the contrary. There was about the guy a quality proud but in no way affected or arrogant. He was handsome, all right—tall, square-shouldered, self-assured, yet not the slightest bit overbearing. When the warden told him that he would have to begin his stretch in, well, *cramped* quarters, until a bunk and a regulation cell opened up, Loach had smiled pleasantly and shrugged. "Whatever you say. I'm sure I'll be all right."

It had infuriated Duffy, the smooth-tongued casual way it had been stated—"I'll be all right"—as though the bastard knew something that nobody else knew, and it gave him an edge. Okay, Buster, Duffy had said to himself, his face reddening: we'll see how long you'll be all right, bent over like a jackknife ten hours a day. We'll see what you talk like in a month or so.

But Loach had not complained, and the flush of angry shame had never quite left the warden. When the man's military record came to light on Duffy's desk some weeks later, the flush burned hotter yet. The bird was a goddamn *war* hero, three times decorated, once by Pershing himself!

13

What kind of fool wouldn't bring that up in his trial? Of course, pleading guilty straight off, nobody had imagined he would get more than a slap on the knuckles for a manslaughter rap, so maybe he hadn't thought he needed to wave his ribbons. Not even the DA had expected the judge to hand down a second degree and slap on twenty years. Two full dimes! It must have been, Duffy thought to himself, that that judge mistrusted the bastard as much as I do.

Duffy groaned again and eased himself into the chair behind his desk. He picked up the old clipping. Though he knew it nearly by heart, he reread the lead:

CHIP SHOTS *by Chick Ferrell:*

—Oct. 24, 1928. San Mateo County Courthouse—

After only twenty minutes deliberation, Judge Winston B. Loy handed down a surprisingly stiff sentence to defendant Dr. Charles O. Loach, Pht.—twenty years in the state penitentiary at San Quentin.

The packed courtroom was plainly shocked. Members of Loach's Society of the Cavern shouted protests. Some broke into sobs. Noted spiritualist sisters Mms. Mona and Ramona Makai swooned simultaneously and spoke back and forth in tongues.

Dr. Loach, who had entered a *nolo contendere* plea at the beginning of the trial, stood unshaken. The occultist had voluntarily surrendered on September 3, confessing to San Francisco police that he had just killed a former society member and colleague, one P. L. Beamann.

Beamann, a noted Las Vegas entrepreneur and photographer, had accompanied Loach on the renowned "cavern expedition" two years before as archivist. His photographs of the tall explorer standing in front of the cavern's painted wall had thrust Loach and his "secret grotto" into the eyes of the world press as well as that of the scientific community.

Loach has never revealed the location of his find, nor has he returned to the cave, choosing instead to reside at the Makai mansion where the killing took place.

Dr. Loach claimed he had sworn an oath of secrecy while inside the grotto, and was "bound by holy oath" to protect its whereabouts. He testified that the killing of Beamann had occurred during "a thrall of rage" when Beamann announced he was on his way to the papers with maps to the area.

The San Mateo County Coroner said Beamann's spine had been broken as though "by the jaws of a gigantic hound." When he was questioned concerning this, Loach, a large man, answered, "It was as though I was transformed into Cerberus, the watchdog of the ancient Grecian underworld."

In a fiery statement at the sentencing, Judge Loy angrily referred back to this canine metaphor when he proclaimed: "Men are not dogs. Men do not kill each other over old bones in the ground."

Dr. Loach gave no answer. He smiled and waved to his crying followers as he was led from the courtroom into custody. An appeal is being considered.

> Second-degree-murder convictions can be considered eligible for parole after eight years with good behavior.

Duffy laughed. Good behavior hardly did it justice. The sonofabitch had walked his time so soft he could have been considered for canonization. This reminded him that Father Paul would be arriving any minute, and this awoke him to his tieless condition. He called again down to laundry about the tie, then began to organize his desk.

Not that the priest would give a tinker's dam how his desk looked, or his clothes either. Duffy and Paul D'Angelo went back a lot of years, and, if anything, the priest was even messier in his ways and less conventional than the warden. They had boozed together in the old days at St. Francis, and they had buddied together ever since, whenever possible. They were colleagues, in a way, in the business of salvation, conferring often in this very office over the fate of many a hapless miscreant up for parole. Duffy had farmed out a lot of San Quentin conditionals into Father Paul's care over the years—some successfully, others not. But this one, somehow, had become a bone between them. Duffy felt it, and it galled him in spite of himself. Paul had always been innocent, as naive as the goldi-locked altar boy he still resembled. He'd always tried to believe the best of people. It was Paul's way. But the way he had been suckered in by this bright-eyed fourflusher—it made Duffy furious! Writing all those letters, all those petitions. All those hours he had spent visiting Loach, playing poker through the bars on a grocery crate. Those were hours that once would have been spent in the warden's office, sipping Benedictine and discussing all the various ramifications of important Catholic issues, like the

16

IRA, or Mussolini, or the prowess of the season's Notre Dame football team.

Yeah, dammit, Duffy admitted with a sigh; he was jealous. And that right there was what burned him the most: he was jealous of a convict, a Murphy man, a backbreaking bullshit artist with bright eyes and good posture.

The box on the table squawked. "Father Paul is here. And listen to this, Warden. This Loach? He don't want his streets. He says they don't fit him anymore. And he won't take no free suit neither."

"Oh yeah?" The warden felt his face getting hot. "Why so?"

"He says that they ain't neither one in style anymore anyhow."

"He said that?"

"That's what he said. Shall I let him walk out in his blues?"

"I don't give a damn if he walks out buck naked! Just get the bastard ready! And send Paul up to my office."

"He's already down the spine, Warden."

"Already down the—? To where?"

"To Loach's Cracker Box, like usual. He said he thought he might need to help Loach carry books or somethin'. . ."

The warden flipped the power switch on the box completely off and leaned back in his creaking swivel chair. Through the barred window behind him he could hear the garbage tug blow its melancholy call, and the gulls wheel out to greet the loaded scow pulling for the open sea.

"Ain't in style anymore anyhow," he said. "Jesus Bleeding Christ."

2

Gaby and the dragon,

Rodney and Chick . . .

Loach unlocks the Temple

and finds the jewel . . .

Gabriela was out of the depot and walking fast along Mission before she was awake enough to know for sure what city she was in.

She was just damned relieved to be off that Greyhound from hell, was all she knew for certain. As soon as the big bus stopped moving, she had climbed over the sleeping sack in the seat beside her and shoved up the aisle, gasping like someone drowning. All night, as the bus had droned its way through the dark, the trapped air had become more and more depleted of value, used up, like the poor boozy wretches that had been breathing it since L.A. If they'd kept going another hundred miles the driver would have discovered he was hauling nothing but husks.

She felt a little delirious as she walked. Queasy. She hadn't been sleeping so much as suffocating the last half of the journey, rationing herself to shallow little breaths until consciousness left her. Now she walked fast, gulping at the good fog-washed atmosphere. When her head cleared she realized she was back in San Francisco.

She slowed to a calmer pace and turned left at the next corner, up toward Market. She still didn't know where she was headed, but any street would be better walking than Mission. Hope hadn't reached as far as Mission; it was the sort of street that would always be stuck in the Depression. And depression begets depression, Gaby knew. You can catch it like the flu. The sleeping sacks in the doorways looked like victims of the same plague that she'd bolted from on the bus. Smelled like it, too. Terminal mankind. She had been the only woman on the bus, and her clothes and hair were thick with the smell of it all, the perfume of the impoverished, the beat-down, the bottom-of-the-barrel.

"Gaby gal," she said aloud to herself, pulling on her hardest grin, "you always used to say you wanted to be one of the boys. Now you got locker room on you so thick you might never get it off."

In you perhaps even worse, she added silently, keeping her grin hard.

She turned along Market Street. When she found a nice, clean doorway of a shoe store, she stopped and lit up a cigarette. She pretended to be appraising the latest in women's footwear. No other shoppers were in the store; it was still too early. Women didn't do much shoe buying before noon. The clerk looked suspiciously at her through the store window, but she stood her ground, smoking and frowning at the purple pumps and the open-toed sandals. She couldn't think of what else to do. It didn't make any sense to go up to the Temple this early. Even if some of the old members were already there no one would open the hall until the Doctor himself showed up and gave the word. That had been the deal. And the paper had said he wasn't officially due to be sprung until one minute after noon. Besides, that spooky cellar still gave her the willies, just thinking about it. Even after six years.

She could go to the Sisters' place on Montgomery—their wire had insisted she stay with them when she arrived—but she didn't much want to tangle with those two witches either. Not this early and this woozy, with this dark clot of uncertainty still in her stomach. They were chore enough, she remembered, even when you were fresh and in the pink.

Then, as she frowned in feigned consideration of a pair of high-heeled, butter-colored horrors, she knew where she wanted to go. She had been planning it all along, she realized, ever since she had purchased the ticket printed SAN FRAN. She just hadn't let herself in on the plan because the destination made her more nervous to think about than the Temple *or* the Sisters. It made her mouth go dry and her throat tighten.

But what the hell, she shrugged; as long as you've got time to kill, you might as well go right for the jugular.

She lit another cigarette from what was left of the first and resumed her walk down Market, her heels clicking and her hard grin going out before her. When she reached Grant she turned up through the crimson arches into Chinatown. She wasn't at all sure where the place was, but she knew she wouldn't have to look for it. She kept walking until a little man slid out of a decorated doorway. He hissed in her face like a yellow snake:

"Tssst! You want tiny blue heron on shoulder? Three dollah?"

"No!" she hissed back, and the figure disappeared back into his den of colored drawings, like a cartoon character being sucked back into the Sunday funnies.

It was him, all right. It had been nearly eight years ago, but this was the place. A girl would think the little devil had been waiting all this time, just for her.

She walked again, slower now, hoping she looked like your typical Frisco tourist, rubbernecking along, peering into those shadow cracks of the mysterious Orient. She had never really liked Chinatown; it was one of those gawdy phenomena that seemed to grow darker as the sun rose higher. Like the ritzy palm-draped streets in Beverly Hills, or the sundecks of the damned frat houses in Pasadena.

She walked until a big lascivious-looking alley tom darted in front of her. Black. That settled it. No sense in trying to get away. If you were going to fiddle with the fates you might as well play all the notes. She swung around before crossing the cat's path and clicked right back to the little shop full of tattoo illustrations. Not to go in; just to look. Who'd said anything about going in?

A faded Chinese lantern hung in the window. An enormous green dragon serpentined up the glass, decorated with red and gold designs. She remembered that the black Chinese characters over the dragon spelled out the word "tattoo." Charles had told her that. But then he'd also told her that it wouldn't hurt and she'd believed him. He was, after all, the Doctor, wasn't he?

She peeked through the dragon window. The tiny room was filled with patterns and templates, everything two-dimensional. At the far end of the shop was a black curtain with more Chinese symbols painted on it. She knew what lurked behind that curtain—that little reptile with the needle

fangs, capable of stitching pictures into skin. A dragon himself. This reptilian aspect was what had first attracted her.
When she'd passed the shop that night with the Doc she had
stopped to look at the picture on the window.

"You like these sorts of things, I've noticed," he had said.

"I should hope you noticed," she answered. "I've been
asking for one for years." All the guys in the troupe had one,
and some of the women. Not her mom, though. Her mom
considered herself too dainty for such a manly decoration.
She didn't even have pierced ears.

"Which one would you get?"

"That little green and gold one."

"Where would you get it?"

She saw his reflection in the window, grinning at her. She
wanted to tell him but, being not quite fourteen at the time,
there was hardly enough room there. So she said, "I'd by
God get the damn thing right here."

She lifted her left foot and touched her ankle, just above
the bone.

"Why then," he said, reaching past her to push the door of
the shop open, "let's by God do it."

A golden bell announced them. The artist emerged through
the black curtain, breathing loudly through his smile. He
looked very happy to have somebody in his pit to hiss at. Gaby
stood, waiting in amazement while Charles spoke to the man
in what seemed to her to be Chinese. The man listened, nodding respectfully. Then Charles took Gaby's arm.

"You sure of this, Kiddo?"

She could tell by his smile that he still expected her to back
out. "Sure I'm sure! But just a little one. Not any big ugly flag
like you got."

Like a lot of doughboys, Uncle Charles had Old Glory on his chest. She wanted to be one of the buddies all right, but not to the point of looking like a member of the VFW.

"Okay," he shrugged. "Let's go. You're still under age, but I told him I'm your guardian."

That was how she'd come to call him Uncle Charles. She had lain on a long table, clenching her fists and her teeth. He stood at the end of the table, watching the process as intently as an intern. Not once did he comfort her. Just watched, those eyes burning like dry ice, not saying a word. Quiet, even for him. He'd been quiet like that for days, it occurred to her, ever since they'd left the show in Bakersfield to do some advance before they opened in Frisco. Brooding about something, even more than usual. His face had come to look more and more like the picture on his banner—DOCTOR DESTINY SEES THROUGH WALLS AND TIME.

And the way his eyes burned . . . she wondered if somewhere, her mother was also feeling that needle.

When the tattoo was finished, Charles spoke to the artist a while in Chinese. He told her that the old man had explained how she must not wear a sock on that foot for a full week. Tiny scabs would form over the tattoo and then fall off, leaving the winged creature perfectly intact. They did and it was. Perfect. And still is, she thought, the delicate threads of gold and green as vivid now as the day they'd been stitched into her—except then there'd been red.

She remembered the first thing she'd asked when she followed him out of the shop, limping and whimpering: "You're sure the damn thing won't come off?" While she could not have backed out at least she could complain. "Because I sure don't want to have to do it again."

23

"Not unless you have it removed. And that's worse than getting it on."

"That's just ducky."

"You said you wanted one," he reminded her, walking. He didn't turn but she could sense him smiling. "In fact, you've been saying so for *years*."

"It's Lydia I'm worried about. She's gonna raise fifteen kinds of hell when she gets here."

Lydia was her mother—Lydia the Lightning Lady. She also belly-danced and sometimes helped the Doctor run a mind-read. Sometimes all three of them shared a Pullman when the show moved by rail.

"Not this time," he said. "She's not coming."

"I thought you said the show was playing Funland this weekend?"

"The show is, your mother isn't. She's found other venues to play."

That was all. Nothing more was ever said. Gaby thought Lydia would catch up in Sacramento, or Redding. She'd missed days before. Sometimes months. But when they got to Portland the Doctor's brother took down the Lightning Lady banner from the flap line. Gaby knew then her mother wasn't coming back again, ever. She was as gone as the little dragon was permanent. The following season Gaby picked up the electric number and Uncle Dogeye put up a new flap: GABRIELA THE ELECTRIC ANGEL. It boldly featured the dragon on her ankle, the limb lifted high and lightning squirting out of it like the bolts from the antenna on top of the world at the beginning of an RKO movie.

Chinese music from an upstairs apartment brought her back to the street. A rickshaw jogged by, the driver just missing her.

"Very sorry miss," he bowed. "Very sorry."

Gaby opened her purse and lit a cigarette. Then she took out the telegram and looked at the address the sisters had given her. She hoped they'd have some hot coffee.

They didn't have coffee but there was jasmine tea in a silver pot and scones at china settings. There were three settings, as though they knew a guest would be arriving soon.

Mona stood smiling in the kitchen doorway. Her sister Ramona sat at the table, reading poetry aloud from a leather-bound book in the bright light of the October morning. She lifted the silver teapot to pour herself a cup of tea. The scent of jasmine rose with a faint plume of steam.

"Sappho!" erupted a shabby green parrot. The bird stood behind Ramona on the domed top of a heavy metal trunk, cracking open pumpkin seeds. The empty shells went popping across the kitchen floor. He flicked his head to one side, one eye concentrating on Ramona.

"Sappho!"

"No, not Sappho," Ramona corrected patiently. "Coleridge. Samuel Taylor Coleridge. Mona, why don't you sit down? You're making Kronos nervous."

Mona, her Chinese robe hanging in the air a step behind her, took her seat; the silk draped around her legs in folds.

"Sappho!" the bird insisted.

Mona unfolded the napkin on her lap. Her sister leaned near the parrot and enunciated slowly:

> In Xanadu did Kubla Khan
> A stately pleasure dome decree,
> Where Alph, the sacred river, ran
> Through caverns measureless to man
> Down to a sunless sea.

Ramona looked up from the book, beaming. "Very fitting, don't you agree?" Neither the bird nor the sister answered. Ramona rubbed her palm over the page and began the stanza again. She was still hoping the bird would learn a verse or a stanza—at least a few words in the proper order. She had been hoping this since she brought the bird from Mexico, more than three decades ago, but the bird couldn't even keep the authors straight.

"Sister," Mona interrupted the bird's lesson. "We are going to need help getting this trunk in the car, you know. He'll surely want it down at the Temple. All the Society will want to witness the opening."

"Help will come," Ramona said with an irritating air of certainty.

"Oh? And from what quarter?"

"That I do not know. Perhaps from Rodney. Perhaps Rodney will come here straight away when his aeroplane arrives."

"Rodney won't help," the other sister was sure.

"Perhaps not. But you must admit that it's wonderful for him to involve himself after all this time."

"Rodney was never much for lifting."

"Perhaps Mr. Juke, then . . ."

"We still have to *find* him," Mona reminded.

"With the way he's billeted himself at the Temple door these last few years, I doubt he's gone far."

"Do you think he even knows about the Doctor?"

"I'm sure Mr. Juke reads the paper—he sleeps under them every night."

"Loach!" the bird called, pumping himself up and down, his thin yellow legs working like pistons. "Loach Doctor Kubla!"

Mona looked up, half expecting to see the Doctor in the doorway, but a young woman stood there instead, her face flushed across her cheekbones from the outside air. "I'm Gaby," she said.

"Gabriela? Is that you, child? I didn't recognize you at all."

"That's because I'm no longer a child," Gaby said. She tossed away her cigarette and stepped into the fragrant little parlor. "And don't call me Gabriela."

"Didn't I tell you," Ramona boasted, putting away her book of poetry. "Didn't I prophesy assistance would arrive? And look how *mature* she's become; she'll be much more help than Rodney ever would."

This prompted Mona to bustle to the window and look at the sky. "Oh, I do hope Rodney has been all right on that aeroplane. I hope he had a nice time, flying."

◇

It had been the worst time of Rodney Makai's life. The two-hour ordeal had seemed longer far than the four hours he'd been waiting, since then, sipping bourbon in Chick Ferrell's dilapidated Nash. His stomach was still in a knot the size of a golf ball.

"Next time I get on a airplane I'm gonna get stinking," he said to Ferrell. The photographer didn't answer. "That's the way to fly." Another minute passed. "That Loach character better get here pretty damn quick." Rodney looked directly at Chick as though he were to blame. "Or somebody's skinny ass is gonna be mud."

Chick Ferrell's skinny ass already felt like mud, as well as most of the rest of him. Had for years. His head felt full of it, and his veins. In fact the only part of him that didn't feel clogged with years of silt was his stomach. It seemed it always felt empty nowadays. When he'd scalped his press pass for the big game this morning, he'd made just enough cash to fill his Nash's gas tank and oil pan, but not his belly. The plate of eggs and sausages had disappeared into an echoless void, leaving him as hungry as ever. He hoped this new assignment with his old boss paid better than it used to—at least enough for three squares.

The Nash was inconspicuously parked at the far end of the block. The only other autos on the narrow street were the squad car and those belonging to the other reporters. Rodney Makai and Chick Ferrell were slumped down in the front seat, hats pulled down nearly level to the dashboard, eyes fixed on the entrance of the Temple. Ferrell drummed his fingernails on the steering wheel as Rodney entertained visions of a police stakeout. Perfect, thought Rodney. Just right. The story was panning out to have all the right ingredients for the premier edition of his crime tabloid—murder, magic, and adventure. Maybe a complete Sunday foldout, lots of drama shots. Potentially, a real blue-chip scoop and—like everything else in Rodney's life—it had all simply fallen into his lap.

Sure, it was going to be a nuisance working with this spongehead Ferrell, but Ferrell had once been at the top of his line. And nobody else really knew the background of the saga as well as Ferrell. In fact, it was the reporter's obsession with the story six years ago that had teetered him off the top. Sloshed would be more like it. Ferrell had taken Loach's fall from the heights harder than Loach had, it seemed, landing in a jug just as deep and in some ways deeper. He had lost his by-line with the *Chron*, then his job, then his rep. Now the name Chick Ferrell was about as respected in the journalistic

28

trade as the name Aimee McPherson in the religion racket. Kook Ferrell would be more like it—the gaunt-eyed ghost of a former great.

Ghosting was exactly what Rodney had in mind for the guy, too, though he knew better than to say as much at this point. A Chick Ferrell by-line would be like the kiss of death by ridicule. An R. L. Makai by-line, on the other hand, would have some juice to it. If the pencil-necked hack could manage to hack out just a few more days of work, a few more inches of respectable copy, the editors in L.A. could take care of the rest. Then let him slosh off to whatever depths he wanted. It would be perfect.

Rodney could feature the saga of Charles Loach along with the stories he had already written—well, almost written, at least commissioned, to other ghosts he'd spooked out of other dingy newsmen's nooks—about the grisly and mysterious ends of John Dillinger, "Baby Face" Nelson and "Pretty Boy" Floyd, all shot and killed earlier in the year. All soon to be more feathers in his publishing cap. "The Final Say," by R. L. Makai—Man on the Move! And now that they'd found the Lindbergh ransom on Bruno Hauptmann last week, the public was drooling for gore and mystery. This Murderer's Secret Cavern edition ought to be a sure smash, especially with him along and in the shots. Just like Stanley in Africa. He might even turn the whole thing into a book, or a movie like the one that drew Dillinger out to the theater in July, when Melvin Purvis shot him down—*Manhattan Melodrama*, with Clark Gable playing the thug, Blackie Gallagher.

Yes, letter perfect, Rodney mused. Get in, get the story, and get out, and at the same time save the Makai family from squandering any more of its wealth. That was important. If necessary he could even use what he gleaned to start the

29

mental incompetency proceedings he'd been considering for years—stop having to wrangle with his wacko aunties every time he needed operating capital.

Rodney knew he would have to be careful as well as clever. And, as always, timing was of utmost importance. They had already shown up nearly two hours late because Ferrell had failed to get to the airport on time, and then the dumb cluck got them lost driving across town. When they finally got to the Temple there was such a small crowd that Rodney thought he had missed all the action. What about all these people that were supposed to be here for the mucky-muck's big coming out? All those Frisco swells that had been so sweet on Loach and his Society six years ago? Gone as sour on the whole business, apparently, as the *Chronicle* readers had gone on Ferrell's stories. Yeah, timing was going to be important. The news of this spook's release would be hot for ten days, two weeks at most, then it would be just more paper at the bottom of the birdcage. Ten days. Get in, get the story, and get out.

Across the street Rodney saw his aunts standing on the Temple steps, a group of reporters and photographers milling around out front, and not much else. Some skirt with her collar turned up and a half dozen winos across the street in the alley. Not what you'd exactly call a throng. But he could get Ferrell to change that: "Irrational Surge of Supporters at Cave Society Scene." Just give the winos two bits apiece to surge a little.

Rodney sipped from his pocket flask and reached for some gingersnaps Ferrell had in a bag on the seat. As Ferrell tilted his head, watching the cookies disappear, Rodney saw that the reporter looked even more haggard than he had appeared at the airport. He wore a loose-fitting summer suit that

30

needed to be cleaned and pressed. There was sweat around his hatband, and his cigarette fingers were yellow. Look at him—guts growling just at the thought of picking up the Loach story again. Practically salivating, like those winos. Gone too far out on a limb before and drooling to do it again . . .

Outside, the fall sun had already dropped over the horizon of tarred rooftops. The narrow street below took on a sudden chill in the shadows. A young reporter emerged from the phone booth down the street and called to the others that he had just talked to the warden: "Duffy said Loach left right at noon with some priest."

"That was hours ago," yelled back another. "What gives?"

"He might have jumped parole," Rodney muttered, taking the last gingersnap. "Perfect. Write this, Ferrell: 'Loach Takes It on the Lam!"

Ferrell shook his head. "Not Charlie Loach. That's not his style."

Rodney was about to say style-schmyle when he noticed the blurred figure of a man round the far corner down the block. It moved along the wall on the opposite side of the street, jerky as a lizard. The man had some kind of case held by the handle in one hand, and in the other some kind of curved tool. Rodney thought at first it was a pry bar, a jimmy. Then the figure stopped and put one end of it to his lips. Smoke billowed from the other end. It was a pipe, the kind shopkeepers smoke in German fairy tales, with a long drooping stem swelling to a bowl as big as your fist. A huge cloud of blue smoke erupted through the sievelike lid of the pipe with each puff, and when the cloud cleared, Rodney saw that the man's face was as blue as the smoke. This creature lurched away from the wall to the curb, where he held on to

31

a street lamp for balance and spit into the gutter. The wretched figure recoiled and snapped, like a snake spitting venom.

"Gawd, will you look at that nasty bum," said Rodney with disgust. "What a cesspool."

"Him?" said Ferrell, lifting his camera. "He's no bum. That's Loach's sidekick, Emmett Juke. He was at the cave!" He held the camera out the window and leaned down to look at the tiny image inverted in the viewfinder. "They were old war buddies," Ferrell mumbled. "They made it all the way to the final offensive on the Meuse River. The mayor of Argonne awarded him that pipe personally."

"What's that case all about?" asked Rodney. "Is that what he carries the nasty thing in?"

"No. He's got a cornet in there. They say he used to be pretty good. Before the mustard got his lungs."

"Gawd," Rodney repeated, shaking his head. "But keep shooting! That's just the kind of color this piece needs. Shoot those two crazy old biddies, too."

Ferrell looked blankly at Rodney. "I thought those old biddies were your aunts," he said.

"They are. But it apparently hasn't helped them a bit . . ."

From where she stood on the steps, Ramona Makai also saw the figure weaving up the curb toward her. Her old eyes couldn't make out the features but she recognized the cough. She watched as the form tacked closer, like a dinghy in the bay looking for a familiar pier.

"It's him!" cried Ramona. She lurched past her sister, toward the street.

"It's him!" echoed Mona. She bolted after her sister down the steps.

The young reporter heard the sisters' cries and started run-

32

ning, shouting, "It's him, it's him!" The others took up the cry and followed.

Juke had just come out of another blue cloud when he heard voices and saw people coming at him through the smoke. They waved arms and notebooks and cameras, bearing down on him in an excited pack. He looked behind him but there was no one else. They seemed to be shouting about him. Even the winos had been stirred to action and were beginning to trickle out of the alley.

"Old Juke is him?" he marveled. He put the smoldering pipe in the pocket of one of his jackets and straightened up. He wished he had a hat.

Rodney and Ferrell were even caught up in it. They both got out of the car and followed in amazement as the crowd bore down on Juke, unable to resist. Then, before they all rolled over the poor man completely, they stopped, and the first reporter said, "It isn't him."

"Not him," Juke agreed, relieved.

"He's Juke," Rodney explained airily to the others. "Loach's flunky. He was at the cave. This must mean the big tamale himself is getting close. And about damn time, if you ask me."

"She said that it was him," said the young photographer, pointing back at the old lady. He swung his camera up and popped off a shot at Juke, just in case. The flash left Juke wide-eyed and blind. When he could see again he saw that the crowd was beginning to drift back toward the mansion. He followed, but kept his cornet case held high, out of harm's way. A reporter fell in on each side of him.

"What are your boss's plans, now he's out of prison?"

"Do you think he can find his way back to the cave?" asked the other, holding his notebook poised. "Do you intend to go with him?"

Juke blinked from side to side. These were hard questions.

"Do you feel your boss's early release was justified justified justified?"

Ramona pushed through the crowd, scattering reporters. She elbowed the young photographer stiffly in the ribs. She took Juke by his trembling shoulders and shook him gently. "Mr. Juke?" His eyes fluttered. He coughed. His skin flickered through various shades, like a cuttlefish. "Mr. Juke? It's Ramona Makai."

With a jeweled hand she raised his chin until his face found hers. She picked flakes of ash from his clothes and smoothed his matted hair. "Mr. Juke? Have you brought the key? Dr. Loach shall need the key, dear."

"Gone," said Juke, remembering at last.

34

"Is this him? Is this Dr. Loach?" said a breathless wire service man, trotting up late.

"However did you ever get such a wild idea, young man?" said Ramona. "This is Mr. Juke."

"Yeah, young man," the other reporters kidded. "How'd you get such a wild idea?"

"Mr. Juke takes care of our Temple."

"Well, where in the hell is this Loach character, anyway?" grumbled the reporter. He folded his notepad and stuck his pencil behind his ear. "I'm getting tired of all this."

At that moment Father Paul's black Plymouth, shiny and worn as a rosary, pulled quietly past. It rolled to a reverent stop at the Temple. A solemn gray face could be seen through the passenger window. "Now *that*," Ferrell said, "is *him*."

The clamor was considerably depleted this time, owing partly to the false start. But another thing subdued it even more—the center of the clamor's attention itself. The face that turned to look out of the car window was not the sort one rushed at with hard questions. There was an aspect to the mouth and chin, a brightness to the eyes that suggested hard answers. The reporters held back, seeming to wait for someone else to start.

"Let me get the door," said the priest, reaching across.

"No thanks, Paul," said the other man. "I better get used to opening doors again."

Charles Loach stepped from the Plymouth. The crowd of reporters parted before his bright gaze, like grass before a snake. Everyone fell in at his heels and followed as he walked through the open gate.

"Make sure you get this down," Rodney whispered out of the corner of his mouth to Ferrell. "He's got them in some kind of trance."

They were overwhelmed by his physical presence. A whole head taller than most of them, he walked with his shoulders back, his torso straight. As he moved, his arms and thighs stressed against the fabric of his prison blues. He stopped and stared up the walk at the front door where the lock clenched tight to the hasp.

"What about the key?"

The sound came up from deep inside his chest, propelled by the bow of his diaphragm.

"Mr. Juke says the key is lost," Mona said. "Gone."

"Gone, gone, gone," the little man reiterated in a thin whisper.

Loach stared at the corroded lock, his hands hanging.

"You look like someone who's not sure whether he's come to the circus too early, or too late," said a voice at his elbow.

He turned to discover a young woman, her face tilted. It was difficult to say if her smile was derisive or merely aloof.

"Gabriela? Is that you?"

35

"Gaby. Gabriela was a little girl you used to know, a long time ago. How ya doin', Uncle Charlie?"

Loach smiled and opened his arms. She pressed against the faded denim of his shirt, surprised how hard he felt for looking so white. He was surprised that she felt so soft. She stretched up and kissed him on the cheek.

None of the reporters had spoken a word. Rodney Makai decided it was time to break this tender little spell with some business.

"Loach? I'm Rodney Makai. Maybe the good Father here told you about me. *The Hollywood Herald*? I'm the sugar daddy that's thinking about bankrolling this little jaunt of yours. R. L. Makai of Makai Publishing? Soon to be Makai Publishing and Productions?"

Loach didn't seem to notice, staring down at Gaby as though trying to reconcile this face with the girl he had left, and the woman who had left him.

"Surely the Father has told you—well, hell, we don't need to be so stiff with each other. Your two old cohorts, Ramona and Mona here, are my *aunts*. That makes us like family, Loach. Put 'er there."

Loach extricated himself from the girl's hug and looked down at the round face with its pencil-thin mustache. He took the offered hand as though palming a pink coin.

"What about it, Loach?" the A.P. man asked, gesturing at the locked door. "Looks like we may have to wait to get a look at the famous Temple, eh?"

"Yeah, Loach. It must be something of a disappointment to get out, then not be able to get in."

"You know what Confucius sez, don't you, Loach?" a third leering reporter asked. "He sez, 'Man who lose key to girl's apartment no get *new* key.' "

The reporters laughed but Loach laughed with them, good-naturedly. Then he turned back to the door. Without hesitation he engulfed the rusty lock in his hand and twisted. The metal seemed exhausted, tired of standing so hard by itself against the battering of time and the salt air. It came apart with a gasp of rust, as though relieved. Loach pulled the creaking door open with a dramatic swing.

When Rodney saw that Ferrell had, like all the other dumb-founded newshounds, missed the shot, he kicked him hard in the ankle. "Wake up, dolt! This isn't some Punch-and-Judy for you to gawk at while you suck on your sourball. I want *shots*."

Chick snapped up the viewfinder of his Hasselblad and maneuvered to get Loach in the frame. When he saw the upside-down image lift its hand at the press of reporters it seemed to be waving farewell.

"And now, gentlemen of the press, if you will excuse us—" Loach was at the door, gesturing those he didn't want back and those he did forward. "Please come in, ladies, Gabriela . . ." Standing with his feet planted apart and the other hand on the metal door, he was both guard and usher. "Come, Paul . . . Juke. I'm sorry, gentlemen; this must be all for the while—"

"*Wait* a minute," the reporters exploded in a shout. "We've been waiting here for *hours*!"

Loach silenced them with another wave. Rust still clung to his fingers and a scrape of blood oozed down his palm.

"I apologize for the lateness of our arrival. The Sunday traffic had the ferries completely backed up. But be assured that a statement will be forthcoming. An official press conference shall be announced later. Monday or Tuesday. I'm truly sorry, but the Father here would like to hold a small service of thanks before this Sabbath is over." He cocked an eye at the last rays of the sun, sliding over the roofs. "So, we must bid you all good day."

Despite the protests and objections the tall man ducked to follow Paul through the door. Rodney caught him by the back of his prison shirt.

"Just a damn second, Loach," Rodney demanded. His cheeks were blazing. "What about *me*?"

"You?" Loach smiled. "What about you?"

"If you expect me to even con*sider* picking up the tab for this little swore-ee, you damn well better not slam that door in my face is what about me."

"Yes, Doctor," one of the sisters called from the gloom below. "Rodney seeks to become one of us."

"He does?" said Loach. "Is that true, Makai? Are you 'seeking'? Or are you merely 'considering'?"

The twinkle behind Loach's question made Rodney's cheeks burn hotter yet. But before he could respond Loach relented with a laugh, clapping a hand on the padded shoulder of the expensive suit. "Enter, Makai. Come on in. There is always room, even for the tentative seeker."

"Ferrell too," Rodney insisted, pulling Chick forward. "This is my photographer, Loach. He's got to come too. Without photos the story, what*ever* it is, wouldn't be worth so much as those rags you got on. C'mon, Ferrell . . ."

Dragging at the skinny reporter brought back some of Rodney's bravado. He bent the man like a puppet and shoved him at the door. Chick paused to shake Loach's hand.

"Chick Ferrell, Doctor. I worked your trial for the *Chron*."

Loach took his hand. "I remember. You got into some hot water for your sympathies, as I recall. Enter. But I must remind you: my cavern and I have not been overly kind to photographers."

Chick ducked through with a nervous smile and Rodney followed. Loach gave a final wave to the remaining pack of frustrated newsmen—"Until *mañana*, gentlemen?"—and ducked through after the others. The door closed like a gong.

Inside, it was vast and dank and dim. Chick Ferrell realized he had brought no flash equipment. A little light was still streaming through the porthole and down the steps but the rest of the place was dark as a tomb. Even the fastest emulsions wouldn't come near it. Still, he thought, I better keep up a good show of clicking and rolling, just to keep Makai off my ass. He'll never know the difference. He's too full of himself to tell an F-stop from a stoplight, anyway. And I got to keep this job, what-so-damned-ever! Because it's *my* assignment. I know Makai is scheming to make me a ghost on it, but let him scheme. I'll free-lance it when the time comes, or give it away. But I'm not giving up my by-line! Not anymore, not this time. This time I got to get it and finish it and put it to bed and tuck it in myself. I got to show them that Chick Ferrell is not through. They starved me down and thought they counted me out, but they didn't know that it wasn't over. Two falls out of three. Even up. All I have to do is keep quiet, keep cool and keep clicking. Chick Ferrell may have been starved, a little gaunt, but he's no damn ghost. Not yet. No, not yet.

He let his camera hang a moment and took out his notebook. Holding it close he wrote one word. "Vindication."

Juke appeared in the vestibule carrying two candles in holders. " 'Lectric ain't on yet," said Juke, handing one of the candles to Loach.

39

Loach took up the light and led the entourage down the stairwell onto the hall's main floor. No one spoke. Loach stood on tiptoe to light the twelve-arm candelabra hanging from the cobwebbed ceiling. Juke was working on the remains of votive candles along the walls.

"Look at all the tracks," said Gaby, tracing the tiny footprints across the hall. She swatted at the wisps of web that hung invisible in the dim light and dust rose with every movement. "Dust and rat tracks."

"Well, naturally it is a trifle untidy," said one of the sisters. "Could that be why the old members didn't show up, I wonder?"

No one said anything, adjusting to their surroundings. The place seemed surprisingly huge and empty. Mona Makai ran her finger across the lectern. "People seem so occupied these days," she mused.

"It's all right, Mona," Loach said. He was strolling slowly about, his candle held before him. "I don't think I would have been ready for a sudden crowd."

Rodney found and lit his own candle, then prowled over to a reading table. Father Paul stood thumbing through a stack of old newspapers. "Rodney Makai here, Father," he said, thrusting his hand across the table toward the priest. "*Hollywood Herald*. I wrote you that we were considering backing this excursion?"

Father Paul gave him a dusty palm. "Paul D'Angelo."

"Still just considering?" Loach commented in an amused voice. Rodney chose to ignore it. He moved instead to the young woman and gave her his hand.

"Gaby," said the woman dryly.

"Gabriela? Loach's niece?" asked Rodney.

She didn't answer. Rodney reached to his inside jacket

pocket and withdrew the packet of photographs that Ferrell had given him at the airport. He spread them on a table next to his candleholder. "Is that Gabriela as in 'Gabriela the Electric Angel'?"

Still she didn't answer and the room was quiet again. Finally, the priest spoke: "There is something wonderfully angelic about the name Gabriela."

"I'm no damn angel," the girl said.

Ferrell was arranging a congregation of candles on the floor near where Loach was looking at the Temple's painted wall, hoping that a time exposure might take. "Reminds me of the allegory of Plato's cave, Doctor," said Ferrell. "Your shadow, there . . ."

Loach regarded the man for a moment, brows raised, then turned back to the wall. His silhouette moved across the etchings of prehistoric animals and ancient symbols. "You have an education as well as an eye for metaphor, Mr. Ferrell. Unusual for a man in your profession."

"Comes in handy with the babes," Rodney put in, using his toughest newsroom smirk. "Every hack knows that. Give 'em a little Tennyson or Longfellow and they think you're either a philosopher or a poet."

"And which are you, Mr. Makai?"

"Neither. I'm just a businessman passing through, sizing up the situation, considering the odds."

"In a way, I envy people like you, Mr. Makai—able to withhold your commitment until logic bids you make your bet."

"I can play it close to my vest, if that's what you mean. For instance, on this cave deal: you won't find R. L. Makai anteing up so much as one red cent until he knows what the game is, what's wild, and what is likely to be in the pot.

Also," he added, folding his arms like Loach, "just what kind of sharpy he's playing with. Nobody pulls a fast one on R. L. Makai."

"Rodney! I'm ashamed of you," said the plumper of the sisters. "You behave as if Dr. Loach is some kind of trickster."

"Trickster? Do you know where the good *Doctor* got his handle? Tell us where you got your diploma, Loach," said Rodney.

"We already know, Rodney," the other sister joined in. "From the Orange County Academy of Theosophy. Ramona and I just happen to have been his sponsors at that occasion if you didn't know. I am ashamed of you for thinking he might be trying to pull a fast one."

"Yes, Rodney; for once I agree with Mona. I am ashamed of you, treating Dr. Loach like he was some kind of, of—"

"Of con man?" Loach finished for her, his eyes wrinkled with amusement.

"Right, Loach!" Rodney said. "You got it. You hit the nail right on the old thumb. Isn't that what they call men just out of the pen? Cons?"

"Rod-*ney!*" the two women exclaimed in chorus.

"It's all right, ladies. Your nephew has every right in the world to keep a sharp eye out for sharpies. That's good poker acumen, and I respect it."

"Right!" Rodney repeated. "Good poker acumen! And not only ain't I sure what the game is, I ain't even sure if you can find the pot."

"I found it once," Loach said. He had turned now, facing Rodney. The others had drifted near the discussion, their shadows crowding up the wall.

"By following a spirit in the form of a bird? So I heard. But it don't look to me like that little bird is leading you around any more, does it, Loach? You couldn't even find the key to your digs. As the fellow says, 'If the hound can't find the coon, find another hound.' Let's see your stuff, Loach."

The challenge hung in the flickering gloom. Loach's eyes seemed to grow brighter as the little knot of onlookers watched. Finally he said:

"You may well be right, Mr. Makai. My powers may have faded. Perhaps we should try a bit of an experiment. Sisters?"

"You don't need to prove yourself to us, Doctor," they said.

"Father?"

"The Voice saith unto Moses, tempt not the Lord Thy God."

"Never mind that," Gaby said. "Let's see your stuff, Uncle Charlie."

Loach smiled round at the candlelit faces, then turned to Rodney.

"What shall it be, Mr. Makai? Flying tambourines and horns? Fairies dancing on the head of a pin?"

"Go easy on yourself, Loach. Something simple. How about just reading my mind?"

"Phoo!" said Mona, turning her back on her nephew. "I can do that, that's no test. Even *Ramona* can do that . . ."

"Something simple? Very well. Ladies, would one of you have a blindfold? Something thick and long enough for Mr. Makai to tie over my eyes? So I absolutely cannot see?"

Mona eagerly pulled an embroidered scarf from about her neck and Ramona offered a long linen sash. Loach stood while both pieces were tied about his head, one over the other.

"There," they both said as though already vindicated. "Even you, Rodney, will have to admit the Doctor absolutely cannot see."

"So what?" Rodney said with a bored laugh. "I still ain't seen no little birds." But in a quick aside he hissed to Chick: "Ferrell, if you ain't getting this, I'm getting me another shutterbug."

"Now," Loach said. "Would someone please lead me away, completely outside the room? While I am away, Mr. Makai, would you please choose some object or article and hide it somewhere? Any object, anywhere. Then bring me back in. When I come back into the room I beseech all of you not to say a word, not to make a sound. Just picture that object in your mind and say its name. Repeat in your mind that name, over and over, and visualize the place where Mr. Makai places it, as though the spot is bathed in light. Diamond light. The name of the thing, and its position, and the light. Nothing more, please. No other thoughts, no other sounds. Now, would someone be so kind?"

44

Rodney insisted on re-examining the wrappings, trying to appear matter of fact. He winked at the others and suddenly threw a haymaker right, straight for Loach's face. The pink fist stopped inches from the tall man's swaddled nose. Loach did not flinch.

"Good enough for government work," said Rodney. "Padre? Can we trust you to lead our blind bluffer outside without slipping him some signals?"

Father Paul nodded and without a word took Loach by the elbow and led him across the room, up the stairwell, then helped him duck through the metal door. He shut the door behind Loach's back.

"Maybe even stand at that window, Padre?" Rodney called. "Make sure there ain't any little peekers out there . . ."

"Rodney, I declare—" started Ramona. Rodney cut her short with a finger to his lips. Then, without a word, he reached deliberately toward the girl Gabriela. Her eyes narrowed angrily for a moment as his hand settled over the scarab brooch. Simpering, he fondled the bauble a moment, then plucked it free. Forefinger at his lips, Rodney began elaborately tiptoeing across the floor. He placed the brooch amid the pile of clippings the priest had first examined on the far table, then tiptoed back to the others. With a gesture, he motioned for Paul to bring Loach back into the room.

Loach shook his elbow free from the priest and made his way alone down the steps to the tiled circle in the center of the room. He stopped. Then he began to turn in a slow circle, his hands outstretched. Everyone watched, barely breathing. Even the snap of Ferrell's camera had ceased. Loach continued to revolve until he was facing the wall where the reading table stood. Again he stopped. One hand fell to his side, but the other stretched higher. He began to follow the hand forward, shuffling across the dusty floor. When his thigh touched the table he stopped and stood. The hand hovered over the scatter of objects. A minute passed in silence, seeming far longer; then the hand abruptly swooped down on the brooch and held it aloft. The whole room relaxed in a mutual sigh.

"Six years," the tall man said apologetically as he pulled down the blindfolds. "I fear my little bird is a little rusty." He smiled over at the group.

"Okay, Loach, okay," Rodney said, shaking his head. "Ya got me, I admit it. For now, anyways, ya got me hooked. Where do we go from here?"

"Moab."

"Moab? Moab, Utah? The cave is in Utah?"

"No, but my brother is."

"Oh, swell," said Gaby. "Uncle Dogeye."

3

Over the border . . .
machine on fire . . .
Dr. Jo gets wire . . .

They were barely thirty minutes beyond the transient block-
ade at the border when a ragtop caught up to them and went
around, honking and shouting: "You're on fire, folks! You're
on fire!"

Not quite half an hour out of California. Nevada looked no
different from the roadside vistas they had been motoring
through since crossing the pass out of Placerville—the same
rolling emptiness; the same sage and juniper and failed farm-
houses. Yet Charles Loach found himself feeling, for the first
time, that he might have finally, actually, made it out. Gone,
escaped, on his way, beyond the grasp of those official second
thoughts he'd been hearing around San Francisco since his
conditional release five days ago, out of reach of the noses of
the bloodhounds and the newshounds.

Out.

Maybe it was just getting out of California. Or maybe the
wide-open emptiness and the road rolling on ahead had at

last convinced his doubting senses that he was free. It was supposed to take a while. Old cons always claimed, "When you been in a long stretch, it takes a long stretch to be out."

But what it really was, he thought, was all those damn state troopers back at the border. A dozen of them at least, like a platoon—all with their fat necks mowed and their boots polished and holsters riding high on their haunches. And their clipboards (the real weapon of the police state, he knew) all fluttering with rules and regulations and records of every incoming license plate and every flivver full of Okies. Keeping tabs on all the hicks heading to the Golden State on this road from Reno, on the Hoosiers and the losers, the Buckeyes and the Arkies. The more southernly transients would be coming in farther down, at Needles, or Yuma. Those might be called Crackers or Cajuns. But they were all Okies, as far as the California troopers were concerned. Whatever the point of departure recorded on the clipboards, all these westward wanderers were still all Okies.

Just like all prisoners were cons.

Their expedition had been bound east, so they had not been bothered; but the unpleasant borderline spectacle had sobered everyone, plunging the carrier into silence. Rodney Makai quit telling Gabriela about his various enterprises. The old sisters ceased their bantering chatter. Even the parrot seemed hushed by the sight, hunching his head down in his feathers and brooding on man's inhumanity to man. They had rumbled along this way until that shout from the convertible snapped everyone from their private reveries. Out the rear windows of the machine's big double doors the road was swirling with smoke. Ned Blue, the hired driver, swerved the machine off onto the shoulder in a gravel-spitting drift. "Battle stations!" he shouted and snatched the fire extinguisher loose from the stairwell, leaping out the door. "All ashore, mates, all ashore!"

Loach was right behind him. He watched the tightly muscled back disappear into the smoke and heard the whoosh of the extinguisher. "Fire in the aft hole!" he heard the man shout, then another prolonged whoosh. When Ned reappeared, his eyes were watering and he was smiling triumphantly.

"All secure, Chief. It was that inside right. She went low and catched fire is all. My fault. I noticed she was responding a little soft when we took them turns back at the border, but I thought it would hang on till we raised Reno. Then I aimed to drydock 'er. My fault . . ."

48

Loach offered him a handkerchief. "I take it you were a sailor, Ned." Loach had liked the bouncy little man from the first moment he saw him in the unemployment lines. He was glad Makai had enlisted him.

"Aye, sir. First stokey on the USS *Des Plaines*." He dabbed at his eyes. "I chased submarines all over the North Atlantic; this ain't nothing. I'm used to smoke." To prove his claim he ducked back into the black cloud and gave the burning tire another blast of CO_2. His voice called cheerfully from the smoke, "Where was you during it all, Chief?"

"I was in France," Loach answered. "Chasing tanks."

"I could tell you was a military man." He reemerged and opened the big rear doors and waved at the other passengers. "All secure, folks. Just some old hot rubber." He pulled out the wooden Moxie case he used for a rear step and began to usher them out. "If you just make yourself comfortable under that nice shade tree yonder, Ned Blue'll have it changed in a jiffy. The smoking lamp is lit."

"Lit?" said Rodney, disdaining Ned's offered hand and nearly falling in the process. "Ablaze would be more like it."

They straggled out, waving at the smoke. The tree was a stunted joshua, offering about as much shade as the skeleton of a starved steer; but the October sun was not that hot, and a hewn plank table gave the passengers a chance to sit while the tire was being changed. They unloaded the basket of apples and cheeses the sisters had packed and spread one of their colored scarves on the wood for a tablecloth.

Ned worked furiously. He had the rear axle jacked up and the outside wheel off before Rodney could uncork his first bottle of wine. The charred inside tire took more time. Ned had to throw water on it to cool it down. It continued to sizzle and smoke. The travelers watched, sipping Burgundy from Dixie cups.

49

Rodney felt obliged to do most of the talking. He had a lot to say about the wine selection he had chosen for their trip, and wanted them all to savor the vintages. Loach liked the wine, but found himself growing more and more impatient with the party. He excused himself and walked out into the sage to a flat rock.

He sat very straight on the warm stone, breathing deliberately. All those hours browsing through the tomes of Father Paul's eastern philosophy had taught him at least that—how to sit straight and how to breathe calm. A good hole card to have in your hand, whether you found yourself pinched down in a tight spot or out in this wild and wide expanse. He stilled his pulse until the trembling left his hands and the horizon ceased to pitch and yaw.

He began to look about at his surroundings. He watched a horned toad scurry from beneath his stone and spin around so it could glare at him for a moment. Then it scurried on, toward the road, as though to give Ned a hand beneath the carrier. Loach saw Juke's head pop up from the nest on the machine's roof, blinking as though he just woke up.

The carrier resembled the horned toad in a way, considerably enlarged. It was a surplus bargain Rodney had tracked down in Vallejo, completely undriven since it had come off the assembly line in 1930. "Tried and true," Rodney had proudly announced when he showed up with the monstrosity at the Temple three mornings ago. "And only has eighty-five miles on it. War surplus, built four years ago. A cracker-jack of a rig."

Everyone had filed out of the Temple to look it over.

"But we weren't having a war four years ago, dear," one of the sisters reminded him. "How could it be war surplus?"

50

"Of course we weren't having a war. We were having a depression. But the military has to keep up, does it not? Keep developing its equipment? This carrier was developed after our involvement in Europe. The army realized if we ever get into another No-Man's-Land we're going to need bigger rigs to carry the casualties. The quartermaster said they were called C.C. Riders."

Gaby gave a derisive laugh. "With those little bitty port-holes I would think they'd have called 'em *no* see see riders."

"You got it wrong, doll. C.C. as in *Casualty* Carrier! This thing is a one-of-a-kind. Unique. And *armored*, too; that's why the little windows. It was built to roll into an active battle zone, load in as many as forty-four casualties through the rear doors, and roll out." He gonged on the side with his little fist. "Take a cannon to penetrate this baby!"

"I don't know, Rodney," the other sister said. "It strikes me as somewhat morbid to have such a vehicle for our expedition . . ."

"Morbid? Comfortable and convenient is more like it. Come round here." He led the little knot of onlookers around the heavy metal siding to the rear. "Double doors, and a ramp pulls out at the tailgate. For sliding in, oh, *things*. I got it so you ladies can slide your couches and crap in. Your trunk you can't get open. That's one of the main reasons I bought it—comfort and convenience."

"Rodney, you never could lie. You got this godawful juggernaut because you got some kind of deal on it. Isn't that correct?"

"Hey, I said I'd bankroll this traveling circus but I never said anything about carrying you clowns first class! In fact, that's what it stands for now. C.C.—Clown Carrier."

Rodney had been so pleased with his wit that he repeated the line to everybody, giggling until Ramona was forced to kick him on the shoes.

"Don't repeat yourself, dear," she scolded. "It's a sign of degeneracy."

"Oh, it is not!" Mona corrected her sister. "It's a trait of the Gemini, double-tongued little imps. And they aren't couches, Rodney dear; they're davenports."

Loach had to smile now, looking at the outlandish machine still exuding wisps of smoke from its nether quarters. It was unique, all right. There was certainly nothing else like it on the road. And it was armor-plated, just like Rodney had claimed— the siding three-eighths-inch thick of riveted steel. They could have loaded it up with Okies and crashed that border back there, pistol shots zinging off harmlessly as they roared on.

Back at the table, Gaby had separated herself from the wine and the group and was walking his way, a cigarette in the long amber cigarette holder in the corner of her lips. She stopped a few feet from him, took the holder out of her mouth, and stood, one hand on her hip, looking him up and down. He was still dressed in his prison denims.

"Well, if you aren't a pip. Why haven't you got you some new stuff?"

"I've been too busy since I got out," he shrugged. He hadn't really had much of a chance yet to talk with her. "Getting stuff for the expedition."

She gave her short laugh. "Well why didn't you get them to give you back that nice baby blue pinstripe you went in with? You always looked sharp in that."

"I didn't even bother trying it on. I knew it wouldn't fit anymore."

"Yeah, you're a scarecrow all right. Were you such a troublemaker they kept you on bread and water?"

52

Loach smiled. "No, they fed us plenty . . . if you like creamed ham and mashed potatoes."

"Gad," she said, and made a spitting noise at the ground.

He raised his eyebrows in mock surprise. "What are you so disgusted about? You didn't have to eat it."

"What am I so disgusted about? What am *I* so disgusted about? Christ on a bike, who wouldn't be disgusted? Six years ago we're all supposed to be on our way to Nob Hill and champagne and caviar and our names in the social register; the next minute you're slammed away practically for life and little Gaby is doing good to scratch up enough for beer and hamburgers! In case you never knew, Uncle Charles, I had hoped for more than beer and burgers."

"I had hoped for more than creamed ham and mashed potatoes," he answered. He had meant it to be humorous but he saw her face redden and her green eyes fill with remorse. She turned aside and ejected the cigarette in the direction of the carrier, like a dart from a blowgun. Then she stuffed the holder in her blouse pocket. She moved around to take a seat beside Loach on the flat sandstone, crossing her legs. After a moment of silence she wiped her eyes with the back of her wrist and stretched her legs into the sun, pulling her blue silk skirt up above her knees.

"Sunshine, that's what we both need. Me as much as you. Look how white I am."

"I thought you had been down around Hollywood. Wasn't there enough sun for you down there?"

"Maybe I didn't get out in it enough," she said. "I always liked the night life, you know."

Loach didn't say anything. They heard a pop from the table beneath the joshua; Rodney had opened more wine.

"But what I really always liked, if you want to know, is the road life. I always liked being on the road with the show, hustling and scuffling and hanging around with the gang. Them were the times, huh?"

Loach didn't answer. Gaby pushed off her shoes and pointed her toes, making sure he could get a good look at her ankle. He still didn't say anything.

"Yeah, the good old days. And maybe I wasn't getting what them Nob Hillies might call a decent education, but at least I always got a good suntan."

"They say," Loach chuckled, "that too much sun isn't supposed to be good for fair maidens. Freckles 'em."

"You!" she hissed, snapping her thighs shut and pulling her hem back down. "You butter-tongued old carney bastard." He smiled but said nothing. After a few moments she took out her package of Chesterfields and offered the pack sideways.

"Want a butt?"

"Thanks, no. I gave them up."

53

"What for, for Lent?"

"For peace of mind."

"You act like you gave up a lot of things in that can."

"You learn to do that. When they've got you locked up they can use your habits against you, is what you learn. If you've got a hard yen for anything, you're vulnerable. Smoking, gambling, drinking—even coffee drinkers are vulnerable. Any hook you have in you is just another place for them to tie another string."

"But *you*, naturally, you showed 'em. You cut the strings . . ."

"As many as I could," he told her. He could feel her eyes on the side of his face, like the desert sun. "Candy bars were tough."

54

"You always did have a tooth for the sweet stuff. Which one was the toughest?"

"To try to do without? Reading, I guess. I found out I was a reading junkie. I never did kick the book habit, to be honest. Luckily, Father Paul kept me in quality reading material. Yes," he said, nodding, "I think reading would have been my toughest thing to do totally without . . ."

He felt the gaze on his cheek grow hotter. He turned on the rock and shaded his eyes again with his palm, squinting toward the carrier. Ned was letting down the hydraulic jack.

"Looks like we're ready to roll again," he said. He stood up, looking down at his threadbare shirt and trousers. "Sorry about my shabby appearance," he apologized. "We were just so busy in Frisco, making all those arrangements, doing those press conferences—"

"Ah, you love it. You big harlequin!" she laughed, shaking her head at him. "Once a carney always a carney—ham it to the hilt. Maybe we can pick you up a nice crown of thorns in Reno."

He laughed, the sound rough in his chest. It sounded almost painful, it was so rusty. Gaby accepted his offered hand and stood, smoothing her skirt. They walked hand in hand back through the sage.

"We'll find lodging in Reno," Loach said. "We'll be there before dark."

"Good criminy, I should hope we'll be there by dark! The last sign said fifteen miles to Reno and that was at least ten miles back. Let's get this show on the road, team!" she called toward the picnic table. "I want to play some slot machine. If we don't make better time we'll all be dead of old age by the time we get to this damn hole of Charlie's. Break camp, campers; let's ride . . ."

At the other end of the long state, Jocelyn Caine was also breaking camp and getting ready to ride. But she was alone, except for her horse. Her horse and the little people painted into the stone bluff. The big bay gelding and those little stick figures had been her only company for the last three months. If such a choice had been possible, she would rather have taken the figures with her and left the animal behind.

She slid her Winchester into its holster on the bay's saddle, tightened the cinch, then gave the place a last look around. She had used this ancient campsite off and on for almost two years. When she was satisfied that her presence had left no significant scar, she led her horse up the slope to the red sandstone rimrock. From here she could see all her little friends, twenty-three square-shouldered petroglyphs. Each of the figures was as individual and familiar to her as though they had been part of her own family photos, preserved in an album of stone. She hated to leave them. It was unlikely that she would find better company with this new project, no matter how fascinating it promised to be.

Dr. Jocelyn Caine had studied the archeology in this part of the West for more than a decade. Even during the Depression when there was no government funding, she kept coming back. She had been dedicated to the dream of finding some foundation for her theory about the migration of ancient peoples in the Americas. Here in Moki Canyon, she had found some slight evidence that the Anasazi, those aboriginal predecessors called by the Navaho "The Ancient Ones," had been influenced by the highly advanced cultures of South America: the Incas, Mayans and the Aztecs. In one of the ruin's rooms she had found the skeleton of a Macaw that could only have come in trade with the Aztecs in the south of Mexico. She had worked this site for two painstaking years, looking for something to challenge the Bering Strait—Land Bridge migration theory, but archeology was a slow process.

56

Also political. For the last six months she had been forced to dip into her own savings to supplement her meager grant from the National Geographic Society, and now a telegraph had informed her that that trickle had been cut off. Other archeologists would be arriving to work the site—a new team, all men, all known for their level-headed qualities. Recent pressures had made it impossible for the National Geographic to further fund these romantic notions of prehistoric soap operas. They had another assignment for her.

Jocelyn propped a laced boot into the saddle's stirrup, took hold of the horn, and pulled herself onto the bay. The horse bobbed its head once and shook its mane as Jocelyn took the reins in her hands.

She was now at eye level with one of the figures on the cliff wall. *"Hasta luego,"* she said out loud. "Someday we'll take up where we left off."

Although her hypothesis had been increasingly ridiculed since she first suggested it to the scientific community, Dr. Caine had held firm to her conviction. She knew her idea about migration was valid and she intended to one day prove it. What she theorized was considered archeological heresy, but she had expected that. But she found that there was a greater heresy represented by her efforts—being a woman in a man's field, that was what the establishment considered the greater heresy. So she had stayed out of the establishment's way.

Then, this morning, as the day's thunderclouds were convening in preparation for their usual afternoon powwow, the pockmarked Hopi who packed in her water and supplies came riding his burro into camp, more than a week before he was usually due. The Indian said nothing, but stared off at the clouds for some time. Finally, he slid off the little animal and extended the yellow envelope to her. She didn't open it right away. She didn't need to. Whatever the word might be in the envelope—cashiered? terminated?—it would all boil down to the same thing. Fired. The Indian knew it as well. He did not meet her eyes as they drank coffee and he didn't answer when she thanked him for his delivery. He straddled his sleepy mount and sat for a while more, staring at the ancient tabloid of petroglyphs, then turned the burro with his knees and rode off in the direction he'd come.

The telegram was from Buckner Harris, the old colleague she'd worked the Moki Canyon site with. At least they'd shown the class to get an old friend to wield the ax. But the terse wording could have come from any bureaucrat and still would have meant the same thing: fired. Exactly what she had expected. What she had not imagined, though, was the second half of the message. Further instructions from the home office. Yes, she was being relieved of duties in her Anasazi pursuit, but she wasn't just being turned out to pasture. Nor were they stashing her away in a token teaching job in some musty home for the harebrained. She was being offered another assignment in another state, if she was interested. Apparently that so-called secret cavern discoverer, Charles Loach, was being freed from prison on the condition that he lead an expedition back to the underground gallery. And the authorities in the correctional community wanted some authority in the scientific community to go along with him to verify if there really were cave paintings and judge whether or not they were authentic. The people at the home office thought it sounded just the cup of tea for Dr. Jo Caine.

58

Just her cup of tea. Some of those old fossils in New York must have cackled long and loud over that. What a ridiculous project. Just right for a woman. But, secretly, she was fascinated; and she felt her excitement rising all morning as she broke camp. She was already quite familiar with the scant amount of material from the previous expedition—mostly newspaper blather and more Tutankhamen horn tooting—and she had developed numerous different enlargements of the few photographs of the wall itself. What a mishmash of symbols! As though someone had devised a paste-together of impossible fossils from all over the globe, combining the spine of a giant sloth from paleolithic Ohio with the wings of a pterodactyl from Iraq and the beak of the dodo. Ridiculous, and almost certainly a fraud. And yet . . . if it were real, and if she were able to prove it, then who would be laughing?

The wire emphasized there was no time to waste. It was already late October and this Indian Summer could not be expected to hold out much longer. If anything was to be accomplished before the snows closed the passes to wherever the mysterious crack in the ground was located, they would all have to move quickly. The party had already left San Francisco, two days before if this telegram was accurate. They were due to spend the night in Salt Lake City tomorrow, Saturday evening, then move on on Sunday. For her to rendezvous with them there, she would have to ride all day south down to Searchlight, get a car to take her east over to Kingman where she might be able to catch the milk spur to Flagstaff. From there, if she was lucky, she could rent a Pullman on the Atcheson Topeka & Santa Fe and get into Salt Lake Sunday morning.

Where to find them in Salt Lake? That was a problem she would have to work out on the way. She could wire ahead. The local papers would probably have some information about their lodging. An archeological expedition into the American wasteland wasn't such big news, but a convicted murderer out on bond was bound to attract some attention, especially in the Mormon press. She would find them.

Jocelyn Caine turned from the painted figures and nudged her horse through the stone ruins down the canyon toward the highway, wondering for the thousandth time why the Navaho had never used these Anasazi structures. Even after countless centuries the structures were still perfectly good shelters, solid stone and stone-hard wood, but never used. She had never understood why. For all her study and all her interviews it still remained a mystery to her, a complete mystery.

The coppery rays of the desert autumn sun were still chipping at the clouds as she rode out of the illuminated canyon, south.

4

Society visits Mormons,
meets Boyle,
escapes Whiteshirts . . .

The carrier chugged and banged up Temple Street from their hotel. Ahead of them, nestled between the ridges of Little Cotton Wood Canyon, was Temple Square. North, and a bit west, the granite cupola of the Capitol Building rose. Gaby regarded the wealthy-looking street scene flowing past her porthole window.

"It reminds me of Reno," she said to Father Paul. "Only Reno makes more sense."

"Reno? However so?"

"Well, just look at it—all these ritzy digs built here in the middle of nowhere. Why is it here? There's none of the usual reasons to build a city. These people let a madman lead them to this no-place place and, at his say-so, they went to building. They don't even have gambling or liquor as an excuse."

"They have religious freedom," said Paul. "That is their true motivation."

"Banana oil," Rodney broke in. He was stirring a flask cap

of bourbon into his coffee. "I'd call millions in railroad dollars their true motivation. Copper and silver also make pretty good motivators, not to mention the lucre that pours in every week in tithes. The Latter Day Saints are currently the third richest religion in the nation."

"Second," corrected Father Paul in a sad voice. "And climbing."

"See? These Mormons are no dummies."

"Well you couldn't pay me to live here," Gaby said. "You realize I couldn't even get a drink at that hotel last night? Who ever heard of a dry hotel?"

"You could have gotten a drink in my boudoir, honeybunch," said Rodney.

"A girl's got to be careful of the boudoirs she visits, sugarbush," said Gaby, turning back to her porthole. "Why are we going on this Sunday School side trip, anyway?"

"We are supposed to rendezvous with our scientist," said Rodney over the brim of his cup. "I got word last night from the editor of the paper; he said the city desk got a wire from the archeologist assigned to us—obviously some old crackpot rockhound from the desert doesn't read the news. He didn't even know what hotel we were staying at. So the wire said he'd meet us at noon at the Mormon Tabernacle." He slouched back in the pillows of the davenport. "I guess he figured the Temple was a sight for us to see and a landmark he couldn't miss."

Father Paul leaned close to one of the portholes. He was curious about this Rome of the Latter Day Saints. Beyond the city he could see the Great Salt Lake smeared across the valley floor. Peaks rose out of the center like incisors and salt marsh surrounded the island like infected gums. There were no trees on the flats, no flowers, no grass; nothing but swirl-

61

ing eddies of dust snaking skyward in the morning thermals. And over it all was that famous golden angel blowing his golden bugle. Paul was impressed.

The street leveled out. They were approaching Temple Square. In the driver's seat Ned eased into a lower gear and slowed. He angled through the intersection traffic and put the carrier into a counterclockwise orbit around Temple Square, looking for a parking place. Near the southeast corner of the ten-block square he found two spaces and pulled over. The front of the rig extended onto the sidewalk.

Juke climbed down from his perch on the roof before the motor had stopped. He smiled in at Father Paul as he passed his porthole. The flat stone wall that surrounded Temple Square stretched out behind him. He extended his arms like wings and let go the rungs, but he didn't fall. Instead, he seemed to hang in the air a few feet away from the rig. It looked to those inside the bus as if he were floating. He tucked his wings in and dug into his garments. He withdrew the pipe. Nonchalant, he carefully poured a load from the bag hung around his neck.

"What the hell is that freak doing now?" Rodney asked, crowding to the porthole.

"Looks like he's packing his pipe to me, Rodney," said Father Paul.

"I see that. I mean, what the hell is he standing on?"

Mona pressed her face against her porthole. "Why he's standing on some sort of pillar."

"Pillar?"

"Just that, Rodney. He is standing on a stone block. It comes right out of the sidewalk. Very odd."

"Well I don't like it. It looked like he was hovering out there, like some sort of spirit."

62

"Rodney, spirits don't hover. You make them sound like vultures. They ascend or they materialize but, in all the lengthy experience I've had with spirits, I've never yet seen one hover."

"I don't know about that," Ramona argued. "Remember when we contacted that sweet Mr. Donnelin's wife? She hovered above the table for a bit. Didn't say anything, which was a real pity, but she did hover. Mr. Donnelin found it very unnerving if I remember."

"As well he should have. Mr. Donnelin was a cad! But I still don't think she hovered, exactly. It was more like she floated—"

The motor shut off and the machine became still. "Ladies," said Loach, unfolding his legs and standing, "and gentlemen . . . I believe that we should pack up whatever we consider necessary for this little excursion and stow away the rest. We will be leaving as soon as we meet our archeologist. I regret that our errand doesn't allow for more sight-seeing but I'm sure you understand." He smiled. "I've only been granted twenty days." He walked to the front of the rig and went outside.

Mona began packing frantically. A star chart, a shuffle of mixed Tarot cards, a rabbit's foot rubbed practically hairless, and countless other pieces of spiritual paraphernalia all disappeared into a flowery carpetbag.

"That should be adequate, Mona," Ramona scolded. "Unless you plan to carry it."

"I *do* plan to carry it!"

"I know you. You always start out carrying it, then the first insignificant pebble or something you stub your little piggy on—"

"Ramona, I need every single thing I put in there! And

they are all small things, unlike that ungodly dogwood cross that fake Indian gave you."

"Jibway was no Indian. He was a Mongolian Shaman and certainly no fake. That cross is a protector against infringing auras. And I sense some very infringing auras hovering around this place. Now auras hover . . ."

The back doors clanged and swung open and Ned put his little step into place. As the Society filed out, Rodney hurried to refill his flask from the big demijohn of bourbon he kept in a cardboard carpet roll for protection. He sipped the excess off the top of the little silver flask and slid it into his suit pocket.

"Protection against hovering auras," he said to himself with a shake of his head and started after the others. He bumped into Father Paul, returning. The priest was nervously unbuttoning his collar.

"No reason to raise more eyebrows than necessary," Paul explained. He tossed the circle of stiff linen into his bag and pushed it beneath a couch with his foot. "Wait up, Mr. Makai."

The pair found Ned at the rear of the group, dawdling before the small pillar of stone where Juke was still perched. Ned was pretending to read the inscription on a brass plaque. As they approached the pillar, Rodney felt an odd current of air sift down around him, and he started to shiver. He flipped up his jacket collar. Something inexplicably cold *did* seem to be hovering about the place. He looked both ways, then snuck a quick nip from the flask. There were a lot of tourists around, but they weren't about to notice *him*, he was confident—not with that blue man on top of that stone post and the black man at the bottom.

"Colder here'n it looks," Rodney said to the priest, wiping his lips.

"I've noticed," Paul said. "The grounds of these religious edifices always seem to be a bit chilly."

"Noticed that myself," put in Ned cheerfully. He sounded relieved to have some company bringing up the rear with him. "I recollect going through Notre Dame one August afternoon and, why, it was hot as pitch on the street but it was miserable cold in that place! Colder'n the heart of a you-know-what. Come on down, Mr. Juke."

"Cold," said Juke atop the pillar. "Cold, cold, cold."

"Yes, please," Father Paul insisted. "Hop down."

Juke obeyed, landing at the base of the pillar with a surprising lightness. After knocking a shower of sparks from the bowl of his pipe he frantically began trying to find a place to conceal it. The curved stem seemed too big and the bowl too hot for him to use any of the usual pockets in any of his various garments. An amiable voice stopped him.

"No need to hide your habits here, little friend." A large man in a seersucker suit was smiling down on the group from the top of a small flight of flower-bordered stone steps. "Inside the Tabernacle we do request that you refrain from smoking, for the comfort of some of the infirm and elderly that often visit. But there's no need to hide your vices. Nobody's going to bother you for carrying a pipe—nor a flask, neither. This may be holy ground but it's still the good old U. S. of A. Of course, *we* all abstain."

His grin was an expression of such meaty magnitude that it looked as though it were the result of long and vigorous training. The cheek muscles looked like biceps. The teeth were equally spectacular, big as dimes, and one of the molars was solid gold. It gleamed like the golden angel trumpeting atop the Temple tower.

"Excuse me," said Rodney grinning back. "We were wondering, what is the purpose of this stone?" What he was really wondering was if the man had seen him take his nip or not. He didn't care for the idea of being lumped in with the likes of Juke.

"This old shin banger? This is supposed to be the very spot where Brigham Young stopped. The cornerstone of the Promised City. All the streets of Salt Lake are laid out in relation to this stone. Was that the rest of you-all's group I seen just go by? I thought so. Let me introduce myself. Name's Boyle."

He came down the steps sticking out a palm so broad Rodney wondered how he got it through the arm of the jacket. "I'm R. L. Makai," Rodney said, feeling quite dwarfed as he watched his own tiny mitt disappear into the hammy slab.

66

"R. L. Makai?" the man exclaimed, pumping Rodney's arm with enthusiasm. "Of *The Hollywood Herald*? Honestly, now, ya mean *the* R. L. Makai?"

"The one and only." Rodney beamed. He was beginning to feel bigger. "My friends call me Rodney."

"Rodney, this is some kind of honor and that's the gospel truth." He turned loose the hand and gestured toward the rest of the group ahead. "So this must be the famous Loach Expedition?"

"That's right," Rodney said. "The Search for the Secret Cave, we are calling it. My paper is backing it, you know."

"I sure do know! I've been following all the news releases. There was a nice photo of you in the Sunday rotogravure. In the park in Reno, all of you eating fried chicken. Even you, Jim." He turned the grin at Ned, but kept his hands in his pockets.

"Yes, sir," said Ned. "I eat chicken just like everybody."

"I'll bet. So, then, Makai; the paper said you was to make a stop at the Temple today, and you did. What an honor and treat—the famous Secret Cave Expedition! On behalf of The Saints let me officially welcome you to Salt Lake."

"The Saints?" asked Father Paul.

"I mean Latter Day Saints. Some of us has sorta shortened it; we refer to ourselves, among other things, simply as 'The Saints.' "

"Lots better than calling yourselves 'The Latters,' I suppose," Rodney quipped.

They laughed together. "You're a regular fella, ain't you, Makai? I can see we're gonna get on just hunky-dory. C'mon, I want to meet the rest of your little regiment."

The man threw a massy arm across Rodney's shoulders and steered him up the drive after the others, leaving Juke, Ned, and the collarless Father Paul standing at the pillar.

"E-specially I want to meet this Dr. Loach hombre. In fact, why don't you let me give you folks a special tour? Save you having to wait in line. There's always a wait on Sundays. I'm big enough of a wheel I think I could manage it."

"You got a deal," Rodney said. "If there's one thing I hate, it's waiting in line. Time's too precious to stand nose-to-tail like sheep."

"Amen to that, Brother Makai," Boyle said, rubbing his hands together. "Let's go!"

The rest of the regiment was standing at the end of a long line of other tour groups, waiting their turn to enter the Tabernacle. Rodney called as they approached.

"You, Chick? Dammit, Ferrell, snap out of it and come here."

Chick spun round when he heard his name called. The festoons of photo equipment swung out from his thin neck.

"Mr. Boyle, I'd like you to meet my man Ferrell. In charge of visual as well as verbal documentation of the adventure. Let's just hope he's up to it. Chick, shake hands with Mr. Boyle. He saw your pic of us eating lunch in Reno."

"Great photograph, son," Boyle said, shaking Chick's hand until the cameras banged together. "Revealed everybody's various personalities right to a cut hair, I thought."

Chick nodded, saying nothing. He didn't exactly know what a cut hair was, nor how this big red rubber inner tube of a man could have known whether the various personalities were revealed or not.

"Ferrell," Rodney said, "what I want is for you to get a shot of me and Mr. Boyle meeting. Right now, on these steps, with those edifices in the background. A picture, Ferrell? Click-click? Think you can handle it? Maybe you better use the tripod."

Chick began bustling nervously with his equipment. As they were posing, Father Paul came up. "You know, Mr. Boyle? This area reminds me a bit of the Vatican."

"I suppose there are some physical similarities," Boyle admitted. Then he reached and twiddled Paul's throat with a finger. "What happened to our collar, Padre?" His grin turned loose and lewd. "Are we trying to travel incognito?"

"I must have left it in the carrier," Paul said, flushing.

"Wasn't any need," Boyle said. "The Mormon Tabernacle is open to all visitors, be they pipe smokers, fried chicken lovers, or mackerel snappers." He laughed and pulled the priest in under his arm on the other side. "Have your man shoot all three of us, Makai. For balance, as they say."

As Chick set up his tripod, Paul tried to overcome his discomfort by making conversation. "I take it then you've been in Rome, Mr. Boyle?"

"Sure. Rome, Jerusalem, the cathedral at Chartres. The Temple of the Thule Group in Luxembourg. All them spiritual centers. It's probably our big wall that makes you think of the Vatican."

"Perhaps. It's quite formidable."

"The young church needed it in the early years. For protection, and I don't just mean from the Indians. Did you notice that cave on the ridge as you drove in? The Temple here as well as the Capitol are connected to that cave. It made for a good lookout and back-door escape hatch, both. Just like prairie dogs, huh?"

The camera clicked. Chick pulled out the plate and reversed it for another shot.

"We still use that hole in the ground, matter a fact—as a vault for all our genealogical records, surplus foods, emergency medical supplies. Never can be too careful, eh Makai?"

Before Rodney could answer, a deep voice interrupted from behind the posing trio.

"It must be quite a solace to be surrounded by such security."

"Ah," Rodney said. "Loach. The very man you wanted to meet, Mr. Boyle. This is the discoverer of the cavern. Mr. Boyle—Dr. Charles Loach. Boyle has volunteered to give us a special tour, Loach, so we won't have to wait in line."

Boyle forgot Chick and the camera completely. He turned and held out the big palm. "A honor, Doctor, and that's the truth. I've naturally heard all about you. Quite the hombre. I didn't realize you were a physician as well as all that other stuff."

"I'm not an M.D., Mr. Boyle," said Loach. "I've just got a minor degree—from a little Theosophical Academy no longer extant, I fear."

He met the man's grip; his hand was as long as Boyle's was broad.

"I'm sure you're too modest, Dr. Loach. Theosophy is quite an involved and exacting study. That old Ukrainian mama was no dummy."

Loach's eyebrows raised. "You've heard of the good Madam?"

"Blavatsky? Sure. I even dropped by her old digs in London, once, for a lark. Shot the bull with that poor flunky of hers. Ouspenski-doo. Just kidding. Actually, I got some close associates in Germany still into the old dame's brand of spiritual soup. Sure"—the man lifted his big shoulders in a magnanimous shrug—"like the hedgehog said as he mounted the hairbrush, 'It takes all kinds.'"

Rodney laughed uproariously at the comparison. Loach smiled and slipped his hand free. The rest of the company began straggling over, attracted by the encounter. Gaby was the first.

"Mr. Boyle, I'd like to introduce my niece, Gaby."

"Pleasure." Gaby nodded to Boyle, then turned to Loach. "Don't call me your niece," she said.

"You call me uncle," Loach reminded her with a smile. "Mr. Boyle has volunteered to give us a private tour."

Boyle made a slight bow. "The pleasure's all mine, Toots."

Before Gaby could object Father Paul said, "You say you have a vault? How interesting . . ."

"Sure, Padre, just like the one the Vatican's not supposed to have in the basement. Only ours is more up to date. We are in the last millennium, you know. New juice acoming. Until it comes we—just like the Catholic Church during the Dark Ages—are committed to saving all that is true and holy. We are currently amassing a huge collection of all the spiritual studies, ancient and modern. That's one of the reasons I went to Europe—to collect the most recent teachings. There is a *new age* dawning in Germany, if you didn't know—a great new order, destined to resurrect old powers. Like screwing a fresh bulb in an old socket. When the juice hits—zingo—we got us a bright golden dawn."

He gave them all the smile, tipping his head just right.

"And until then," Gaby said, "the golden tooth'll have to do."

"You got it, Little Sister."

"I'm not your sister, neither," Gaby said. Boyle pretended not to hear, swinging his attention back to Loach.

"Anyway, we are all honored that you all have chosen to stop by our humble Temple on your way to yours. I consider it fitting and reverent."

"It wasn't exactly by choice," Rodney said, leaning close to the big man in an intimate display of confidence. "We are to rendezvous with a very important member of our expedition here. Our archeologist. An authority on caves, you see, some egghead who's supposed to be able to tell if those paintings are the real megillah or just another flimflam, like the Cardiff Giant."

"I read about that egghead," Boyle told him. "Somebody called Caine. It figures, having a jasper called Caine assigned to travel east of Eden with you, to check out if you got the right place."

"Dr. Joseph Caine," Loach corrected, "is probably the foremost authority on ancient petroglyphs on this continent."

"Just spoofing, Loach. I'm a spoofer. Actually, I wish your whole endeavor and all of you the best of fortune. Absolutely. In fact, I admire everything about the whole business but for one *leetle* problem."

"And that is?"

"I don't know as you noticed or not," Boyle said, leaning close to Loach and mocking Rodney's tone of intimacy. "But some of your group ain't entirely what a fella could call white."

After shaking hands with the rest of the group the big man asked them to wait a moment, then pushed through the shifting throng and past the guard with a quick salute. They could see him through the glass doors in the plush lobby, hunched over a pay phone. When he returned he was beaming.

"Everything's set. As the fella in the front half of the dancing horse act says to his partner: 'Folly me.' "

He led the group around the crowd and tapped on an LDS ONLY door. A young man in black suit and tie opened it from within. Ned held back, his face blank.

"If it's all the same to you, Chief," he said to Loach, "I think I'll just wait out here."

"Are you certain, Ned?"

"Yes I am," he nodded. "From here, I can keep an eye on our rig down the driveway, see nobody tries to board her while she's in the slips."

"Very well, Ned. Perhaps you can keep an eye peeled for our archeologist. The wire said we would recognize him by the full field pack he'd be wearing, army issue."

"I'll do it," Ned said, brightening. "A field pack is something Ned Blue can recognize."

While the rest of the group filed through the door, Loach held back to speak briefly with Ned. The driver nodded, then dug something from his trouser pocket and handed it to Loach. Loach turned and walked briskly through the doors to catch up with the Society. Boyle was already into his spiel.

"Friends, this here Tabernacle was built in 1862. This smaller building next to it serves as a meeting hall and for overflow from the Tabernacle when we get particularly popular services. Like Easter. That grand structure out them windows yonder is the Temple, our most holy place. It was begun in 1853 and completed in 1893, forty years to build. Follow me."

Loach fell in behind the man's broad back and once more followed, frowning slightly. Maybe the feeling of mistrust aroused by Boyle was nothing more than prisoner's paranoia. Another old con adage of advice to those hitting the streets after serving a long beef was "Yer bound to feel paranoid. The trick is, make yer paranoia work for ya." There was something suspicious about this snake in the white suit, but he still might prove useful. Besides, there was nothing to do but wait with the troops until this archeologist showed up.

Boyle turned out to be a jovial and informative guide. He explained how the massive Tabernacle was built entirely of materials harvested from the unforgiving Utah desert. He told about the wooden pegs used in the construction instead of nails. He related the tale of the pilgrims' first year, when the new city and its surrounding croplands were smitten with a thunderous swarm of locusts, threatening the young religion's future.

"But in his infinite wisdom and mercy, Moroni sent us a flock of seagulls. Those birds ate all the bugs and the crops was saved. The birds stayed, too, blast their feathers. A messier beast never lived. Quiet, now. We can slip in here through the side . . ."

He led them on into the organ-booming hall and bade

them wait in a group at the rear. He bent to say a few words to an usher and the usher bent to say a few words to a group of Baptists from Kentucky. When the usher stood up so did the Baptists. They filed out, looking confused, and Boyle motioned the Society into the empty pew.

The enormous hall was completely packed, every seat filled and people waiting in the wings. Music was booming out of the bouquet of carved walnut pipes raised at the other end, stately and mesmerizing. The Toccata and Fugue in D Minor. Loach let himself slide down on the polished bench. How long since he'd heard Bach? Father Paul had been allowed to bring in a Victrola a couple of times, but that's not the same. Bach has to come out of a church, or a hurdy-gurdy, or a calliope. Real steam, through actual pipes, that was the way Bach had to be heard.

The music covered him like a mother's hand, and time slid away. So did Boyle. As the last chords of Jesu, Joy of Man's Desiring faded, Loach sat up with a start and realized that the fat man was no longer at the end of their pew by the aisle. He was nowhere to be seen. The crowd was standing and beginning to file out, subdued and considerate after the inspirational concert. Loach followed the rest of the Society into the packed aisle, nodding as the sisters gushed accolades over the organ. He kept looking for Boyle. Then, as they reached the lobby, Loach heard Boyle's voice over the crowd's shuffle and murmur. And a lot of other voices, coming from the wide steps, outside the building. It sounded like a mob. He stretched his height above the exiting crowd to see what was happening. It was like something caught in an aquarium—a school of white-bellied flounders had one little catfish pressed up against the glass. Boyle was the flounder at the head of the school. The catfish was Ned.

74

"I *knew* that fat bastard had a joker up his sleeve. Juke! Juke, come here! They've got one of our boys pinned down. You prepared to take on a tricky detail? I'm talking to you, soldier; can you still follow orders? Yeah? Here take this and listen good—"

Juke takes the key. He listens good. He hears the trouble. People. He sees where the crowd surges and boils around Ned the driver, like soup around a potato. Boils boils boils.

"Can you do it?" Loach demands. "Can you?"

Right, says Juke. Juke can do it A-okay. Double A-okay. All he needs to do is first things first—find the key, get the tempo, let it roll. Let this flood of white shirts and Temple attendants and agitated tourists pick him up and roll him by, whirl him like a leaf toward his objective. Try not to attract no attention. Yes sir, no attention. Juke can do that. Whirl along easy, out to the machine, remember the orders, save the day. Be prepared, yes sir. First things first. Too much evasive action? Already on the carrier, all alone. Not on top, in the driver's seat. Slipped back for a little smoke. "I'm late, Lewis Carroll!" Ramona's old bird. Never could remember his name. Salt Lake. Right. Beautiful music even if it wasn't jazz. Johann Sebastian. Right. That's a start. First things first. But orders is orders. Ned pinned down. Another puff now the blue cloud. Then there's the white shirts. The white shirts. The white shirts. Well, twist 'er tail and throw her in gear, any gear'll do. If you can't find it, grind it! Grind it and drive. Drive drive drive!

After bumping the car in front of him three times, the little man at last found reverse and backed into the street. He threw the stick forward and the huge machine moaned, almost dying. He gave it more gas and picked up speed, the engine beginning to whine.

75

It came up the drive, hunched and heavy with its metal plate and bulletproof glass, its gearbox screaming. The crowd fled from its impending scream. The gate and barricade disappeared beneath the wheels like a cymbal crash. The airhorn was blowing a rhythm reminiscent of "Take the A Train." Juke drove it, still in first gear, all the way to the top of the steps. The Whiteshirts and the tourists and the Society scrambled like ants in a kicked-over hill. As the front bumper reached the glass doors the engine died. Loach was already at the rear, throwing the two doors open and shouting. The last one to board was Ned. He had gone back to get somebody. It was a tall woman with an expression of suntanned amazement. She had a pack on her back.

76

"Here's your scientist, Chief," Ned shouted over the confused babble of the crowd. "Anything else?"

"That'll be fine, Ned. Hop on. I'll drive."

But Juke had the motor turning again. A scream rose from passengers and bystanders alike—he was going to drive right on into the Tabernacle! But reverse appeared magically and the machine began to back down the steps, its big rear doors still flapping open like mandibles on some monstrous insect. From inside the parrot was able to screech "Into the Valley, Kipling!" before his cage splattered to the floor.

Ned managed to scoot in behind Juke by the time the machine had backed its way to the street. He swung around and headed down the tree-lined street, everything still bouncing behind him in the armored enclosure.

"Her name is Dr. Caine, Chief," the driver called without turning around, "Dr. Jo Caine. And she ain't no man, though she sure can sock like one. She socked the snot outta that fat feller back yonder. Hot damn if she didn't! Hot dingy damn!"

5

The Moab Museum of Natural Curiosities . . . opening trunk and having seance . . .

Dogeye crunched across the parking lot, passing before the long low wall of the compound. It was just high enough to convince even a tall man he'd have to shinny over to see in, and it was decorated with garish candy stripes of danger: red bars, orange cuts, and gaping black-paint tears, and ritualized portraits of slobbering animals. Impressive as could be, though Dogeye had only managed the front edifice yet. The remaining three sides of the property were strung with salvaged barbed wire. Only a small part of the actual dream had so far been realized. But it was sure enough open for business, should any happen past. Beneath a hound's face, all purple and green brush strokes, was an inscription that read: "If You Can't Stop Roll Up Your Windows and Honk."

At one point the wall was broken for real, the way the stylized angular shapes all along it had promised. A drunk Californian driving a Studebaker with bad brakes had rolled up his windows, honked, then rolled right on in. Almost. His car still loosely plugged the hole, but it had looked so bad and embarrassing that Dogeye had gradually entered it into the design.

Dog squeezed between the Studebaker's flank and the broken bricks and stood outside the wall, grinning on all he surveyed. This was the best site on the property. He kicked through the weeds and sagebrush, checking his wire traps until he found a full one. Then he bent and snatched up a live rat by its tail. It twitched and squeaked, feet pedaling in the air. Dogeye squeaked back.

Dogeye held the rat suspended between his fingers and regarded the sporadic light of the neon on the roof of his main building. He was proud of that neon. It said ICE. And though he had no ice he left it on day and night, flashing blue and pink, nurturing the sky just the way the sky nurtured the weeds that had grown up around this California car. The weeds were still prospering nicely, no doubt encouraged by the mulch of garbage and bean cans rusting in the ruts, by the crippled furniture, the fractured door frames and so on. Excellent weed food. And the finest weed light, left on as long as the gas in the generator's tank held out, in the brightest, cleanest, emptiest sunlight north of Antarctica. Left on even though the word ICE would probably overheat one day, and explode.

The light reminded Dogeye of the old carnival midway. What a wondrous galaxy that had been, green and blue bulbs whirling, useless illumination in a skeleton turning, alleys laced with webs of orange and blue, red glares screaming down rails, colors and banners making you stiff with wonder: Clarissa the Illuminatrix! Lydia the Lightning Lady! The Hall of Mirrors! Glass tubes twisted into a pink wing-spread, soaring rapture. Christ, yes!

The rat had gone into a paralytic stillness, waiting. Dogeye flipped it, deftly caught its neck, and it was dead. He popped

78

it into his shirt pocket. He was about to go back through the wall when something stopped him.

In the distance, he heard a low murmur, like an angry crowd approaching. His eyes narrowed. Through the waves of heat he saw a black shape hulking across the face of Blowout Butte, so named for the many tons of flinty rocks its faulting had liberated. A moment later the hulk was even larger, lifting a tail of road dust like a horse running from flies. Must really be loaded. All those loud people. Pilgrims? Tourists? Customers? Citizens out of the office for their two weeks a year and fired up to see the Museum? Not likely. Dogeye sighed and shifted his weight to his left heel. He knew it wasn't customers.

This land wasn't right for the fourteen-day vacation. That's where he'd gone broke. This land was the disappearance of systems and structures, time tables and agendas. The disappearance of quests, for this land had disappeared a few. Dog knew the hulk had already rolled past shanties and bits of square dirt strung with barbed wire, dangling hanks of hide, past the plots and parcels, out where there wasn't any shelter for the odd hobbyist. Where there was only miles and hills and sky. And then just sky. That was the main thing out here, everything else simply lifted a little off the ground to meet it. And it was the same for tourists as for the pilgrims, because the only thing offered up here in the air was something you couldn't want ahead of time. You had to get trapped out here and let it grow on you. Mulch it and water it right, afford it the proper illumination. Then it would grow.

That big whatever-it-was, clearly no make or model of any wheeled vehicle Dogeye had ever seen, was getting bigger. Dog threw his shoulders back and struck a little pose, back straight, chin up, chest out. Because, after all, it had to be

79

Charlie. That telegram hadn't left much room to squirm—but Charlie's orders never had. Dog felt down the front of his clothes, checking, then turned quickly to button his fly. When he turned back, they were right on top of him. And then that big-rumped rig went into the most frightening, top-heavy, six-wheel drift Dogeye had ever seen. A simply apocalyptic road maneuver that made that bloated conveyance grunt and should either have left the metal monster of Dog's stone wall on its side or at least shredded all of the beast's rubber, but nothing happened.

When the dust cleared, Dogeye saw the whitest grin he had ever seen grinning at him through the thick front glass of the machine, like a bright new moon. The motor hushed, then the thing, all flat black paint with thick welds like scabs, finally opened up and dropped something.

Something long and oddly angular, blinking in the withering glare Dog lived in and was unaware of. It was his brother.

"You're looking thin as fishline, Charles," Dogeye said. Loach smiled, standing there in worn denim. It was oddly unsettling. Then it struck Dog: what was so unsettling about his brother, batting his eyes under this sun Dog hadn't noticed in years, was his brother's color. Not his skinniness nor his duds. He was still in his prison blues, but that didn't matter out here. It was his hide—as pallid as a gecko's underbelly. He didn't look unhealthy, though. Thin as he was, he looked somehow larger, as though his big bones had grown bigger. But big wasn't enough when the man was practically translucent. The ghost of the Charlie that went to prison, that's what it was.

Nevertheless, Dogeye said, "You're looking all right, though, Charlie-O."

"Bull," Loach said. "I look like six years of strained peas

and eight foot miles." Loach peered around, scanning the length of Dog's wall. "You got the telegram? We're not a surprise?"

"Sure I got it," Dog said. "But you're still a bit of a surprise."

"And this is your welcome? Six years in the can and you don't come jumping into my arms?"

"Well hell, Charlie." Dogeye stuck out his hand. Loach took it and they shook for a second and a half. Then there was a loud voice from the machine's innards that sounded like it was regurgitating an undigested article.

"I don't give a good God*damn* what he said nor *what* kind of weird thing that is out there, I'm stretching my legs! And *you*, boy, you're goddamn lucky I'm drunk, or I'd pummel you black and blue for that driving stunt."

Loach glanced back over his shoulder. Out of the corner of his mouth he said, "Rodney Makai."

On cue, a rumpled little man in a pink tie and banker's linen spilled from the doorway and landed out in the sun, flat on his face.

"You're fired, boy," he said into the dirt, then struggled awkwardly up onto all fours.

"Why, that didn't hurt an ounce," he said. "I could have broken my spine."

Dog looked back to the rig with growing interest, anxious to see what would appear next.

Next was a young woman in skirt and blouse the color of electric storms. After an instant survey of the scene, she extended a long, stockinged calf and stepped down from the machine. She took her time crossing to where the first fellow was still down on all fours. She blew a spent cigarette from her holder and then, astonishingly, one-handed the fellow by his collar to his feet.

"Stand up straight, Mr. Makai. You're a much handsomer man on two feet."

Dogeye recognized the voice, though nothing of the sixteen-year-old girl the voice conjured up could be seen in that form. It was Lydia's sprat. An even more amazing transmogrification than Charlie's. Another ghost, resurrected out of that thin little girl that had mooned around the midway all those afternoons all those years ago.

"Why if it ain't the Gaby—really," Dog shouted with honest delight. "Darn it all, girl, don't you know you've become the finest young lady I've ever seen?"

Gaby glared at him without answering.

"Well, don't you?" Dogeye insisted.

"Doggy." She laughed suddenly. "Isn't there one drop of B and B we could squeeze out of this ratty, dry old place?" She looked a little wobbly, Dog thought, but that didn't diminish her beauty.

Next, the doorway dropped those two old bats, the Makai sisters, shoving each other along. Their needles were still skipping merrily, Dog was happy to note. There is at least some permanence in the world. Somebody aboard that rig wasn't drunk.

But now it was really getting queer. A priest hopped down, pretty as a painting and nervous as a sparrow, cleaning a pair of specs. He walked straight over to Dogeye and offered to shake, pushing his glasses back on his nose. Suddenly the priest stopped in his tracks, his hand stuck out like a spike stuck into a post. He had noticed the garish enclosure. He spoke very slowly, in a voice as pretty as his face.

"Isn't this a very fascinating thing," he managed, with a kind of sickly approval. "It's a . . . wall of some artistic sort?"

"It will be someday," Dogeye said, a little hurt.

"Father Paul, my brother," Loach said. "Mr. Makai, my older brother, Dogeye. And this is our newsman, Chick Ferrell."

Loach indicated a hungry-looking fellow with a red-nostriled nose who was fooling with a camera as he backed away from the group. The man spoke without looking up from his viewfinder.

"Glad t'meetcha. Get that other lady doctor out here and we'll have a nice shot. Stand up a little straighter, Mr. Makai. Better button your fly, mister."

Dogeye turned from the camera to work on the front of his pants again. The problem, essentially, was that when he'd patched that hole the coyote bit out of the seat, he'd taken in too much material. They bound up a little across the front, plus the fact that one button was missing and the two others he replaced in a slipshod manner, one with a button that was just too small, the other with a short twig. They were always popping. When Dog finally looked up he was glad he happened to be wearing underwear, because there was a woman in the stairwell in front of him. She wasn't blushing, and she stepped up to him boldly, holding out a hand. Dogeye took it, tongue-tied.

They froze for the shot, Dog almost unbearably uncomfortable in the presence of the woman six inches from his right elbow. She made him feel like he was suspended. Many times he'd seen hawks float for hours, nearer the sun than the earth, then plummet as if a string had been cut. It was like going through a dip in the road too fast—left his stomach behind.

When Ferrell finished his shot Dogeye cleared his throat and dug a ring of keys up from his hip pocket.

"All right, everyone," Dogeye began, "you no doubt would

like to freshen up. We're short of cabins. Here's how we'll double up."

He handed a key to Ramona, or Mona—you never could be sure. She stared at it a little blanker than usual, Dog thought. "You and your sister'll be together, Miss Makai." She started to whisper something but Dogeye was already parceling another space out to the little drunk banker.

"You and Mr. Ferrell," he said.

"Ferrell can sleep on the bus," Makai said peevishly.

"I'm sorry, but no," Loach said. "We may need to do some rearranging."

Loach went on. "Dr. Caine? You won't mind rooming with Gabriela?"

"Gosh, yes," Gaby said. "We'll have loads of fun. Especially if we can squeeze Doggy for some cactus juice to unbend with."

"I'll bend you, girl," Dogeye said, leering. "Right across my lap."

"Father Paul," Loach smiled. "I'd like you to minister to this old sinner. Room with him."

The priest wasn't paying much attention. Or rather too much attention, for a priest, and not to any old sinner. The wobbly Gaby had hooked his eyes and he watched her with a helpless smile. He kept offering to support her but Gaby was having little to do with it, and anyway, she was still a jigger or so from the actual falling-down stage of drunk.

"By George, I'm looking forward to it, Father." Dogeye clapped Paul so hard on the back his glasses slid down off his oily nose and dangled from one ear. "It's been years since I cornered a man of the cloth."

"It will all work out, I'm sure," Father Paul said.

"Folks," Dogeye went on to address them all, "I'm honored by your presence. Take a moment or two to find your bunks, none of the doors are really locked. Move in your bags, freshen up. Plenty of water in those shower stalls yonder. I've got a holding tank as big as this ugly heap of tin here"—Dog slapped the carrier—"plus a water heater I built myself and I've been shoveling juniper rounds into it all morning, so *some*body better take a shower. But don't dally or you'll miss chow. What I mean to say is—"

Dogeye turned toward the setting sun and held his hand at arm's length, counting the number of fingers between the sinking orb and the horizon.

"—Four and a half fingers. Dinner in forty-five minutes."

The four dumpy little cabins were clustered in a ring, each front porch facing out, as if they were wagons in a western under Indian attack. If they'd been strung out straight along the road, Dr. Caine thought, and if it hadn't been for that larger first building with the neon flapping on the roof, the cabins might have been mistaken for a motel. No tribe, Anasazi or Apache, would have dwelt out in the open like this, but then Loach's brother didn't seem exactly tribal. Jocelyn led Gaby to the number 2 that matched their key.

The door wasn't locked, but it was definitely stuck. "It's got to give," Jocelyn observed.

The archeologist leaned against the cabin's wall, out of the way. The girl brought her ample hip sideways against the partition. The door banged open and flecks of paint fell.

"Looks like nobody's been in here since Methuselah was in short pants," Gaby said, staggering across the dark, hot room to drop her bags bedside. "But I'll be damned if these aren't fresh sheets."

Jocelyn set her pack just inside the door, then crossed straight to the blind and sent it flapping upward. The sun was beginning to singe the far ridge, ballooning and reddening and cooling like there was something wrong with it. And, in fact, Jocelyn knew it must be fifteen or twenty degrees cooler out on that baked plain than it was inside. She loosened her collar and tried to bang the window open with the heels of her hands.

"It's stuck too," she said. "Painted shut." She turned to see if Gaby was still in the room. She had a funny feeling she was alone, but there the younger woman sat, on the bed, dribbling bourbon from a pint into a jam jar she'd dug up somewhere. Jo had thought she was gone because of the quiet of Gaby's concentration.

Jocelyn found her pocketknife and turned back to the window. She folded out the small blade and began chipping at the paint.

"How'd you get hooked up in this?" she asked without turning from her task. It was a long time and a couple of clearly audible swallows before the girl behind her answered.

"Just climbed on board, is how."

"I mean Loach. And his brother and those sisters. You seem to know them all."

"We were all in the carney bit together. Not the sisters. They came later, with the cave business."

"You were in the cave with them?" Jocelyn asked. She began to work on the bottom edge of the window frame.

"Naw, not the cave. They didn't need me. But I was fully qualified as a real carney lady."

"But how'd you get started?"

Gaby shrugged. "Grew into it. Oh, at first I lacked the body and the bull. Just a skinny little thing. My mother ran off on me. She'd been the aerialist and Lightning Lady act, you know. After she left I tried the trapeze but didn't have the strength. I could handle the Van de Graff, though, so I got onto the bill doing the lightning bit. But what I wanted to do was trapeze. You know, that was the biggest disappointment of my life—when Lydia ran off without teaching me to fly. That was the end of my future as an acrobat. I loved those costumes."

That was about all Jocelyn wanted of Gaby's past. She concentrated on the window. But Gaby was still talking, pausing only occasionally to dribble liquid into the glass.

"So, how do you get to be a lady doctor, anyhow, Doc?"

"I guess you go to school," said Jo, turning from the window.

"Do you have any men patients," the girl asked, "or is it all just the ladies?"

There was an odd little silence. Jocelyn went back to work. She finished the last of the bottom edge, where the paint had puddled. She started on the left side, chipping toward the sunset with renewed vigor and concentration. Inches peeled away at a stroke.

"Did you start out as a nurse of archeology?"

Jocelyn set her knife on the sill and turned away from the sunset. Gaby was flat on her back, drink on her stomach, counting on her fingers.

"Loach's brother said there were showers," Jocelyn said. "Why don't you go first?"

Gaby didn't appear to be listening. She folded the last finger and lay still. "Nearly six weeks," she said. "What rotten luck." She sat up on the cot and looked at Jocelyn. "You haven't got that thing open yet?" The girl stood shakily, looked about the room and, before Jocelyn could move, picked a glass ashtray off the bedside table and hurled it at the window.

Air began to move within the room.

Outside of his cabin, Rodney was trying to grasp the significance of the bizarre fence he was pissing through. Hard to believe it was possible, but the fence was weirder than that weird damn wall up front. There was all kinds of, well, *stuff*, hanging off it: twisted rabbit skins like picked scabs; rusted sickle blades painted pink; crankshafts trailing black satin ribbons; a stocking cap; a framed formal portrait of a man in an admiral's uniform of the last century; a section of twisted lead pipe spelling GILL, such as fish have; and then a lot of bones and torn-up tree roots. Like the inside of an ax murderer's twisted mind, and they ought to get some snaps of it, just in case.

Chick, on his second trip from the back of the carrier, came around the corner of the cabin dragging heavy bags. His eyes were red and his nose was running. "Sage," he sniffed. Rodney pulled in his legs to let him by.

"Don't you have the sense to get that colored boy to help you?"

Chick shrugged and banged through the door, breathing hard. Makai staggered to his feet and followed Ferrell in. He pushed the door shut.

"All right," he said. "Looks like we got a minute or two. Get cracking. I want some shots of that maniac's fence out there."

Chick dropped his bags on the bed under the window and sat down. Makai's were still out on the porch.

"Look," Ferrell said, "we've only got a few minutes before supper and I'd like to get cleaned up. Besides, we've lost the light for any good shots."

"God almighty, Ferrell, no wonder you got canned! If Hearst heard that line of gab he'd kick you into next week—

88

into a whole other line of work, too. If you can't give me some pictures, then give me some goddamn words in sentences in paragraphs on a page. Ain't that what you're here for? I want a record of *all* this weird stuff, savvy?"

They locked eyes for a second, then Ferrell turned one of his bags toward him and popped it open. He unfolded from it a notebook, took up a pencil, and licked its tip, as though to take dictation.

"That's better," Rodney said. "I'm going to get cleaned up. I'll be back out in time to clean up your grammar."

The shower was exceptional, maybe a little rank and rusty but, Rodney had to admit, piping hot and wonderfully refreshing. He leaned up against the side of the plank stall and relaxed. Things were looking up. He stood under the water until he felt like tipping another drink. He got out, toweled his skin pink, wondering if there was time to trot over for another nip with the gorgeous Gaby. He wondered if they could contrive to be alone, and whether there'd be time to slip it in. She was sure as the world hot enough for it, rubbing around all plump and sweaty inside those tight duds all day, her goodies poking against the damp fabric. What agony that'd been. He wasn't putting up with another day like this, gnashing his teeth. He'd nail her if he had to drown her in hootch and drag her off into the rubble.

He left the bathroom combing his hair and whistling.

"All ready," called Chick from their open cabin door. He held up his notebook.

"No time now," said Rodney. "I'm fired up. I'm going to slip over to the women's cabin and slip into something more comfortable, like with wiggly hips. Don't try to dissuade me, she's weeping for it. Where's that little pint of bourbon whiskey?"

"You gave it away," Chick said petulantly. He folded his

89

notebook. "You were fired up for this damn copy twenty minutes ago."

"Ah, ah, *ah*-ah." Makai waggled his finger. "Take it slow, boy. Patience. You're going nowhere with this kinda frantic nonsense. Rewrite. Put in some more action verbs and purple adjectives. I'll look at it as soon as I'm done. Ta-ta."

Chick sniffed and turned to go back into the cabin. At that moment they heard a loud ringing, insistent as a fire alarm in a match factory.

"What the hell is that?" Rodney wondered.

"Let's hope it's dinner," Chick said. "I'm starved as hell."

"Starved, impatient and sniveling," Rodney said with disgust. "Wotta man."

90

Father Paul was the first of the party to reach the main building. He hadn't gone to the shower. He rarely showered, because he rarely got dirty. He had changed out of the collarless priest's shirt and into a light blue pullover. His face shone in the dying light and his taffy bright curls bounced on his forehead. He looked like a model on his way to a cologne ad.

The building before him stood blocky and broad beneath the quivering neon. At the entrance the word "MUSEUM" had been chiseled into the front double doors, half on one door, half on the other. Paul pushed through the "E-U-M" door. Inside, he encountered an explosion of eccentricity that made him think, for an inexplicable instant, of the poor Mexican cathedrals he had visited—haphazard and garish and at the same time somehow pious.

Yet it was apparently a real museum. There were dioramas and displays, each carefully labeled. The high wooden walls were draped almost completely with what looked like the remnants of canvas freak-show banners: The Living Skeleton came rising like a starved Lazarus from the gloom of an abstract coffin; Seal-O the Seal Boy balanced a beach ball on his nose and clapped hideous flippers together; Lydia the Lightning Lady held illuminated light bulbs over her sequined bosom, sparks shooting up from her cleavage; The Human Jukebox displayed a being with hinged arms and a puppet's mouth, an old-fashioned mustache painted across his face and a black derby jammed on his head. Seated with arms raised at the keyboard of a tiny toy piano, the apparition looked like the kind of doll one might expect to find in a fun house.

Exhibits had been pushed back against the banners to make room for a long plank table—cases and cages and terrariums stacked two and three deep. Living and dead animals seemed to be incarcerated everywhere, some in full view, others hidden from sight. He saw an armadillo with a handle on its back, and a coyote with eyeless red sockets. Judging by the snarls and whimpers, a few of the captives had come into closer proximity than they were used to. There were all sorts of things glued to boards, from butterflies to arrowheads to intricate maps of nations Paul couldn't place—and ancient scribbled charts with arrows linking columns of numbers and symbols. There were skulls and skeletons and skins of all sorts of unrecognizable species piled in odd corners, including one thin, hairless piece of leather that looked distressingly human. This was tattooed REMEMBER THE MAINE.

The long table was covered with a roll of antique Spanish lace, so old it looked like it might dissolve at any moment. An extravagant setting of mismatched but elegant bone china was laid out down both sides. Crystal gleamed and silver shone, obviously polished, Paul realized, for the occasion. As haphazard as it all was, it was evident that a great deal of care had gone into this preparation.

The door banged open behind him. "Smells like a God-damn barnyard in here."

That was Makai, banging in with his flunky close behind. Paul was pained by the crudity of the remark. He walked out of the way and pretended to be examining the inhabitant of one particularly dark cage.

"It smells like all sorts of things, I reckon."

This was Dogeye, literally a blur of activity at the big stove at the other end of the room. He didn't turn from his labors.

"That's the breaks with animals," he went on. "Alive or dead, they exude all sorts of things, like nobody's business."

The sisters came in. The room was filling up, beginning to surge with steam and chatter. A sudden wild screech at the cage made Paul jump and screech back. Everything else in the room went quiet, listening to the cage. Dog rushed over and bent to the dark enclosure, then picked it up. Inside it was a black ball of feathers and fur, whirling from corner to corner. Whatever was inside had snaked a paw out through the tight weave of its wall to pull its neighbor in with it—a jackdaw. The bird was plucked nearly clean. Dogeye shook the cage until the creature dropped its victim, then put the demolished bird back in its own cage. He kicked the bars of the unruly perpetrator of the crime.

"That damn lynx," he said to Paul as though apologizing. "The poor thing's in heat. A little confused by her own appetites. Which reminds me—"

Dogeye crossed to the room's other side and lifted the screened lid of a glass box. He reached in and looped out a long green and yellow snake that was as thick as Paul's neck. Dogeye held it just behind its jaws. It writhed lazily until it looped part of its body over Dogeye's shoulders. It waited while the man fumbled something out of his shirt pocket, then opened its long mouth and accepted whatever that something was. Dogeye began to roughly massage the snake's throat, as if working an egg down a garden hose. When it was far enough in, he coiled the snake back into its box and closed the lid.

"Jee-zus," whispered Makai. The room began to chatter again.

"They generally won't eat dead meat," Dogeye explained. "And this fellow needs his energy."

"Jesus H. Christ," Rodney repeated. He was somewhat relieved to see Dogeye stop briefly by the washbasin on his way back to the stove.

The door opened and Paul also felt relieved. It was the girl, Gaby. She was followed by Dr. Caine. The girl looked around, rolling her eyes at the spectacle of the hall. The older lady looked absolutely delighted, however. She walked immediately to an iridescent feather robe hung on a wire hanger. Dogeye beamed.

93

"That's one of the best pieces I've got. Belonged to Hawaiian royalty."

"I know," said the archeologist reverently. "Made from the feathers of the oi-oi bird, now extinct."

"Well I didn't exterminate 'em. I just won it from a passing Polynesian who happened to think he was hot stuff with the poker cards."

"I've only seen pictures," said Jocelyn.

"Now you've seen a real one. Go ahead, try it on."

Jocelyn picked up the beautiful feathered robe. It was tremendously heavy. She draped it around her shoulders. Though she was on tiptoe, its hem touched the floor. It was alive with yellows and iridescent reds that puffed and shivered delicately with the garment's movement.

"Makes you look royal as butter," Dogeye suggested without a hint of sarcasm. But the woman pulled it off as if something obscene had been suggested, hung it back in place.

"It is beautiful," she said. "And very well preserved. It must be at least a hundred years old."

"You can have it if you want. Looked better on you than on that hanger."

Jocelyn was completely nonplussed by the sudden offer. She laughed. "I don't accept gifts that are worth more than a year of my salary," she finally said.

"Suit yourself," Dogeye said. "But any time you change your mind, she's yours. I never seen a woman before that was man enough to wear it. I mean, what I mean is—"

He couldn't go on. An odd tension filled the room.

"Will you look at Uncle Doggy," Gaby whispered to Jocelyn in mock amazement, "pitching that ostrich-feather woo. I think you've got him completely smitten."

Jocelyn didn't answer and Dogeye resumed his cooking.

"My land!" said Mona, walking around the table to change the subject from scales and feathers, "Just look at the table. I certainly didn't expect to find cut crystal out here."

"It's very elegant, Dogeye," agreed Ramona, looking about. "And you know, I think your paintings have improved. They rather remind me of the Cubist work in Paris. Don't you agree, Father?"

The paintings looked to Paul like poor Dogeye couldn't draw straight, but he agreed. "Even Surrealist." He nodded. "Some of the images are reminiscent of the classic Dutch painter, Hieronymus Bosch."

"They are the faces of our subconscious, Father," said Loach's voice. "The sideshow always struck me as a mirror of mankind's hidden face."

If the priest had been asked which door the man had come in, or even if he'd been there before, he would not have been able to answer.

"I've noticed that similarity before in Dog's work, to some of the creatures in Bosch's 'Garden of Earthly Delights.' "

"If this is the Garden of Earthly Delights," Gaby said, "I hope to God I go to the other place."

Everybody laughed and the tension dissolved.

"My brother must be some kind of genius," Loach kidded. "Because every time he tries to do anything else—run a motel, or carney, or farm—he goes broke."

"But I can cook! You got to admit that, Charlie-O; I can by God cook." He turned from his stove, gesturing at the room with a steaming wooden spoon. "Just you folks sit down and see if I can't! It's chow time."

95

Before they were seated, Dogeye had swooped down on them, a steaming platter high in each hand. Paul had never seen such an eye-bulging quantity and variety of food. There were beans and greens, steaks and corn cakes, and a cheese-crusted casserole teeming with something the man called mountain oysters. Even Rodney was impressed, so much so he sent Ned to the carrier for one of the cases of wine he had packed on when they passed through Sonoma.

It was a marvelous meal. Dogeye kept the food coming and Makai kept the corks popping. They finished up with apple dumplings and a little after-dinner wine that Dogeye had vinted himself, he said, from prickly-pear cactus. Paul had never heard of prickly pears or wine being made from any part of a cactus, but the more he drank, the more he believed him. By the time it was completely dark all the animals had gone to sleep and the people seemed equally placid.

Chick was the last to finish, helping clean up the leftovers.

The clink of glasses and silverware died, and finally only the growl of the generator outside invaded the animal contentment within.

Mona, directly across from Paul, was sitting back in her seat, agitating her half glass of wine with a nervous circular movement of her wrist. She finally spoke up.

"I have a premonition that this is the moment we've been waiting for, Doctor."

"I must agree with my sister," Ramona said. "I feel it too."

"I'm the one who felt it, Ramona! Don't you try to hop aboard my premonition."

"What appropriate moment?" Rodney wanted to know. "What premonition?"

"To unlock the past, Makai," Loach said. "Dog, if you'll get the key Ned and I will carry it in."

"Carry *what* in?" Rodney demanded.

"The *trunk*," the sisters cried together, "the trunk from the *Temple*—that Juke had lost the *key* for!"

Jocelyn didn't ask any questions. She went to work clearing the table. Most of the dishes were piled in the big tin sink by the time Loach and the stocky driver thudded the heavy chest in the center of the room. Dogeye was waiting with a crude brass key. Jocelyn looked around her at the room full of attentive eyes and sat down. This wasn't just some after-dinner game she hadn't played before, she realized. They seemed serious.

The trunk looked big enough to hide a folded man. With everyone in a circle around it, Dogeye handed over the key. Loach knelt and inserted it in the rivet-ringed keyhole. It turned with a satisfying scrape and both sisters gave simultaneous sighs.

Loach lifted the lid and an aroma of camphor and cast iron

wafted out. Tissue-thin silk scarves bloomed upward, like a rainbow taking a breath after years of waiting for the storm to pass. The silks began to drift over the trunk's edges and float to the floor where they undulated with the slightest puff of air, they were so light and insubstantial. They kept coming, geysering purple, green, vermilion . . . Finally, one of the sisters uttered a happy sob and dug her jeweled hands into the erupting colors. She drew up a small crystal ball, no bigger than might have been used in a game of croquet, but breathtakingly brilliant. The myriad scarves surged and ebbed within the globe as the sister held it high.

Jocelyn had never seen a real crystal ball before. She found herself having to look away from it. It was hard enough to watch those scarves swimming around like gypsy trout, without the glass curving them into nightmarishly magnified poses.

Then, with her own little cry, the second sister located her prize—some kind of machine, all gears and nested spheres. At first Jo thought it was an astrolabe, but it was only the outer shell that was etched with constellations and stars. The inner rings were inscribed with Roman numerals and arrows, and the whole thing seemed to be built about a surveyor's sextant. As Jo looked, she saw the old lady's eyes moisten. She held it cradled for a few moments, like a baby, then began to turn a small crank and say her sister's prayer out loud. It sounded like a hen cackling over an egg.

"That's a model of the universe," Gaby whispered at Jo's ear. "Not the current universe, some *other* universe, with the sun at the center."

"Ptolemaic," Jo whispered back, and the girl said, "Right."

Now everyone was digging into the trunk, as though suddenly bent on getting their share of an exhumed body.

Dogeye found a skull that Jocelyn thought looked prehistoric, even *Australopithecus*. But she couldn't tell because the skull had been painted with gold lacquer. With a laugh Loach untied a bundle of old clothing—khaki shirt, tall boots, jodhpurs. Gaby found a cut-glass bottle; eyes closed, the girl took the stopper out and smelled the contents. Even poor Juke located a personal prize, a little derby made of some kind of hard black synthetic, like horn players used for a mute. He stood looking down into its dark cavity as though he thought some of the notes might still be trapped in there.

Now Loach was up to his shoulder in the iridescent cloth-embalming fluid, feeling for something on the trunk's bottom. He finally located what he was after—an old canvas-bound book with a snap-flap to keep it closed.

98

"Doc Destiny's famous *book*," Gaby explained in another loud whisper, putting the stopper back on her bottle of perfume. "Where he keeps all his famous mysterious *secrets*."

Loach chose not to notice the friendly derision. He walked back to the table with his book, eyes shining like the sisters'. He unsnapped it and began to leaf through pages filled with notations penned in an ornate cipher. For a time the only sound was the turning of the pages and the distant flutter of Dogeye's gasoline generator.

Other articles were emerging—more clothing, bundles of roots, bones set with rhinestones and glass, canopic jars sealed with wax, more books. Finally, from the very bottom, a heavy lathed pedestal and an oval slab of dark wood nearly as big as the trunk itself. "Our altar," one of the sisters breathed; Jocelyn could not tell which.

The pedestal stood on three little legs, carved griffin paws with talons of ivory. The oval slab slid intricately into three carved slots at the top, creating a table. The top of the table was absolutely writhing with symbols and glyphs. It looked to Jocelyn like someone had shaken the illustrations out of a copy of the *Arabian Nights* and shellacked them into the wood right where they fell.

"Oh, Doctor," the sister with the crystal ball asked, raptly polishing the tabletop with a scarf, "shouldn't we have a little seance?"

"My thought exactly," the other woman put in. "An inquiry, to see if the spirits are in accord with our endeavor."

"I don't see why not," Loach said with a gentle smile. He closed his book. "But I certainly hope the spirits are more understanding than my warden was, or we might never get out of here."

The priest laughed and Rodney hissed an order to Ferrell to go get his camera. The photographer didn't move. Without another word the sisters began to drape themselves in scarves while the room watched. Even more disturbing, Jocelyn realized, were the articles of their underclothing that were beginning to turn up on the floor—petticoats and corsets and bloomers. When they were completely enfolded in silks and sashes, even their blouses and walking skirts lay in drab piles at their feet.

Dogeye had gone out for a second, and now he returned with a wrought-iron candelabrum. He set five thick candles into its sockets, three black and two red, and lit them. The sisters were following him, fussily changing the placement of each candle until the arrangement suited them. Then they began to light fistfuls of incense sticks and fix them in the wire mesh of the cages. Smoke was beginning to blanket the hall, stinging Jocelyn's nostrils. Some brand Episcopalians haven't discovered yet, she thought.

Without a word the sisters pulled up chairs and sat on

either side of the oval table, knobby bare toes poking out of the florid fabrics as though playing footsy with the griffins. They let their eyes unfocus and raised their palms toward the five candle flames. The jeweled fingers shuddered for a few moments then were still, spread, seeming to hold an invisible globe between the two women like a big beach ball.

Nobody moved. The incense was having quite an effect on Jocelyn, making her tear and blink. She hated this ceremonial stuff, especially when it stank. If there were dogmatic words and dogmatic images, this was surely a dogmatic smell, sweet and cloying and sanctimonious.

Outside, the generator began to sputter and die, the electric bulbs in the room suddenly fading. People hardly seemed to notice; something was happening to the sisters. Their eyes had rolled back beneath their penciled eyebrows and a noise was beginning to come from their throats—a mutual growling buzz, like a gathering swarm of electric bees. It reminded Jocelyn of the noise she'd heard the Australian Aboriginals make with their didjeridus in the dark outback.

This is different than I expected, Jocelyn was forced to acknowledge with a shiver. Something more than incense and old silk. It was a shocking thing she was witnessing. The two old women were twitching, growling, shuddering, their eyes so far back that nothing showed but the veined whites. And the animals were waking up, agitated by the throaty buzzing. It rose to a din, a cacophony, the pitch and volume lifting toward some sort of unavoidable climax. At that moment something behind them bayed.

It had to be the blind coyote, surely. But the effect could not have been more profound had it been a werewolf. And it had the intended effect. The sisters suddenly quieted. Their irises rolled back down and they were staring into each other's eyes, their mouths gaping as if they saw some mutual manifestation, some vision there for them to use, and were about to use it.

Then Loach spoke, his voice low, pitched seemingly outside of the sisters' realm.

"It helps to hold hands," he said. "To unite the energy."

As by command, all the witnesses linked up, tightening the circle around the sisters. It was a little too close for Jocelyn's taste, but she joined in. She couldn't resist. And they had seemed like such nice middle-aged ladies. A little dim, but other than their foolish talk and trinkets they'd seemed reasonably conventional, of a type Jocelyn might have recognized among her mother's friends in Philly. Hobbyists. Dabblers. Older ladies pottering around in the other world when they weren't tending their hydrangeas. A pastime while unloading their inheritances.

But none of her mother's friends had growled. The echo of that sound still reverberated in the room's dank corners, with the incense smoke, though the sisters made no noise at all. They had also stopped breathing, Jocelyn was convinced. Maybe they'd even managed to hush the pulse in their veins. The only live things about them were their eyes.

"I think they're in contact now," Loach went on. "And the ladies really don't have the stamina for an extended session." His eyes closed. "Spirit . . . are you there?"

Nothing happened, nothing at all.

"If you are there, Spirit, please help us."

Even the animals waited in silence.

"If you are there, please, there is a question we need an answer for. Is this endeavor in accord?"

Still nothing. Somebody shuffled in the gloom across. This should have been the obvious moment for the slicker who was bankrolling this show to crack wise, but when Jocelyn looked over she was amazed to find Makai's eyes as glassy and his mouth hanging as slack as the sisters'. Jocelyn cleared her throat, as quietly as she was able. Well, if that pink-tied loudmouth wasn't getting impatient with this mumbo-jumbo, she sure as the world was.

"Who do you think we have contacted, Doctor?"

It was the priest, the priest, for heaven's sake! And there hadn't been so much as a squeak since that coyote howled.

Jocelyn spoke up. "Is there any chance we might put out the incense, Doctor?" Loach didn't seem to hear. His eyes remained shut. It was all beginning to irritate Jocelyn considerably. She had known from the start that in hooking up with Loach and his band of whatnots she had taken a huge risk with her career. There was no question that if this was an archeological expedition, it was one Barnum & Bailey couldn't have improved on. Here they were, holding hands and asking for guidance. They were going to need it, too, if this smoke got much thicker, spinning around in this wornout Ptolemaic foolishness. That's not how you make your mark in archeology. If you're an archeologist, you make your mark by measuring variations in the diameters of ten thousand examples of fossilized avian metacarpals, by watching your step as you go sifting through the detritus of real ages, not by careening through the desert with a convicted murderer and two old bats in silk. And if you're a *woman* and an archeologist, Jocelyn thought, you had *really* better watch your step.

Unless you actually do find something, something so absolutely undeniable that you won't just offend the establishment, but rattle it completely down.

And you'd better find it. Or all the growling and howling and smoking and other spurious high-level directives won't help.

One of her favorite professors had told Jacelyn that the way of true science is the plodding way, the way of Newton, or Galileo, or Darwin. That intuition was best left in the kitchen, especially female. That all those so-called suffragette scientists like Madame Curie was just flukes who had fallen through the cracks. She wondered wryly what he would have said to her about this bit of research, in this ramschackle laboratory of the libido.

"If the presence of this group," Loach intoned on, "or of any of its members will not be tolerated in the cavern, we will not go forward. Will we be tolerated?"

Jocelyn was about to clear her throat again, but suddenly there was a sound—loud and clear as a rifle shot. The whole room shook beneath the report. No one, nothing had moved. The sound had seemed to come directly from the nearest of the sisters, though neither had moved at all as far as Jocelyn could see. She leaned forward, intent on watching them closer.

"Thank you, Spirit," Loach said. "Now. If this expedition has been improperly composed, or if our visit at this time and season will be improper, or if the visit of any member of our expedition will be improper, we will go no further. Does the Spirit consider this endeavor to be in any way improper?"

There were immediately two more knocks, deeper than the first, and seemingly closer to the other sister, loud and conclusive, as if someone were knocking skull-sized rocks together; but again, completely without movement. Out of nowhere, out of absolutely nowhere!

"If the conditions under which this journey was commenced are tainted, if the funds which have supplied it are tainted, if I myself am tainted by my incarceration among unclean spirits, we will go no further. Is there such tainting?"

Again, the two deep cracks. Jocelyn felt her skin begin to prickle.

"It is your judgment then, Spirit, that we are clean enough to go on?"

The first report cracked again, like a boulder divided by the frost. Then dead silence. Jocelyn set frozen, stuck between belief and incredulity. This could not be happening! But here it was, not three feet in front of her. Her mind spun and she felt for a moment that the large supper she had just eaten was about to find its way back into the room. Her lungs were paralyzed. No one else seemed to be breathing, either. Even the animals back there beyond the candles were stunned into silence. She heard the tall man whisper, "Thank you, Spirit," and suddenly there was sound and movement again. The sisters began to wilt in their chairs, all the silks and colors going limp about them. The coyote started whimpering.

"I'd call that a definite affirmative," said Dogeye, turning loose Jocelyn's hand and standing to yawn.

The rest of the evening, the scarves turning on the floor, the sisters shaking it off, and Loach's sonorous voice—all of it was a raveled tapestry in Jocelyn's mind: it wouldn't hang. The weave of it had a theme she couldn't work out. She'd never been very good with tapestries.

Jocelyn was the first to head to her cabin that night, leaving the others explaining to the sisters what had happened during their trance, and the dishes still in the sink unwashed.

◇

As the other diners were leaving, Dogeye and Loach took the opportunity to step onto the porch and look at the stars. Dogeye fell to kicking at the post that he knew harbored termites.

"If you keep them bugs moving they can't do nearly the damage," he said, thumping away. "Can't chew good."

"Feels good to clear the lungs," Loach said to Dogeye. "They burn that incense like they're having gas warfare."

"Maybe we should get them to sign some sort of treaty," Dogeye said.

"Not those two," said Loach. "They're stuck in their smoky ways."

"Plugs up my snoot," said Dogeye. He bent over to dig with his long, naked nails at the post where it joined the porch. Nothing unloosed yet. Would be, though, if he kept kicking.

Dogeye's sinuses began to clear and the world dribbled in. Smelled like a dropped tent, he thought. Not pleasant, but not offensive. He stood by his brother, smelled the sage. He used to stand shoulder-to-shoulder with Charlie, he seemed to remember. Now Dogeye was a foot shorter, like something in the desert had shrunk him. He was turning into a desert rat just like he'd been warned.

The sounds and the lights from the cabins died. Dogeye heard Rodney, a hundred feet off, flaring orange on his cabin's back porch, light a cigarette. In the stillness he could hear the burning tip crackle as Makai pulled.

"Did you ever get the feeling there might be something funny in that incense the sisters use?" he asked. His brother didn't answer. Loach was caught up in his thoughts, and the amazing stillness of this desert night.

Dogeye sighed. "It just beats the hell out of me how those dingbats do that damn knock," he said. "Do you really think it could be the incense somehow? I always do feel pretty damn odd after they run their act."

Loach shifted his weight and the floorboards squeaked. "No, I was just joking about that," he said. "I don't know how the hell they do it. It's something a man can think about for six years."

"Want to hear my objections to your little expedition, Charlie?"

"No."

Dogeye sighed again.

"Then tell me what we're up to out here. Enjoying the night air?"

"No," Loach said, stirring himself. "We've got all kinds of work ahead of us tonight. We might as well get at it."

The brothers stepped off the porch together.

Only an occasional coyote howled to help the rising moon. It was an off night for coyotes. The dreams of the travelers in their cabins were tinged with engine roar and the rhythms of rubber on asphalt. Dream machinery. But it was the sound of real metal on metal that woke Father Paul.

$$\diamond$$

He peered through the darkness of the room to the other bunk. Empty. He rose, lit the lantern, and walked naked to the cabin's back door. Across the gravel path a light came on in cabin two and Paul could see the silhouettes of Gaby and Dr. Caine. They too were trying to hear what was too dark to see. The sound commenced booming again but Paul couldn't take his eyes off the shorter of the silhouettes. Behind the gauze that held the light around her, she was naked. Even as he. Paul found nothing in his eyes but that dark shape within the light. The sound continued, like thunder. Someone was out there, Paul was almost sure, beating on the rig's side with a stick just to hear it boom. But it seemed to him the lightning that caused it came from that dark form. He had to pry his eyes away or have his heart beat through his chest.

He could see nothing but bobbing lamps. The hammering stopped and the steady grinding of a saw replaced it. Dogeye could be heard, laughing, then the voice of an older woman, either Mona or Ramona, trying to shush him. He wouldn't shush. He kept laughing. Whatever was going on out there amused Dogeye.

The light in the other cabin went off. Paul hung in the doorway a moment, then he too crept back to bed. It seemed safest. Paul brooded on that vision he'd seen—the cornucopia of Woman, like a spiraling tunnel, and he could see no bottom to it. He spun face-down on the mattress and pulled the pillow over his head, hoping to stifle the noise from outside and the pictures within.

When they were finished, Dogeye went back through the crack in the wall and crossed directly to the Museum. He squatted in the center of the room. It was serious, turning these animals loose. Most wouldn't live, some that shouldn't would: it was like letting go of the wheel at highway speeds. But there was only one way to do it—open up your hands.

He pivoted on his heels, memorizing the features of each animal just in case he met up with it again, in this life or the next. He savored the quiet stillness. All the renovation had been fun but noisy. It had put him on edge, too. The smell of this animal stillness soothed him, the way it always did. The room was peacefully rank. Whatever spirits the sisters had conjured up were gone now, forced into the night by the smell of nature.

107

Dogeye went first to find the rooster. This finely rounded yellow beak was any or all beaks, except for the white slash near the corner, where the animal had been hurt somehow on the first day or so of its life. Besides, it had four wings. Unmistakable flight pattern, like a living eggbeater. Dogeye lifted the top of the rooster's box, carried him under an arm to the door, and tossed the bird onto the ground.

Next came the lynx, wriggling its hips, and horny. A condition absolutely endemic in its race. But this one had a knot in its bobtail, a broken spot near the tip like a surgically implanted golf ball. Dog would recognize this animal in an hour or in sixty years. He unlatched the small side door of the cage and the big cat ran to the door, sniffed, and trotted out into the open air.

108

Dog went down the rows of cages, propping doors open. He rubbed the python's cold head as he lifted it from the cage. He wondered if the snake was smart enough to find its own rats. Or if the rats were stupid enough to find the snake. He wondered what would eat the rooster. Or what the lynx would find to couple with.

Just got to open your hands.

He opened the door of the last cage, an armadillo. He lifted the animal out, grinning. The beast reminded him so much of the armor-plated vehicle he decided to keep it, for a mascot. He carried it out to the dark shape, pleased with his work.

All was quiet until dawn's first light. Then a sound awakened Rodney. He thought at first it was Chick, strangling on his tongue or something. But when he sat up in bed, he saw the photographer stretched out, peacefully breathing little plumes of vapor into the dawn chill. Then Rodney heard it again, it lifted him from the cot like the jerk of a hook. It was definitely not human. Stuck in an agony of stymied transfiguration, half howling, half crying, like a thing damned, yet denied entry to Hell itself!

He pulled the quilt about his hips and crept to the window. It was too dirty to see out of in this early light but he could hear the thing—huffing and moaning. Carefully he leaned one eye to an empty triangle of broken pane and peered out. He saw a heaving hump of fur with two heads; the eyeless coyote from the zoo had mounted the horny lynx. The animals were galvanized together in hideous, unnatural lust.

Rodney gasped, as much in envy as disgust.

The lynx twisted, snapping at the coyote's legs wrapping around her, moaning deep in her neck. The coyote's tongue lolled from the side of his muzzle, wet and flopping. "Lucky dog," Rodney said, and returned to bed.

109

Dr. Jo dreams and wakes . . .

It rings. The pink limestone secretary waits for it to ring
again, standing there, chiseled in naked glory. But what's all
this bellowing, coming down the corridor? This is supposed
to be prehistoric France, not some bull festival in present-day
Spain. Yet here they come, thundering in her door, brows
low and nostrils flaring—a protein stampede! She stands,
sweating, unable to move. She can't drop her phone and run
for cover—her pride in her position is stronger than her
fear—and she can't carry it with her.

The cord isn't long enough.

Fortunately, before the horny herd can close around her, it
rings again. It is that bandy-legged brother of Loach's, ringing
his chuckwagon triangle. And hollering. The racket provokes
a long groan from the cot across the room.

"Tell them to knock it off, would you?" It's the cigarette-
smoking Jane with the cheap perfume. "I'm sick of this banging and clanging all night."

"I think this time it's breakfast, Gabriela."

"It's the middle of the night."

"It's dawn. The sun is rising."

"It's freezing is what it is! I froze all night. And don't call me Gabriela. I'm no damn angel, that's for sure."

Jocelyn raised up on an elbow to look at the huddled form on the cot. Indeed, the girl was visibly shivering under the pile of blankets she had pulled over her head. Her chin and lips were all that poked out of a crack in the covers, chattering a stream of vapor. It reminded Jocelyn of the way baby seals breathed in the frozen bays in the Baffins, their breath tooting out of tiny ice holes. The temperature in the room was probably freezing.

Why then had she found herself covered with perspiration when she woke?

111

Her head ached on the musty pillow and her mouth tasted bitter, bitter with more than the remainder of the quantity of wine she had drunk last night, too. Much more, she remembered through a fog. She had been suckered into swallowing far worse stuff than that immature Burgundy of Makai's. That silly seance! Listening to those daffy sisters play knock-knock. It pained her to remember. Table rappings, good God! One of the oldest, one of the hokeyest—well, she could think of a dozen ways she'd seen medicine men fake it. *Two* dozen!

She hadn't really been that drunk, either. No, her only excuse for swallowing that kind of hokum had to be the tired old alibi that it is the duty of an inquiring scientific mind to observe all phenomena without bias. One should study these bizarre beings and their rites as one would study any deviate cult—with an open mind, a courteous mouth and a lot of keen-eyed skepticism. What had slipped her skepticism such a mickey? Oh yes, she'd been dulled by more than bad wine. She had allowed herself to become so entranced she had actually gone along when Loach made them swear that ridiculous oath of secrecy.

She squeezed her eyes shut against the humiliating memory. She would rather have that dream of the naked secretary and the horned bulls, if it came to rathers. She knew what the dream meant, at least. The nude figure was the famous carving in the cave beneath Dordogne, dubbed by the anthropologists the Venus of Lausell. Jocelyn had visited the figure on her European sabbatical five years ago. She had several photographs in the folder in her pack. Life-size, in fact; because the chiseled bas-relief was only seventeen inches tall in its crude actuality, rising only a thumb length from the doughy stone as though kneaded there. Tiny. But in historical significance and mythic power, the figure was a giant—a giant*ess*. A sign of the Siatic Isis, from one of the oldest cults in prehistoric Europe. And if the photos of that cave were accurate, from somewhere in America as well.

Gaby punctured Jocelyn's thoughts with another shivering groan. Jocelyn sat up. The sun's rays were slicing through the grimy windows into the room. She rubbed her aching eyes with the heels of her hands. Ah well, she sighed; as humiliating as these foolish little after-supper seances might be, they were not what counted. The expedition was what counted. Soon they would be under way to an actual location, hopefully to unearth something truly new and significant. If those photos were a halfway honest indication, the prevailing old mutton-chopped theory of cultural migrations would be turned on its ear! Whole world histories would have to be reconsidered. One had to take risks and suffer indignities with the possibility of such a prize at stake. For such a treasure it was worth having to drink a little too much young wine and swallow too much old baloney.

She heard the brother call again—"Git it now or go without!" The triangle shrilled a final command and was still. She drew a breath and swung her thin legs out to the floor. She reached over to put a hand on Gaby's shoulder.

"Come on, Sweetheart, up we go. A good cup of hot coffee will make things a lot better."

"Don't call me Sweetheart, either. And where are we going to get a good cup of coffee in this hell's half acre? Uncle Dogeye wouldn't know good coffee beans from prairie-dog turds."

Jocelyn didn't answer. She hurried to dress in the chill. Gaby made no move to come out of her nest. As Jocelyn was pulling on her boots, the girl finally rolled over and looked at her.

"What time is it, really?"

The girl's voice irritated Jocelyn. "It's morning," she answered. She didn't know the precise time although she could have made a very educated guess had she wanted to. "Morning," she repeated, driving her heels down into the stiff leather.

By the time Jocelyn was ready to leave the little room, Gaby had made it out of bed. She was standing in her slip at the basin, shivering bountifully and dabbing that perfume under her arms. The artificial scent made Jocelyn's nose wrinkle. Lavender! Just like a kid with a voice like that to use a lot of lavender. She told the girl she would wait for her outside and stepped out into the October morning.

Jocelyn drew a deep breath of the chilly sagebrushed air. The shadows of Dogeye's stand of totem poles stretched long across the bald courtyard. No other creatures were in sight. The generator was working again and the neon once more burned in the bright daylight, proclaiming ice Dogeye didn't have. Across the courtyard the big military contraption was parked in the same dusty clutter just like they had left it. Then, as she continued to look, Jocelyn saw that something had changed. She blinked in amazement at the sight, unable for a moment to believe her eyes. All the porthole windows along the side had been painted over flat black. The rear door windows as well. Only the front windwings and the windshield had been spared. And through the windshield she could see that a partition had been constructed in back of the driver's seat. One small door was all that accessed the rest of the carrier. Loach had ordered the whole passenger section blacked out, like a city in a bombing raid!

"I guess he didn't put any more store in that oath of secrecy than I did," she said to herself.

114

Suddenly, the metal roof of the armored vehicle thundered and the little man they called Juke came scampering along the top and down the side ladder. He stood in the dust by the front door, his head bobbing. He was dressed in layers of dark clothes. Around his throat he wore an incongruous silk ascot, once red, with the ends stuffed down into the layers of clothing. His mottled blue face peered this way and that. Suddenly he bent over, paralyzed by a terrible coughing. When there was a let-up he reached into an inside pocket and pulled out an ornate meerschaum pipe. He cupped his hands to protect a match from the morning breeze and lit the pipe, stilling his cough. The silk neckpiece fluttered for an instant on a morning breeze. The exhaled smoke mingled with his icy breath. Jocelyn caught a whiff of the smoke and recognized it immediately: deadly nightshade leaves and berries. Some of the Navaho bucks back from the war used it. She was sure that the powder Juke was smoking was a government blend called Asthmador, a mixture of the belladonna derivative with other herbs. She had heard that the Veterans Administration was issuing it free to those unfortunates whose lungs had been damaged by mustard gas. The smoke dried the mucous membranes and allowed the victims to breathe more easily.

The little man moved to the side of the carrier and leaned against it, one ankle crossed over the other, nodding to an inner rhythm. Suddenly he noticed Jocelyn watching him and froze dead still, staring into the clutter of tools and cans and paintbrushes on the ground. At last he brought his chin up in a sort of acknowledgment. Jocelyn nodded back. The man stood a few moments more, overcome by the unexpected observer, then spun round and scurried back up the metal ladder and across the roof of the carrier. He disappeared into the tangle of packs like a rat into a trash pile.

Jocelyn had scarcely begun puzzling over this curious encounter when she was distracted by another oddity. This one was much nearer, rubbing against her leg. It was the lynx, rubbing its hindquarters up and down her boot.

"Scat," she said, kicking sideways. "Get *away!*"

The big cat backed away with a disappointed yowl.

"Don't you like wildcats, Dr. Caine?" a breathy voice asked. Jocelyn turned and found Gaby's eyes on her through the cabin's screen door. The girl was having her first cigarette of the day, a Chesterfield in a sturdy amber holder. The smoke strained through the grimy screen.

"I love wildcats," Jocelyn answered. "In the wild. This poor thing's not right."

"Cage-crazy," Gaby said. The girl pushed the screen open and stepped into the frosty sunlight. She stretched, yawning smoke. "It happens."

Jocelyn noticed that some of the pout had gone out of the

girl's voice, and the face seemed almost sweet, still honeyed with sleep as it was. Even beautiful. On the other hand the desert light could be quite deceiving at this time in the morning, Jocelyn knew. With the air still pale and the long shadows still jeweled with frost, anything might seem beautiful.

The girl let the screen slam and fell in beside Jocelyn. She didn't seem to notice the carrier and Jocelyn made no mention of the painted windows. They walked side by side in silence toward the long main hall. Purple smoke was arrowing out from the rough stone chimney at one end of the roof, and Jocelyn could smell coffee coming from the front door.

"Smells like your Uncle Dogeye's found some good coffee after all," she ventured.

Gaby grunted a grudging agreement. "Before I try it I think I'll make a little trip to Uncle Dogeye's powder room."

The girl cut off the cinder paths toward the cluster of outhouses situated behind the cabins, leaving Jocelyn to stroll on through the morning alone. She took her time, examining the courtyard's bizarre gemstone creations. The effort and detail that had gone into the lapidary displays was incredible. The centerpiece of the yard was the NRA Eagle, complete with the New Deal slogan: WE DO OUR PART. It spread its wings over the ground eight feet across, made entirely with tiny blue aquamarines.

At the front door she paused, her hand on a doorknob made from the kneebone of some large animal. The smell of frying bacon came to her like a blast, smoky, full. It made her mouth water. Still, she hesitated, listening in. There was a morning softness to the sounds—the scoot of a chair, the occasional thump of a mug, a muffled laugh. Live humanity, she thought, in all its warty glory. She remembered Cervan-

116

tes's evaluation with a smile: "Every man is as God made him, aye, and often worse." She heard the high-pitched scraping of the fire door being opened on the stove, then the voice of the man Dogeye.

"Fire's goin' down, folks, Gotta put my boots on, fetch more wood. Be back in a flash."

"Take it easy, Dog," said Loach. "I'll get it."

Jocelyn immediately stepped from the porch to the woodpile. She already had an armful when Loach came out.

"Good morning, Dr. Caine," he said. "Looks like you beat me to it."

"Good morning"—she didn't want to call him Charles or Chuck, or Charlie-O, like his brother did, so she had to add—"Doctor."

"Look at this, Dog," Loach called, holding the door. "Dr. Jocelyn on the spot."

Dogeye turned from the stove. "Well good *morning*," he said. His face lit up with his wolfish leer. "Say, Charlie-O, I have to give you credit. When it comes to putting together an adventure you know how to pick your adventure-ers."

"Your brother didn't pick me, Mr. Dogeye." She tried to sound cheerful. "It was the National Geographic Society. Where do you want this?"

"Oh, sorry." Dogeye started from his leer. "Right yonder."

She dropped her armload into a wooden box and stood, brushing the bits of pine bark from her shirt while she took in the scene. The spiritualist sisters sat at the near end of the long table with a plate of toast and jam. A teapot snuggled under a cozy at the skinny one's elbow. The crystal ball was resting next to the stouter one, set like a huge bauble in one of Dogeye's polished roundbone napkin rings. Rodney and Chick sat at the other end, sipping coffee and talking guardedly to each other. Ned the driver sat in a rocker by the stove, a mug in one hand, a home-rolled in the other. Smoke curled up his alert face. And Loach had at last shed his prison togs. He was packed into the clothes from the trunk, a stiff khaki costume of the typical British explorer of the past—lace boots, bat-winged jodhpurs, military shirt with buttoned epaulets to keep the straps of important map cases from slipping off the shoulder. All he needed was a pith helmet and a whip and he could have joined Frank Buck in the Big Cat cage. With a stiff spin on his heel he took a seat on the counter, his long legs dangling casually over the side.

Dogeye bustled over from the stove with a cup of coffee. "You want cream or sugar with your mud?"

"Black is fine, thanks." She looked at the man grinning eagerly in front of her. His bright green eyes were rimmed with red. "Were you up all night? Gaby says she heard people moving around at all hours."

"Sorry if we kept you awake," said Dogeye. "Charlie here decided we needed to modify the rig a little for the next leg of this adventure."

"Oh, you'll just love it, dear," the plump sister piped up. "We made it so *cozy*. We have draperies, now. Bookcases, a wash stand—"

"*Not* a wash stand," corrected Mona. "We set up an *oracle* table. We can consult the Ouija while we ride . . . for spiritual interpretations."

It was too much for their nephew to let pass. "Interpreta*tions?*" he hooted, looking up from his huddle with his photographer. "Of what? All this exciting scenery we been traveling through? We don't need an Ouija board for that; I can look out the windows and interpret sagebrush all by myself."

Evidently, Jocelyn realized with secret amusement, Gaby

wasn't the only one who had yet to notice the vehicle's blackened portholes.

"We also wired in some interior lights," Dogeye informed her. "Else it'd be dark as a coffin in there."

"Dark in where?" Now it was the goose-necked photographer, looking up and chewing. "How do you mean, dark?"

No one answered him. "Got to keep the location hidden," Dogeye went on to Jocelyn seriously. "I don't hanker to see this place get found by the public any more than Charlie-O does. Oh, it will someday, I know. But we want to protect it as long as possible. You can see that, can't you?"

"I can see the necessity for precautions, yes. I'm sure you did what you considered prudent."

"The necessity for *what?*" Rodney wanted to know.

The photographer stopped chewing and chimed in. "Yeah, *what's* very prudent?"

No one chose to pay any attention to the pair. Dogeye scurried from the stove to the counter where a huge rasher of bacon stood cooling on a newspaper. He pulled his knife from its sheath and began cutting long strips from the side that hung by the sink. He put the bacon into a large cast-iron skillet with a handle at least a yard long.

"Can I help you?" Jocelyn asked.

"Sure, ma'am, sure. I was going to make some cakes. If you could do that it'd be a treat. I get tired of my own fare day after day."

She rummaged through the cabinet and found a large clay bowl. Pictographs of the Navaho Sun God wavered around its edge but she did not think it was native-made; the design had the same telltale flare she had noticed in all the motel's signs and designs. She cleared a place for the bowl and began with a dash of salt and baking soda. Then she added whole wheat flour from a coffee tin on the counter. Above that she found a rack of dry goods. From these she added wild rice, raisins, an oozing puddle of Blackstrap. With these in the bowl she began opening cabinets and drawers.

"What ya needin', Dr. Caine?"

"Please, you can call me Jo."

"Okey-dokey, Jo, you can call me Dog. What was you looking for?"

"For some eggs."

"Well we'll have to walk for that." Dogeye began pulling a boot on, hopping around the plank floor.

"No, you're busy here, Just tell me where to go."

Dogeye grinned up at her, then dropped the boot. "Well fine. You'll need a light." He rummaged through a drawer on the sideboard and produced a long silver flashlight. "About twenty feet out the back door you'll see the entrance to the cellar."

A path led her to the slanted cellar door. Jocelyn pulled the leather handle. A shaft of light revealed a narrow stair cut into the stone. He must have chiseled these steps by hand, she realized, day after day down through solid rock. Obviously had a lot of spare time, waiting for that brother of his to get out of jail. Glad to see he didn't waste it moping.

She descended into the cellar, letting the door close over her head. There was no way to prop it open. When darkness enveloped her, she fumbled with the light switch. Nothing happened. She started backward for the door. When she moved the light flickered. She shook it until a weak yellow beam trickled out.

At the back of the hole was a small spring, diked off with stones. In this shallow pool she found a tub of butter, a basket of odd-sized eggs and a stone crock, its lid held firmly in place with a wire clamp. She opened the crock and the unmistakable smell of sourdough bloomed up. She smiled, thinking of Dogeye. A real sourdough, all right, starter growing in the basement and everything.

She resealed the stone crock and put half a dozen mismatched eggs in her pocket. Rising, she shone the light around the room. On the far wall was a rack. It was filled with canned vegetables, pickled beets and cucumbers, bottles of French wine, and sealed Mason jars of some golden liquid. She checked the wine labels. Some were better vintages than the selection Rodney was so proud of. And those jars must be the cactus brew.

She climbed the steps, closed the cellar door, and returned to the kitchen to find Dogeye cutting more bacon. Juke had emerged again from his rookery atop the vehicle and come in. Ned had given up his rocker and found another chair. Dogeye handed the strange little man coffee in a glass tumbler with a big spoonful of cream. He obviously knew that was the way Juke liked it. Juke stirred the thick cream and rocked, humming to himself.

"I brought in the starter," Jocelyn said. "I hope you don't mind."

"Hell no. Love sour cakes. Got that starter in New Orleans, years back. Remember that place Juke used to play, Charlie? Kneewalking Jackson's?"

Loach smiled from his perch on the counter. "I remember." He turned to Jocelyn. "He was the only colored that owned a club on Bourbon Street. The band from our show used to play there when we were in town."

"Used to blow," whispered Juke, staring into his murky drink. "Blow, blow, blow."

Dogeye popped his eyebrows up and down for Jocelyn's

benefit. "Anyways, that's where I got this starter from, from Kneewalking. Ten, twelve years ago. Taken it with me all over the nation plus Canada, regular as religion. Makes the best biscuits you ever ate."

"I'll bet it does."

"Best I ever blowed," Juke recalled, rocking over his glass.

Dogeye ignored the man. "Funny how a little thing like mold can become so dang important."

"Good starter is hard to come by," Jocelyn reassured him.

While she was mixing the starter and eggs, Gaby came in, followed closely by Father Paul. Jocelyn nodded to the priest as he stopped by the stove, his hands held out. Gaby wrinkled her nose as she passed behind Dogeye.

122

"Uncle Dogeye, you smell like a goat," she said, giving him a thumb in the ribs.

"Goats ain't so ba-a-a-ad," Dogeye bleated without turning around.

Gaby flopped full length on a bench across from the sisters. Dogeye poured off two cups of coffee through a small basket stainer.

"Good morning Father, Gaby," said Dogeye.

"What were you lunatics up to all night?" Gaby wanted to know. "I barely got a wink."

"Yes, what was all that commotion?" Paul asked.

He hadn't noticed the painted windows either. It always amazed Dr. Jo how blind the untrained eye could be. Or how selective.

"Why, we were fixing up that hideous old army machine, honey," said Ramona. "Making it more comfortable to travel in."

"Modifying it," Mona added.

"I can hardly wait to see," Gaby said, hunched over her

coffee mug. Jocelyn crossed the kitchen and lifted the cover to the bun warmer at the top of the stove. She put the batter inside to rise.

"Better leave the front open," Dogeye advised. "Them yeasties can get too hot if they's too cooped up."

She thanked him and turned away, hoping her irritation didn't show. She wasn't accustomed to being told how to cook, especially by a man.

When Rodney and Chick had finished their third cup of coffee, the decibel level of their conversation rose to include the whole kitchen. Rodney was still berating the photographer for not getting any shots of the debacle with the white-shirted zealots at the Tabernacle yesterday. Jocelyn felt sorry for the skinny man nodding to his boss, his Adam's apple working up and down as he listened. She would not have been able to take any pictures, either, even if her Brownie had been unpacked. It was all such a sudden hubbub of noise and animosity. The mainline Mormons were arguing with the radicals; the Baptists were in conflict with the little troupe of nuns who had come out from St. Louis for a tour of American holylands. A full-scale dogma fight had erupted on those steps. Then the way Loach moved when the machine came grinding up the drive like some kind of avenging garbage truck. He had been such a blur of furious action that she had been swept into the guts of the thing like all the rest of its passengers, in spite of herself. She could no more have taken a photograph of the event than she could have painted a picture later. There is simply no way to capture on paper that kind of sudden storm.

As the talk rambled on, Jocelyn began spooning batter onto the griddle Dog had wiped down with bacon fat. They puffed out instantly, firm on the hot grill. Bubbles immedi-

123

ately appeared in the center of the cakes and she pushed the griddle off to the cooler side of the stove. Juke watched from his rocker.

"Wake and bake," the little man sing-songed. "Bake and blow."

The serenity of the morning was lost now that the kitchen was full. The room took on the air of a group girding itself to move—determined and hurried. Dogeye piled bacon on plates and Jocelyn served up the cakes as they browned. There was a jar of sage honey for syrup and a bowl of cultured butter. Chick ate ravenously, still at the table after the others had left to pack up their bags. Dogeye scraped the serving plates onto Chick's place and the gaunt photographer ate every morsel. Everyone was impressed by the man's bottomless capacity, especially Rodney, returning from his cabin with his shaving kit.

"I hope you intend to bring the rest of that porkbelly along," he told Dogeye. "It might keep Chick here from eating one of us alive."

If Juke ate at all, Jocelyn was unaware of it. He rocked and sipped until his glass was emptied of the milky coffee, then crept outside to light his pipe.

She and Dogeye did the dishes silently. When they were through drying, Dogeye moved over to the stove and closed down all the drafts. It smoked briefly and then the roar of flame inside quieted down.

"Sure appreciate all the help. You ever need a job you can always feel free to come here. Or just want to woodshed a couple of weeks."

"Woodshed?"

"Lay back. Clean up. Ooze down."

"Why thank you, Dogeye. It's always nice to know of an

oasis in the desert, where one might ooze down. You must have other duties. I'll finish up here if you want."

"All right. I need to get a few things together. I'll see you out at the rig." He padded through the back door, his boots in hand.

The room became quiet; the smoky air filled with sunbeams sliding through the cracks. She took her time finding where the dishes went and putting them away, then she took a dishrag to the countertop and table. She was all but done when she heard someone outside finally exclaim; "*Jesus* H. Jumped-up *Christ!* Willya look at *this!* Oh, *no. . . !*"

Jocelyn smiled to herself. They had noticed the painted portholes at last.

When the party of explorers was at last packed and loaded and rumbling back out to the highway, Jocelyn found herself for the first time with an opportunity to really study the faces of her fellow travelers. There was little else to look at once one had gotten over the first shock of the bizarre furnishings of the metal cylinder they were to travel in. The sisters had decorated their accommodations with all the trappings they had so joyously resurrected from the big trunk—scarves and rugs, pillows on the floor, drapes, tapestries, icons on the walls. Even the ceiling had been softened; a Sufi flag hung from the corners like an old-fashioned four-poster canopy. But at last it was the faces you were forced to look at. There was no way to avoid it. The seating had been arranged along the walls with the couches and pillows and rugs—everybody facing the oval table in the center with its crystal ball rattling ridiculously in a wooden salad bowl. Even if you concentrated on the glass sphere you still saw the same faces, only shrunken and upside down.

The sister she thought was called Ramona sat directly oppo-

125

site her, cross-legged on a Buddhist meditation pillow, with her eyes closed, mumbling some sort of incantation. The other one waved a stick of incense in the air like a band leader with a baton. Mr. Makai, sitting plumply next to them, was tilting his head from side to side and frowning at his aunts' antics. When the three of them sat close the family resemblance was clear. Thin, plump, or mustached, all three had the same broad forehead and long European nose. Their skin was of the same olive shade. They could have been a trio of Gypsies trying to slip out of town in mufti.

Chick Ferrell was next to Rodney, chewing a hangnail and frowning. His long face looked like a bird of prey, frantic and frustrated to be imprisoned in this cage. His camera bag was piled uselessly between his feet. What good was a camera without windows? Its doorless cage swaying on a precarious stand, the parrot looked as peeved as the reporter. Both birds rode in a wordless sulk for miles on end.

Gaby was seated next to Jocelyn with a down comforter pulled to her chin. She couldn't see the girl's face but she could imagine it—a look of studied distaste. Father Paul was at the rear, his angelic brow haloed by an undulating curtain of orange silk. The curtain had been hung to provide some privacy for anyone daring or desperate enough to try the five-gallon-can commode that had been welded over a hole in the floor. That had been the arcing flashes last night that she thought she dreamed.

The long tubular shell of the carrier was suffused with an eerie purple light from the swag lanterns the sisters had hung. The interior wiring had not worked. Still, the air felt electric, charged with excitement. Dr. Jo noticed that everyone appeared innocent in the light, childlike. Like young Scouts about to begin their big adventure.

Jocelyn felt them reach the main highway and turn. She had been confident that she would be able to tell which direction, whether left to the south or right to the north, but now she was not at all sure. The way the big machine rocked and swayed through the task it could have swung all the way around. They could be going toward Canada or they could be going toward Mexico. All she could discern for sure was that they were on pavement.

The transmission progressed through the gears and settled into a long, steady growl. No one spoke. Someone will break the silence soon, she thought. But they didn't. The motor droned on. She closed her eyes, careful to keep a vague smile on her lips. She saw in her mind the composed, professional Vassar woman, dressed for class and in control, the way she would be when lecturing her anthropology seminar.

Someone will talk soon, she said to herself again.

The sound of the air rose to a faint, high whine. Already it was getting warm. She could feel the desert sun burning higher in the sky, beating down on the sides of the bus. We must be going south. It's going to be like an oven in here in a few hours if we're going south.

I'll never make it.

Finally she opened her eyes and drew a breath. Smiling, she turned to the nearest sister:

"Was that a prayer you were saying, Miss"—she didn't know the first name, and she couldn't remember if she had ever been told the last—"Makai?"

Ramona looked at Dr. Jo and nodded. The old lady's round face was quite composed, radiating contentedness in the purple gloom.

"A mantra, my dear," she explained in a careful voice. "A Sanskrit invocation. I was asking the spirits to bless our journey and protect us from the snares of Maya. *Om mani padmi hum, Om mani padmi hum* . . . I am, I am aware, I am bliss. Swami Denanda gave it to me himself when he toured the country in '28. A wonderful man, simply wonderful. A world teacher."

"I didn't know you were also schooled in the Hindu religions," said Jocelyn. She was well acquainted with the childish Indian litany but she allowed the woman to go on.

"All the religions are based on one truth," said Ramona. "Though there are many paths that approach the Oneness. The Hindu are some of the most ancient. Much of what's in the Sacred Secret Doctrines is directly derived from the Sanskrit. Jesus studied in India for quite a long time, you know."

128

"No, I didn't know that," said Dr. Jo, hoping she had not placed too much emphasis on the word "know." No one had ever substantiated that worn-out tidbit of religious gossip, nor any of the so-called Secret Doctrines. "How would he have gotten to India in those days?"

"Trade routes!" Mona piped up. "They had trade routes. Jesus learned everything he knew from the Indian disciples of Buddha."

"He did no such thing!" snapped Ramona. "He learned from the Essenes of Egypt. That's where he was given the holy maps."

"Are there actually records of Jesus' travels?" asked Dr. Jo, trying to seem academically fascinated.

"Madame Blavatsky goes into it in quite a bit of detail. She says—"

"Ramona!" hissed Mona. "Remember your vow! I'm sorry, Miss Caine, but my sister is really not at liberty to discuss these things. There is quite a bit of training one must go through before one can impart such secrets to the uninitiated. She has not achieved that degree."

"It's quite all right, I wouldn't dream of—"

"Horse feathers! Doctor, I'll have you know I've achieved more degrees than that old hen has feathers!"

"Achieved them how, sister dear? By going through honest rituals of ancient astrological societies? Or by staring into that glass croquet ball like a loon?"

"All the cosmos can be concentrated into a single crystal," Ramona cried. "And it's a better place to stare than trying to locate the one golden grain of sand on an endless beach of ether like you people do . . . gawking up at these zillions of stars."

"Crystal gazer!"

"Star gawker!"

"The stars are the macrocosm. The Milky Way is the Grand Path."

"So is the crystal, only reduced for efficiency's sake. I can carry my Milky Way with me, like a box of Cream of Wheat, a picture on the box of a man holding a box with a picture of a man holding—"

"Macrocosm!" Mona insisted shrilly.

"Microcosm!" Ramona maintained.

"Marconi," was the parrot's considered opinion. Everybody laughed at this feathered proclamation, except for Rodney.

"Malarky is what to call it, if you ask me," he declared. He met Jocelyn's eyes. "I've been hearing this bushwah for years, Doctor. It doesn't add up to anything. They just like to dress like kooks and talk spooky."

"Kooky and spooky," echoed Juke.

Both sisters sniggered in their hands. There was a good-natured side to the pair, Jocelyn had to admit. Their nephew, on the other hand, was a sneering pig.

"I take it you don't believe in things of the spirit, Mr. Makai?"

"Let's put it this way, Miss Caine," said Rodney. Jocelyn sensed he was trying to sound like John Garfield. "I believe in what I can see with my own two peepers. I've got no patience for speculations as to what kinds of ghosts might be knocking around in the 'ethers' or who gave Jesus maps or even where he may have wandered. I'm an empiricist and a businessman."

"I see. And what is a businessman doing on a trip like this?" Dr. Jo asked pleasantly. She was hoping to relax into the role of interviewer.

130

"I am also a newspaperman. And this caper of Loach's is news, wherever it wanders. If we find something to support his alibi, it's a scoop. If we don't, the bird goes back to the coop and *that's* at least second-banner news. Get it? Just so long as we get some good shots and hack out a decent lead my rear is covered. This wagon could end up in the Tunnel of Love at Coney Island for all I care. I could still pump a story out of it."

"I don't know if I could get pictures, though," Chick said morosely. "Not enough illumination."

"Dimwit here forgot to bring flash equipment," Rodney said to Jocelyn in mock confidence behind his hand.

"I was rushed!"

"You was a boob! I thought you were supposed to be a photographer. You didn't get so much as one shot of them damn crazy Mormons."

"I never signed on to be a combat photographer. I'm a

sports photographer. What would I need flash equipment for at a Saturday afternoon football game?"

"You think *this* doesn't have enough illumination, wait till we go down in that hole. What are you going to do then, dummy? Light matches?"

"I'll pick up some magnesium powder the next town we go through."

"*What* next town? Listen to that road out there. Does that sound like the outskirts of anyplace?"

Indeed, the highway had been singing uninterrupted beneath their tires for some time, empty.

"I'll bet there won't *be* any next town."

Everyone sat quiet for a while, listening. "Maybe we can focus a bunch of those miner's lights of Dogeye's," the photographer said unhappily. Rodney snorted and pretended he was masturbating. Jocelyn was relieved when Dogeye stuck his head through the opening in front of the bus.

"Everybody comfy?" he called. He was carrying the armadillo by the handle on its back, like a bowling ball in a case. He stepped inside and closed the little door behind him. He went immediately to Jocelyn, grinning.

"How you like the new decor, Doc?" he asked, taking a seat beside her. "Is this the cat's pajamas?"

"Very," she agreed.

Dogeye looked at her closely. His grin went away. "You don't look like you agree with me, to tell the truth."

"I'm sorry. I've something of a headache." Without warning, Dogeye reached out and felt the back of her neck. She stiffened. His palm was as hard as the hide of the animal in his lap.

"You're knotted up like a crazy sailor's rope, lady. You need a massage."

"Oh no, please! I'm fine."

"Sure you are." He put down the armadillo and, without warning, hopped up on the back of the couch behind her, nimble as a monkey. "Let old Dog work you over."

"Could you please first remove your boots, Mr. Dogeye?" Mona asked. "That antimacassar was woven by a Sufi master more than two centuries ago."

"Happy to oblige," Dogeye said, kicking off his dilapidated boots as he balanced on the couch back. To Mona's dismay, the socks were full of holes, and the toenails poking through looked nearly as dangerous as the steel-tipped boots.

"If you would remove your socks I'll bet you could talk Ramona into darning them," Mona said.

132

"That's right," her sister said. "I may not be of Mona's degree spiritually, but I'm a darn good darner."

He removed the socks and handed them on, then he squatted behind Jocelyn. She could not see him, but in her mind's eye she was reminded of paintings she had seen in the grottos of Rome—imps of the pit. The fingers fastened on her neck.

"Now, let us see if we can't unravel some of those knots."

He began massaging her neck and back. His hands were as strong as metal tools, but gentle. In spite of herself she began to relax. Her eyes closed and her head rocked from side to side.

"I understand that you are the actual discoverer of our famous cave," she said.

"I found the entrance, the hole in the ground, yeah. But Charlie was the one that sorted out the particular passage that led to the paintings."

"Are there lots of passages?"

"Dozens. A maze of switchbacks and circles, and side spurs to nowhere. Charlie's got the only directions recorded in that book he carries." His voice dropped, conspiratorially. "He claims he was led to the Temple gallery by a spiritual guide hovering before him in the form of a little yellow bird. 'Course, *I* couldn't see nothing."

"Spirit guides *can* hover," one of the sisters muttered. "But they generally waft."

Jocelyn didn't open her eyes to see which one of the pair had made the distinction. She tipped her head farther back, into the hands behind her. "How did you happen on the entrance?"

"Prospecting," he said. "Just pokin' around and panning, looking for that old mother lode. It's how I passed my time while Charlie and Juke were over in the war."

"I wondered if Juke was a casualty of that awful time."

"Yeah. Him and Charlie both got gassed in France. It affected Juke worse, especially in the head. He always had been a little, let's say, *precarious* in that category."

"You knew him before?"

"Oh sure. He was in the show with us."

"The show?"

"The Congress of Worldwide Wonders." Dogeye moved his hands farther down her back, kneading the muscles like lumpy dough. "Gaby was with us too, weren't you, hon?"

Gaby pretended to be sleeping.

"We all ran the flap box."

"Flat box?"

"Flap. A flap box is carney for sideshow." Dog lifted his eyes at the ceiling, toward the spot where Juke had nested on the roof. "Yeah, Ol' Juke; he was all 'round. Even after they came back from France he still rousted and played in the band. He was eventually able to do his old act again, but it just wasn't never the same as before."

"That's too bad."

Dogeye shrugged. "He was somewhat tetched before he went to war, anyhow. Matter of fact he was considered to be what some called 'a gifted.' "

"That's hard to imagine."

"Not really. Where's the line between a gifted and a freak? I couldn't tell ya. Him and Charlie's always been tight. Ol' Juke come through good for him in Salt Lake from what I hear."

Jocelyn wasn't ready to talk about that. "So they both enlisted?"

"In 1917 about this time of the year. They claimed it was patriotism but I think the reason was that they wanted the glory of being a Yank in Europe . . . if you want to know what I think. Charlie's always had a hankering for glory."

"And you chose not to join them."

"Naw. I ain't much of a joiner. When they went patriotic, I went prospecting. I guess I like gold more than glory. But then I guess none of us found much of neither no way—just bad lungs and a hole in the ground."

"A very interesting hole, though," she said, thinking suddenly of her dream, and how much the woman with the horn resembled the carving she had seen in the limestone cave in Lausell. She decided this was not the time to pursue that angle.

"And you say Juke used to be a functioning member of society?"

Dogeye laughed. "Sure. Even after the war. Functioned real good, considering. Until this damn cave business. Yeah, Juke was all 'round."

"I find that rather difficult to imagine," she said. "What kind of act did he do?"

134

"Juke's act?" Dogeye giggled. "Well now, I find that rather difficult to describe . . ."

The door from the front of the bus opened and sunlight came pouring into the dim chamber. Jocelyn opened her eyes and turned quickly, hoping to glimpse the landscape they were moving through. But the light from outside was blinding. When she could bear the glare, she saw Dr. Loach's stiff silhouette duck through the doorway and close it behind him.

"What are you doing, Dog?" Loach asked. "Some kind of Barbary ape imitation for the folks?"

"Therapy, Charlie-O," Dogeye said, and hopped nimbly down from the couch. "I always had the tender touch, you know. Whatcha say, Jo?"

"I must admit the headache is better," she said, realizing that it in fact was. "And your hands *are* much more—uh—"

135

"Tender than they look?" he finished with a laugh. He grinned down at his spread hands. "They are horny lookers, I guess. I always was a scratcher and scrabbler. Unlike Charlie here, who never had honest dirt under his nails in his life. Look at him. Six years in the pokey and he's still got his manicure."

Loach put his big white hands behind him.

"Dr. Loach, your brother and I have been talking about the cave. Perhaps you can let us in on what our prospects are. Our best hopes. What's down there? What do you think returning will accomplish?"

"Dr. Caine, I'm somewhat surprised at such a question, especially from you, a searcher into ancient ways. Surely you respect, as I do, any form of discovery?"

"Get off it, Loach," Rodney spoke up. "That's no answer, you're dodging the question. You're like the cat that ain't ate the canary yet, but's got plans. Come on; give. What is our best hope?"

"Yeah, Loach," Chick chimed in, "give. There's no way we can let any of your secrets out, now that you got us all bottled up in here. Where are we headed? When are we going to hit a town with a photo shop?"

"I'm afraid we're not, Mr. Ferrell. Salt Lake was our last town large enough to offer such equipment."

"I told you, noodle brain," Rodney said, elbowing his partner in the side.

"Then what about a little town with a drugstore? Even a tiny little burg has got to have a drugstore, don't it? I can *make* powder," Chick wailed.

"We are not stopping at any burg of any size, Mr. Ferrell," Loach answered, not unsympathetically. "What would be the sense of bottling you all up in the countryside, then letting you roam the towns?"

"What about gas?"

"We have two seventy-gallon tanks. We filled them in Moab."

Now Rodney was getting worried. "What about food and drink? What about lodging?"

"We're rigged to cook our own meals," Dogeye answered in a proud voice. "Fact, I'm gonna start whuppin' up some sandwiches right now."

"We have bedrolls for camping," his brother continued, "and a water supply for washing and drinking. Not to mention those cases of wine you loaded on in California."

"What about let's say somebody might feel the urge to *relieve* themselves, for the love of Christ?"

Dogeye answered again. "For that we've got the emergency W.C. at the back," he said. "Lid and everything. I bolted 'em on, myself."

"I'm sure they are first rate," said Rodney. "But we kind of wandered off the subject, didn't we? We were asking what our best hope is, Loach. And I don't mean *your* obvious and understandable hope of staying out of the clink. *Our* hope. What do you think verification of this find—say we find it—is going to mean to the common American Joe? Is this another Tut's tomb?"

"Yeah," said Chick, flipping his little pad open to take notes. "How does this compare to, say, the discovery of the fossils of the Dead Sea Squirrels?"

Jocelyn thought she detected the slightest flick of humor playing at the edges of Loach's solemn mouth, but his voice betrayed none of it.

137

"Those were scrolls, Mr. Ferrell. But I think that is a good comparison. This discovery could be as momentous. If we find the key to the cavern's symbols we could well unlock the mysteries of much of this continent's past. There may be clues to the meaning of the Mayan Codices, the Hopi picto-graphs . . ."

Loach swung his gaze around the circle of listeners. He motioned toward the altar Mona and Ramona had set up in the center of the bus. The crystal ball had been removed (Ramona was using it as a darning ball in the toe of Dogeye's sock) but the incense still curled out of the brazier and the ornate letters of the Ouija board shimmered in the smoke.

"We might find the origin of our own alphabet," he said. The machine hummed on uninterrupted for a few moments. Then Loach added, "I mean to evade nothing, Mr. Makai, but

I've had six years to dream of this journey. That's not easily condensed into a brief response to such a question."

He rubbed his brow between a long thumb and finger for a moment, then raised his head. When he spoke his voice had changed in pitch and rhythm, the tone lower, barely audible over the motor.

"Since the earliest days of man those same questions have possessed our species. Where are we heading? What do we hope to find when we get there? It may be that these questions, the ability to ask them, is the destination itself. That I do not know. But I do know that seeking is what distinguishes us from the lower animals."

"For the worse, I'd say," Dogeye interrupted in a whisper, winking at Jocelyn.

138

"Yeah," Rodney snorted. "For the worse. What a bunch of hooey."

"Rodney Makai, you shush!" Ramona clunked him hard on the kneecap with the ball in the sock. "Let the Doctor speak."

Loach went on. "If my analysis of the symbols in that cave has been at all correct, then whoever painted them had access to the symbols of many, perhaps all, of the whole world's major spiritual systems."

This brought the priest to attention. "You mean whoever painted those pictures had traveled the whole world before coming here?"

"Right," Gaby laughed. "To some God-forsaken wilderness to paint in a cave? That's rich."

Loach didn't seem bothered by the question. "It's even more astonishing than that. I took a scraping of pigment from the cave to a chemist. He estimated the paint to be older than any known—in Iraq, in Persia, even in Egypt."

He looked from face to face. "Perhaps tens of thousands of years old."

Dogeye suddenly began to cough and sputter. Jocelyn patted him on the back. "Do you need some water, Dog?"

"No, that's okay," Dogeye gained control of himself. "But I'd better go up front and get some air. Getting a little thick in here for me."

He stood and left the chamber. All eyes turned back to Loach. He had moved the brazier and seated himself on the little table with the incense. The comical scoffing from his brother had not seemed to ruffle him. If anything, Jocelyn noticed, it had lent Loach's words a deeper note of authenticity. She could imagine they might have been doing this act since boyhood—Loach spieling on in his affected style; Dogeye snorting and snickering in the background, like Pancho Sanza behind Don Quixote.

139

As soon as Dogeye slid the door closed, Father Paul went back to the subject:

"How in God's name is such a thing possible, Charles? Vestiges of old religions in the New World? They never taught this in any of our seminaries."

"Unfortunately, Father, the religious studies the Catholic Church provides are not particularly, well, shall I say, diversified. The hierarchy of the Vatican suppressed certain teachings labeled heretical or occult which we now accept as simple science. As you know, those teachings have been my field of study for some time—"

"Get to the point, Loach," Rodney snapped, "we know about your doctor's degree. What's at stake? What's up for grabs?"

"The point, Mr. Makai? Very well. Let me ask you a question. Do you know anything about the Akashic record?"

"Never heard of it. It must be ragtime . . ."

"There is said to exist," Loach went on, "somewhere in the universe, a library that archives all the events of all time, a chronicle, if you will, from the dim mists of the past to the far, far future."

"Are you trying to say that some Sioux or Cherokee or whoever had these asthmatic records down there in that cave? Bunk."

Loach chuckled. "No, not exactly. The Akashic records do not exist in such a corporeal way. Perhaps they are kept in Heaven, by wise old angels with big books and fleecy robes; perhaps they are stored in the mystery of our own cells. We know they exist because we have unearthed, over the centuries, countless cross-references. Card catalogues that refer to different though corresponding spiritual and artistic and scientific data, across vast centuries and seas. But they exist, nonetheless, and can be perceived by certain individuals in advanced states of consciousness. Despite insights gleaned from my studies, I have never been able to penetrate this realm. But I once felt its nearness. In that cave, standing in front of those paintings, I began to feel myself transported, ah, into the higher dimensions. It was as though—"

He frowned as his big hands labored to shape the thought. Everyone watched, fascinated.

"—as if the cavern contained not knowledge itself—that is, not *facts* about the past, chronicles of lost civilizations and such—but rather, that those paintings were the process of initiation itself. The Irish poet, Yeats, has a theory about symbols: that when viewed in a proper setting they can serve as keys to hidden parts of the mind, and finally to the universal states of consciousness—to the Godhead itself! My own theory is that ancient masters used that cave many thousands of years ago. Their powers of prescience must have been so great they were able to perceive the course of mankind in its entirety. That would explain the pictures from conflicting times and beliefs. They left those symbols for us so that we might unlock the doors of our own minds and fulfill our spiritual destiny—find out just where we *are* headed. Perhaps even have some control over the fate that transports us there. You can see how important it is that such powers not fall into evil hands. You can see why I—" Loach suddenly stammered. His eyes dropped to his own hands. "—had to do what I did."

No one spoke. Jocelyn realized with a start that her mind was glazed by the outpouring of words. Just like the others, she thought with chagrin: suckered in.

"I'm sorry," said Loach, standing abruptly from the little table, "you'll have to excuse me. I'm not used to talking at such length."

Without further words he strode to the little door and ducked back out the way he'd come. Jocelyn thought he appeared genuinely shaken. Ah well, she reminded herself; it comes in all kinds of wrappers.

The rest of the day droned by uneventfully, without further visits from the control chamber. When the bus finally lurched to a skidding stop, Dr. Caine was the first one on her feet. The big double doors at the back of the carrier swung open and the silk curtains billowed out past the makeshift commode, revealing an open prairie. Ned was there with the Moxie crate for a step. Dogeye rushed up as she came out, offering her a hand. "Welcome to nowhere," he grinned.

"Are we . . . *where* are we?" she asked.

"Like I say, Jo, nowhere in particular." He shifted a toothpick to the corner of his mouth, his eyes never leaving hers. "Just a stopping place."

The Makai sisters followed her, then Chick. Rodney stirred inside, wallowing up from a pile of paisley pillows. Gaby was awake, with her hand on the shoulder of the sleeping Father Paul, shaking him. A distant grunting from the other side of the road startled Jocelyn. It faded away in a measured rhythm: Huff huff hup. Huff huff hup.

"What was that?"

"That's just Jukie."

"Sounds like a code," she said.

"He's probably talking Morse to the moon," Gaby said.

Indeed, a bright three-quarter moon had risen already, though the sun was far from down. The front door opened and Dr. Loach stepped out. "We're going to set up camp now," he called. "To give everyone some relief."

142

Everybody cheered. "Praise the Lord," said Gaby, and the parrot added, "Forever without!"

The cool evening air against Jocelyn's face was so exhilarating she felt faint. She closed her eyes, leaning against the machine's armor plate to steady herself. The others began to spill out of the bus, stretching and stumbling.

"Why it's nearly sundown," Rodney said. "My watch must have stopped."

As her pulse slowed to normal Jocelyn felt her head begin to clear. Everyone was moving quickly, as if to make up for the hours of confinement. Ned was charging to and fro gathering what wood could be found among the scrub, and Dogeye and Dr. Loach were unloading camping gear down from the roof. The sisters were spreading blankets and unpacking food. Jocelyn walked a short distance away from the commotion and stood, turning a slow circle to study the horizon.

"What do you see?" Dogeye asked. "Anything recognizable?"

"Nope," she said. "Could be any of a half dozen states. Open land, cloudless sky, the moon and stars."

"Polaris," he said, pointing a stubby finger.

"Yes," she gave a shiver, "the north star. There's always that."

"Gotta help Ned build a fire. Can I get you something? You look like you could use a drink."

She let him lead her by the elbow toward the circle of faces gathered around the sputtering fire. The sisters scooted a few inches to the left to make room. Mona handed her a box of saltines.

"Hors d'oeuvres," the woman said.

Jocelyn took the box and thanked the old lady. In spite of herself she felt a sense of familial closeness building between them. She munched her crackers, looking up at the darkening sky. The north star still glowed comfortingly. She sighed, stretching her legs out toward the fire. Dr. Loach and Ned approached, laughing together about some shared story. "Coffee'll be a while yet," Dogeye told them. "Then supper." Jocelyn passed the box of crackers to Dr. Loach, who passed them on to Ned.

"Sit down, Doctor," she said, and again everyone scooted to make room.

The passengers did not seem at all cranky or harsh, as one might have expected. Like her, they had been bludgeoned into a daze by the hours of swaying confinement. Emptied. The tuna fish sandwiches Dogeye had passed out for lunch were long gone. The travelers sat quietly, watching the fire get bigger. Dogeye unpacked his cooking supplies and was unwrapping a bright, thin filleting knife he'd strapped to the ridiculously long handle of his skillet. He began whetting the blade on a butcher's stone, humming happily.

143

Even Rodney Makai seemed in good spirits. He stepped out of the back of the carrier holding four bottles of wine by the necks, two bottles of red in his right hand and two of white in his left.

"Whatcha say, Chef?" he called to Dogeye. "Is this repast to be red or white? Cabernet or Chardonnay?"

"Red," Dogeye answered. "In fact, here it comes now."

They all looked the way he pointed with the knife, past the carrier back toward the highway and the setting sun. The huff-humping sound was returning. Through the sage a hump of twisted animal components was bouncing its way toward them. Antlers swayed and eyes glowed and forepaws jiggled loosely against its chest. Jocelyn gasped in a swirl of confusion. It looked like one of the creatures escaped from her dawn's dream, arisen into some kind of twisted half-life. It stopped at the edge of their stunned circle and swayed there, huffing, its shadow stretching out to them.

144

"Antelope," Dogeye announced proudly. "Not a better meat on earth. Young antelope steaks carved from high up on the tenderloin. Mmm—boy! Your young Burgundy'll set it off just dandy, Makai."

Juke huffed and dumped the animal into a limber, broken pile before them. "Dear God," Father Paul said in awe. "However did he get it?"

"Juke? Juke never got it. It was Ned, here."

Ned grinned. "Easy as pie," he explained to the inquiring eyes. "Mr. Dogeye says, 'That un!' and I just cut through the gap. Just like pickin' a halfback out from the blockers. Right through the gap. Ka-flooey."

"You ran *over* it?" Rodney blurted.

"Naw," Ned beamed. "Just tenderized it."

And before she realized it, Jocelyn found herself slapping

her leg and laughing with the others, like she could not remember doing in ages. And found herself remembering something, a truth she did not even know she had forgotten during all these years of solitude, avoiding the fellowship of fools:

That, for all the nuisance and irritation and suffocation they could provoke, fools could also be quite amusing.

7

Boiling and skidding . . .
Juke sings . . .

The white DeSoto sailed across the barren Utah desert. Inside the car, a fat man wearing a soiled white shirt sat with one hand on the steering wheel and a sunburned elbow protruding out the window. Shifting his weight he pulled a red handkerchief from his hip pocket. He wiped the moisture from his forehead and upper lip without removing his eyes from the vehicle a half mile ahead.

He eased off the throttle. He was getting a little too close. Maybe they had already spotted him. Maybe they were leading him on a wild-goose chase. Why else would they drive south two hundred miles, then turn right around and head notheast toward the Wyoming border, then veer west in the direction of Idaho?

It didn't matter if they did spot him. He was resolved to follow that devil's wagon to Hell and back if necessary. It didn't matter to him whether the newspaper stories about a cave of mystical secrets were true or false. Either way it constituted a wrinkle in the fabric of his people's philosophy, and it had to be ironed out. History would form you if you didn't form it, and the history they were involved in forming showed that only the fair races had the intelligence to advance human consciousness. The dusky tribes had demonstrated pockets of power over the ages, certainly, but these were aberrations, like illegal radio stations transmitting from the bush, creating wavelengths that were the work of the Old Boy Himself, or some even darker and more alien broadcaster. It made no difference if the message the station was broadcasting was as simple and accurate as the multiplications tables, the broadcast was a lie at the source.

A war was being waged; vast forces held in check for centuries were stirring, planning to darken the new age. The idea of a cave right here in Utah or Wyoming that contained artifacts of an ancient culture was a blasphemy even if it was authentic. Authenticity often was not the truth. Witness this guy Scopes and his simian fossils. Could the bones of a few dead apes outweigh the gathered glory of ages? No, no more than a few scratchings in a dirty hole could discredit the writings of Joseph Smith. But they could dirty the water and they had to be eliminated; authentic or false, they constituted a blemish that had to be eradicated.

Boyle recalled his speech two days earlier to his fellow members in the Order for the Preservation of Racial Purity. "There is a time to consider and reflect," Boyle had told them, waving the picture from the Reno paper, "and a time to study and plan. But all those times have passed, my friends. When the Devil is before you and the floodwaters are racing down upon you, the time for action has come. And now is that time. Now is the time to rise up and strike down the enemies of the angel Moroni, Joe Smith's avenger. We must follow those enemies to their lair, the fount of their poison, and destroy it utterly!"

Those enemies were slippery. They almost got away in Salt Lake. When they moved, he had to admit, they moved fast. Fortunately, he had VIP parking and had been able to get to his car and get after that Devil's wagon before it had pulled out of sight. He had hollered after some of the boys but they were too stunned by the machine's sudden maneuver up the steps to react. He had been able to phone in directions from time to time, but he was riding alone. Three times he thought he had lost them, but checking the various highways out of the city and asking a few questions had always put him back on the trail. There were no other vehicles of their description.

148

He had trailed them to their perverted lodge outside of Moab and slept in his car on a windswept ridge where he could keep an eye on them. And last night he had spent behind a Orange Crush billboard, not a quarter mile from their campfire. When they started again he was once more on the trail, belly rumbling. His fuel gauge showed he was down to an eighth of a tank. The fill-up he had pumped in at Green River was almost gone, a third of it burned up by the speed he had to drive catching up. But they'd have to stop somewhere soon, for gas, water, supplies. As soon as they stopped he would be able to put in a quick call to The Saints in Salt Lake. The boys would intersect with him somewhere along the way, in Parkerville, or Buffalo Wash. At full force they would be able to put a stop to the heresy these demons were planning to perpetrate, once and for all.

If these demons ever needed gas!

Behind the wheel in the carrier Ned Blue drove as if in a trance, gazing across the flats to the gray mountains ahead.

Next to Ned, Dogeye sat with his back rigid against the partition that separated them from the passenger section, and next to Dogeye sat Loach, his face turned to the little windwing. His long hands were cupped on his knees and he hadn't spoken in over an hour. Ned didn't mind. Even though Loach was not looking out the front windshield, he anticipated every junction and turnoff, giving Ned instructions at exactly the right moment.

Ned heard the slight change in the hum of the engine as the carrier strained to climb a long grade into the mountains. He looked in the side mirror. Yes, that white car was back. He thought maybe it had given up. He hadn't seen it for two hours. It looked like a brand-new DeSoto. What kind of folks could afford a new luxury car these days?

Same kind that can afford to spend days following a load of loopy explorers with a colored driver, he guessed—the dangerous kind.

The sky ahead was clear and blue, but big thunderheads could be seen gathering in from the southwest, as though summoned there by the white DeSoto. With any luck they could lose the bad folks in the DeSoto, but the bad weather? That might be harder to outrun, especially in this neck of the woods in this season.

Ned glanced again at his side mirror. The black road curled across the glass like a snake, and at the top of the mirror where the head of the snake would be, there was the white DeSoto.

Ned eased up slightly as he saw the road split ahead. A sign pointing to the right read: PARKERVILLE 60 MILES. He turned his head to Loach.

"Take the right fork, Ned," Loach said without opening his eyes.

The whine of the engine grew louder and higher-pitched as the grade became more severe. The road wound upward, through several turns and switchbacks. The carrier leaned and groaned.

"How's she doing, Ned?" Loach asked.

"She's fine, Chief. Just fine," Ned said. "You got no problems with this machine. Freely believe it."

At the top of a ridge Ned looked in the mirror again. He saw the white car coming up the switchbacks, and further down he could see the road snake across the desert for miles and miles.

"Ned," Loach said suddenly. "I want you to speed up."

"Chief?" said Ned with a start.

"Speed up." There was a whiplash of command to the voice. "We're going to put some distance between us."

Ned grinned. "You been onto him, too?"

"Since Smithville. Dogeye, wake up."

Dogeye drew a deep breath. "I'm awake, Charlie. What's up?"

"We're about to give Mr. Boyle the slip. Pour it on, Ned. About a mile ahead, if memory serves, you're going to see a religious billboard on the right—The Wages of Sin Is Death. Pull behind it and we'll let the hounds pass by."

"It's more than hounds I'm worried about, Chief," Ned said. "Them clouds says we're climbing into a bad squall before dark."

"We'll cross that squall when we get to it. Right now we are going to deal with Mr. Boyle. Get ready. He's falling back . . ."

Ned realized Loach's eyes had been fixed on the windwing, rolled open to act as his own little side mirror. Fox and hound for a fact. Well, let's see how this big fox handles.

He swung toward the signboard. The machine rumbled over the weedy embankment, scattering rocks and grit as it drifted enormously toward the corner of a rickety scaffolding. At the last moment it veered to plow into the snarl of tumbleweeds that had barricaded themselves behind the sign. Ned switched off the engine and it sat, shuddering in its nest of dry weeds. The only sounds were the furious demands for explanation coming from the other side of the little door. After a few moments they could see the DeSoto flash past through the cracks in the billboard. The two brothers grinned at each other. The protests from the passengers grew louder. Ned sat motionless, waiting for his next orders. Again, Loach spoke suddenly:

"Get after him, Ned."

"Chief?"

"Get right on his fat rear. Let's see how *he* likes being tailed."

"That's the spirit, Charlie-O," Dogeye cried, clapping his hands. "Now you're talking!"

Ned started the carrier and plowed on through the pile of tumbleweeds. They bounced back onto the pavement, picking up momentum. When they crested the hill they saw the DeSoto gaining speed, roaring away from them down the road.

"Hee-hee," Ned snickered. "Hound still thinks the fox is ahead of him, and gettin' away."

"Wonder if he's going to realize?" said Loach.

"Don't look like it," Dogeye said, sounding disappointed. "Looks like he's gonna keep highballing clean to Canada. Shoot."

The car disappeared around a bend. For good, they thought. But less than a mile later they saw it again, pulled off the

151

pavement, the hood raised. Boyle's enormous backside protruded from under it. It looked as though the car was eating him.

"Hell of a mouthful," Ned said. "Give that car an awful bellyache."

"Ease down, Ned," Loach told him. "Pull over and stop right behind him." Ned stepped on the brakes. The machine rumbled to a stop behind the car. Disregarding the pounding from the passenger section, all three men climbed out together.

As they approached the DeSoto, Boyle pulled out from under the hood and faced the trio. He did not seem the slightest bit surprised to see them coming up from his rear. He smiled and waved a long wicked-looking screwdriver, grinning as if he had been expecting them. Muffled calls could be heard coming through the metal place of the carrier and, on top, Juke's head poked up from his nest. The blue man was wearing the little derby, tied beneath his chin with a shoestring.

Loach spoke first. "What a pleasant surprise, Mr. Boyle. I never got a chance to thank you for our private tour of the Tabernacle."

Boyle tapped the screwdriver against his palm, his broad smile never faltering. "Yeah, you made a kind of quick getaway, as I recall."

"Let's call it a hurried departure," Loach went on. "What seems to be your trouble, way out here in the wilderness?"

"I'm not sure, Dr. Loach. Overheating."

"Probably the water pump," Dogeye offered. "A sudden acceleration will sometimes overwork the water pump."

"Or the fuel line," Ned suggested. "You can get a vapor lock if you get too hot, then stop on a hill too quick for no reason. Has you stopped on a hill too quick for no reason, Mr. Boyle?"

152

Boyle regarded him for a moment. "I don't do anything for no reason, Jim." He looked past them, toward the carrier hammering in the heat. "Sounds like your livestock's getting a little restless in that iron box of yours, Loach—yammering and hammering."

"Boyle, let's be straight," said Loach. "I've got a proposition for you. By every indication you have some kind of an interest in our expedition. Now you're broken down and—"

"Am I?" interrupted Boyle, his tooth glittering. "Am I broke down?"

Loach ignored the insinuation. "—and we cannot leave you alone here in the wilderness. Why don't you come aboard?"

"You mean aboard that landlocked submarine?"

"Yes. Join us, instead of following us. You want to see the cave, that is clear. And quite understandable. This holy place could hold secrets of particular interest to the adherents of your faith. Come along, join the party, see the truth."

Boyle glowed with amusement. "The truth, Loach? I learn the truth here, in God's word." He tapped the screwdriver against the car's rear window where a little black book could be seen. " 'For I will show unto them,' " he quoted in a booming voice, " 'that my wisdom is greater than the cunning of the Devil.' Joe Smith's truth."

"Be that as it may," Loach said, "the offer still stands. It will save you spending any more money on gas—or phone calls."

"Yeah, Boyle," Dogeye prompted, "you want to stay here dickin' with this car or want to join the yammering herd?"

Boyle looked from face to face for a moment, then tossed the screwdriver in the car's trunk and closed it. "I'll go with you," he said, "and much obliged. First, let me get my equipment—"

He started to reach through the rear window for a bundle. Loach stopped him with a hand on his big freckled forearm.

"We've everything we need on the carrier, Mr. Boyle. Fully equipped. Even a double-size sleeping bag . . . "

Boyle looked down at the hand. "Let me grab my coat then," he said at last. Loach didn't let go of his arm.

"Please, Mr. Boyle. Allow us. Ned? The man's coat?"

Ned reached past the steering wheel and picked up a crumpled seersucker coat. He began patting the pockets.

"What's these here?" Ned asked, withdrawing three metal tubes.

"Corona Coronas," Boyle said with pride. "Cuba's finest."

"I didn't think Mormons smoked, Boyle," Dogeye said.

154

"We don't. But we feel it strengthens our character to have temptation handy to resist."

"Sure enough," Ned announced, dipping into the inside pocket. "Here's more of it." He held up a tiny silver flask.

"This is rattlesnake territory," Boyle explained with a shrug. He took the flask from Ned and tipped it up for a quick swallow. "I believe in being prepared, just like the Boy Scouts."

"I'm beginning to appreciate that, Mr. Boyle," Loach told the fat man. "Now let's be on our way, before some other Boy Scouts show up."

Loach and his brother fell in on either side of Boyle and escorted him toward the back of the carrier, Ned bringing up the rear.

Loach swung open the double doors. The crowd that had been banging on the door at the other end swung round and came toward them, everybody talking at once. Loach silenced them with a raised palm:

"You all remember Mr. Boyle from Salt Lake? He has elected to grace our company with his presence for the remainder of the expedition. I'm sure you will make him comfortable."

Before anyone else could comment they had pushed the fat man into the machine and were closing the doors behind him.

"We'd make formal introductions," Dogeye said to Jocelyn, "but we're in a kind of a hurry. There may be Boyle Scouts after us."

The doors rang shut and Boyle smiled about him at the surprised faces. "Once more, folks, a pleasure, an honest-to-God blue-ribbon pleasure."

The engine roared to life and the machine began to move. He looked at the blacked-out windows.

155

"A honor, too," Boyle went on, swaying dangerously, "a know-nothing outsider like me getting accepted on the Sodom and Gomorrah express." He stepped deeper into the purple light, kicking the meandering crystal ball out of the way, grinning at his surroundings. "Real nice. Especially the way you've blacked out the windows so's you ladies won't get a burn. That ol' sun can be right nasty at these altitudes. Whups, there's that embankment again. Maybe we best all sit down before we fall down."

With that he pitched his coat over the back of a couch and plunged down in the heaving moil of pillows and scarves, like a sea lion into the surf.

"Wasn't intending to impose myself on you nice folks this way, but when Dr. Loach here extended the invite, why it was just too good to pass up. We don't get excitement like this every day back in Salt Lake." He patted a pillow beside him. "Better plop it down, Honeybuns, before it falls down."

"I think I'll plop it down over here, thanks," said Gaby, seating herself in the davenport across. "And don't call me anything."

Outside, the black clouds gathered and shouldered, pushing for a better view of the object droning toward them up the winding highway. They were growing in size and stockpiling icy ammunition as they grew. Lightning was beginning to fly back and forth between the troops like signal flags. They watched the carrier coming closer.

Ned watched them watching. The sun had dropped from sight behind the bunker of clouds, darkening the mountainsides. Whatever was coming would cut loose soon, Ned knew. He hoped they could make it over the pass first. Loach said it wasn't much farther—up to the summit, then downhill to a T and a crossroad that wouldn't have so many twists and turns and yawning dropoffs down each side.

"Which way when we hits the T, Chief?" Ned wanted to know. "I surely hope it ain't east. East is where that squall look like it's really squallin'."

Loach was studying his canvas-bound book, frowning. "I haven't found the answer to that yet, Ned. My handwriting is shaking here."

"Probably was goin' through a storm when you wrote it," Ned said. "What about you, Mr. Dogeye? You recollect?"

"You got me, Ned. All I remember is we crest at that saddleback yonder, then get down outta these damn mountains. We'll make it. We're nearly over the top."

But when they reached the summit they found the clouds were already there, just over the rise, waiting in ambush.

Suddenly the thunder seemed to be right in the cab with them. The downgrade was inches deep in hailstones big as golf balls, and more coming. Ned had to shout to make his questions heard:

"Shall we stop, Chief? Oh Lord, she's fishtailin'—"

"Steady as she goes, Ned!" Loach shouted back. "Keep way! Brakes could spin us out of control!"

"Spin us into Hell is what they could do," Dogeye added. "It's two hundred yards down on either side. Grab a lower gear and ride 'er out, Ned!"

Ned managed to find second. "Best I can get, Mr. Dogeye. Hang on. Whoo-ee! Just like sleddin' back in Omaha."

Dogeye opened the partition door and shouted for everyone to hang on. No one could hear a word. They sky had let loose a full salvo. Ice and electricity boomed around them in continuous detonation as they fishtailed down the slope. Like a battle at sea, thought Ned, lights flashing and death laughing and the depths waiting on both sides. Oh Lord!

The hail beat on the roof. It pounded the hood and the sides and bounced up from beneath against the floorboards. Men were cursing and women's mouths were wide with screaming, but no sound came out. It was swallowed up by the roar of the storm. Tongues were muted by the blast. And the hail got larger. It hit the pavement so hard that cracks were created deep in the roadbed. It ricocheted off the windshields and sparked off the fenders. It hammered into the sides of the machine as though the hailstones were being fired from cannons hidden on the slopes across. It pounded so hard that one of the bulletproof portholes finally cracked beneath the bombardment.

Ned let the machine find its way down the ribbon of ice, trusting the roadmakers. Sometimes he saw the roadguards

flicker by, a silly little fence against this kind of inertia. Sometimes he accelerated a little to keep making way, like a boat
had to do when running with a tide. He kept telling himself
that it couldn't last, that the bottom had to be down there
somewhere, that he'd been through worse, but finally he felt
he was about to pass out. The hailstones had entered his
skull. They were banging around in there like firecrackers in
a syrup can. He couldn't stand it much longer. Yet the banging increased. They were under attack and the attackers were
under orders to take no prisoners. Wipe them out utterly.

During a momentary let-up he heard something from the
passengers' section, above the whine of the gearbox and the
rattle of hail. It sounded like laughter.

158

Gaby heard it too. She opened her eyes long enough to see
it came from the photographer, Chick Ferrell. He was laughing as though he didn't know how to stop, as if his laughter
were part of the hail, out of his control, and beating at him
from the inside of his head while the storm beat on the
outside. While she was watching him, she noticed the broken
window. At least there's that, she said to herself; fresh air at
last. Maybe I can even see out. It's like we're in a drum,
pounded on by madmen.

She peered out the window, for the first view of the countryside she'd had since boarding the carrier that morning.
There was not much to see, a cyclone of silver hail, and the
shadowy figure of something in the distance—bushes, or
even mountains, so nondescript within the storm that she
could not tell one from the other. Someone yelled. Gaby
looked around as Rodney jumped from his seat.

"Stop!" he yelled. He ran to the door at the front of the rig.
"This din is maddening! I've got to get off."

Then the floor of the carrier dropped from beneath Gaby's

feet like an elevator and slanted forward in a frightening pitch. Gaby had to grab ahold of the couch to keep from sliding into the Father. "Jesus," she said, "Oh, Jesus." She looked at the Father.

The carrier hit something and bounced, tossing Gaby two feet above the couch. When she came down she left her stomach behind. She swallowed her stick of chewing gum. Her ears were ringing with the noise and the pounding hail.

The carrier lurched sideways and the Father was thrown into Gaby's lap. He grabbed her knee to keep from being pitched forward and to the floor. Bottles and tins of food rolled around the floor of the rig. The crystal ball plopped between the Father's feet. The bird few overhead, landing in a flutter on a swinging lamp, then took to flight again, squawking and beating its wings.

159

The sisters, putting aside their spiritual differences for the moment, clung together like children wrestling on the floor. The table, the Buddha, and the candles had long since been tossed to the back of the carrier by the swinging and bouncing motion.

"Stop this thing, stop this thing, we can't ride out a hailstorm like we're in a boat," one of the sisters yelled out as they tumbled back to the other side of the carrier.

The hail pounded down like mortar fire in the Great War.

Across the aisle Chick held tightly to the arms of a chair, his teeth rattling as he tried to imagine a headline for this latest episode in the trip—"Expedition ends in disaster! Famous reporter killed!"

"We're sliding," Gaby screeched.

"I can't hold 'er, Chief," she heard Ned shout. "This is the end of the road!"

With a sickening lurch the carrier slid over the road's end, the front end dropping with a crunch. Everything at the back of the carrier clanged against the metal roof—trunks, shoes, canned goods, the brass Buddha—and fell back to the floor. The oval top of the seance table ricocheted off the wall and crashed one end out through the already cracked window. Air rushed in, then, all at once, everything was still. The carrier and the storm had crashed to a simultaneous stop.

Pale afternoon light fell in through the broken window and illuminated the wreckage. The silence was almost as deafening as the din. Father Paul held his right forearm in his left hand and bright red blood oozed from between his fingers.

"Something got me," he said at last. Everyone stared at him, but no one moved. "Bird, I suppose. It's not bad, just a flesh wound." He grimaced as Gaby tore a strip of cloth from the tail of his shirt and wrapped it around the wound.

"Mona, darling, where are you? Are you all right?"

"I'm just fine, dear, I'm right here, under the tapestry."

Loach peeked through the doorway. "Is anyone hurt? I want everyone to count off."

"What do you mean, count off?" Mona asked, bewildered.

"I need to make sure you're all fine. Gaby? Ramona, Mona? Dr. Caine?" The women answered in a chorus. Loach stepped over the pedestal from the altar table, kicking aside pillows and scarves.

"Father? Makai? Ferrell?"

"What the hell happened?" Rodney asked.

"We hit a stretch of ice. Are you all all right?"

"I think I hurt my wrist." Rodney flapped his left hand.

Loach felt Rodney's wrist. "Not broken, but it's swelling a bit. We'll pack some hailstones around it."

"Don't you have a first-aid kit? My God, this is supposed to be a casualty carrier and it doesn't even have a first-aid kit? Wouldn't you know."

"You're the one that bought it, Rodney," said Ramona.

"It probably has one, but right now I'm not sure where it is," Loach answered. "Is that everyone? No other wounds?"

"Mr. Boyle!" Mona cried. "What has happened to Mr. Boyle?"

"Boyle?" Loach called. They began to search among the debris. "You still with us, Boyle?"

"Here's his shoe," Chick said, "but there's no foot in it."

"Boyle?" Loach dug through the jumbled mass of pillows and piled luggage. A muffled groan answered him. "Here he is. Dog, give me a hand . . ."

Loach pulled Boyle's head into view from the rubble. The man looked much deflated. "Maybe he popped," Gaby said, "like a football under a pile-up."

161

Loach loosened Boyle's collar and leaned close. "No, he's still breathing."

"Breathing?" Gaby asked. "Or you mean leaking."

"Be sure he has no spinal injuries," Dr. Caine put in. "It could hurt him even worse to move him."

"I think he's just knocked cold," Loach said, leaning close again. "Boyle, can you hear me?"

"Of course I can hear you," Boyle answered. "You're hollering right in my ear."

As Boyle moved, the machine teetered forward, creaking.

"Everyone off," Loach said. "Chick, help me and Dogeye get Boyle back on his feet."

"Give him a drink," Father Paul volunteered.

"Good idea," Rodney said, reaching for his flask.

"Damn good idea," Gaby said. "Let's have a belt all

around." She had located her amber cigarette holder and was feeling some of her spunk returning.

"Everybody off!" Loach repeated. "She's tipping."

But the front end came to rest and the tipping stopped. The rear was angled into the air, both doors open. It was too steep to get out the back. The passengers had to work their way through the partition and out the front. As soon as they had all dismounted, the machine creaked again and tilted heavily back. It was high-centered on the embankment, like a teeter-totter. Neither the front nor the rear wheels touched ground. The passengers stood in the sudden still among the melting hailstones, watching their transportation teeter back and forth.

"Jesus, what a spectacular mess," said Rodney. "And I'll lay odds Ferrell left his equipment on board."

"I never thought—" Chick began. Rodney cut him off.

"Some photographer. I'd have done better to hire a cartoonist."

"Look at all this stuff," Dogeye said. "Hey, somebody better check up top and see how Juke fared."

"I'll do it," Ned said and started up the side ladder.

"Careful," Dogeye cried. "Any shift of weight seems to teeter her."

"We're gonna need to get them rear wheels back to earth before we go any place," Boyle observed. "Gonna need a pry pole." He began looking about him, rolling his shirtsleevews back from his beefy forearms. "Everybody'll have to pitch in . . ."

"Ned," Dogeye shouted. "Get Juke down here. We're going to try to tip the rear wheels down so you can back her out."

"Just a minute," Ned called back. He was rummaging

through the storage platform at the rear of the machine's roof. Suddenly he stood up. "Mr. Juke ain't here!"

"You sure, Ned?" Loach scrambled up the embankment and hurried back to where Ned was standing.

"Certain sure, Chief. Looks like his whole nest has been jarred loose."

Dogeye scrambled up the ladder to the top of the carrier. "Ned's right. Juke's clean gone." He shaded his eyes to look back up the ribbon of melting ice. "Christ. It could have happened any place, all the way back to the summit." He started back to the ladder. "Come on, everybody, we'll have to— No, wait! Look! Look yonder!"

They looked the way that Dogeye was pointing, ahead of the carrier, down the rutted embankment. They saw a dense grove of aspen trees. One of the trees was bent nearly to the hailstone-covered earth. The topmost branches had been tangled and weighted down by a formless gray mass. The mass hung among the pale yellow leaves like an enormous bee swarm.

"Oh my stars," cried Mona.

"Your stars indeed!" her sister said. "They certainly never predicted anything like *this*."

Dogeye and Ned climbed down and followed the others toward the dangling mass. Everyone could clearly see what had happened: when the machine's front end had dropped over the embankment, the hindquarters had banged skyward. Juke had been catapulted into the air like an acrobat off a jump board. He was still in his filthy sleeping bag, the bag inside its khaki cover. The loose lashings must have snarled in the first tree top they struck, bending the long white trunk pendulously to the ground. It hung there, heavy and motionless.

"Gimme a hand here," Loach said. His ability to suddenly

move had brought him to the bag far before the others, but he couldn't lift it and unsnarl the lashings at the same time.

Paul was the first to reach him. "Is he still with us?" the priest asked, wringing his hands.

"How the hell do I know?" Loach snapped. "I can't even tell which end his head is at. Lift here . . ."

Dogeye arrived, panting. Without a word he unclasped his Barlow and slashed through a canvas cartridge belt. This dislodged a cascade of various objects from the bag. Tins of Army beef, a canteen, a selection of clay mugs . . . but no Juke.

"Cut the other one," Loach said. "He could be suffocating."

Before Dogeye could free a second belt the cornet fell free, dinging on the hailstones. This lightened the mass enough that the tree sprung up slightly, further jarring the load. Juke came sliding out, right on his head. Luckily, his little Bakelite derby was still tied on. It cushioned his fall like a helmet. The tree snapped standing, waving the sleeping bag back and forth at full mast, like the flag of some shabby regiment.

Dr. Jocelyn came skittering through the hailstones and touched Juke's neck. His skin was icy cold and his face was even bluer than usual.

"He's got a strong pulse," she said. "Here, lay him under the trees where there's no hail."

"Is he all right?" both sisters called in concert.

"He's alive, but I can't tell if anything's broken. I'll have to—"

She stopped. They all stopped. The figure on the ground was moving, and moving strangely. They all watched as it rolled to its knees and started standing—slowly, like a rusty doll. The eyelids fluttered slightly, but remained closed. When it was fully erect the arms began to spread, the way a performer might welcome an audience. In the stillness, the last rumble of the storm could be heard far away, like applause from the balcony. Everyone stood, staring at the little man with his arms spread and his eyes closed. Then they heard a thin, airless sound, a sound they all were forced to recognize as a voice, though nothing at all had moved. The voice was half-reciting, half-singing:

> A long time ago
> A million years B.C.
> The best things in life
> Were absolutely free . . .

All the passengers stood transfixed by the eerie spectacle, even Boyle. Juke's blue lips had not so much as trembled. The words seemed to come from some place beneath the throat, mechanical, hidden, a black disk turning under a tiny needle:

> But no one appreciated
> A sky that was always blue
> And no one congratulated
> A moon that was always new.

The leaves of the aspen had ceased quaking. There was no sound from horizon to horizon but the thin, airless words:

> So it was planned that they
>   Would vanish now and then
> And you must pay before
>   You get them back again.
> That's what storms are made for,
> But do not be afraid, for—

At last the smudged sockets came open; but the eyes stared at nothing, like a doll's. The head swiveled, facing the listeners. The hands began gesturing in jerky pantomime and the lips began to move. And Juke's voice rose in a sweet, throbbing tenor, clear as the storm-cleaned air around them:

> —every time it rains it rains
>   Pennies from heaven
> Don't you know each cloud contains
>   Pennies from heaven
>
> You'll find your fortune falling
>   all over town—
> Be sure that your umbrella
>   Is upside down
>
> Trade them for a package of
>   Sunshine and flowers
> If you want the things you love
>   You must have showers
>
> So when you hear it thunder
>   Don't run under a tree
> There'll be pennies from heaven
>
>   for you
>
>   and me

166

Dogeye was the first to speak. Turning to Dr. Jo, he popped his eyebrows up and down.

"See?" he reminded her. "I told you it was rather difficult to describe."

8

Sisters purify expedition . . .
Loach consults spirit compass . . .
Boyle gets whammied . . .

The skidding machine had landed at the bottom of a steep downgrade in a pocket of the fault-block mountains they'd been climbing into for the whole of the day. Their highway junctioned at a road along a stream. The stream cut along a pass. Judging from the ruts in the roadbank, their rig hadn't been the first to roll down that steep grade and fly straight into this grove of aspens. And, judging from the fire circles scattered in the little meadow between the aspens and the stream, they weren't the first to make camp here.

On the far side of the creek, up the limestone and siltstone mountainsides, knotty red pine and thin, straight bristlecone pine gray. Scattered among these trees were clusters of kinnikinnick, fireweed and sledge—all casting their shadows up the creek.

The storm crashed and tumbled on up the stream, away from the disheveled intersection. The sky slipped from lapis to cobalt. And to the southeast, over the granite ridge, Venus shot up like a flare. The sun eased from beneath a thunder-head. Warm light filled the draw.

On the ground hail sparkled and flashed—arrangements of diamonds set among the beige-brown rocks. The mountain air was so dry the hailstones were evaporating about Juke's unlaced boots, right before everybody's eyes, glistening one moment, gone the next, without a trace. A warm breeze washed off the melting highways, shimmering the leaves along the trunks of the aspen like coins being spun, gold heads, silver tails.

The little audience that had been transfixed around Juke at last began to stir.

Boyle resumed his search for a pry pole. He located a length of peeled pine and wedged it beneath the front bumper. "Had to do plenty of this in the war. No problem for a man of my strength. I might need a little help pushing it off where it's high-centered, though. Get in and start 'er up, Jim. We'll be loose from here in a cut hair. Who's gonna help me?"

Dogeye stepped up. "Right here."

Father Paul said, "Here too," and Chick Ferrell added, "Here three."

The Makai sisters spoke out in unison, "We'll help."

"Don't talk nuts," Rodney called to his aunts. He had remained alongside Juke, waiting for another tune. "You'll just strain some flappy muscle or other."

Mona Makai put her hands on her hips. "We don't mean to use our *muscle* power," she said.

Loach joined the crew Boyle had gathered around the front of the vehicle. Rodney and Juke continued to stand in the little glade beneath the aspen, estranged from the proceedings at the roadside. Ramona and Mona walked a few feet closer and halted, facing each other. They closed their eyes and simultaneously raised their outstretched arms, their hands open and their palms upward. They began to growl. Ned climbed back behind the wheel, looking dubious.

Boyle, Dogeye, Father Paul, Chick and Loach took positions around the front grille. The engine chugged to a start and Ned shouted out the driver's window: "Lift!" As Boyle pried, the others put their shoulders against the fenders. The front slowly lifted until the rear wheels found solid ground.

"Into the rear, ladies!" Boyle grunted. "Weight is more important than telekinesis right now. Everybody, in the rear!"

Rodney and Juke stayed where they were. The four women hurried around to the back and helped each other over the rear bumper. When they were all inside, Ned carefully put it in reverse.

"All right," Boyle grunted again. "Heave!"

Ned gunned the engine. Boyle pried and Dogeye, Father Paul and Chick leaned into the fenders. Loach put his back to the grille and hooked his long fingers under the bumper. They heaved. The rear duals spun and spit hailstones until the treads reached pavement. The big machine began to scrape backward over the dirt embankment into the intersection. When the front tires bumped over the little bank and back on the road the women inside cheered. From somewhere out of the depths of disarray Kronos the parrot cheered, too.

Loach followed along with the machine until it stopped, then he leaned against the dark metal to catch his breath. Down the embankment, Chick was bent over with his hands on his knees, wheezing hard. Boyle steadied himself with his pole as though it were a crutch. Dogeye lay flat on the ground, looking up at the sky, whistling and hee-hawing like a jackass.

At the bottom of the ditch, Rodney was puffing and holding his hand to his spine as though he had hurt it helping. "Damn back," he shouted up at the others. "Goes out on me at the first sign of physical labor."

Ramona and Mona had crawled back out through the rear doors.

"Never mind, dear," Ramona called back. "We understand. You were always such a delicate child."

"A lazy little loafer, that's what he was," Mona snorted. "Never lifted a finger his live-long life."

Dogeye rolled to his knees and stood up. Ned eased the machine forward along the highway east to a little rutted off road and parked. The passengers began shuffling through the parcels scattered about the trees. Chick was finding film boxes and Gaby was gathering the packs of Chesterfields from demolished cartons. Ramona thrust up her arm and cried, "Hooray!" The crystal ball glowed in her palm. Loach and Jocelyn helped Juke into the carrier. They made him comfortable on a couch. Joselyn removed the dented derby and examined the little man's frazzled white head. "Nothing seems upset," she announced, thinking: Except the little citizens that resided there.

Dogeye separated from the others and walked out into the middle of the intersecting T, examining the three possibilities—west, east, or back. He began strolling down the T one direction, then turned around and walked the other, pursing his lips. Gaby finally looked up from her rummaging and shouted to him:

"What's the matter, Uncle Dog? Lose the trail?"

"No," Dogeye answered "Lost that damned armadillo. No tellin' where that bugger's rolled off to."

"Well, come on back," Father Paul fretted. "I'm sure as we clean up this mess we'll find him."

"Yeah, Dog," Loach called. "We might make camp here as we clean up. What do you think?"

"Okay, sure," Dogeye said. He reached up behind his braid and scratched his neck. "But damn me, Charlie, I hate a thing being lost."

This brought Rodney to life. "Lost? We're lost?" He had walked over to join Boyle for a sip from one of the flasks. "Damn you, Loach, you said your brother had the senses of a bloodhound—could return to anyplace. I think you exaggerated—"

"You know what *I* think, Makai?" Boyle confided in a loud voice, "I think a couple of little boys are lost, is what I think. Lost and humming up their sleeve to hide the fact from us."

"Is that right, Loach?" Rodney demanded. "Are you two lost?"

"Could be, Makai," Loach answered. "But we're camping here regardless."

"Well if you want to know what *I* think—" It was Mona, stepping to Loach's side in a show of confidence. "—I think Mr. Dogeye's armadillo will come out, just like the stars."

"That'll be helpful," Boyle went on. "Leastways our navigator should be able to figure whichaway north is."

To take the sting out of the fat man's sarcasm, Father Paul suddenly turned toward the scavenging women and shouted through his cupped hands: "*Camp*-ing! Camping *here!*" like a Scout leader whose pack had somehow missed the news. "We'll want a nice fire. What do you say we divide into two groups? One to make camp, the other to gather the spilled equipment? How does that sound?"

"Sounds ducky," said Gaby and plumped herself down in a pile of bedding. "Call me a campmaker."

Ramona picked up a walking stick and poked around the piles of leaves in case of snakes. Mona squatted at Juke's bag and began gathering everything within arm's reach—maps, pitons, hammers, carabiners, ropes, tent stakes like a jumble of pick-up-sticks—and shoving them in the canvas bag. Suddenly, she screamed and fell back, beating at the canvas with a stake. Ramona rushed over to join in the pummeling.

"Hold it, hold it!" Dogeye shouted. He picked up the bag and began to shake it empty again. The last thing to roll out was the armadillo. "You rascal. What was Juke using you for, a footwarmer?"

His animal found and stored back in the carrier with Juke, Dogeye was even able to devote himself to the evening's meal. "Wood! Lots of wood. I seen a dead scrub cedar down that left fork. Come on, everybody! We got antelope kebabs in our future!"

◇

Supper was finished and cleared away, but it was still too early to turn in. Though the night was clear and calm, the recent bombardment of the storm and the careening shriek of the wreck still echoed in everybody's ears. The group dallied, sitting about the fire on decaying aspen logs that Dogeye had found piled near an abandoned fencing project.

"They ain't worth beans for burning," he had told the people, "but they make nice furniture."

He and Father Paul had shouldered one of the pulpy posts and carried it up to the campfire—a shaggy pole about the size of a tall man—and Loach and Ferrell brought up another.

Boyle had scoffed at the effort. "Little sticks," he laughed. "Pencils. My posterior's too commodious to sit on pencils."

Boyle tramped off down the ravine toward the pile. When he returned he was carrying a jackpine log, bigger by twice than the one he'd pried the carrier with. It crashed to the ground in a blizzard of dust and sparks.

"Now that's what I call furniture," Boyle said, much too loudly.

Boyle had grown louder during Dogeye's supper, especially with sips from his flask and the addition of Rodney's wine. He winked at Gaby, watching with her hands on her hips, and patted a smooth spot next to his commodious rump. "Come on over, Toots," he said, displaying his teeth in a meaty grin. "I don't bite."

173

"I do," Gaby said. She took a place on Dogeye's log, next to Dr. Jo. "And if you keep calling me Toots I just might have to show you how hard."

"That's the spirit," Boyle laughed. He poured himself another tin cup of Burgundy.

"All this imbibing, Mr. Boyle," Ramona said. "It doesn't seem like the Mormon way?"

"Why, Miz Makai, don't you know? We're not in Utah any longer." He slapped his thigh and sparks jumped from the fire.

"How do you know that, Mr. Boyle?" Chick asked, pulling his notepad from his hip pocket. "Just how familiar are you with this territory?"

"Familiar enough, Fido. Look at the lay of the land; by now we're in Wyoming, I'd bet on it. Those peaks yonder is probably the Tetons. I'm not precisely sure of our location, but I know the lay of the land. And this land you folks are on lays treacherous."

"I don't understand—" Chick said.

"Of course you don't. You wouldn't know the lay of the land from the lay of the town."

"Our Mr. Boyle is in good spirits," Paul said to Loach. Loach was seated between the priest and Ned, engrossed in his canvas-bound ledger, his bare feet stretched toward the fire. "He's not at all as I anticipated," Father Paul went on. "A funny man, really."

Loach made no comment, but Ned muttered, "Yes sir, real funny."

"Say, Makai? How about uncorking some more of this Devil's Blood? Long as we're all tenting on the old campground, let's get acquainted, tell tales, sing campfire songs. Jim here can accompany us on the mouth organ. You do play mouth organ, don't you?"

"No sir," Ned lied. He had a nearly new harmonica in his Dopp kit. "Sorry."

"Then let's exchange *his*tories," Boyle persisted, looking about at everyone with his lewd leer.

"I'd rather keep my histories, if you don't mind," Ramona said. She sat on her log darning one of Loach's socks. "And let you keep yours."

Boyle ignored her. "We got time to spare, don't we? Let's tell each other our life stories." He turned to Loach. "What about you, Charlie boy? What do you do in real life?"

Loach didn't appear to hear. He was turned, holding the ledger up so the firelight fell on the pages.

"How about *some*body," Boyle persisted. "I bet some of you got some whoppers for us, eh?"

"Very well, Mr. Boyle," Jocelyn cut in. "Let's start with you. What do you do for a living? You must be something more than a tour guide and bad detective."

It came out sharply but Jocelyn didn't care. The fat man had been needling them ever since he had almost single-handedly heaved the teetering machine back onto the road.

"*Moi?*" Boyle said, delighted by Jocelyn's interest. "Why, I'm a brickmaker, Doc. The Boyles is always been brick-makers. My brother's a brickmaker and my son's a brick-maker. My daddy's a brickmaker in Cleveland. My grandpa was a brickmaker in the old country. We've been brickmakers clear back to Boyle the Great." He gave Jocelyn a wink. "Great as in Big, that is. They say you could put Great-Granddaddy Boyle on one end of a teeter-totter and a full-blown bull on the other, and the bull'd go to rising."

"That was a real nice flivver you was driving, Mr. Boyle," Rodney observed. "So it must be a pretty lucrative profes-sion."

175

"Brickmaking? It's the pits, so to speak. All my illustrious ancestors was always as broke as they was big. Died poor as beggars and spitting brick dust. But, you're right, Makai; this Boyle's doing all right. I'm as rich as blood pudding, as they say."

To everybody's surprise, the next question came from Loach.

"Then tell us, Mr. Boyle"—Loach kept his eyes on his book—"how is it that you were able to rise above the fate of your predecessors?"

Boyle swung his muscled grin back on Loach, making sure the firelight caught his gold tooth.

"Why, I had me a *vision*, Charlie boy. Just like you musta had, eh? The basic primary number-one vision? Only I had two of 'em." He leaned back, lacing his fingers behind his fat neck. "I was with C Company in a little town in France—Pont à Mousson on the Plateau Lorraine. We was mopping up. Street-to-street, dirty business. It cost us eight days not to mention eighty percent of C Company. Dead Frogs and Krauts and Yanks everywhere. A hell of a world, I says to myself. Then, on the eighth day, while I was picking my way through the rubble sorting things out as they say, I got to noticing the bricks. What I noticed was the *difference* in them, from one building to another. I noticed that the bricks they used in the *churches* was a whole lot better grade of product than what you found in your everyday Frog hovel. Better than from your big municipal buildings, even. Right next to a cathedral was what was left of the Pont à Mousson Library, fer instance—completely leveled. Pulverized. The bricks was tore up worse than the books. Cheap bricks, barely baked. It also came to my attention that the dead priests looked in a lot better shape than the dead librarians. Better dressed and better fed. Right then and there, all of a sudden, I seen the light. I says to myself if I get out of this mess I'm damned if I'm going back to Dad's yard in Cleveland, eat red dust all my life so's a bunch of hoity-toity contractors can vacation their winters away in Florida. No sir, I says to myself; not me, not this Boyle. I'm going someplace where bricks are by God considered *holy!*"

176

"And you came to Utah," Jocelyn said.

"Right!" Boyle said. He swiveled to her. "You're pretty keen for a doctor, Doc. Yep. Moved the whole shebang to Salt Lake, lock, stock and barrel. Everything but Daddy. He simply wouldn't go for it. Said he could not abide Saints, Latter Day or other wise. He maintained that the Mormons was just more of the same old sneaky Sons of Abraham who'd figured a dodge to get more than one old lady. He cussed me over the decision, too, from the time I sold the house to the moment me and my brood was pulling out in the family Ford. Said I didn't stand a snowflake's chance in Hell of making a go of it among the Mormons. He said they'd Jew the socks off a brickhead like me inside of a year. He was very nearly right. Me and the Boyle brood got right down to our last dime more times than once that first year. We was slicing our bologna so thin it only had one side." He leaned forward again, grinning. "That's when I had the *second* primary vision—that if'n you can't Jew 'em . . . join 'em. Now *that* vision, Charlie Boy, is one I'm not sure you've yet visioned."

Loach closed his book, marking his place with a thin half-black, half-red marker. He picked up a stick and began poking the fire, frowning into the orange flames. He refused to raise his eyes to the man's pointed challenge. Sparks stirred upward into the aspen leaves. Down the bank the rocky little creek rattled and splashed. Boyle continued:

"I became a church member," he explained. "I took to reading Joe Smith and I joined some clubs. And you know? My fortunes commenced to rise. I did my brickwork by day and my churchwork by night. I even bought salvation for those Boyles who had departed (Dad took his mortal leave of Cleveland that winter), departed without the benefit of God's Word as revealed by the angel Moroni. We can do that, you know? Buy passage into Heaven of the souls of bygone loved ones. And in less time than it takes to tell it I watched my business grow to be the third largest brickyard in all Utah and Idaho. In terms of the Great American Greenback, that ain't exactly hay. Six years ago I was able to take my *own* winter vacation. I went *back* to Europe and that little town where I'd seen the light—left my son in charge of the business and took my wife, my four daughters, and enough of them greenbacks with me to rebuild *both* their goddamn churches, the Jesuit and the what-the-hell-those-other-ones are, plus endowed them to rebuild that library into the best in western France."

He sighed. "So. That is my success story. Now it's your turn, Charlie Boy," he prompted. "Where did *you* go to vacation six years ago?"

"Benedictines," said Father Paul. He looked up, his spectacles firelit.

"What?"

"That's the name of the other major order in France."

"Gee thanks, Father," said Boyle. "I'm glad we cleared that up."

Nobody else spoke. They listened to the creek and watched the sparks. After a while Boyle drew another long breath, still waggling his toes, but before he could resume his monologue, Loach spoke.

178

"You mentioned something about the Golden Dawn."

Boyle's tiny eyes widened for a moment; this wasn't the response he had expected his needling to produce.

"The Golden Dawn," Loach repeated. "Didn't I hear you saying something at the Tabernacle the other day? About the New Order of the Golden Dawn?"

"Could be, why? What do you know about the New Order?"

"Not much. Just what philosophy I've managed to piece together from the few periodicals the good Father was able to bring me." Now it was Loach's turn to raise his eyes and smile. "The library in my vacation land was not so well endowed. Naturally, I am acquainted with the works of Spare and Crowley." He turned to Father Paul on the log next to him, smiling. "When the guard brought me *Magick* he asked if I would tell him the secret of the linking rings when I was finished—that he'd always been particularly mystified by that one."

Paul laughed, and so did Dr. Jo. Boyle didn't think it was funny.

"Piece together what philosophy?"

"Oh, just the barest bones, Mr. Boyle. A skeleton, really. But enough to know the creature for what it is."

"Yeah? And what is that creature, Mr. Loach?"

"The same old dragon that's always lurking behind these moldy old Teutonic Orders. Behind the Knights Templar. And the Cagliastrians. And the White Brotherhood. Western civilization's same old dragon, as near as I can see."

Loach's voice was gentle, almost conciliatory, but it was clearly a gauntlet thrown. Everyone watched Boyle, waiting.

"Yeah, Loach? And what dragon is that, exactly?"

"Greed. Greed for possessions, power, even light. Greed for enlightenment is still just mercantile mysticism. Yes, Mr. Boyle, it's that same scaly old nightmare that always hides itself under the banners of tradition. And one of those banners is usually racial purity, or do I read you wrong?"

"No, you read me correctly." Boyle's big pumpkin grin was gone, as well as his uneducated drawl. "Though I take issue with your characterization."

"I imagined you would," Loach said, and was quiet. Thunder mumbled far up the ravine, like an afterthought.

"You don't understand," Boyle protested, his voice rising. "We *aren't* racists! Traditionalists, perhaps, yes; but not racists. Mankind is at present in a darkened time, groveling in a shadow of ignorance. The New Order is attempting to bring forth light by establishing contact with the powers of the past. It's like, say, a *tele*phone line, connecting us with the mighty signals that used to be, and that will be again. That phone line to the past is our very blood! But the line has to be clear, you see? If you want a clear signal. You know about spirits. You wouldn't want to be talking to important spirits and risk having a foreign power run a tap on the line, would you? For the signal to be true, the bloodline *has* to be *pure!*"

Loach didn't respond. Boyle was becoming more and more agitated on his log, rocking to and fro, rubbing his palms on his thighs.

"Other bloodlines have other signals—their *own* racial messages. Ain't that right, Jim? You folks have your own powers and your own way of contacting them, right? Drums and voodoo and such? You wouldn't want a bunch of outsiders mixing into that, would you?"

180

Ned shrugged uncomfortably. He was beginning to wish he'd gone ahead and got his harmonica.

"And you, Loach—" Boyle leaned forward. "—don't you believe the Sons of God?"

"No," Loach said.

"Don't you believe in a *Chosen People*, as it says in the bible? *God's* Chosen People?"

"Not particularly," Loach answered, still refusing to look at Boyle's face blazing across the fire at him.

"Then what the hell *do* you truly believe in," Boyle wanted to know.

Loach answered without a pause. "I believe in poker," he said.

"*Poker?*" Boyle pulled his feet under him, as though to rise. The grin was still there but his wide orange brow was knotted in frustration. "The card game?"

"Poker," Loach affirmed.

"I don't get you."

"Poker. As in plain old American five card stud. Where the same rules apply to everybody. Where three of a kind beats a pair and a full house beats a straight and the Joker goes with the aces straights and flushes. Poker. Where everybody gets the same number of cards I don't care who his daddy is or what kind of blood he has. *That's* what I truly believe in Mr. Boyle. Poker."

"Hear that, folks?" Boyle spread his hands to the firelit faces, attempting to regain his hold on his audience. "Hear that? Your leader believes in *poker!* A cardsharp, that's what your famous leader is. Boy, he must've drawn some hot hands in that pen."

"Not particularly. I played a lot but I was never much of a winner. Even you used to take all my Tootsie Rolls, didn't you, Father? Mr. Boyle, I'm not a great poker player. I just admire the rules is all I say."

181

"Well, I hope you're a better poker player than pathfinder is all I say. Because I think all this talk is just so much pissing up a rope. I think the bald-assed *truth* of it, Mr. Loach, is that we are at the crossroads and you do not have any more idea than a *duck* which way to take us. You nor your crazy brother, neither."

"Say now, Boyle—" Dogeye started to stand from his seat next to Dr. Jo. "I'd watch that fat mouth if I was you—"

"It's okay, Dog." Loach raised his hand toward his brother. "He could be right. We all saw you scratching your head out there in the road. I'm not sure, either. I am sure, however, that the direction will be revealed to us if we seek it correctly." He turned to the sisters. "Isn't that right, ladies?"

"Right!" they both answered in a loud voice, agreeing completely for once.

"You're sure, Loach? And just how will it be revealed? We gonna cut high card to see who picks a direction?"

Loach frowned at the man's agitation for a moment, then turned to Jocelyn. "Doctor, didn't I see you looking at a compass before supper? May I borrow it?"

Boyle slapped his knees and hooted. "A *compass?* Hear that, Makai? A compass! Who the hell needs a compass? I can tell you which way north is," He pointed above the aspens. "That star yonder? That's north, north, the same direction we were headed when your black Barney Oldfield here run us off the end of the road."

"He's not my Barney Oldfield, Boyle," Rodney made it clear. "I would have fired him back in Moab and driven the thing myself, were it not for my back."

"And there are more influences in this world than the stars, Mr. Boyle," Ramona said, unable to resist. Her sister was too fascinated by the duel between the two men to notice the dig.

"Dr. Caine," Loach repeated, "your compass, if you please. And if you sisters could perhaps loan us the use of your altar table?"

"By all means!" Mona exclaimed, already standing. "Come, Douglas; I'm sure we can put it back together."

"I'll get the incense," Ramona said. She started after them, the sock swinging pendulously in one hand like a loaded sling.

"Whoopee!" exclaimed Gaby, making little circles in the air with her cigarette holder. "More boogity-boog."

"Goddamn you, Ferrell." Rodney threw the last of his wine

at the photographer. "You think you can maybe wake up enough to get some shots of this?"

Chick Ferrell wiped his face and started searching for his tripod, muttering, "Not enough light." Father Paul began to clear a little space next to the fire, as though preparing the altar for communion. Ned tossed another twisted cedar branch into the flames. Jocelyn found the surveyor's compass at the bottom of her purse, but before she could hand it to Loach he walked away, treading barefoot toward the carrier.

Jocelyn was relieved by all the movement; she hoped it would break the tension and defuse Boyle's mounting contentiousness. But, if anything, the man's eyes only got brighter as he watched Dogeye affix the oval top to the pedestal, his grin more malevolent. When the sisters started walking about with their incense sticks and mumbling, he laughed out loud.

183

"Mr. Boyle," Ramona cautioned, "don't laugh at the spirits. They can hold a grudge, you know?"

"Forgive me, lady," Boyle said, pretending to stifle his derision with a fat hand. "But it ain't the spirits I'm laughing at."

When Loach walked back into the firelit circle he was wearing fresh socks and carrying the Moxie case Ned used as a rear step. He put the box in Paul's cleared circle and seated himself on it.

"Dr. Caine? Could you please place your compass in the center of our altar. I mustn't touch it. Dogeye? Can you scoot your log a bit closer. Sisters?"

The sisters immediately tossed their smoking sticks into the fire and resumed their places on the log. Boyle rubbed his hands together.

"What about me, Loach? You want me to shuffle? Deal?"

"All I need from you, Mr. Boyle, is silence. Do you think you are capable of that?"

"I'll try not to laugh," Boyle said to Rodney out of the side of his mouth.

There was a sustained click from Chick's camera, then everything was quiet. Loach closed his eyes and let his head tilt slightly back. The fire lit his features from beneath.

"Now. Everybody. Imagine in our sky a *different* pole star, a beacon from our collective subconscious. See it burn and spin. Everyone, try to see it. Let it shine above our destination."

" 'O, little star of Bethlehem—' " Boyle began. The sisters hushed him with a mutual hiss.

"You're the one who's been there," Chick said. "What good is our subconscious?"

184

"We've all been there, Mr. Ferrell," Loach replied without moving his head. "Just concentrate. Imagine the cavern . . . the opening . . . the wall. Focus it, just like your camera."

"Still not enough light," Chick complained under his breath.

Everyone had grown still, even Boyle. Loach opened his eyes and tilted his head back down. When he looked at the oval table, every eye followed his. They stared at the compass.

"It's here," Loach said. He relaxed and crossed his legs.

"What's here?" Rodney demanded. "Damn your eyes, Loach, they were right. You're nothing but a—"

Rodney's breath stopped in his throat. The needle on the compass was beginning to tremble.

Jocelyn felt her skin prickle with goose bumps. Not again, she thought, not again. But it was too late. The needle was swinging, undeniably turning from the north she knew to be to the pole that this man had created out of nothing. Out of absolutely nothing. The dial swung east, west, east again, then full circle, and then stopped. Trembling, the dial held, pointing exactly the direction the road to the east ran.

Loach looked at the faces around him and said, "That's it." The needle swung back to normal, pointing at the star through the trees. Loach drew a deep breath and stretched.

Boyle's face had turned even more crimson. He was shaking with rage and drink. "I can't help but noticing," he said through his teeth, "that your altar looks a little wobbly. Let me fix it . . ." He leaned a hand on the table and the top flipped into the air like a huge Tiddlywink. "Oops, sorry," he said maliciously, picking up the wooden oval. He gave the underside a quick examination.

"Mr. Boyle!" Mona scolded. "Do you think we would stoop to tricks? At a time like this?"

Boyle drew in an exasperated breath and sailed the tabletop away, toward the darkness of the creek. "Let's check this damn stand."

"Boyle!" Dogeye stood. Again Loach waved him off. As Boyle held the pedestal high above the firelight his feet became tangled in one of the cedar branches. He appeared to lose his balance, stumbling and staggering precariously. At the last moment, before stepping into the blazing boughs, he released the pedestal. It fell into the fire in a splash of sparks. Mona cried out and Ned jumped through the flames, rescuing the piece of lathed wood with a nimble sweep of his foot.

"I'm *so* sorry, ladies," Boyle said, unbearably sincere. He held out both hands, puffy palms up, turning from the sisters to Loach and back again. "Can you folks ever forgive me?"

"Probably not," Mona said. "I fear our altar has been permanently defiled."

The group watched the big man teetering about the fire. Anger could almost be seen steaming from his soiled suit coat. He tried to goad Loach with his eyes, but the tall man evaded his glare by resuming his seat on the Moxie box. He picked up a crooked stick and commenced stirring the embers, waiting for Boyle to cool off. Boyle continued to mutter and sway.

"You were so good controlling that compass," Mona said to Loach. "Don't you think you can do the same for Mr. Boyle? He's working himself into a terrible state."

"She's right," Chick said. "We can't have him stumbling around all night like a drunk bull in a china closet. I've some expensive equipment here."

"Expensive but unused," Rodney groused.

Boyle loomed over the fire. His grin was ominous. "Pilgrims, I must take issue," he said. "This is a long stretch from being a china closet and I am not drunk. That little dab of dinner wine you forced on me? I used to *spill* that much with a meal."

"I noticed," Rodney said. He was beginning to edge away from his newfound friend, toward the safety of Ned.

"Why, I could drink the whole phony lot of you under the table if I took a notion. Control *me?* What would you have the good doctor do to me, lady? Give me the evil eye? I could outstare the sun itself, let alone this whey-faced charlatan. More wine, Makai!"

"Dear me, no!" Ramona protested, "If you don't calm down, you cretin, I'll calm you down myself."

"Yeah? How?" Boyle wanted to know. "With gobbledygook and incense? Horse piss!"

"Doctor?" pleaded Ramona. "Can't you help?"

"Yeah, sure! Let's have us another trick from the famous Doctor." He planted himself in front of Loach, his feet spread.

"Whatcha got, Doc? You think you got a little trick for a big stumble bull like me? Or are you all mouth and magnetism?"

Loach picked up a second cedar branch and continued poking at the fire, a stick in each hand. "Physical magnetism and animal magnetism are much the same, Mr. Boyle. The concentration of energies. This fire is only a concentration. Disperse it, spread the heat and the light apart, and it goes out. One stick may smoke, but it will not burn. *Two* sticks, however—" He brought the twisted sticks together, raising them out of the embers as he stood to confront Boyle "—two sticks are the beginning of a fire."

He lifted the flame high, stirring it among the stars, then brought it down until it was inches from Boyle's bull's-eye of a face. "The hot and the cold," he said matter-of-factly. "The light and the dark. A solitary point of energy, independent yet interdependent. Together, they manifest energy; apart, they grow calm and go out."

187

Loach tossed the sticks into the darkness behind him, one over each shoulder. Boyle tried to follow the twinkling arcs, his eyes crossing, his mouth going slack.

When he at last blinked, he saw that most of the members of the group were in their bedrolls, sleeping. The fire was low, the thin clipping of a moon was sliding down the valley, and he was tied up.

9

Abandon ship . . .

"Let's get this show on the road!" Rodney shouted from the inside of the carrier where he sat fuming. These kinds of adventures—drunk Mormons whooping and hollering, compasses mysteriously moving, disorder and debris everywhere—these kinds of adventures always aggravated him, though he had never been on one before in his life. He sat stiff and at the same time limpish, uncomfortable in his double-breasted suit and pink tie. His back hurt like hell. All that wild activity yesterday, all that work. Well, he would *not* help today, he decided, no matter what anybody asked him to do. He was paying to ride this damn circus wagon, not push.

"Loach," he shouted again, "let's get moving! Do you think we've all developed our patience sitting in prison for years? Well, we haven't."

There, he'd said it. Just what he felt and it felt good. Get the show on the road and get it over and get back to L.A. Time was money. That's all there was to it.

Rodney reached into his shirt pocket and pulled out a

White Owl. His next-to-the-last. Then what? Maybe bum one of those Corona Coronas that Boyle was always bragging about. Trade him a drop of what was left of his bourbon. What a circus. A blue mechanical man, a pair of growling aunts, and a dissipating Mormon.

He lit his cigar with an agate lighter a lady friend had once given him. He smiled, thinking of her expression when he had told her she wasn't good enough for him. Tasty.

"I *am* sorry, chérie," he distinctly remembered telling her, "but this is the end. *La fin. Fini la guerre.*"

He'd memorized the words from a script he'd read, and had waited years to use the lines. He had even practiced the pronunciation with Pierre Pied, the limpwrist from Switzerland who had convinced him he would some day make a great movie producer. Makai Productions. Chérie had only understood "this is the end" but that was enough. She had thrown herself on the director's chair in his living room and leaned over it like a rag doll, her blond wig falling to the floor like a basketball. It was the best bit of acting Rodney had ever seen her do, and he almost relented and told her she could stay if she'd go to acting school. But she ruined it all by opening her mouth and calling him a spoiled little pig. Naturally, he couldn't forgive her for *that,* so he threw her coat and wig out the front door and told her she had better go get them before the Doberman ate them.

Rodney was consoled by the memory. It made the cheap agate lighter worth something. He turned it over in the palm of his hand while he sat inside the carrier's clutter, being impatient, silently daring any one of his insufferable traveling companions to come aboard and berate him for smoking inside. He'd smoke if he wanted to. His aunts be damned, and all the other puritan snips he was forced to abide on this absurd journey to some secret hole that, in all probability, didn't even exist.

The only other person already in the vehicle with him was Boyle, trussed up like a fat turkey and grinning like the village's fattest idiot. He hadn't said three words since Loach put the kibosh on him at the campfire last night. Just in time, too. He had to give Loach that—the man had a great sense of timing.

"Loach, we're late," he bellowed again. The man had no damn notion of time at all, not its value nor its worth. They needed to locate a laundry pretty soon, too. Or a haberdasher. Wonder if they had haberdashers in—in wherever they were? As if to prove his point, a suit button popped off and rolled onto the imitation Persian carpet.

190

"God damn it to hell," he yelled, "let's *go!*"

Loach, standing outside with the others, turned toward Rodney's voice.

"What's that, Makai?" he called through the rear doors. "You sound impatient."

"Impatient? Oh no, Loach, not at all. Not the frigging slightest. I enjoy sitting here like a fool. Take your Goddamned time. You're accustomed to it."

"We're almost loaded, Rodney dear." It was one of his aunts. "Compose yourself. Tranquility is a virtue."

"I didn't come along on this trip to be virtuous," Rodney said to Boyle. The fat man just grinned. Rodney couldn't tell if his wit was getting through or not. He resumed his shouting toward the curtained rear of the vehicle. "Let's roll! Where's that black-assed driver? C'mon, c'mon, c'mon!"

The curtains suddenly parted and Loach appeared. He glanced at the Buddhalike figure of Boyle sitting on the floor, then turned his attention on Rodney.

"That's enough out of you, Makai. The color of a man's skin has nothing to do with his heart."

"I didn't say his heart," Rodney asserted in a cloud of smoke. "I said his ass."

Before Rodney could puff out another word Loach grabbed the cigar out of his mouth and tossed it through the broken porthole. Rodney's face reddened and his eyes bulged like he had a thyroid problem, but he said nothing. Loach returned to Boyle and checked his bonds.

"How are you doing, Mr. Boyle?" he asked.

"Never better," Boyle said. "Just fine. Best I ever been tied up, 'cept for once in France." His lewd grin spread across his face. "And that was by professionals."

Loach looked at the pair, shaking his head. "I'm damned if I know which of you is the worst."

191

"That's easy," Boyle said. "Me. Makai's just an amateur." He was trying to act calm but his face was redder than Rodney's.

Loach walked back and parted the curtains and tucked them out of the way. "All right, everybody. We'd better get moving before one or the other of these firecrackers in here blows up. Everything inside."

"Everything inside?" Dogeye's voice called back.

"Everything important goes inside," Loach told his brother, standing at the open doors ready to load. "Gear, boots, helmets, everything. And that goes for Juke, too."

"Say, now," Juke said. He had been about ready to climb up his ladder.

"Inside," Loach repeated. "Now."

"We got to wait. I can't find my pipe."

"Let's go, fool," Rodney called. "Loach'd just throw it out the window, anyway."

"Inside," Loach said to everybody. "Now. Warm 'er up, Ned."

Loach was not in a mood that anyone wanted to argue with. The party hastily threw together their belongings and joined Rodney and Boyle in the machine's interior. At last everyone was on board but Chick Ferrell. Loach called for him but he was nowhere in sight, not at the cold campfire, not at the creek where everyone had been washing. He was about to call again when he heard someone say, "Shit!" Loach walked around to the other side of the vehicle. He saw the photographer, down on his knees, looking beneath the carrier. The inside rear tire was sitting squarely on a demolished cardboard suitcase. Without warning, Loach broke into loud laughter. Ferrell jerked his head around.

192

"You think this is funny?" Ferrell sounded as though he were about to cry. "That's all my extra lenses and stuff. No wonder I couldn't find it last night. You wouldn't be laughing if this was yours."

"It *is* mine," Loach said, laughing louder. "Yours is already on the rig. Leave it. It's nothing but my old prison duds."

Now Ferrell was laughing along. "It looked just like mine."

"Cheap birds of a feather," Loach said, clapping him on the shoulder. "Let's go."

By noon they were eating cold shish kebabs and rolling along as though they had been doing this for years. Mona was feeding Boyle as though he were a pet. Rodney was sipping wine, refusing leftovers. Father Paul sat next to Gaby, watching her chew. Finally he spoke:

"Gaby, let me borrow your shoe a minute."

"My shoe?"

"Yes. I need the heel to break out the rest of this window."

He was sitting directly in front of the only window that had been damaged in the accident.

"I'd like to let some air in. And watch the countryside for a while." He picked at one of the shards. The bus hit a bump, jarring his hand. A thin line of blood welled up across the back of his index finger. With his good hand he reached in his pocket for a handkerchief. Instead he found only the stone from his broken chalice.

"Could you lend me a hankie, Gaby?"

"You want a hankie or my shoe?" She was gesturing with a black pump, the heel extended to the priest. He looked up from his cut to find Gaby smiling at him. She gave him the shoe. Father Paul tapped out the rest of the glass. Juke answered the beats with a rhythm of his own. Chick, listening like a bird dog, tried to translate.

With the glass tapped out, both Father Paul and Gaby had a view of the land and the trees and the rocks they were passing. Cold air blew in through the broken window but the sky was blue—not a cloud interrupted the color.

"This is remarkable country," Paul murmured, sucking on his bleeding finger. "I once spent some time on a retreat in a place like this."

"What?" Gaby said. She put her hand on his wrist and pulled his arm down to his lap. Her hand stayed there, resting casually on his.

"What did you say? I couldn't understand you with your hand in your mouth."

"I said I once spent two months on a retreat in a place like this. It was lovely."

"What do you mean, a retreat?"

"A religious retreat, away from society, getting to know

yourself. Almost always in a place like this." His eyes drifted from Gaby to the mountains outside. "I was silent for almost two months."

"What's that gonna do for you?"

"It's hard to explain. It slows you down, so the singing of a bird can almost make you weep. It was the final stage of my training. When you decide if you can commit yourself and take the vows of the order."

"I don't think I could do it," Gaby said.

"Remain silent for two months?"

"No. Any of it. No sex. No money. Someone always telling you what to do. God!"

Paul laughed and stuck the finger back in his mouth for more nursing. "I do know what you mean," he said. "We're *all* human. But generally, I've been happy. My life is limited, but it's peaceful. I don't have many of the social pressures, for example—"

"A real rose garden, hah?" Gaby said. "Well, you can keep it." Her face changed. She had soured on him and he didn't understand why. He let his eyes drift back out the window.

Some of the crew were beginning to doze off. Rodney bent at the knees, easing himself down onto the mattress they had arranged for him on the floor. To his astonishment, the pile of clothes next to him stirred and coughed:

"Ain't nothing wrong with Juke," it said. The pile swelled and Juke arose. "Nothing that a puff from Juke's bag wouldn't cure." Juke slowly rubbed the sides of his head, caressing the temples with his fingertips. "Excuse me, Mr. Makai, but I's asked everybody else. You didn't happen to see a big old pipe laying on the ground somewheres?"

"What?" said Rodney, cupping his hand to his ear. "Eh?"

"A pipe. Like you smokes. It got lost in the commotion."

194

C A V E R N S

"You ought to be thankful you're alive, instead of whining about some damned pipe."

"Well, Mr. Makai," Juke said. "There's alive and there's alive with some enjoyment."

Rodney pursed his lips and nodded. There was more to this little blue freak than met the eye. "Buddy, as far as Rodney Makai is concerned, the word 'enjoyment' dropped out of his vocabulary when he stepped on this rig. I swear I wouldn't be here if I didn't think this would make one hell of a movie. I'm a producer, you know? That Ferrell chump? He's doing my screenplay. If it weren't for me having to keep an eye on him, I'd be in Palm Springs right now *really* enjoying myself. You wouldn't happen to have a bottle, would you?"

"A bottle?" Juke asked. "Of what?"

195

"Whiskey, wine, anything. My demijohn is suddenly empty. I think that Boyle bird has been tapping it."

"Sorry, Mr. Makai. I don't study alcohol. I smokes." Juke's eyebrows wrinkled and he leaned closer to Rodney. So close Rodney could smell the dust and sweat in Juke's pea coat.

"Ain't no reason Juke can't ride on the top," he confided. "Juke ain't no cripple."

"That's right," Rodney agreed. "No reason at all." Rodney felt like he ought to smack the impertinent little beast, keep him at a respectful distance. On the other hand, it was nice to have somebody to talk to. Besides, he had an ace up his sleeve. "Y'know," he said slyly. "It might be that I did happen to see somebody toss something on board that could have been a pipe . . ."

Juke's eyes brightened. "You did? Sir, I'd give *any*thing—"

Rodney touched a finger to his lips, then began feeling beneath one of the couches where a lot of the rubble from the accident had been tossed. He withdrew the curved pipe and held it against his chest, shielding it from the other passengers' view. Juke made a reach for it.

"Ah, ah, *ah*-aah," Rodney teased, moving it out of Juke's reach. "You said you'd give anything for it. Anything like what exactly?"

Quick as a monkey, Juke sprang to his feet. He scurried up the cluttered aisle of the carrier. Rodney watched him bob from side to side, stepping over the feet of sleepers and nodders. Finally, the little blue man stopped in front of the metal trunk that had held the scarves and crystal ball. After checking both ways, he eased up the lid and all but disappeared into the depths of the trunk. When he surfaced, his tiny monkey fingers were clasped around a pint fruit jar filled with Dogeye's cactus brandy.

196

"There aren't but only two of these in the whole world," Juke whispered when he returned to Rodney. "And this is one. Did I do right, Mr. Makai?"

"You've never done better, Jukie," Rodney crooned, reaching for the pint jar.

"Ah, ah, *ah*-aah," said Juke, dancing from one foot to another.

"Oh, yeah, Sure. Here. Take the disgusting thing." He handed over the pipe and Juke gave him the jar of golden liquid.

The two men resettled themselves in silence. Rodney pried the lid off the Mason jar with thick impatient fingers. Juke rustled down the throat of his pea coat until he found an oval cannister with a Veterans Administration label. He stuffed some of the contents into the bowl of the pipe. With trembling hands he lit it, took a puff, then released it into the smokeless air.

Rodney took a drink of the brandy and made a face, but he

felt better instantly. Looking up, he saw Chick staring at him from the end of the carrier couch. Grinning wickedly, he waved the jar in Chick's direction.

"You know I can't drink, Makai," Chick told him irritably.

"Oh, excuse me, Ferrell. Forgot about your little weakness. I'm truly sorry." He took another big swig and Chick turned away.

He didn't need much of Dogeye's home brew before he started feeling ready to throw Ferrell out that broken porthole. He felt powerful. The brandy was tasting wonderful and his back as good as new. Numb was more like it, and he wouldn't quibble with the medicine. He loosened his pink tie and leaned back against the arm of the couch, smiling. He noticed that Juke was smiling as well, his eyes closed. When they opened they were looking directly into Rodney's.

197

"Try some of this," Juke said in a gesture of goodwill.

Rodney felt good enough to take him up on his offer. The smoke wasn't as good as his White Owl, of course, but it was better than nothing. It dried out the mouth; that must have been why this little lamebrain used it—to keep from drooling. Rodney laughed at his own dry wit. He found it all ridiculous to the point of hilarity; he was actually sucking on Juke's nasty calabash! Well, one good turn deserves another. He offered the jar to Juke.

"Try some of *this*," he said. "That goofy brother of Loach's is a better distiller than he looks."

"Why not," Juke answered and tipped it up. Some of the juice dribbled down his chin. He only sputtered a little.

"Not bad," Rodney said, retrieving the jar. "For a beginner." Then it suddenly seemed to him that this whole trip was not only the most ridiculous, but also the funniest thing he'd ever done in his whole life. His shoulders began to shake with bottled laughter. This movie didn't have to be a thriller, he realized; it could be a comedy.

He laughed out loud. Let them think what they would. Juke laughed along, his eyes closed. The laughter changed to a rhythmic snorting, the strains of a jazz melody—"Take the A Train." The saxophone part. When it was time for the drum solo, Juke's right hand starting slapping his legs. For the bass, he thumped his index finger against his voice box while popping his lower lip in and out. Finally the blue freak put everything together—the humming, the strumming, the thumping and the slapping.

Rodney watched this human ensemble with a dawning admiration. No doubt about it, this goon had talent! There would be a spot for him in the movie. "Yeh! Yeh!" Rodney said, snapping his fingers.

"That's it, sir," Juke encouraged. "You got it. Yeh yeh yeh!"

"Ack ack!" echoed Kronos from his swaying cage. "Ack ack ack!" Before they knew it they were making music together as though they had been doing it for years, never missing a beat.

The jazz trio worked like magic on the drowsing passengers. Things came to life. Chick stood and let the squawking parrot out of its cage. The bird flew excitedly around the bottled interior, calling, "Ack ack ack!" in perfect tempo. Then the bird perched on Boyle's shoulder and went into a dazzling solo of trills and whistles. Boyle, his hands still bound, tossed his head at the insolent parrot, but could not deter it. When Gaby laughed at the spectacle the fat man laughed along.

Mona stood up and began to move to the rolling of the music and the rocking of the bus, her stockinged feet shuffling, her eyes closed, her hips swaying. Ramona located two

198

pieces of carved ivory in her bag of occult accoutrements and
started rattling them together with a proficiency that betrayed previous practice. A wordless warmth came over the
passengers. Chick Ferrell whistled through his teeth. Father
Paul removed his glasses and fluttered his eyes shyly at Gaby
as though working up the courage to ask her for the next
dance.

Even Boyle was enjoying the musical interlude. The bird
notwithstanding, Boyle was nodding contentedly up and
down in his bonds like a fat baby strapped in a spring romper.
Suddenly he threw back his head and burst into song:

> Oh, ship me somewhere east of Suez
> Where the best is like the worst,
> And there ain't no regulations,
> And a man can raise a thirst—

"I swear, Mr. Boyle," Ramona Makai exclaimed, giggling
uncontrollably, "if you aren't the oddest creature."

Boyle winked at her, clacking her ivory three places down,
and sang even louder:

> On the *road* to Mandalay,
> Where the *flying* fishes play,
> And the dawn comes up like thu-u-nder
> Outta China, 'cros-s-s the bay.

He stopped as suddenly as he had started and turned to
Paul, mooning at Gaby: "Tell me, Padre, ol' top, ol' bottom,
ol' rusty, ol' boots, ol' snake-in-the-grass, ol' skunk-under-
the-cathedral—you ever been to Mandalay?"

The priest started at the sudden confrontation. He turned away from the girl, his cheeks burning. "I'm afraid not, Mr. Boyle."

"You oughtta do yourself the luxury," Boyle advised, leering like a pirate. "The Orient's the place for a man who needs some rocks hauled. I know a little spot there by the docks—whoo-eee! I mean, there's girls there can tie a Roundeye's shoelaces without benefit of hands."

Paul was speechless. The little improvised jazz session began to fumble down.

"Yep, Mandalay's the place for you, Padre. You strike me as a man with a tremendous surplus of unhauled rocks."

"You certainly seem to be worldly for a Mormon, Mr. Boyle," Jocelyn said.

200

"There's Mormons and there's Mormons, Doc. Some's old hat while there's others that are the cat's tailored pajamas. Now me, I got fitted for my pajamas last year in Hong Kong." He grinned at the other passengers. "So listen to this: if Mandalay is where to go to get your rocks hauled, and Hong Kong is where to go to get your pajamas tailored, you know where this nut wagon oughtta go to get itself fitted out?"

Nobody answered. Juke ceased his scatting and waited.

"To Tibet. I been to Tibet and I tell *you*, there's some brothers there who know how to haul those spiritual rocks, if you get my drift. Yes sir, Padre, you ought to just veer right on over to the Himalayas and let those Buddhists give your old soul a rubdown, if you want my opinion. Be better than beating off here in the northern Wyoming nowhere." He threw back his head and launched again into song, louder than ever: " 'O, on the *road* to Man-Da-La-a-ay—' "

"That's enough, Boyle," Jocelyn said, though she felt he

was just warming up. She was glad when the partition slid open and Loach ducked into the compartment.

"What's all the commotion?" the tall man asked.

"Just a little revival, Loach," Boyle answered. "Want to join in?"

"Thanks, no," Loach said. He offered Kronos a finger and the bird hopped off Boyle's shoulder. Loach walked to the bird's cage and sat it back on top. He looked down at Juke, on the floor alongside Rodney. "You seem in fine fettle, Juke," Loach said. "What's up?"

"Nothin'," Juke answered, wiping his mouth.

"We were just making a little music," Rodney said. "That against Loach's Law, fun and music?"

"Not at all," Loach said. "But I suggest you might better spend this next little while preparing."

201

"Preparing for what, Doctor?" Jocelyn asked.

"To disembark," Loach said. "This road is the last leg of our drive—"

" 'On the *road* to Mandalay—' " Boyle began.

"Can it, Boyle," Chick Ferrell said, suddenly nervous. "Where are we, Loach, or is that still a mystery?"

" 'O, sweet mystery of life!' " Boyle sang, " 'at last I've found yo-o-ou . . . ' "

"Shut *up*, Boyle," Chick said, "or I'll shut you up!"

Boyle swiveled his mountainous torso toward Chick. "Is that right, Ferrell? And just how do you intend to accomplish that?" Without waiting for an answer, he began to sing 'Onward Christian So-o-oldjers"—then stopped abruptly when Chick pulled something out of his pocket. It was Chick's gray handkerchief.

"Wait a minute, Ferrell," Boyle said, recoiling from the rag as though it were a poisonous reptile. "Whatcha got there?"

"My hankie, Boyle," Chick told him. "My *only* hankie. But I'm willing to sacrifice it if you don't shut that God-damned gaping hole of yours!"

Boyle's mouth closed with a snap.

"Thank you, Chick," Loach said. "Now, to resume. It may be that my penitentiary training has made me overly cautious, but I believe our expedition is in increasingly grave danger."

"What in the hell are you talking about?" Rodney demanded, suddenly sober. "What dangers? Is Barney Oldfield up there planning to wreck us again?"

"No, Mr. Makai. We are being followed."

"Bull pucky!" Boyle laughed. "Don't listen to him, folks. Once a carney always a—" His mouth closed as Chick moved toward him again with the balled-up cloth.

202

"Are you sure, Doctor?" Jocelyn asked. "I can't for the life of me see how. We've been winding around in the wilderness for hundreds of miles. How could anyone follow us? Who would want to? Or *why?*"

Instead of answering, Loach dropped to one knee between Gaby and Father Paul, his face to the broken porthole. Then he stood and motioned the archeologist over. "Take a look at the ridge across, Dr. Caine. That's our road, about five miles back."

Jocelyn bent to the breezy opening. Across a deep ravine of jack pines and huckleberry she saw the thin gray line of their highway, switchbacking up the mountainside. As she watched a tiny dot came into view, followed by another, and another. The leading dot was white.

"It's the DeSoto!" she said without taking her face from the hole.

"What DeSoto?" Rodney cried. "You mean Boyle's DeSoto?"

Boyle started to sing "Old Dog Tray" but Chick's threatening handkerchief shut him up before he had finished the first line.

"Four . . . five . . . I count six of them," Jocelyn said, moving aside so the others could look.

"Dog counts eight," Loach said.

"Jackals!" Ramona hissed.

Her sister shook a sparkling fist out the opening. "Pirates! Doctor, I say come about and ram the blackguards to the bottom!"

Loach smiled. "A courageous thought, Mona. But Dog and Ned and I have a better plan."

203

◇

Back in the cab with Dogeye and Ned, Loach said, "I think the rest of the crew is ready."

"Oh mercy, *how* can they be ready?" Ned fretted. "*I* ain't ready and I'm a veteran! Abandoning a ship ain't something you can just up and do. It takes drills, practice drills, and lots of 'em!"

"You're probably right, Ned. But this is one we are going to have to do cold. All you have to worry about is getting up steam when we make our dash."

Dogeye chuckled. "And you got to admit, Ned—we *have* practiced that."

"Oh mercy, is all I says. I wish I was back in the boiler room. I never wanted to be no helmsman, anyhow."

"You're doing fine, Ned," Loach told him. "I shouldn't wonder if you get the Navy Cross for this maneuver."

"If this maneuver works, that is," Dogeye added.

"Oh mercy, mercy, mercy," Ned said and pulled his little white hat tighter on his head.

They droned along in silence for a few more minutes, then Dogeye squinted and leaned toward the windshield. "I think I see the sign," he said. Another mile closer Loach and Ned were able to read it as well:

CAUTION—ONE LANE
SULFER CREEK BRIDGE
2 MILES AHEAD

"Here we go, Ned. Pour the coal to 'er!" Loach slid the door open and shouted into the rear: "This is it, folks. Hang tight and be ready. Two miles and counting."

204

Ned double-clutched into the next lower gear and floored it. The big engine shrieked and the machine lunged forward. This wasn't like when they'd tried to ditch Boyle; that had been flat highway with gentle curves. Nor was it like tobogganing down the hail-slicked slope where he had been using the engine's compression to try to slow them down. This was a mountain road with 15 mph warnings at every turn, and turns every few hundred yards. He kept it in second so he could hold back going into the curves, then gunned it hard as he came out. The big contraption squealed and swayed and blue smoke boiled from the rear. The temperature gauge was pinned all the way to the edge of the red by the time the bridge came in sight.

"Scoot it right across, Ned, then hit the brakes," Loach barked. "Try to stop with our ass-end sticking right over the gully."

"Aye aye, Chief," Ned replied. He was getting into the spirit of this business. When he reached the one-lane bridge he locked it up, footbrake and hand, and cramped the wheels hard left. The rear of the machine drifted perfectly into place as it crossed the bridge.

"Just like bringing a launch into dock," he grinned.

Loach and Dogeye flew forward into the windshield and everything in the back pushed up against the partition door. While Ned and Dogeye sat dazed, Loach moved back from the glass and, not missing a beat, climbing over Dogeye and pulled the dividing door open.

Rodney was sitting on the floor of the carrier next to Juke in the midst of one long last lungful of the stuff in Juke's pipe.

"All right," Loach yelled, "everyone off, and fast!" Almost instantly, the carrier doors were pushed open and everybody fell out.

"Here, Auntie," Rodney said, giving Mona her glasses. "Put your glasses back on."

"They're cracked, Rodney. Everything's jagged. Oh, Rodney. What happened? What can Dr. Loach mean by this?"

"You can bet he's got a plan. Always does. Not one we'll necessarily like, though."

"Shush, Rodney."

"Jesus, they've dumped us out and left us here. We should have guessed. Loach is nothing but a god-damned criminal after all. Loach and rascally brother. Who the hell's shaking me?"

"That's enough, Mr. Makai. Straighten up. This is a time for discipline."

Loach was crouched in the shadow of the wash, his eyes fixed on a point above it. Beneath the wooden bridge ties their boot soles sunk in the dry creekbed. Tires passed across the planking overhead like gentle growls, rumbling in the dry air. Finally the growling faded and Loach rose and made his way to the top of the wash, scree falling around his hands. He edged toward the summit.

Behind him the passengers waited, silent, eyes upturned. Curtains of dust streamed through the planks and settled on hats, scarves. Loach turned to them. "All right, move." His voice filled the void. Everything was still. The crew remained motionless. Even Boyle seemed to be holding his breath.

"Now!" Loach shouted, scrambling down the hill and approaching Juke. "Juke, you stay with Boyle. Prod him up the hill. If he gives you any crap, brain him. The rest of you, load up." Loach bent down and grabbed a backpack, slung it over his shoulders. He took hold of two ammo cans, adjusting his fingers on the handles as though they were sticky with resin. Dogeye moved now, as did Dr. Jo. But the rest of the crew remained motionless, not sure the growls wouldn't return.

Loach shouted again. "This is what we came here for. Move now or stay where you are, forever." The explosion brought them to life. Mona helped Ramona. Father Paul brushed the dirt from his knees. Focusing his camera on Loach, Chick framed him between the bridge beam and the walls of the wash. He snapped a picture and shoved the camera into his case. Everybody grabbed something and fell into line behind Loach. Gaby, slower than the rest, reached down into a clump of sagebrush before moving off. She retrieved a faded leather satchel, thrown off the carrier with everything else. She put it in her pack, then trailed along behind Dr. Caine.

Loach motioned them closer. They crowded together, one behind the other. He pointed to a spot on the near horizon. "We move hard to that ridge. There are trees there . . . cover. I want you to move fast and don't stop until I say so."

They fell into an imitation of order, a ragtag military unit out of step. Juke obeyed Loach's orders immediately and grabbed Boyle's elbow, leading him like an old lady. They moved up the wash, climbing the bank. Loach paused, allowing each member to pass. He tapped Dogeye on the shoulder.

"Take the lead, Dog. Get them out of this wash and into the brush. Make sure none of the tourists stop for flowers or picture taking." Dogeye nodded and laughed quietly. Suddenly, his smile fell away as his vision lowered to the sand.

"Charlie?" he said.

"Damn it!" Loach hissed, looking down. "Don't say anything to anyone. No use scaring the natives." Dogeye adjusted his pack straps. "And talk to Dr. Caine, that's something she'd notice for sure."

"Right. You're right there. Dr. Jo and me, we've got an understanding of sorts." Dogeye smiled oddly.

"By the way, Dogeye," Loach laughed, "did we remember ammunition?" Dogeye laughed, too.

"Hell, let's see. We got a crystal ball, a lot of gumption, a little bit of brains. We got ammo boxes, but ammo? I doubt it."

Jocelyn looked up the steep hill. It gave her neck an odd feeling, like sitting in the front row of a movie theater. They were making their way toward the rim of a crater, awkwardly climbing over porous lava rocks. She saw the backs of the people ahead of her, straining with boxes and packs. Dogeye in the lead, then Boyle, unbound now, carrying the largest load. After him, Chick, Rodney, Juke, Loach, the sisters, Father Paul. She did not see Gaby. She turned and saw her a few paces down the hill. Gaby had set her boxes down and was holding one hand over her sides, breathing hard. Jocelyn approached and gripped her shoulder with a firm hand.

"You don't feel well?"

"Not really," Gaby answered, trying to sound tough.

"Are you nauseous?"

Gaby stared at the older woman, her face softening. "Sort of, but I think I'll be all right."

"Here, carry this one," Jocelyn said, handing one of her smaller boxes to Gaby. "It's lighter than yours. Can you go on?"

"I think so." Gaby lifted the box and together the two women progressed slowly up the slope.

As they walked, Jocelyn scanned the hills they were on and the terrain around them. The black rock of ancient lava flows; live trees and dead; everything trying to survive the stringent earth it was fated to grow in. Jocelyn recognized the area as part of lava beds that stretched east from Oregon and Washington into Idaho and Montana. She made mental notes of the variety of trees, shrubs, plants. She noted the size and color of the lichen growing in the rocks. If this was Idaho, she was not sure exactly where. She could try to find out later, when she had her books.

As they reached the top of the hill, they could see a cabin. Dogeye paused for a moment to allow the stragglers time to catch up. Pointing at the cabin he said, "That'll make a good camping spot." Back down the slope there was a sudden scuffling that startled them. They turned just in time to see the armadillo disappear down a hole in the lava.

"Ah," Dogeye sighed. "I wish I'd a brought a pair. We'd come back in a few years and the whole hill would be overrun with lava-dillos."

They walked on, laughing, toward the cabin. It was nothing more than a carefully constructed lean-to; weathered, sun-bleached; claw marks scarring the walls. Over the open doorway hung a hand-carved sign: PEG-LEG'S PLACE, it read. Mona creaked the door open and looked inside.

"This is lovely. We won't have to sleep in the cold."

"We can't all fit in there," Gaby said. "It's no bigger than an outhouse."

"I wonder who Peg-Leg is," Dr. Jo mused. Mona and Ramona exchanged glances. "We should help set up camp and fix supper," Mona said, changing the subject abruptly. "I'll ask Mr. Dogeye what we can do."

"I'll come with you," Ramona said.

Dogeye was building a small fire and Rodney was lying flat on his bedroll. Mona knelt down beside her nephew. "Rodney seems to be having problems." She tried to make him comfortable.

"Who isn't?" Gaby snorted, as she strolled up to the campfire. "Hey, Uncle Dogeye, what's for chow?"

"Pork and beans," Dogeye chuckled, "or pork and beans?"

"Well, now, Dogeye," Jocelyn joked, "I think I'll try the pork and beans, if you don't mind." Then she said, seriously, "Are you sure they can't see us from the road, if they come back?"

"Not here." Dogeye handed her a plate. Gaby looked at Dr. Jo's plate of beans and blanched. She turned her head away. "I'm not really hungry. I'm going for a walk."

"Where's that brother of mine?" said Dogeye.

"Last time I saw him," said Mona, "he was sitting alone over there by the little cabin, going over some documents."

Dogeye told people to help themselves if they wanted more dinner. He had some matters to discuss with the good Doctor. He walked away from the campfire, through the shadows, toward the lean-to. Loach was sitting Indian style on a pillow, a kerosene lantern by his knee, and maps and papers spread out before him.

"What's up, Dog?" said Loach.

"Not much. What are ya lookin' at?"

"Just some pamphlets, stuff about cave art. Just info, you might say."

Dogeye raised his eyebrows and puckered his chin thoughtfully. "I see. Worried ol' Jo Caine might start hammering you for facts?"

"I'm not worried about Dr. Caine," he said.

"Who then? Chick?" Dogeye burst out laughing.

"Hardly." Loach smiled. "I can handle photographers."

"Boyle?" Dogeye tried again.

210

Loach shook his head but said nothing. Dogeye looked down at the papers. The oil-lamp light made them look like old documents from an archival vault.

"See you got some maps, too," he said. "You concerned about finding the cave? We shouldn't have any trouble."

"No," Loach said. "That doesn't concern me."

"What *does* concern you, then?" Dogeye asked his brother. "That track we saw?"

"No. What concerns me is our Electric Angel. She's acting odd, for one thing. Sickly. For another, I think she's copped my ledger."

10

Gaby reads the book,
Father Paul sees the light . . .

Dogeye sat at the edge of camp, watching everyone settle down for the night. Nobody had elected to use the cabin. The fire's hissing and popping was echoed by the sisters' whispering as they spread their bedrolls and wriggled into their sleeping bags. Mona's bag was a trifle snug, and she rolled from side to side like a big moth trying to get back into her cocoon.

Rodney was hunched down in his bag, the fire reflecting off of his shiny scalp where the carefully plastered hair had fallen aside. Next to him sat Boyle, sleeping cross-legged under a horse blanket. His head was tossed back and his mouth hung open to the firelight. If that gold tooth of his attracts moths, Dogeye thought, Mona will be a goner.

Dog lay back and stared at the sky. He liked the night. In Moab, when the generator went off, he would sit outside and watch the stars until dawn. He thought of the animals he'd let loose. He wondered how they got along their first night out—did they feel safer caged up, or out under the stars? He pulled his blanket tighter, feeling winter not far off.

Back at the fire, Gaby was the only one who hadn't yet settled down. She was still fooling around with her knapsack, her loose hair hiding her face. She looked up, as if she knew she was being observed. She saw Dogeye watching her. Her eyes met his and held until he surrendered and slid beneath his blankets.

"Nighty-night," he mumbled from his bedroll and was quiet.

Gaby's fingers felt along the rough canvas spine of the ledger, deep in her bag. Her mind turned far back to the carney days, remembering Loach holding the book. She saw him hunched over it after the show, a pencil stub gripped in his fingers, scribbling away after the carney people were in their wagons and the townspeople had returned to their homes.

Gaby looked about her. The fire was fading. She stood and moved quietly through the camp. She paused at the pile of equipment and gathered a second wool army blanket. After another quick look she dropped one of Dogeye's carbide lamps in her bag.

She stepped behind the wall of the lean-to and quickly walked away. The sound of the twigs crackling beneath her feet was loud to her, but she was out of sight. She drew a deep breath. For the first time in days she was away from the sights and smells of people.

The wind knocked the branches above her, a dry, hollow sound. She adjusted herself on one blanket with her back against a slab of rock, then pulled the other blanket across her lap. She removed the lamp from her bag and held it in her hands. She turned on the water drip lever, the way Dogeye had shown them, and waited until she heard the faint hiss of carbide gas. She cupped her palm over the reflector and felt the flint roller with her finger. Just like the turquoise cigarette lighter she used to have. She spun the roller with a quick jerk of her hand and the captured gas popped in the concave reflector; a tiny spear of blue flame stabbed into the dark.

Carefully, she placed the flame on the rock over her shoulder, like a reading lamp. She arranged her bag on the pine needles beside her, conveniently open. First, she pulled a crumpled carton from her bag and removed a pack of Chesterfields. The last. She opened it with a broken thumbnail. Shit! That manicure was fresh less than a week ago, that carton full this morning. What a bastard touring could be.

She put a cigarette between her lips and flicked a match with the broken nail. She exhaled and nestled deeper into her blanket.

She could not see them clustered around the fire on the other side of the lean-to, but she could imagine them. Most of them already asleep. Rodney, passed out. That Boyle, still sitting propped against a box, still trussed up and bamboozled. Now *that* had been something—the way they had outsnaked that snake. *That* was the old carney dash!

At last, she withdrew the ledger from the bag. It still carried a whiff of the show—sawdust and horse shit and the creosote reek of poles and canvas. She opened the book slowly, pulling her hands across the cool pages. She felt a jolt of fear and excitement, and something else. But she could not stop now. The till was open, her hand on the money; the crime was already taking place.

She flipped rapidly through the pages, her guilty eyes as much on the darkness around her as on the writing. Finally, one image snagged her attention like a barbed hook. It was a drawing of a man's foot. A crude sketch, in pencil. She

213

leaned closer to the page. When she had skimmed the words beneath the illustration, she immediately read them again. Her breath stopped in her throat. Over her shoulder she heard the gas flame hissing and whispering. She brushed her fingers over the face of the page to see if the words might vanish at her touch. Why had she stopped at this particular page, on this night? Then she cracked the ledger wider open and found the bookmark, a flat hard object, red and black, with a single letter printed at each end, just like in the illustration of the foot—a capital "S" and a capital "N."

Everything within her view began to realign itself, bringing memories into sharp focus. She suddenly saw him clear, in his black hat, on the midway working the marks. She saw his hands and heard his voice, the way they stroked the mark. Everyone went for it, especially her mom. Until she finally had to go away from it for good.

She slammed the book closed on the little magnet and began to laugh. She didn't care if they heard her or not. She laughed until her chest heaved and her head pounded.

"Marks," she muttered. "All of us. Stupid, gravy-sucking marks!"

Tears poured from her eyes as her laughter turned into loud sobbing. God, she hated to cry. Such a baby. "Stop it!" she said aloud, sitting up straight. "Hush! Hush up!" She stifled her sobs until she was once more able to hear the intimate hiss of the carbide fire at her ear. Then she heard something else . . .

Father Paul stood, at the edge of camp, zipping up his trousers. He hoped no one had noticed. But then, why should they? No one had really noticed him much since he'd removed his collar. At best, he was only a nondescript priest; and without his priestly attire he became virtually invisible.

Gaby had seemed to notice him, now and then—but not nearly as much as he wanted her to.

He wondered where she was. He had not seen her with the rest of the huddled sleepers. In fact, she had grown more remote than ever during the last few days. Especially this evening. Withdrawn. Not like when she tended to his cut hand. That was nice. What had happened? Where had she bedded down? Could something have happened to her? She could have wandered off in the darkness and fallen, hurt herself.

He took a few aimless steps this way and that, trampling the twigs. Where would she go off alone? Why? Then he realized what he had just been attending to and felt his face reddening. Ladies must have bodily functions, too, that are best performed alone. Perhaps he should wait a little longer.

215

Turning back toward the camp, Paul stumbled over a rock and bumped his head on a low branch. He had always had trouble seeing in the dark, especially without his glasses. He stopped a moment, feeling his scraped forehead. He didn't want to go back to the fire. He wanted to talk to her alone, with no one else listening. He could endure rejection, but he couldn't endure ridicule. Rodney would make a snide remark, Dogeye would grin and slap his knee, the sisters would gasp and pray to who knows what daffy deity. No, it would be better this way. If he could catch her alone, somehow, then she could laugh like she did and make some crack and it would be over. They could walk back to the camp together.

He leaned back against a tree, taking a deep breath of the clean, clear night air. The stars spun above him. Here in the wilderness he felt the presence of the Living Christ more than ever before in his life. The stars were like the Spirit of Truth itself, burning beneath his ribs. This was the Garden, the true Temple of Earthly Delights. Why had he never realized it before? All those years bottled up in that cloister, mildewing like a rancid dream. One had but to *step outside,* into the *sweet high sky,* to see *God in every leaf,* every star, every breath. *God's light is out of doors!*

In fact, at that very moment, he saw it! About a dozen steps to the right, off through the jack pines and lava—a bright blue pinpoint that framed the face of the Madonna herself. Oh, why hadn't he brought his glasses! At long last, the Light itself, and he had left his glasses in his sleeping bag. On the other hand, glasses were just more of mankind's cumbersome impediments. The sin is to turn your back on nature. Grace is to go forward, *unfettered.* The steps of *Grace* are *always lighted.* My God, my dear sweet *God!*

"What?" said Gaby.

216

Father Paul scooped up a handful of soil from the ground and let it sift through his fingers as he walked. "Dirt, we call it. The word is dirty, but the earth is clean. Thank you, Lord. Thank you for giving us dirt."

"Right," said Gaby.

He was among the sacred trees, grazing their trunks with reverent hands. He paused before a white aspen and caressed its milky bark, peeling away long strips like curved sheets of paper. "Oh, brother *tree,*" he said, "we are *all* children in the Garden of the Lord."

"You bet," Gaby agreed.

Feeling clean and sure as never before in his life, he walked on, washed by the dark magic of nature. "Yes," he said. "But a magician never reveals his tricks. No more light is needed. It's perfect, absolutely perfect!"

"Well, it flickers a lot," said Gaby, "but you can still read by it."

The wind rattled the branches above them, like bones of

the saints. The pendulum of the moon was swinging low and cold. Gaby looked up at the specter.

"Hey, Padre. You always sneak up on people in the dark?"

Paul moved closer, squinting against the lensed light. "I didn't realize I was sneaking," he said. "What are you doing out here, if I may be so bold?"

"Catching up on my reading," she said. She pulled the notebook out of the folds of her skirt and held it open to the light. She scooted over to make room on the blanket. "Put your naive butt down," she said, "and get a load of this."

The priest settled beside her like one of the scarves from the trunk, insubstantial as the starlight.

"Well," he said, snuggling in. "What are you doing way out here?"

"I said I was reading." She looked up at him. "What are *you* doing out here is the question, Father?"

"I saw your light and wondered if you were all right."

"Me? Why, I'm swell, Padre. Dandy." She spread her hands over the open ledger, as if to emphasize it.

"Are you?" he asked.

"Sure," she said, "why not?"

"Why are you out here alone?"

"Because there's nobody with me," she said. Then she relented. "I guess I needed to get away to think." She hesitated. "And to read this." Again she indicated the book.

"Is it yours?" he asked.

"Of course not!" she said, offended.

"I didn't mean anything," he said with a feeble shrug.

"Maybe not," she growled, "but *he* did. In this damn book the cagey bastard means every word he says!" She flipped through the pages until she came back to the place with the bookmark. "Here!" she said excitedly. "Look at this!"

217

Paul looked. There was a flush to Gaby's throat that made him giddy. *Madre mía.* The Flush made Word.

"All that power we think we see? It's a lie, Father!" Gaby stabbed at the picture of the foot with her broken nail. "There isn't a shred of truth in any of it!"

"I know, my dear, I know." He was wiping away her tears with a trembling thumb. "And yet, here we are."

"Yeah, here in the middle of nowhere! With nowhere to go."

"And hasn't it always been that way?" he asked her with upraised eyes. "Yes, it has. Amazing."

"Amazing my pink rear end! Look, damn you. *Here* it all is. This is even a *picture* of how you hide the magnet in the toe of your sock. He was rigging this caper ten Goddamn years ago! The sneaky sonofabitch."

"Now, now. The fault lies not in Him, but in ourselves."

"I *believed* in him, damn your myopic eyes! For *years!* And now he turns out to be just another hustle." She wiped her nose on his sleeve.

"Now, now," Paul said. He was feeling the priest within him rise. "You must never turn your back on Him. He is the Real One. The Real True Light. Closer and realer than we can ever know."

"Sweet Jesus," Gaby said.

The Father put his arm around the shivering girl, drawing her close in the crisp night. Her skin was like the benediction, its odor like heaps of wheat. "The Temple of Earthly Delights," he said.

"Come on, Father." Gaby tried halfheartedly to push away from his embrace. "You don't understand! You've got to listen to me. You've got to look—"

Paul listened and looked. He liked the soft sweep of the

218

writing, and the sound of her fingers on the paper. He could almost make out a letter here and there—a looping "l" or a capital "I." He wasn't sure which.

"Get it?" Gaby went on. "What a complete swindle this is?"

Paul let his eyes roam upward from the book. "Wheat," he said.

"What?"

"Piles of ripe wheat. Song of Solomon. Thy mouth rubies."

"Sure," Gaby said. "But look. It's *every*thing, don't you get it? Not just the carney bit, but the whole suck-egg business!"

Yes, verily: a Madonna's. Clear as a gemstone. Yet not pure. Impurities give the gem its color and uniqueness, like the lone drop of black paint in a gallon of white enamel that painters claimed was supposed to make it whiter.

219

Her hair brushed his nose, and her fragrance slipped over him like a warming aura. He took a deep breath—full of her warmth, her clothing, her taste.

"You know what gets me? It's how alike men are, the rats. I don't mean you, of course, Father. Are you comfortable?"

His arm was fumbling against her back. She leaned forward to help him. Paul's head fell back.

"Yes, thank you." His voice was thick. "I am. More than ever in my life."

But then, how little he had ever known of himself, or his life. How little he knew still. A tin Christmas tree, a decorated fabrication. Nothing had been real before—just words on parchment. But this, this motion, float, swim as a child, tossed by waves, feeling of falling backward . . . hung, in space.

He didn't know how it got there, but the chalice jewel was in his fist. The woman seemed to be fading and the stone began to pulse as he gripped it. He was aware of the sound of a sleeper's breath near him, his own or someone else's, and tears:

"Ah shit, Father, I'm sorry. It's been forty days is what it really is. I'm sorry. I hate to blubber. Forty God-damned days and counting . . ."

Had he heard voices? He strained to hear. The little light was gone. He was alone. The moon was down and the blankets were gone. The chill of dawn was near. But he wasn't cold. Heaven's spark had caught deep in the dry old kindling of his bones. It would never go out. He whispered aloud:

"Words, nothing but words. Midnight vipers, morning vespers. Before the cock crows three times."

◇

Somewhere down the hill Gaby saw the glow of the dying fire. It meant nothing to her, not warmth or people or safety. It was a place like a hundred other places that she no longer cared about. Behind her the priest lay where she'd left him. Whammied. I wish I could sleep like that, she thought. I wouldn't let anything wake me. Even when it got cold, I'd force myself to just keep on sleeping, on and on and on, naked or dressed, full or empty. I'd keep my eyes closed and feel the wind freeze me. Piss on it. I wouldn't move. I'd pray for snow to come and bury me. When the mountain climbers finally found me I'd be sleeping under the snow, not moving, still fresh, like a trout on ice.

She shivered again, and stepped among the sleepers. She spread her blankets as near as she dared to the ember-edged firepit.

11

Hike to hole,
the fat's in the fire
and the priest disappears . . .

Chick Ferrell sat on a log near the creek with his notebook opened on his lap, early. He was watching the Society members scattered around the camp in their sleeping bags. He wrote in his notebook:

> Plumes of steam from olive green cocoons. Bluejays dance down from the twisted pines and peck among the lava rocks. The sky a troubling promise. Been awake since before first light, don't know why. It could be the happy knowledge that we no longer must be bottled in that carrier, it could be the heady mountain air. Perchance it is the prospect of finally reaching our long-sought objective—the Secret Cave. Maybe it's just that Makai is still asleep. Feel absolutely splendid, whatever the cause. What a morning! No, not even that parasite Makai could awake and ruin it.

At that moment the round lump of Rodney's bag began to move, as if, Chick thought with a sinking feeling, there was an invisible wire connected from the moving pencil to Makai's brain, triggering an alarm. Chick watched as a plump hand appeared from the mouth of the bag, then the wrist and expensive gold Bulova, then the sausagelike forearm. The hand tested the temperature for several seconds, then disappeared. The sleeping bag began to unzip.

"Morning, Makai," Chick said. "Glorious day, don't you think?"

No answer. Just a rumpled gob of linen and flesh, wriggling out and pulling itself into a sitting position. The man was still fully dressed, even to his tie and shoes. The only part of his wardrobe he wasn't wearing were his spats. He started pulling these on as soon as he had them located.

"It's *Mist*er Makai to you," Rodney grunted at last, worrying at his shoelace. "And it's a long damned way from a good morning. My left foot is appreciably swollen."

Chick rose from the log and approached Rodney, folding his notebook away. "Loach's brother brought extra boots. It might be a good idea to use them."

"Boots? What do I look like, a clodhopper?" Rodney struggled up to his feet, unsteady on his thin legs. He scratched his pot belly, blinking about at the cold camp. To Chick, Rodney's bulk seemed like a water tower built on broom handles. He laughed in spite of himself.

Rodney made a gawky attempt to brush the wrinkles from his suit, giving Chick what he considered a withering scowl. "You're acquiring an attitude, Ferrell. Don't stand here giggling. Come on. I want you to help me make a big fire."

Chick didn't move. Rodney changed his scowl, becoming conspiratorial. "Okay, then, make a little fire. Do that like a nice boy and I'll share a little secret with you."

"Yeah? Like what?"

"Like that sugar-cured bacon you went ape for back at Moab? I rolled up what was left of it like a smart fellow. I got it squirreled away in the bottom of my knapsack. Listen, we can share it before these goons see the light of day if we're careful. What do you say?"

Chick shrugged. "Sure, why not."

He eased down the slope and returned with an armload of small dry branches. Rodney was hunkered down on the back side of the lean-to wall, among the equipment they had piled there. He was blowing on some dry grass he'd gathered. He was trying to blow as quietly as he could, in quick, measured puffs. Chick watched from behind as the seams in the seat of his pants accordioned in and out, like a bellows. Chick felt a little ashamed of the secrecy, but he admitted that the chunk of bacon Rodney had unrolled from the butcher paper was small—barely enough for two. He sighed and hunkered down beside his boss.

223

"Here, you try," Rodney commanded. "I brought home the bacon; least you can do is get us a fire going."

"Sure," Chick said. He began to blow on the coals and a little yellow curl of smoke wiggled out, sliding up the wall of the lean-to. A breeze had come up from down the hill, bringing the odor of the milky green creek with it. It smelled like overcooked cabbage.

The snake of smoke grew longer and hotter. By the time Rodney had returned with Dogeye's skillet the branches were blazing. He eased the blackened metal into the flame.

"That's probably enough fire," Rodney advised in a whisper. He plopped the chunk of bacon in the pan. "Here, hold this handle and don't let it roll out. You can handle that, can't you?"

Chick knelt to one knee and took the long handle. Rodney

sat down on a coil of rope ladder and leaned against the split-plank wall. He laced his fingers behind his neck and closed his eyes, sniffing at the rising odor.

"Yeah, man, smell that. The real trick with great bacon isn't the smoking, you understand? It's the glazing. Honey, that's the secret. That's the way they preserved the pharaohs in ancient Egypt, you know? Stick 'em in a big stone coffin and pour it full of honey. That's why all those grave-robbers were always after those mummies—the meat was esteemed a once-in-a-lifetime delight by gourmets, went for big bucks in culinary circles."

Chick had no comment about Rodney's bit of historic curing information. He was looking at the pan in growing dismay. The branches were blazing higher and the meat was sizzling louder. He wished Rodney had sliced it, the way he'd watched Dogeye do it back in Moab. He wished he had at least cut that hairy hard part off. But the chunk was already simmering too deep in its own pool of fat to do anything about it. What he mainly wished was that they had woke Dogeye up to start with, and used the main firepit. He hated to be a sneak. He knew his appetites were his weakness, but he nevertheless hated to be a sneak—especially a weak sneak.

"Makai," he heard himself saying, "this is the last flunky job I do for you. The very last!"

"Come again?" said Rodney. He thought the high mountain air was distorting the acoustics.

"This cave job. I know you're planning to run it under your name. That's standard. But I've been writing my *own* observations, apart from the story. I intend to bring this out as an adventure travelogue—with *my* photographs and *my* name. Then I'm going to get Robert Flaherty to help me and it's going to be *my* movie."

Rodney didn't even unlace his fingers from behind his head. "What's with you, Ferrell? Maybe *you're* the one dipped into my demijohn? You better be glad you got *any* kind of job, flunky or whatever. What the hell's got into you? This outdoor living and camping and bacon smell giving you delusions of grandeur?"

Chick didn't know what to say. Makai had always been able to tongue-lash him into a daze. And the smoke was making his eyes sting. All he could do was turn his back on the situation and stand there, fists clenched in silence, hot tears stinging his face. The bacon smell eddied about him but he didn't feel hungry.

"Ah, forget it," Rodney said. "We'll divvy up this cave pie when we're done baking it. Right now we better tend to this porkbelly, before we ruin it. Pour off some of that grease."

The wad of meat could be heard hissing like an electric snake, demanding attention. With another defeated sigh, Chick turned back to his cooking. But his eyes were still awash. The toe of a boot caught beneath the surplus of branches he had carried up from the draw, and he stumbled.

Rodney saw it coming. He had sensed Chick's innate clumsiness and knew that that foot, like a magnet to iron, could be headed for no place but the handle. He saw the pan flip overhead into the blue sky above him. He tried to dive sideways but he was too late. The glistening shower of hot grease began to rain down like tiny bombs, exploding on the wooden wall, on the packs, on the coil of rope he had vacated—mostly on Rodney's rapidly ruining suit. Some drops splattered on his bald spot where his hair had become unplastered, only a few,

225

but enough for him to rise up in a smoking roar and go for the apologizing Chick. Chick screamed and ran. Rodney roared and took after him, murder in his eye and the smoking skillet in his hand like a Norseman's ax.

It was this riotous reveille that mustered the other campers from their sleep. By the time Loach had sorted out what had happened, the lean-to wall was ablaze. By the time everybody had dragged the equipment clear, the shelter was a collapsing pile of embers. Dogeye decided to cook right on it.

"Grits and sorghum," he announced. "Nothing fancy but it'll stick to our ribs. Meat's all gone less somebody wants to gnaw on this."

He kicked the wad of blackened bacon across the pine needles toward Rodney and Chick, like a battered ball toward opposing rugby wings—let 'em fight for it.

226

Gradually, the Society members began to calm down and wake up. Loach and Father Paul heated a kettle for shaving. The two sisters sat back to back on a shiny throne of obsidian, brushing out their long black hair. Jocelyn and Gaby walked down to the stream out of sight and found a hot spring bubbling up where they could wash. Gaby stripped and sat in the steaming pool to her shoulders still frowning over the ledger. She was getting the stinking water all over it, but she didn't give a damn.

Boyle sat cross-legged on the ground, untied and spooning in heaps of the mush Dogeye had prepared. "Our final feast before this cave is exposed, eh Loach? Our Last Supper?" His smile worked as he chewed the undercooked pieces of corn.

"Hardly," said Loach, dipping his own panful from Dogeye's stew pot. "It's still a good half-day's hike to the entrance. But any further meals will have to be taken from cans."

"Bully beef?" Boyle said. "Great. A soldier never loses his love of bully beef."

"Makai," Dogeye called to the fuming publisher. "Better get some of this. Or you and your flunky won't have nothin' but the crow you've already et."

The women returned from their hot springs. Dr. Jo had brought a portfolio from her backpack, and she was examining its contents spread on a rock while she nibbled at Dogeye's grits and syrup. Gaby was still studying the damp ledger, obviously for Loach's benefit. The tall man chose to ignore her.

"Are those references to the cave painting, Dr. Caine?" Loach asked, approaching Jocelyn. "Would it bother you if I had a look?"

She gave him a long stare. "No, Doctor," she said at last. "It wouldn't bother me for you to have a look."

She was kneeling down, the contents of her saddlebag strewn about her: maps and charts and sketches and pages of notes in small precise handwriting that resembled somewhat the style of the Anasazi drawings. Loach knelt alongside.

"I'll tell you what *does* bother me, though, and I'll bet it isn't what you think. It isn't the conflicting drawings. It isn't even the geocultural discrepancies, though I've found quite a few. No, Dr. Loach, to be perfectly frank, *this* is what bothers me."

She took her portfolio from the pack again and removed a large manila envelope. There were lots of detailed enlargements of sections of the famous cavern wall.

"I was fortunate enough to have received these enlargements from Washington." Jocelyn leafed through the photos, spreading them among the other papers on the ground before her. She seemed to be looking for a particular one.

Noticing this activity, the other campers began to edge near. The Makai sisters bunned up their hair and walked over. Boyle bulled his way in close. Dogeye carried a pack over, adjusting the shoulder straps. "What's that one there, Jo?" he asked.

"This? Well, this isn't the one I was searching for," Jocelyn said, "but what it is is an enlargement from the lower left-hand corner of the newspaper photograph." She held it up in the morning light. "It was taken approximately 22.3 inches above the cave floor, if my calibrations are correct. Are you six five or six six, Dr. Loach?"

"Six six," Loach answered.

"Anyway, as you can see, the figure is purely symbolic in nature, an ornate 'X' with bent arms which resembles a rood. This is just one example of how this cave painting doesn't make sense. The images do not correspond with one another, nor do they correspond with the other rock art of the ancients in western North America."

Jocelyn paused as Juke approached and handed her a cup of coffee. She thanked him with a smile. After a quick sip she set the cup on the ground and continued:

"Anasazi rock art, while fairly advanced, is limited in its variety of topics. Most North American rock art is either anthropomorphic or animal in nature, or totem designs combining the two. Or simple circles. The closest example we find of this design in North America is at burial mounds in Ohio. But they are recent artifacts, no more than nine hundred years old."

She laid the photo on the ground with the others and returned to the bundle in the envelope, dealing out one at a time. Each one was a perfect enlargement of a symbol from the cave painting—a maze, a serpent, a spiral, a human hand. She piled all of these together and evened up the edges like a big deck of playing cards.

"No, Doctor, what *really* bothers me is not the content of the art so much as the inhabitants of the cave." She held up the last two prints from the manila envelope. It was an enlargement of a pair of obscure though familiar blurs. She put it aside and displayed the last photo. It was an even larger and more detailed enlargement of the blur on the left.

"This appears to be a bat, a tropical bat—to be precise, an *Artibeus aztecus aztecu,* or aztec fruit eater."

Loach looked puzzled. "I'm impressed by your knowledge of flying mammals, Doctor, but how come this photo bothers you so much? Surely you've run across bats in your caving before."

"Yeah, Doc," Boyle said. "If bats bother you, looks to me like you'd find another line of work. What difference does it make whether this is an aztec fruity or an arty floparoundus? They may be uglier than usual, but bats is bats."

Jocelyn turned to Boyle, studied his face for a moment as if trying to decide whether he was of the genus Cro-Magnon or an earlier extinct descendant. "Mr. Boyle, I must take issue with you. Bats are not ugly. Neither is it as simple as 'bats is bats.' The aztec is a denizen of the tropics. If my interpretation of these blurred images is correct, these are examples of a breed of bat never found at a latitude farther north than the Yucatan Peninsula." Jocelyn pointed beyond them at the snow-frosted volcanic peaks rising above the far ridge. "And, as you guessed yesterday, those must be the Tetons. Or the Canadian Rockies. These tropical fruit bats could not have come from this area—at least not in this millennium."

Jocelyn turned to look up at Loach, and everybody followed her gaze. He slid his hands into the pockets of his jodhpurs, like a little boy. For a second it seemed that Loach had no intention of responding, then he said: "Those blurs always puzzled me as well. I have no recollection of ever seeing any bats of *any* kind, anywhere in the cave. What about you, Dog?"

"No, me neither! Nary bat one. In fact I always kind of wondered if Peg-Leg hadn't put 'em in later in a retouch job. because I'd have noticed real ones. I *hate* bats, whatever latitude they come from."

People were quiet, waiting for further explanation. Then, from a few yards away, a voice rose. It was Gaby, sitting on a shiny lump of obsidian, her wet head still bent over the ledger. " 'Rule Number twelve:' " she read aloud; " 'always be vague. Let the pigeons connect the dots for you.' "

230

Ramona turned to Gaby, "Please, dear, we're having a scientific discussion."

Gaby shook her head and continued reading to herself.

Jocelyn packed her pictures and maps back in her portfolio. It was obvious the scientific discussion was at an end. The members wandered away to clean up after breakfast and prepare for the hike. While Dogeye was kneeling to his pack at the edge of the campsite, Loach strolled near and stood, shading his eyes as he looked up the rugged slope of the volcano ahead of them.

"I told you," the tall man said at last out of the side of his mouth. "I knew we should never have brought them damn bats."

"Maybe they can get together with the armadillo," Dogeye snickered. "We could have flying armadillos."

"Tropical ones," Loach added.

A few yards away, Juke, his shiny black derby tied securely

atop his head with string, took off walking up the narrow trail of red gravel and pumice, singing, "O, the moonlight spots the night along the Wabash . . ."

Boyle hoisted his pack and joined in: "From the fields there comes a breath of new-mown hay . . ."

Soon they were all hiking and singing, even Loach:

"From the sycamore the candlelight is gleaming . . . on the banks of the Wabash, far awa-a-ay."

Paul had fallen in inconspicuously at the rear of the group. His amice was thrown back from his neck like a faded serape. In his hands he carried his prayer missal; pine needles protruded from the pages like quills. He stopped in back of the Society members, kissed the book and extended his hands. Nobody noticed.

"O, this sacred ground . . . O, this most sacred of endeavors, let us pray." He closed his eyes, and trudged on this way until he fell. Still, nobody noticed.

231

Father Paul rose and walked again, reading and dribbling pine needles. "O, Lord here with us, trudging this meadow of wildflowers. O, Christ here, today, in your burlap tunic and cowhide huaraches! O, wait!" He struggled awhile with the book. He could find nothing in it that resembled the words coming from his mouth. He sent the book fluttering away, a scriptured dove in the mountains.

"O, Almighty, I heard You knock in Moab. I heard You come in the mountain dark. Now I ask that You allow us the grace to find Your sanctuary and the purity to enter. No, not the purity. The fortitude. Allow us to complete our mission, Almighty. Though we walk through the valley of the shadow of the valley, give us this day our daily bread. *Et cum spiritu tuo. Et cum . . .*"

Up the trail ahead, Mona said something that might have
been "Amen."

Father Paul kissed the jewel and walked on.

◇

Dogeye eventually moved out in front of Juke and led the
group, moving at a strong steady pace; the oldest man in the
group, yet the most healthy. A few yards behind, Loach was
shorter of breath, feeling the tightness in his thighs and ham-
string muscles, but walking well. As was Jocelyn Caine; hiking was nothing new to her. The rest of the Society members
fell into a single human strand that strung out as long as an
eighth of a mile. Sometimes the order changed, and sometimes there were halts but, once started, the pace remained
the same. The morning's confident smiles wore away and the
faces reddened with sweat. People were feeling the effect of
the thin air. The need for rests became more frequent for all
of the climbers.

All except the reporter. Chick had been somehow invigo-
rated by the shower of grease he had created. After his initial
fear of Rodney had fled, he found himself secretly delighted.
His nose ceased running for the first time in years. He was
charged with energy. He dashed ahead, paused to shoot a few
shots, fell back, scooted up the hill off the path to find better
angles and write in his notebook. He was seeing things more
clearly than he could ever recall. The mountain air was like a
polished German lens, etching every sprig of tundra, every
chip of lava. He could see the spines and coulees on the far
ridge as sharply as the dry burrs on the miniature flora rattling
underfoot. The pockets of remaining snow against the black
lava looked like mathematical formulas, scrawled with chalk

on vast blackboards. The stunted pines among the lichen-spotted boulders looked like hands lifted in bleak prayer.

And the people. For the first time, Chick saw his companions strung out on the trail as a caravan of pilgrims, priceless beads on a single strand—at once ridiculous and noble in purpose. Dogeye, in the lead, his ash-gray hair in a braid down his back like a trapper in a historic novel; Loach, tall, dark and mysterious; the two sisters in their ankle-length walking skirts with their new leather boots peeking out from the fabric; the jack-Mormon Boyle, puffing and sweating right through his seersucker jacket, but still grinning like a car salesman about to close a deal; Makai limping along in his spats and his bespattered suit, about as far out of his world of cute talk and cocktail parties as a Hopi would be in New York City; and the skinny, bronze-skinned lady archeologist followed by the voluptuous pink tootsie. Good stuff.

At the far end of the string was the Jesuit, looking a bit wan, but his smooth white skin was beginning to show some color, and the smile he was mumbling through bespoke hidden spiritual delights.

The only one who didn't seem to fit into Chick's view of the group was the little blue man. His role as the singing leader had been short-lived; he now weaved on and off the trail, his lungs wheezing in the thin air, his face like a dob of clay. No matter what angle you took with him, Juke was not the sort of character they wanted to see on the cover of *National Geographic.* Chick cropped him out of the frame whenever he could.

The Society trooped on. As they climbed higher on the trail and the sun arced lower in the sky, Dogeye heard the beginnings of discontent. At first it was mainly from Makai, but gradually it began to infect everybody. Now there were few things in the world Dogeye outright hated. He could count them on one hand. And the first finger of that one hand was bitching. And when the grumblings turned to groans and the groans started edging toward bitches, Dogeye suddenly could abide no more. He turned on them:

"Listen, damn all your eyes," he shouted at the startled faces. "Nobody ever said this was going to be any picnic. It's tough now and due to get tougher, but jawing about it won't change the fact."

Dogeye hitched his shoulder straps and started to walk again, but there came a dreadful gasp and a cry. Everyone whirled around in time to see Rodney finish a pinwheeling tumble. He came to rest on his back in a patch of last year's snow, one leg crumpled beneath his body. The grease spots and the bulkiness of his pack made him look like a speckled turtle flipped on its back. "God damn it!" he screamed. "My leg is broke! God damn it and God damn this mountain and God damn the whole miserable lot of you to Hell!"

At the end of the column, Paul rolled his eyes and crossed himself. Dogeye hurried back through the group and down the lava. He bent next to Rodney. "How bad?"

"How the hell do I know? I'm no doctor, I'm a movie producer!"

"Can you walk on it?"

"And you aren't a doctor, either!"

Dogeye scratched his jaw. "Hey, Charlie, this man wants a doctor."

"I want a real doctor, blast you! Take me to a hospital."

Jocelyn had worked her way down to Rodney. "Can I have a look? I've treated everything from snakebites to gunshot wounds."

"Well"—Rodney studied her face—"I guess a doctor of archeology is okay."

Jocelyn pressed and probed the ankle and each time Rodney let out a yell. Finally, she stood and delivered her opinion. "It's not broken. Probably just sprained. We'll have to immobilize it."

"What does that mean?" Rodney asked.

Jocelyn tore some strips from the lining of Rodney's suit and wrapped the ankle. As Jocelyn worked, Ramona approached her nephew, "He's always having things like this happen. It's his karma."

"Destiny!" Mona called from the trail.

"Never mind the psychic diagnosis," Rodney wailed. "I stepped in a hole was all! The question is what do we do now? I can't possibly go on."

"We could walk back to the treeline and get material for a stretcher, I suppose," Jocelyn said. "But then what?"

"There ain't any more cabin, remember?" Dogeye reminded him. "You and Ferrell burned it down for breakfast. And if we go back it's a day lost—"

"A *day?* You're talking about a god-damned day when I could lose a *leg?*"

There was a momentary lapse when, for perhaps the first time, each member of the Society realized there was a possibility they might not reach the cave. Before vague suspicion could work itself into full-blown worry Boyle eased his pack off and announced, "Don't worry about it." He started crunching down the lava toward the fallen man. "I'll carry our poor fallen comrade."

"Seriously?" said Dogeye, impressed.

"Seriously," Boyle said. "I lugged two casualties out of No-

235

Man's-Land one time, one over each shoulder. Help me get him up. I'll carry him piggyback."

A look of astonishment replaced the agony on Rodney's face. "You must be joking. I'm not riding on anyone's back."

"Suit yourself."

"What's that supposed to mean?" Now Rodney's face went pale.

"It means we don't have time to wait all day," Dogeye grinned. "You been offered a ride. You want it or not?"

"Come on, Makai," Boyle said. "Things are just getting interesting. I didn't come this far not to get a look at what's down that hole."

Before Rodney could protest Dogeye and Jocelyn had slipped their hands beneath his armpits and lifted him to Boyle's back. Boyle bounced once and hooked his arms around Rodney's knees.

"You're light as a fat little feather, Makai," Boyle said. "Just latch on like you used to do around your daddy's neck."

Rodney cursed and wrapped his arms around Boyle. The man turned and headed back up the hill, seemingly without effort. When he reached the trail he stopped and waited for Ramona and the others. Everyone was staring at the spectacle. A pronounced click broke the silence.

"God damn you, Ferrell! You print one picture of this and you'll *never* work in this town again."

Boyle trudged along easily. But with the added burden of Boyle's pack, Dogeye's pace was slower. They were climbing steadily higher and higher, the air and the vegetation getting thinner. Nobody complained. Boyle's demonstration of strength and endurance acted as a source of inspiration. He was third in line now, behind Loach, and everyone else trudged along behind without speaking. When they reached a level shelf where the rim of the volcano used to be, Dogeye called a lunch break.

The group straggled up to him, sucking hard at the thin air. They let fall their packs and collapsed on top of them. Dogeye broke out the cans and a church key was passed around and they started opening the Bully Beef. Gaby retched in disgust.

"I can't eat this crap."

Rodney said, "Institutional swill! Maybe you're used to this, Loach, but *I'm* not."

"Eat it or don't," Loach said. "I don't give a goddamn." The edge in his voice surprised everyone.

"This is a nice place," Mona said diplomatically. "A wonderful view. Perhaps we could make a shelter and leave poor Rodney up here while we go on."

237

"A shelter out of what?" Loach wanted to know. "Lichens and tundra?"

"Well, we can't expect Mr. Boyle to carry Rodney all the way and *back*," she said.

"I have a feeling by the time we start home your nephew's foot will be healed."

Rodney looked at Loach with a dawning respect. "You're cold, Loach," he said. "Cold."

Leaning against a tree, Chick spoke up, "It can't be far to the cave, right, Dogeye?"

"It's got to be somewhere nearby," Dogeye said, slowly settling to the ground. "But I just can't remember for sure where."

"Dog, I'm beginning to have suspicions about your memory."

"Yes, Dogeye," Jocelyn said. "You couldn't remember which one of those forks back at that T."

"Years of living alone, Jo. It takes its toll. What about you, Charlie-O? You been here before, too."

"Maybe he doesn't want to find the hole," Rodney whimpered. "Maybe there isn't a hole."

"There's *always* a hole, Makai. You found one, didn't you?"

They waited for Loach to say something, but he just turned and stared off across the volcanic wastes, his hands on his hips. It made everyone feel strange to see Loach act this way. Everyone except Boyle. He picked up Gaby's rejected can of army beef and licked it clean in a gulp. Gaby made no comment. She was browsing through the book again. Loach had picked up his pack and announced they were ready to continue just as the priest came straggling up in his shirtsleeves.

"Lord, Paul," Loach said. "We almost forgot about you. We've just had a bite—"

"That's all right, Charles. I'm not hungry."

"You want a little rest?"

"No. I'm not tired, either."

"What about chilly?" Gaby asked. "You've left your jacket somewhere—"

"I'm fine, Gabriela. Don't worry, please. I've never been better."

"Then we better haul it," Dogeye said. "Those clouds yonder are still sniffing around after us. It's nearly November, you folks realize. We shoulda done this down at Twenty-nine Palms or someplace."

When they strung out again on the trail Gaby took up a place in front of Loach, the book in her hand. He tramped along at her heels for a while in silence, then said, "I'm a little worried about Father Paul. He seems to be sort of shedding things."

Gaby answered without looking around. "We're all shedding things," she said, turning a page. She looked up to see if Dogeye was far enough ahead to be reasonably out of earshot, then began to read out loud. " 'Barnum was wrong,' it says here. 'It isn't that there's a sucker born every minute, there's a sucker born every *birth*. All you have to do is find out what particular sugar tit they want to suck.' Is that all that ever mattered to you, Uncle Charles? Rodney may be right about you, for a fact."

When she didn't go on he asked, "How so?"

"You're cold. Colder than I could have ever imagined, even for a stone-eyed carney."

"Well," Loach said after a dozen steps of silence, "ya pays yer money and ya takes yer chances."

Gaby laughed and Loach went on in a strange voice:

"Besides, that was written a long, long time ago. You know the only thing that matters to me anymore?"

"What's that?" Gaby asked. Her interest was genuinely piqued by his tone.

"Open sky. That's what matters."

"Aren't we getting closer, Douglas?" one of the sisters called from back along the trail. Dogeye didn't answer. "It's not that I'm complaining, mind, it's just that I certainly didn't expect us to be going all day."

"Oh, really?" the other sister retorted. "I thought you could see the future."

Nobody turned around to see which was which. Dogeye kept walking and said nothing.

"Don't be testy, Ramona," Mona said.

"Why shouldn't she be testy?" Rodney cried from Boyle's

back. "In fact why shouldn't we all be? I know I didn't sign on to suffer out here on some modern-day Trail of Tears!" He seemed to have forgotten that he was riding piggyback. "Look at me! My head is all speckled with burns! My suit is ruined, my leg is broken—"

"And you smell like a smokehouse in a bacon factory," Boyle added pleasantly. "Ain't it all wonderful?"

"No. It is not all wonderful! My back is killing me, too, if I haven't mentioned it. And for all we know, we are all hopelessly lost—*lost!*—on some half-baked hoax to Hell! What a sucker I was."

"There's one born every minute," Boyle observed.

"More often than that," Gaby corrected, laughing.

From across the clearing came the voice of Chick Ferrell. "Wait! I've found something."

"At last," the sisters said together.

"I don't mean the hole," Chick said, hurrying along the path to catch up. "I was back there on that rim to get a good establishing shot, when I saw something. This is what I picked up . . ."

It was Father Paul's collarless shirt.

"I think the rest of him's missing," Chick said. "I scanned all back up the trail with my telephoto. Not a sign."

An uneasy quiet followed. Boyle allowed Rodney to slide to the ground where he lay, panting, his wrist thrown across his eyes to shield out the sun.

"Well, that about tears it, don't it. Priest lost, us lost, hole lost. Well, well, well." His voice faltered. It sounded as though he might start to cry.

Gradually the members began to group about, waiting to see what would happen next. They took seats on the rough lava boulders, resting their legs and feet. Chick continued to snap pictures, especially of Makai, lying on his back.

"Shouldn't we send someone back to look?" Jocelyn finally asked.

"He was nowhere on the trail," Chick said.

"I'll bet you he eased off for a little rest," was Dogeye's opinion. "He looked awful drained this morning."

"Wouldn't there be dangers for the poor man to face out there alone?" a sister asked.

"Oh, rattlers in heat . . . sunburn. And frostbite if those clouds ever locate us. But that's no more trouble than all of us face." Dogeye shook his head and let out a giggle. "He ought to be all right, of all people; he's got *God* on his side."

"You're cold, too, Uncle Dogeye," Gaby said, but there was no more anger in her voice.

"He couldn't have gone far," Jocelyn said.

"One way or another," Loach said, "we're running out of options." He seemed to be at as much of a loss as anybody.

"Hey, Loach," Chick called and raised his camera. "Can I get a shot of you holding Father Paul's shirt?"

Loach glared at the reporter.

"I mean no disrespect for the departed," the photographer went on, "but I'm a professional."

"Great," said Rodney from the ground. "Now he's a professional."

They waited. Nobody had any suggestions. The autumn sun angled toward a jagged horizon.

"I think we're close," Loach said.

"Close to what?" Rodney gasped. "Annihilation? Do we just keep wandering around up here until we drop, one by one, naked and broken and greasy?"

241

"C'mon, Dog." Loach turned to his brother. "You must have some ideas."

"Fresh out," Dogeye said.

Loach turned in a slow circle. His long shadow stretched out across the snow-patched lava like the marker on a sundial.

"Perhaps some of us should go ahead and scout for the entrance and some of us stay here," Jocelyn suggested.

"Right," said Gaby. "And some of us go back and some of us just go ahead and go crazy."

"No," Loach said. "We better stick together and keep going."

"Is that wise?" Jocelyn asked. "We're all exhausted."

"It'd be dark before we got back to camp. If we could find the entrance of the cave we could go down—"

"Now?" Chick let his camera hang. He was beginning to grow concerned. "It'll be dark in an hour."

"It's always dark in a cave, Mr. Ferrell. And in this particular cave, warm. At least warmer than it will be out here in the open. If we can find the entrance, we can use the warmth."

"Loach," Boyle said, "if ifs and wishes were horses and fishes, we'd all ride fat. But it sounds to me like we are even short of ifs."

A few members nodded, the rest continued to stare at their feet. Rodney had the only concrete suggestion: "Shoot me now and get it over with."

Again they waited, looking toward Loach and Dogeye. The voice they heard came from beyond them, atop a small rise.

"Pillar of clouds," Juke said. He was standing completely stiff, one hand out like a metal jockey on a lawn. "Makes me think of that cave we went down in a while back. You remember, Charles?"

242

12

Going down . . .

"Line up." Loach clapped his hands together. "One by one, now. Let me check over your gear."

Chick grumbled at this. "We're not school kids, Loach."

"Ferrell, your life may depend on your equipment. Now line up, everyone, and let me look you over."

One by one they stood while Loach examined the fit of their knapsacks, checked their supply of carbide pellets, explained for the third time how to reload and light their lights. Gaby lifted herself up on her toes so Loach could check her helmet and for a moment their eyes met. The secret she had exposed in his book still burned there, but she was smiling. He returned the smile and moved on to Jocelyn.

"Okay, Dr. Caine?" he asked. He was sure her equipment would be in order.

"Fine," she said. "I'm always a little nervous before a descent. Anticipation, I guess."

"Dog, you got that electric spot?"

"Yep."

"The blankets and first-aid stuff?"

"Got 'em, Charlie-O," answered Dogeye.

"Say, if it's going to be warm like you said," Boyle asked, "why are we going to need blankets?"

"You'll see," Dogeye grinned.

"Once inside," Loach said, "I want to remind you all to stay close together. One missing member of our troop is enough."

"If Paul hasn't gone back to camp," Gaby said, "I bet he finds us here. He's onto my scent."

Though it was still daylight, brilliant stars already gleamed in the sky. Some of these points of light were strangely defracted by the steam that rose in erratic puffs from the entrance of the cave. No one spoke as they watched Dogeye unroll the rope ladder down the hole.

"It don't go all the way to the bottom, Charlie," Dogeye said, jiggling the ladder, "but I think it'll be close enough. It's a sixteen-footer and I don't recall it being more than a yard or so more than that."

"We'll have to chance it," Loach said, straightening up. "We can't wait for Paul much longer. Gaby's right. He's likely gone back to camp. The trail from the rim is clear enough. Rodney?" Loach said without turning to look. "You are possibly going to have to be Paul's lifeline as well as ours. Are you up to that?"

"I think so," he answered weakly. He was piled in the rumpled nest of equipment where Boyle had dumped him. "I wish I had some wood for a fire. Perhaps one of you could—"

"No!" said Chick. "There's no time. You've got two down-filled sleeping bags."

"Use your miner's lamp for a signal if you hear the Padre call," Dogeye told him in a bright voice. "You'll be fine."

"Well, don't get all choked up if I perish," Rodney said. "Believe me, I won't shed any tears if I never see a one of you again."

"Okay," Loach said, turning away. "So who's first?"

Juke touched the brim of his derby in a salute. "Never volunteer," he said, and stepped forward.

Ferrell snapped a quick photo, then started scribbling furiously in his journal, talking aloud as he wrote: "First intrepid explorer to make the treacherous descent: Emmett Juke, war hero and singer. What a guy!"

"Ferrell, get over here," Rodney interrupted. Chick looked up, irritated.

"For*get* about that little freak. This story ain't about him, it's about Loach and me. Come here." Chick clambered over the rocks to Rodney, the notebook tucked under his arm.

"Now listen close, you jellybean. I'm not going down that hole. Somebody's got to stay up top in case you guys have a problem. Like for example that crazy brother knocking you all off? That fence back in Moab? Remember I told you how it looked like it was done by an ax murderer?"

"Knocking us all off?" asked Chick.

"Yeah, then saying you had some accident, see. Some kinda cover-up. Somebody's got to stay back, so the truth can be told. You better let me have your notebook and what shots you got."

"I don't think so," Chick said.

"Listen, dummy, this is the point; *you're* going down in that hole and *I'm not*. Something could happen to you, then where would I be?"

Chick looked at his employer. "All my exposed plates are in my bag there. The one with the bacon spots. I'm keeping my notebook."

245

Before Rodney could protest Chick was walking away, already writing again: "R. L. Makai incapacitated . . . guarding our rear."

Across the lava Dogeye broke into a laugh and clapped Juke on the shoulder. The little man had marched to the hole and was standing at attention. Loach helped him secure his lamp to the band of his derby. He flicked it on. He watched the upturned blue face descend into the hole. It slowed jerkily.

Juke was feeling the pressure in his chest again. He was hoping even the smallest change in the elevation, like the descent into the cave, would ease up on the blood throbbing in his temples. But his thoughts of relief jerked away from him when he breathed the cave's warm air. Chemicals! Hydrogen sulfide and something worse. His throat thickened. He remembered. He'd been in this cave before! But he didn't remember the smell being this bad. There was something else, something new and *worse* than rotten eggs, fetid, straight from Hell like the flap of dirty Bibles. It was all around him in an invisible dust. He could feel it on his skin. It weighed on him like ash that landed after a bomb blows. He flinched and could move again.

Loach was next. He descended quickly. He hovered on the last rung of the ladder, searching with his foot for the floor of the cave. Then he stepped down to a dark firmness. After the swinging descent, the first thing that hit Loach was the smell. From above he had remembered the smell of sulphur coming out of the cave, but now this smell at the bottom was a surprise. A new essence had been blended in, an even darker scent. He adjusted his light. Crouched in the rubble he saw Juke playing with a box of matches like a pyromaniacal child. Loach was reminded of Juke's specialty in France, the

246

best in the world at it. But there you are. After a war, who wants one of those around, head full of death and detonation? He watched the little man light a match, throw it to the ground. Light another, throw it to the ground. Little truths, flaring and burning out, one after another.

Loach walked toward the sporadic flashes of light. "How are you doing?" he asked.

Juke smiled. "Better, Charles, better." He struck another match. "You remember that guy that went down with us way before?" Juke's eyes never left the matches. "You know, the one that ain't here, with the limp. What was his name? Somethin' about pirates."

The match nearly touched Juke's flesh before Loach answered. "Peg-Leg," he said.

"Yeah, Peg-Leg. Where do you think Ol' Peg-Leg is now?"

Loach looked away from his friend, up at the ragged opening above. They were waiting for his call. But, looking up at the hole, he felt as though he were falling away into the black rubble below his feet. He thought he'd overcome the feeling, with his studies of yoga. It was demeaning, this primitive fear; it robbed a man of all his civilized character. The grandeur of thousands of years was negated by one simple punch to the belly. Shakespeare and Bach—obliterated. Pythagorus, Galileo, Abraham Lincoln—kayoed with a single low blow.

He hadn't experienced the sensation since the trial. Then, too, it had come as a surprise. Throughout the entire proceedings he had not really been worried. Until the judge tolled out his sentence, he had not seriously considered the possibility of taking a fall, especially not a fall of the magnitude the judge had in mind. Twenty years. It was too much time to even seem finite.

When he had finally arrived at the solitude of his little Cracker Box in Quentin and could once more think clearly, he vowed he would never leave himself open for a punch like that again. Knowledge provides light for those battles against dark fear. Wisdom. Spirit over dross. He had trained himself in the long days and nights that followed—meditation disciplines. He could drive pins into his thigh and never flinch; he could hold his breath for nearly ten minutes and slow his heart to a crawl. He could keep a straight back in the full lotus position for hours on end. He thought he was in shape, yet here it was again.

Loach tipped his head so the lamp lit the rubble at his feet—just the floor of a cave, with crap cluttered about—new stuff and old, cans, packs, bags, ashes, and—Christ!—that pair of Beamann's orthopedic shoes, twisted by the seasons. Beamann had left the shoes after being forced to wear the boots that Dogeye had made him put on.

Beamann had been a hurried man who wore an expensive but ill-fitting suit with enormous cuffs and lapels. He could have been mistaken for a two-bit gangster if it weren't for the photography equipment he lugged around. He had to balance the tripod and camera carefully because his posture was already so lopsided. Beamann hated the named Peg-Leg. He was ashamed of his handicap. When he did portraits in his studio he always leaned against the big developing sink for support, his leg out of sight, talking around a cigarette in the corner of his mouth:

"So what's in it for me, anyhow?"

"You'll be famous," Loach had promised. "You'll get to do portraits for royalty, movie stars, presidents—name your own price."

"My own price varies. What do I get for this job of yours is

248

what I want to know? I don't usually go crawling down holes."

Loach stood calm. He had always been able to stand his ground. "How about ten bucks a day?"

"Don't be absurd," Beamannn had laughed. "How about a hundred?"

"We aren't working with that kind of nut in our pocket, Peg-Leg; you know that."

"All right, we can work something out. How about I get a percentage of your share? Every time you use my pictures, I get a share."

"What kind of share?"

"Fifty-fifty?"

"All right," Loach relented. "But keep this in mind; that fifty-fifty is for more than your god-damned pictures. It's for the zipper as well—"

249

"Zipper? What zipper?"

"On those flappy lips of yours, Beamann. I know you. You're a lip-flapper. On this job there'll be no big talk down at the newshounds' hangout. The location of this cave has got to remain secret. Understand?"

"Absolutely," said Beamann.

"It's essential we protect this place from scavengers and defilers."

"Sure, sure, sure," Beamann said impatiently. "I promise."

He should have known then that such a promise would never be kept. The truth had not been in P. L. Beamann. He had no time for it. And truth is time, Loach was thinking. Time! Loach's hands grew hot, hanging loose and useless at his sides. He stared at the burning match Juke held. Little truths. He noticed Juke had only one match left. He threw it out and looked up. The two men's eyes met, illuminated by the firepoints in their mutual lamps. Loach saw twin reflections of himself, the double image of a little man contained in the small holes.

"Old Peg-Leg," he heard Juke say. "What do you suppose Ol' Peg-Leg has been up to all this time?" Loach was silent. "I guess it doesn't matter, does it?"

"Probably not," Loach answered, and walked back to the ladder.

"Okay, Dog!" he shouted. "Start 'em down . . ."

Up on the mountainside Dogeye stepped back and bowed. "After you, girls." He gestured with his hand toward the hole. The three women hesitated at the entrance. Gaby stepped a bit to the side to collect herself, like an actress a minute before her cue. The sisters were holding hands; they glanced at each other stoically, then turned to look down the hole together.

"You may go first, Mona," Ramona said. "You're better at this sort of thing than I am."

"Ramona! You were *always* the athletic one."

Ramona smiled stiffly, "Not *really,* dear. You learned to ride a bicycle before I did."

"Ladies!" Dogeye interrupted. "We don't got all day."

"Look out, for the love of Pete." Gaby stepped up, fiddling with a canvas pouch she had fastened at the belt of her dress. "Just let me make sure I'm all together," she explained.

She leaned over to look down the hole. Dogeye gave her a pat.

"Don't call me Patty," Gaby told him and started down the undulating ladder. As she eased down the first rung, her hand slithered on the greasy rope. It was that stinking old bacon grease those two simps had spilled. The smell made her want to vomit. She forced herself to keep going. When she thought she could go no further she saw Loach's face below her.

"Drop," he said.

She bit her bottom lip and dropped. The beam from her headlamp reached into the steamy gloom. Nasty! She decided those two old women could handle a gloom like this if she could.

"C'mon, Aunties," she called up.

"Yes?"

It was Ramona. The answer was not far above. The old woman was already halfway down the ladder.

"Yes, dear?" Mona's voice was right above her sister's. "We're here. Fear not."

The others followed rapidly, eager to get it over with. At last there was a circle of headlamps watching Dogeye. When he was down, Loach released his hold on the ladder. It swayed in the steam.

The warm sulphuric atmosphere spread out around them. Gaby could imagine that the six of them were standing on the only island in the world, surrounded by space. If she were to step backward she would tumble into emptiness.

"Jocelyn?" she whispered.

"Right here." The archeologist was next to her.

Chick patted his trouser pocket. He could feel the notebook's spiral spine through the thick cloth. He liked these expedition trousers he'd been issued. Maybe he'd get himself a few pair when he got home. These pants would look good in a black-and-white glossy. Maybe he should even get somebody to handle the camera so there could be a shot: Ferrell at the Finish.

"You need help with those bags, Ferrell?" Dogeye watched Chick fiddle with his network of camera straps.

251

"No, thanks, I've got it. I'm ready."

"Me too!" Boyle cried, stamping and grinning.

Dogeye tilted his head at him, scowling. "What the hell *is* it with you, Boyle? You're always jumping up and down like a man with a frog in his pocket."

"You never know," Boyle said.

Jocelyn seemed to be the only one holding back. She had returned to the ladder and taken hold of the bottom rung.

"Listen," she said. "I've been thinking. Makai might not be able to fend for himself too well. He's not so familiar with the out of doors—"

"Why, Dr. *Caine*," Dogeye teased. "I'm ashamed of you. As an archeologist, aren't you curious to see the wall?"

Jocelyn released the ladder. "Of course I am."

252

"You're not frightened?" he asked, concerned.

"Not the way you think. I . . . I do have a . . . fear."

Dogeye snapped his fingers. "I knew there was something about you every time you talked about this caper. You're scared of caves! That's why you were so antsy about getting that carrier. A cave doctor scared of caves. Wait till they hear about this at the Explorers Club—"

She had to laugh at the man's kidding. "Buster, I've been in more caves than you'll ever see in your life."

"What is it?" Dogeye's natural curiosity wanted to know. He waved at the steam that billowed between them. "Is it the smell? The heat?"

"It's not the heat," she said, laughing again. "It's the humanity. I'm an anthropophobe."

"A what?"

"It's a kind of sickness," she shrugged. "I have a fear of being around people."

"That ain't a sickness," Dogeye confided, leaning close. "That's a blessing."

Loach had walked through across the antechamber to a man-sized crack in the wall. Steam was wafting out at the top and streams of the snow runoff were rushing into it at the bottom. "Ready?" he called to the others.

"Ready or not," Juke called back and started after him.

Dogeye raised a hand. "Hold on a minute. This calls for a bit of a toast, don't you think?"

Dogeye removed two jars of cactus brandy and eyed first one and then the other. The dark liquid refracted light from his headlamp.

"Say, this one jar is half full or half empty. Someone has been pumping the handle on the sly."

All the headlamps turned toward Boyle.

Boyle shook his head. "Nope. I been incapacitated, if you'll recall."

"Rodney!" Dogeye called up the ladder. "You been sipping from my spring, you skunk?"

"Piss on the lot of you," the call came back.

Juke dropped his head. "I was in on it, Dogeye," he said without being accused. "I think I *did* have help from Rodney."

"Well, don't worry about it. There's still aplenty to go around. Let's kill it."

Dogeye pried open the lids and passed the jars around. They all drank solemnly. When one of the nearly empty jars reached him, he lifted it high and called out: "Here's to adventure!"

There was a meager cheer of approval. Then an abandoned voice leaked down from the steam above. "Hey, wait a minute you guys!" It was Rodney's voice. "I think someone ought to stay here."

Loach turned from the fissure he had been about to enter and walked back. He called up toward the swirling face. "I want to thank you, Mr. Makai—for everything. For financing the trip, for the good wine and pleasant company, and especially for your unwavering support. You will always remain for me a shining inspiration."

"Wait a minute!" Rodney yelled louder. "What am I supposed to *do* while you're all down there?"

"Keep calm, keep warm and keep singing out."

"What is that supposed to mean?"

"It means keep calling for Paul," Dogeye explained.

"Loach!" Rodney's head poked down through the hole. He had managed to crawl to the rim of the pit. "What if you don't come back? I need to know where the hell we are!"

"America," Jocelyn answered, feeling a thrill of mischief. She was getting into the spirit of this business.

"That's it? America?"

"That about covers it," Dogeye answered. Laughter rattled around him.

"This is all pretty funny to you bastards, isn't it! Well listen to this: I'm giving you twelve hours. No, *eight* hours, goddamn it! One night! As soon as it gets light and my leg's healed, I'm getting *out* of here, back to Los Angeles. If you want to be portrayed favorably in my movie you better be up here to go with me."

"Sing out for the priest," Gaby reminded.

They could hear him begin calling as they followed the little creek into its crevasse: "FAWWWTHERRR . . ."

254

13

Pool and plug . . .

Chick stepped through the fissure into a spacious tunnel. A sandy pathway crunched under his feet; shadowy walls curved away on either side. The little creek burbled along at the base of the wall to his left, leaving plenty of room for people to walk two or three abreast. This wasn't so bad, he decided. Despite the dust and stench that clogged his nostrils, he was at least finally free of that spoiled idiot, Makai. He'd suffered under more than his share of stupid bosses since his fall from quality, but Makai was really the prize yahoo. With him out of the way, things could start to develop.

Yeah, develop. Chick followed out the pun in his mind, imagining lines on a photographic plate slowly appearing under the swirling emulsion. This cave was like an enormous darkroom. The explorers were the plates, each of them awash in the solution. Whatever vision had been captured when the picture was taken would soon develop, now that they were immersed. What was needed, though, was a good group shot from the front. Give the viewer the feeling.

"People?" Everyone was chattering. Chick had to raise his voice to be heard. "People, please. Before we go any farther I want to get a shot of the group. Let me get in front for a moment."

"Sure, Ferrell," Boyle said, allowing him to squeeze past. "But will anything be visible without a flash?"

Boyle's question had the sting of a taunt. Chick wished he could snap back an answer full of authority, but the cave walls soaked up the sound.

"My plan is, if everyone will take off their helmets and point the lamps toward their faces and stand still, I think I can get a time exposure."

He tried to arrange them into some sort of group portrait position, huddled beneath the curving apse of lava boulder that was riddled with holes like a piece of black cheese. Chick placed Loach and his brother on one knee in the foreground, with Jocelyn sitting on a pack between them.

"Now you two sisters stand in back, please. Gaby, you get between them. You can lean back against that wall."

"Ouch!" Gaby said. "This damn rock is like an onion grater."

"We best mind our tongues in here," Ramona admonished her. "Cursing will bring the wrong spirits out."

Gaby rolled her eyes but kept quiet.

Chick had Boyle stand behind Loach. The man's voluminous seersucker provided a good backdrop. "Now, Juke, over here, on the other side of Mr. Boyle. Please stand still—"

Juke was too excited to stand still. He was rushing around like a cave monkey, scrambling over rocks, muttering in a voice like a file working against metal, "I been here *before*."

256

They finally got Juke close enough that Boyle could throw a beefy arm across his thin shoulders. Chick readied his tripod, secured the camera, and set the aperture as wide as it would go. He bent over to look through the viewfinder. Upside down and underlit by the eerie light of the acetylene flames, the little faces looked like confused ghosts. Chick's attention riveted on the phenomenon of Loach's brother's eyes. He looked up from the viewfinder with a start to be sure he wasn't seeing things. But there they were, blood-red as a pair of eyes one might find staring in from the African night. Jackal eyes. Loach saw the photographer staring and smiled: "Now you know how he got his name."

Chick looked back down at his viewfinder thinking, with a bit of self-pity, how seldom the photographer gets into his own picture. Sometimes a tiny scrap of shadow in the corner reveals his presence, but that was usually all. When the pictures of this expedition were published, he wouldn't be in them. His name would be at the bottom of each one, of course, but it wasn't the same. It was as though he were already a ghost.

The name would probably be spelled wrong, too.

He tried to estimate the exposure time—too much and the details would be stillborn in the darkness. "Okay . . . hold it!"

The shutter opened just as Juke spun away in a rapture of excitement. Juke simply wouldn't be in this one, Chick thought as he heard the shutter close—except as a blur. Appropriate.

Before the group broke formation they heard a sound—that same loud rap they had heard at Dogeye's Den. It did not seem to come from any specific place, but to emerge from the rock walls all around them. Everybody jumped. Chick almost tipped his camera over. Jocelyn gasped out loud in spite of herself. Everyone stood, waiting. No further sound was heard.

"Still sounds like yes to me," said Dogeye.

"What the bloody hell was that?" Boyle wanted to know.

"Old friend," Dogeye said. "Before your time."

"Now you've done it," Ramona said to Gaby in a whisper. "I told you your cursing would bring out hostile spirits. I think that was Peh Zahzoo."

"Oh, balls," Gaby said.

Mona disagreed with her sister's identification. "That was not Peh Zahzoo! I think Gaby may have been right. It sounded to me like Balis Loondree, from Indonesia. You know how that little imp loves adventure."

258

Loach spoke loudly to quiet the flurry of voices.

"We're wasting time. We have a long evening's walk ahead of us. Ferrell, gather up your equipment. Dog, you think you can remember the path? You scout ahead with the photographer. Mona and Ramona, you two next, then Boyle, you follow behind them with Juke. Dr. Caine and I will keep the rearguard."

"Where does that leave me?" asked Gaby. "Alone as usual?"

"You better come along with us, dear," Mona took Gaby's elbow. "We'll all watch out for each other."

Dogeye had noticed Jocelyn's sudden start at the knockings. A worried, almost childlike look remained on her face. Scared of ghosts, too, he almost asked, but thought better of it. Better let worried dogs lie, he thought.

The first part of the cave, Dogeye remembered, was easy going—tall and wide as a train tunnel. The walls had a pebbled surface, like textured masonry. The porous stone soaked up sound, muffling the tramp of their feet and sucking away words like a blotter.

Chick scurried along behind Dogeye, equipment clattering, stopping now and again to scribble something in his notebook. Dogeye glanced back at him. He'd never liked anything about the man, except maybe the way he could eat. Always admired a real appetite. But now, watching him struggling over the rough path with his snarl of cameras and tripod, and his knapsack, and his damned notebook, Dogeye had to grant him persistence as well. A wild determination had come over Chick's face these last few hours. It reminded Dogeye of a wolf he'd seen once, chewing off its own foot to get out of a trap. He'd reined his horse behind a stand of creekwillow to watch the damned thing chew. The animal had caught his scent and glared at him—a peeping Tom on horseback—then had gone right back at its leg. Not a whimper came from the bloody jowls, just that determined look and a steady grinding noise. When Dogeye could stand no more, he put a stop to it with a 22 slug.

Soon the tunnel would begin to fork, if Dogeye remembered right; but all they needed to do was follow the water. Other streams would join in. He could hear them already. Much louder, too. This wasn't the trickle he remembered. This was louder, more violent, a small river cascading down into the tunnel from a new split in the roof. Maybe the recent hailstorm had flooded underground rivers they didn't even know about.

Soon, the water completely filled the sandy path they had been walking. Sometimes it was warm and sluggish, sometimes deep and fast and so cold it hurt the ankles when they stepped in it. When they reached a dry spot Dogeye took a seat on a boulder and waited.

"You know, unless I am gravely mistaken, this is a bunch more water than is usually here," Dogeye said to the photographer. It was a longer speech than Chick had heard from him since Moab. "The usual path is what you'd call inundated. We'll have to mountain-goat it along these rocks, next to the wall. You want me to help you with some of that stuff?"

"No, thanks," Chick panted. "I got it. Let's keep going. I'm enthusiastic. This is what I've been after all along."

"I better wait on the rest. Those two old gals can't travel as fast as young enthusiastic bucks like you."

"Suit yourself," Chick said. "I'm going ahead."

Dogeye watched the skinny man clatter away into the darkness, shaking his head.

Back in the tunnel, Boyle paused long enough to mop the steam from his face with the sleeve of his suit. He could hear Juke's wheezing breath in the darkness behind him, harmonizing with the hiss of the gas lamps. That wheeze. Boyle turned to look at the small ruffled man approaching. Juke walked in a jerky, roosterlike stride, staring straight ahead, like something wound up that wouldn't run down.

"Say, buddy. What time was it, perzackly, when we started down here?"

Juke swung his head around. Boyle's lamp made the man's face stand out from the dark rock walls around them. Boyle could see the blue tint of Juke's lips under the white stubble. It looked like he'd been drinking ink and licked his lips with a blue tongue. Boyle had seen these symptoms before, in Europe. "Gassed," he said to himself. "And didn't quite survive."

Then Juke spoke. "Time was it?" The blue lips pursed in

thought, laboring to remember. "As I recall, it was rag. Three-four. Nineteen-twenty-six. Ragtime. Lost my pipe."

Boyle suddenly felt warm toward the smaller man. He wished he could offer him a smoke from one of his cigar tubes, but he was saving those.

"I was over there too, you know. In the war. I never realized till now you was a gas victim . . ."

"Smells like war in here," Juke said. "Rot and cordite. Fear and excrement and sulphur."

"Sure does and that's a fact," Boyle chuckled. "What was your duty over there, anyway?"

"Oh, Juke did this and that. I could blow," he said, his voice dropping. "blow, blow, blow."

So many mysteries in God's world, Boyle thought, and this little man just another. Blow, huh? Well, out of the mouths of babes, he marveled. Half-breeds, too.

They walked on. As they rounded another bend they came upon Dogeye, standing with Gaby and the old sisters. Water gushed out of a crack in the rock and filled the sandy path that had made such easy walking. Dogeye was explaining to them what this next stretch of cave could do to their old knees.

"The pilgrims on their way to Carcassonne need no protection," Ramona insisted. "Women older than me crawled for miles on their knees seeking miracles. How dare you suggest I lack the fortitude!"

The old lady's face was furious in the flickering light. Dogeye was cringing back in mock fear.

"She's exactly right, Douglas," Mona pitched in with her sister. "Of course we'll go on, even crawling. Why I feel a religious ecstasy coming over me this very instant!"

261

Dogeye surrendered to this salvo. "All right, ladies, all right. But don't say I didn't warn you. And go slow, for God's sake! Religious ecstasy notwithstanding, this sorta rock can slice you to ribbons."

Loach and Jocelyn could hear the arguing voices before they could see the group. Jocelyn paused at the sound.

"I'm sorry," she apologized. "It's the jumble of voices, I guess. Sounds like hundreds."

"I think you're doing really well, Dr. Caine," Loach told her.

She answered him slowly. "I know you must think it ridiculous, for a scientist like myself—"

"Nonsense, Dr. Caine. We all have our fears."

262 She glanced back at the tall theosophist. "You seem to have no fears at all. If that's what all these occult studies have given you, perhaps I should take them up myself."

"Please, Doctor—" His eyes dropped. "—grant me my humility."

Jocelyn stared at him. "I didn't mean to embarrass you. But you always seem so in control, so confident."

Loach looked up at her, steady, the way someone would look into a gold pan for a glint of color.

"Six years ago," he finally said, "I stood in a San Francisco courtroom and heard two words spoken. Ever since that day I have had to live with fear."

"What do you mean, Doctor? What words?"

"Twenty . . . years. The bastard said a lot of other stuff, too, but those were only words I heard—Twenty years. Then the knock of the gavel on that wooden block. Clock, like that. *Clock!*"

He mimicked the sound perfectly with his tongue on the roof of his mouth.

"That sound knocked around my noggin for six years—the sound of my time being taken away. It still freezes my gizzard." He smiled at her, his face oddly vulnerable. "Tell me, Dr. Caine; you're the scholar. Is there a Latin word for the fear of time?"

They moved on. When they reached the spot where the stream widened the others were already moving ahead, scrabbling over the rocks. Only Dogeye stood there, waiting for them to join him. He looked up from the surging stream and shrugged at the pair. "Wet but safe," he told Jocelyn, gesturing at the opening. She hurried past to catch up with the rest of the group.

The two brothers hung back, standing close.

"Dog," Loach said when she was out of earshot, "things have changed."

263

"You're tellin' me!" Dogeye said. "I don't remember this much water. Or this smell, neither. Maybe we're down the wrong hole."

"This one will have to do," Loach said. "There's no persuading them to stop now. You got any ideas what we're going to do if it is the right one?"

"Hell, Charlie, I don't know." Dogeye giggled. "All I know's I ain't had stage fright like this in twenty years. Just like old times, huh? I guess we could always declare a 'Hey Rube' and back out."

"No, Dog, we can't. We have to go through with it. My future's on the line on this one."

"That's true," Dogeye said. "I keep forgetting." He scowled a moment and scratched at his jaw. Then one corner of his mouth twisted up in a half smile. "Not to change the subject, Charlie, but let me ask you something. What do you think of this Dr. Jo dame?"

"You mean can she spot a ringer? Hell, Dog, she's an expert . . ."

"Naw, I don't mean that. I mean, you know, as a *lady?*"

Loach laughed. "Good Christ. Here we are halfway to a hell of our own making and you're getting romantic. Isn't it a little late?"

"You mean for an old dog like me? Charlie, let me tell you something I learned from all them animals. It ain't never too late."

"Douglas Dean!" Loach put his hand on his brother's shoulder. "Far be it from me to tell you what to do, but the fact is you're a grizzly old prospector and she's a college professor. And the truth is I think you'd go together like vinegar and soda."

"Foamy. Good. I was hopin' you'd see it like that." Dogeye straightened his back and puffed out his chest, grinning broadly. "Vinegar and soda."

They stepped into the surging water and followed after the others.

Mona and Ramona were helping each through the ankle-deep water that rushed down the rocky tunnel, fussing. Their dresses snagged and tore on the jagged rocks. Several times they almost fell, scraping knees and elbows.

"You going to make it, Aunties?" Gaby asked.

"Absolutely!" said Mona.

"This was not part of the itinerary as I imagined it," her sister added, "but I wouldn't miss seeing that painting for the world."

"Ramona, you're beginning to sound a bit like Rodney. What *did* you imagine? A cable car to take us to the sacred wall?"

"Of course not. But no one mentioned raging subterranean rivers, either. I haven't been so wet since our honeymoon."

"Ramona! You promised never to mention Niagara Falls again. Just the memory could conjure up evil forces and doom."

"Balderdash! He was supposed to be *my* bridegroom! I'll mention it if I want."

"Very well, darling," her sister said. "I'm willing to talk about it if you are. You say it is this water that reminded you? Of the Falls, I mean . . ."

"Yes, I'd say so! Being soaked to the bone, being cold and hungry, being eager and expectant. It all reminds me of Edgar—"

"Ramona, *really!*" Mona gasped. "Expectant? Shame on you."

Both old ladies stopped walking. Mona sat down gingerly on a rough rock. Ramona leaned up against the wall beside her, breathing hard. They were glaring at each other.

265

"Don't you two get your ovaries in an uproar," Gaby advised. She had no idea what had happened at Niagara Falls, or who Edgar was. She didn't expect she really wanted to know, either. "Come on, we're all expecting something." She staggered past them, her jaw tight beneath the strap of her miner's helmet.

"Poor dear," Mona whispered when Gaby was past.

"She's changed," Ramona said.

"Ramona," Mona began again, "about our honeymoon. . . . You know we *should* really talk about it someday. It was painful to both of us to lose Edgar so suddenly—"

"He just slipped over the side into the Falls," Ramona said, a catch in her throat. "There we were, only eight hours after the ceremony—"

Mona cut her off abruptly. "I don't want to talk about it!"

"But you're the one—" She stopped and was quiet, listening to the water. She could see the bobbing lights of Dogeye and Loach approaching. "Anyway," she said with finality, "I have remained absolutely faithful for thirty-five years. To dear Edgar's memory."

"Me too," her sister said. They resumed walking.

The cave bent sharply ahead, and the roof lowered. The old women were now knee-deep in the fast-moving water.

"This water stinks to high heaven," Ramona said.

"Smells like something dead, is the truth of it. It's awful!" Mona answered, pulling up her thick walking skirt, heavy with the pungent water.

They were all soaked and scraped and exhausted by the time they found Chick. He was waiting for them at a split in the tunnel. The main cave bent to the right while the stream splashed down a steep passageway to the left, not more than three feet high.

"If those ancient angels or whatever came down here to do their doodling, they must have had something on us," Boyle said, looking around the rag-tag group of them.

"Nothing on us," Juke said. "We been here. They got nothing on us at all." He didn't explain himself, but kept moving in his jerky fashion from rocky perch to rocky perch.

When Loach and Dogeye joined the group Chick began to talk.

"What the hell's going on here, Loach? I've been down to the end." He gestured toward the tunnel on the right. "And it's a *dead* end. Nothing but dust. What are you trying to pull?"

"Can it, Ferrell," Dogeye spoke before Loach could. "You went the wrong way, is all. The cavern is down through there." His thorny hand pointed to where the stream disappeared into the narrow crawlway.

"Down *there?*" Boyle asked.

Gaby laughed out loud. "Ha! You'll get stuck in that tunnel like a cork in a bottle."

"Are you suggesting that my girth is excessive?" Boyle asked. He slapped his belly and laughed.

Dogeye pulled an old wool blanket from his pack and began cutting it into strips with his knife. He handed the strips of thick cloth to everyone.

"Tie these around your knuckles and your knees."

One by one they knelt and entered the low passage. It was excruciating, inching along the sharp rock. Tiny vents along the wall alternately sent steam and frost onto the crawlers. Sometimes a breeze off the fresh snow, sometimes a blast of gas from the bowels of the planet itself.

"Lordy," chuckled Boyle. "These hot and cold winds. Is this Hell, or am I dreaming?"

Nobody answered him. Those creeping along in front of him couldn't turn to respond, and those following Boyle's big muddy rear end were unable to hear the question. They grunted and cursed and groaned, and gasped when a helmet hit the ceiling, knocking out the light.

It was an agonizing crawl, even with Dogeye's kneepads, but there was no turning around. If they paused too long to breathe or relight the carbide lamp, the flame from the crawler behind was stabbing at their tail. They had to slither along in the rushing cold current, sometimes across rock that caught at their clothes and skin like tiny hooks.

"This stuff'd work great for zippers," Dogeye grunted to no one in particular, "if you could fasten it to the cloth."

Then the incline of the tube's floor steepened sharply and the little river went hissing down a shelf of obsidian, slick as a black mirror. When the explorers came out of the stifling lava

267

crawlway, they encountered a gentle slide. "It's okay," Dogeye said. "This is the front stoop." They slid down the obsidian onto a sandy ledge and found themselves at last in an enormous echoing limestone grotto.

The change in the cave's sound was as startling as the change in its size. The porous lava tube had absorbed sound like acoustical corking, making the ragged walls seem even closer than they actually were. Now the distance vaulted away through the dark mists, far beyond the reach of their tiny lamp beams, reverberating with immensity like a vast Roman bath. And when they had stopped gasping they discerned another sound.

"What the devil is that?" Loach asked, muting his voice. "I don't remember any sound like that."

268

"Me neither," Dogeye said. "It sounds like a giant slurping a bowl of soup."

"Smells like good soup, too," Gaby said with perky sarcasm. She was damned if she'd reveal her discomfort. If those two old dames could crawl all this way and never utter a gripe, so could she. "Rat soup, garnished with rotten eggs and coal gas. A giant's favorite meal."

"Yeah," Chick agreed, "and I can't even get a picture of him. These damn little lamps!"

"Well look here," Dogeye said, removing his helmet. "If you polish the soot off the reflector, it helps." He shined up the little convex disc with his cuff and put it back on. He leaned forward, staring at something in the darkness.

"Jesus Christ, Charlie-O, lookit there! There's something I *know* didn't used to be here."

As the other eyes adjusted they could see a shining expanse before them, as big as a gymnasium floor, reflecting the glow of their lamps.

"A lake!"

The group wandered down to the water's edge. A thick crusty substance lined the shore, lumps of black and white streaked with vermilion, like dried blood. Chick reached out with the tip of his boot and prodded the bank. A small edge of the crust broke off into the water.

"Looks like snow, doesn't it?" he said.

"Like grimy black city snow, been sitting by the road for a week," Dogeye answered, chuckling a little. Chick looked at him with sudden suspicion. The prospector seemed almost glad to find the cave filled to the gills with crusty water. Jocelyn walked over, obviously interested in the phenomenon. She hunkered beside Dogeye, looking intently at the strange aggregate.

269

"I've never seen anything like it," she said. "It appears to be mineral but smells organic. What could have leached in here and caused it?"

The smell was like burnt fireworks soaked in turpentine. It reminded Chick of Fourth of July, back in Illinois, all the kids circled around him, hollering "Chicken Ferrell, Chicken Ferrell," until he'd taken the dare, the firecracker in his hand, before he had a chance to reconsider. It was this odor of cave gas that brought it back to him now—powder-seared skin and singed hair. "No more Chicken Ferrell for me," he thought grimly to himself.

Scouting along the bank he found a long, smooth pine pole sticking half out of the water. Several more like it were scattered about.

"How did poles like this get in here?" he asked.

Loach answered. "Beamann used those as scaffolding to photograph the painting."

"We had a hell of a time gettin' 'em down here," Dogeye added.

"Let's see these paintings," Chick said. "Where are they?"

They stood silent a moment, all of them listening to the continuous, sucking roar.

"The wall must be directly across from us. We'll have to circle this lake, over these boulders. The old trail is gone. Mona, why don't you stay here with Ramona while we scout ahead."

"Yes, Doctor," Ramona said in the dark. "Perhaps we will rest here a moment. We'll follow the progress along by the sounds."

"Sound and no sights," Chick complained. "A photograph won't be worth shit without some more light."

"As a matter of fact," Dogeye said, like someone laying down a straight flush over a full house, "I happen to *have* some more light."

"What?" Chick spun toward him. "*What* did you say?"

"I said, I got a light." Out from his pack Dogeye pulled the electric spot. A squat, square box, jet black except for the shining curve of the reflector. He held it toward Chick.

"Jumping Christ, a light! How long did you plan to hide that thing? Turn it on. For God sakes turn it on, man, turn it on!"

Dogeye flipped a toggle at the top of the box and a dazzling beam shot out, caroming from one amazing sight to the next.

Everyone was completely transfixed by what they saw. They stood gaping, dwarfed by the vastness of the chamber. This cavern was as different from the lava tube as the earth from the moon. Great columns of liquid stone swirled up out of the lake. The cave walls looked alive, like the inside of an enormous craw, slick and purple-mauve, covered with an iridescent slime. Stalactites hung like molars above them.

"My God," Chick gasped. In a second his camera equipment was out. He followed the swing of Dogeye's beam, clicking photos as if every moment of time was worth its weight in diamonds, aiming his lens indiscriminately at the walls curving up into a great dome above them, at the rock formations, at the murky surface of the lake swirling with streaks of maroon and carbuncle.

"Okay, I'm warmed up," he said. "Where's this famous wall?"

"Over yonder," Dogeye said, swinging the heavy box around. "But I'm afraid it ain't gonna make you none too happy."

271

The beam located the source of the sucking noise that filled their ears. At the far end of the echoing gallery, a glistening funnel spun, big as a merry-go-round. And beyond this whirlpool was a swooping white wall of stone. Blank. A few curved lines of paint were all that still showed above the subterranean lake's surface.

"The water's come up and covered the painting completely," Dogeye said.

It was like a vaudeville stage, Chick thought—brightly lit at last but nothing on it. He climbed over the rocks toward the wall, feeling suddenly very empty. Despair was spreading beneath his ribs, hollow as this awful hole itself. Nothing at all! A good thing that rat Makai wasn't here; he'd find some way to blame this on Chick, sure as hell.

When he stepped into the beam he saw his shadow projected huge on that wall like a cut-out of Errol Flynn, his dark cape swashbuckling out behind. The frothing whirlpool near the wall was like something from a nightmare, sucking on the shadow. It rotated slowly at the outer edges, bits of the scummy crust bobbing about, then churning and bubbling faster toward the spout in the center.

"Dammit," Chick said, "I've just *got* to get *some*thing!"

"Ferrell!" Dogeye shouted. "Calm down."

Chick kept going, over boulders big as Frigidaires, as Buicks. He found a shelf of flat stone against the wall that he managed to crawl out on. On his hands and knees, he could look directly down into the water.

"Yes, Ferrell," Loach had joined his brother at the light. "Come on back. It's gone."

"No!" shouted Chick. "It's not gone. It's still here. I can see it down through the water, clear. It's beautiful, absolutely beautiful! My *God!*"

He sounded as though he might break into weeping. He scrambled closer to the edge, pointing his camera down at the surface.

"I'm going to be able to get it! The water's clear here. Dogeye, please! Bring the light closer. Come on, everybody. It's unbelievable. You've got to see it! You've just no idea—"

Carrying the light, Dogeye started forward. He felt a hand in his.

"Wait a minute," Dr. Jo said. "I didn't crawl all this way to miss this."

Already she could see what she thought might be the outline of a huge antler, or perhaps the Eye of Horus.

"Hurry with that light. We must document this. I'm a professional journalist, you know."

Dogeye wasn't so sure about that, but he hurried, swept up in Chick's enthusiasm, pulling Jocelyn along. He could hear the others following behind. As they worked their way over the boulders, the maelstrom below them looked like the mouth of a monster.

"All right, now, Ferrell, take it easy," Loach shouted above the sucking noise. "Those pictures have been there for thousands of years; they're not going to disappear today."

Gaby followed with the sisters, feeling cold to the bone. The wall still looked like an empty stage to her, and she'd been ready for the curtain to come down for days. But she knew she had to see the show through to the last act. She hoped it happened soon. She needed some popcorn.

"I don't know what that crazy reporter sees," she said to Mona, struggling along beside her. "Looks like a big bathtub draining to me."

"Oh, I think I can see the top of God's Eye!" Ramona exclaimed. "Just like it is in the photograph. It's stunning."

"Positively stunning," echoed Mona. "We've found the source at last, just like in my vision."

They pressed forward on the narrow ledge where the photographer was situated, muttering over his equipment. "I'm gonna get it, by God, I'm gonna get it after *all*. Here! Shine that light right down in it. It's damned fantastic."

In the glare of the spot, shapes were beginning to materialize beneath the shimmering surface—animal shapes, symbols, stick figures rippling in the flow. The camera clicked and clicked. "Yeah, by Christ, it's whirly but I'm getting it!" Then he saw something hiss past in his viewfinder. It sounded like the bacon in the pan.

"Look out!" Dogeye shouted. "God *damn* you, Boyle!"

Chick put aside his camera, the better to see the hissing object. It looked like a cluster of cigars, bound together with a white leather belt. A fuse protruded from one end, seemingly

273

propelling the bundle along the water's surface like a model motorboat.

"Everybody back!" This was Boyle's voice. "God's will be done!"

Chick watched the dynamite hiss past, taking a slow lap around the perimeter of the whirlpool. He still could not believe what he was seeing. He began to remove his shoes.

"No, Ferrell!" Loach was shouting. "Don't do it!"

It wasn't as though he had a choice. It was his assignment. He *was* a professional. Without a second thought, he found himself already swimming after the bundle, stroking in a wide circle behind its wake. He was not at all worried. He'd watched dynamite before. This was a long fuse—at least a minute. There was plenty of time. And he was damned if he'd lose this opportunity. He had barely begun to work. He was going to need to change lenses. Film, too. All this light, he would need slower emulsions—penetrate better, deeper.

His hand closed over the sizzling bundle just as the carousel of water carried him past the glaring spot on the shelf. He wouldn't want to toss it that way. His gear was up there, and his friends. He trod water leisurely, ignoring the shouts as he waited until he was on the far side of the circle. Then he threw it. He saw the little trail of sparks arc over the water and bounce among the dark boulders. "I got it! I got it!" That was the little man, Juke. Not a bad fellow. Conscientious in his way. Almost like a professional. All of them, not that he thought about it—each in their own way: reliable. The old ladies could growl and make things knock in the night. That Dogeye, you wouldn't think it, but the sucker could cook. Even Loach. Diving in now. Classic. Once a hero, always a hero. Reliable. . . .

Dogeye began tearing at Jocelyn's pack. Before she could

ask what he was doing he had pulled out a length of rope and was looping it around his waist.

"Dogeye, you can't—" she began. Loach had already been sucked into the maw of the whirlpool after the photographer. "It's too late!"

He was handing her the free end. "Belay me, I'm counting on you." He, too, was gone into the swirling darkness.

Jocelyn braced her foot against a rock as the rope tightened in her hand. Somewhere in the darkness behind her, amid the screaming women, she heard Juke's voice—"Disarmed!"— and heard the sharp crack of the blasting cap go off harmlessly. She could not turn to look, and she knew none of the others could make it up on the shelf in time to help. She felt Dogeye's weight like an enormous fish on the line, fighting her with its life. She wrapped the loose end of the rope around her own waist, closed her eyes and fought back. Just when she thought she couldn't hold on any longer, she felt the weight ease in her hands. She opened her eyes, thinking Dogeye must have broken free.

Instead she saw that Boyle had stepped up beside her and held the rope in his hands.

"You! What are you doing?" she shouted at him, trying to pull the rope away. It was like tugging on a mountain.

"I want to help," Boyle shouted back. "I'm sorry. I never meant for all this to happen. In God's name, I didn't. . . . "

He began to haul the rope in, hand over hand, so easily that Jocelyn still thought it was attached to nothing. Dogeye came sputtering free of the water's grip and onto the rocks. He was holding his brother's unconscious form by the seat of the jodhpurs.

"Didn't see Ferrell," Dogeye at last managed to cough. Boyle helped him lift Loach's frame onto a level rock. The tall man looked deathly white in the harsh glare of Dogeye's lamp, and smaller. Dogeye bent over Loach, pushing at his chest until his brother began to gasp and struggle for air. Loach curled in a ball. He looked like a baby to Jocelyn. Dogeye turned his head up and met her eyes.

"Sounds like he's alive," he said. He tilted his head, listening. "What's that? What in the hell's that?"

There was silence. Dogeye stood and rushed once again to the edge of the lake. The whirlpool had stopped its sucking swirl, completely. The water was slowing into separate eddies where the maelstrom had been. Jocelyn stood up from Loach's shaking body when she heard Dogeye speak.

"It's plugged," he said, his voice forlorn. "Ferrell's plugged it."

14

Lost in the dark,

found in the flower . . .

When Boyle opened his eyes, he was tied up again.

When Loach's ears were cleared of water and scum enough that he could hear again, what he heard was a huge silence.

When Jocelyn had calmed her mind so she could look back into her memory and review what had just happened, she wondered if she had seen anything at all. Had she seen a painting? Hints of a giant eye, submerged? A weak man become strong enough to die, a tainted man clean enough to try to stop him? It was hard enough to remember, let alone believe. What existed, exactly? Shock and water and thwarted breathing. No one spoke.

Dogeye's words finally jarred the silence. "Turn that damn spot off." The bright light had been a kind of security. Now it seemed almost intrusive, useless. Reduced to the nervous illumination from their swarm of lamps, the faces of the explorers once again collected as masks, flaring sporadically when one person turned to look at another—portions of people: a quivering cheek from one sister, a hand to the throat and an oh-dear from the other.

Dogeye spoke again, feeling the need to somehow explain. "We're liable to need what's left of that battery later."

Jocelyn put one hand on the prospector's shoulder, feeling somehow the need to reassure. "You're right. One never can tell."

Gaby felt the need to feel her belly. It didn't seem any different, under the sliding of her palm. Still, she did not move her hand away. She noticed she was also feeling a little sick, not to mention confused, anxious, pissed off and thirsty, though she was at that moment standing in a pool of water. The pool hadn't been there before.

278

"I hate to break the mood, folks, but I think this water is rising." She stepped to a higher stone.

Loach was on his feet now. He sloshed a few steps one direction, then the other, headlamps following him. The liquid floor reflected their lights like dancing demons. "She's right," he said.

Chatter started up then, like a light wind. Ramona and Mona paddled around like nervous ducks, mumbling about spirits causing calamities.

"We have to head back," Loach said. "Now. Time to roll up our tents."

"He didn't have to dive in after them," Juke said. "They weren't weighted. They won't sink if they aren't weighted. They woulda just popped on the surface and our ears woulda rung for a while is all. He never needed to jump in."

It was the longest sentence anybody could remember hearing from Juke, and without one repetition.

"What about this snake?" Dogeye asked, kicking water at the squatting figure of Boyle. "We searched him good and he's de-fanged for sure this time. Looks like those four sticks and that one cap and fuse was all the venom he was carrying."

"What about it, Boyle?" Loach asked the man. "Can we have your word that you won't try anything else?"

"I'm tamed, Doc. Swear to God. Matter of fact, I'm impressed. How the dickens did you put the whammie on me this time? Post-hypnotic suggestion?"

Gaby laughed. "No, you dope. It was Ramona clipping you from behind with her crystal-ball-in-a-sock—just like the other time."

Boyle laughed with her and rocked himself into a standing position. He turned his back so Dogeye could reach his bonds. "Well, I'm still impressed," he said. "Besides, I've blown my wad. Cut me loose, folks. I'll be good."

Loach nodded and Dogeye sliced the rope with a wave of his knife. As they were leaving the grotto Gaby turned for one last look at the echoing expanse of water. "One thing's sure, Uncle Charlie; you're a damned bear on photographers."

Resolution pulled everyone to begin groping their way back to the lava tube. Resolution and uneasiness. Like when you don't have a direction, but you move anyway, just to keep anything uncomfortable from settling on you—like dust. Dogeye took the lead, the others fell in behind. One by one back into the crawl. Once again body parts became hindrances. Ribcages scraped, knees dragged, hands, shoulders snagged. Once again the hard breathings.

What had been difficult had also been exciting, on the crawl in. The mind could anticipate wondrous surprises— monsters and lost cities, treasures and creatures. Crawling back was much less moving. They were quiet. The dark leveled their differences, as if they were one creature, centipedelike, inching along, measuring each handhold by the darkness they were headed for. Together, they were cold and damp and tight, like one body. Together, hands found cracks and knobs to cling to. Slippery traverses, untrustable ledges, un-eternal weight. Pieces of rock giving way in a touch. Fear either pushing or pulling them. Making a rhythm, giving direction. Crawling back up the throat of the unknown erased their individuality. Only Gaby noticed consciousness, and that not even her own. Nothing particularly remarkable about any of this, she thought.

Gaby bumped face first into the crouching form of Mona ahead of her. "Listen," the old woman said. "Listen." A strange whirling whisper stopped their crawling.

"Sounds like . . . radio static," Gaby said as they broke free of the tube.

A hundred yards ahead a dim figure stood, arms outstretched. "My word," Mona said, "It's Rodney. I'd know that limp shape anywhere."

"Why would he come down here?" Ramona asked.

"Perhaps the bats drove him in," Mona suggested.

The figure did not move. They were only twenty feet away before anyone realized he was trying to call out. His voice was thin and raspy, vaguely familiar. His words were unintelligible. He looked glazed over with something. Shock.

"Rodney?" Mona called. "Dear, is that you?"

The figure started, as if noticing them for the first time. His whispered calls grew more urgent.

"What is he saying?" Ramona asked Mona.

"I can't quite make it out," Mona said back.

"Makai," Loach's voice filled the cavern.

"He seems to be in shock," Jocelyn told him.

Rodney took a step toward them, illuminated from behind and above by the light from the entrance. His hands seemed animated.

"Makai?" Loach repeated.

"Father Paul," Rodney raspily whispered. He felt around in the air with useless gestures, like a blind man. "It's you, isn't it, Father?"

"Oh, my dear, he's lost his mind," Mona cried.

"And his voice," added Dogeye.

Rodney whispered, almost like a sly secret, an aside, to Loach, "I'm so glad to see you, Father."

Gaby walked straight up to his face, "Hey, what the hell is wrong with you? You're beginning to sound like Juke!"

"Listen!" Jocelyn's elongated voice from the front answered, "I suggest you all lie down." Bodies obeyed. Now there was no one crouching in Gaby's light, though she knew they were all there. She tilted her beam further down the crawl into the black air. Something was coming, like a breath down a windpipe, coming toward them, alive and pounding; and flapping. Wings! and wind, brushing their backs and legs. Furry bodies brushing and beating against them. Most of the group closed their eyes tight, pursed their lips, tightened their muscles waiting for the feeling to pass.

Gaby tried to raise her head once or twice, then her arm. They kept coming, by the thousands. Winged movement pinned her. If she hadn't felt so disgusted, she might have felt massaged.

When the last of the flurry brushed over them, Mona or Ramona murmured, "How perfectly *awful*. What horrid little creatures! Why do they *do* that?"

Her sister answered, "They're just animals, dear, they don't know that it's rude." Gaby rolled onto her back near the end of the line. Dogeye turned to Jocelyn at the front.

"I thought you said them batus floperandus couldn't exist down here, Dr. Caine." He was smiling.

"Most peculiar phenomenon," Jocelyn returned. The crawling continued.

Fresh air washed over them. Jocelyn stood and inhaled gratefully.

They could see the ragged hole through which they had entered, now a dazzling circle of light.

"Must be morning," Dogeye said.

"Is that a person standing up there, or just a rock?" Gaby yelled.

"Makai, why in hell did you decide—" Loach began, and broke off. Rodney was pointing up at the light at the cave's entrance.

"They're after me, Father," he whispered. "I'm so glad to see you."

"Who's after you?" Dogeye asked.

"Bears," Rodney rasped. "Bears, bears, bears."

Gaby's voice rose, and she pointed. "And now what's *that?*" The tiny carbide lights followed her finger. "It looks like snow," she said. Floating down from the hole, little white things.

"It's not snow," Jocelyn said, and they all realized at the same time, "it's feathers . . . sleeping bag feathers!"

Then they heard the growling, grunting, thrashing, ripping. It was bears. Just then the ladder jerked up a few feet. Dogeye bolted for it, but in the middle of his "Goddamn," the ladder jerked up again, then disappeared altogether. Shot up from the cave like a pulled tooth.

"They're after that bacon fat," Gaby said. She glared at Rodney. "You simp."

But Rodney waved his arms around frantically. "Would you rather they had gotten me?" No one spoke. The words hung like the carbide lights in the dark.

A long minute went by and then Gaby said, "The real question is, what the hell are we going to do now? Any of you geniuses have an idea on that?" She faced each of them separately, waiting for a clear response. "Well, Uncle Charlie?"

"I'm open to suggestions. The water's rising behind us, the wild beasts are waiting in front. And they sound unfriendly even if we could climb up to where they are, which we can't. Yes, I'm open to suggestions."

He stood in the cone of light pouring down from the entrance above, looking from one person to the next, his expression bemused.

283

"If only I hadn't been so hasty with my dynamite," Boyle said.

"We still got the dynamite," Juke said. He withdrew the four sticks from inside his coat, where he used to keep his pipe.

"Dynamite's no good without a way of blowing it, Juke," Loach reminded his comrade. "You don't happen to have another fuse-and-cap stashed somewhere on you, do you, Boyle?"

" 'Fraid not," Boyle said.

"How's about *inside* you?" Dogeye asked. He wasn't sure he was finished with Boyle and he kept his hand on the butt of his knife handle.

"One try was all I vowed," Boyle said. "One was all I brought."

"Then those sticks are worthless," Loach said. "Why don't you get rid of the damn things?"

"I can blow them," Juke said. "I know a way."

Loach and Dogeye turned together to look at Juke, waiting.

"Carbide," he said.

The two men blinked, but the little blue man's eyes were steady, the way they had been before this cave business . . . before the war. Dogeye looked at his brother and raised his shoulders in a what-the-hell shrug.

"Blow, blow, blow," Dogeye said.

"Oh, I had a vision that we would live," Ramona sighed.

"Oh, you did not," Mona said. "So be quiet. This is serious."

"You ain't just whistling Dixie it's serious," Gaby said. "But I'm staying here, even if I have to stay by myself. No more crawling."

"You can't just wait here, dear," Ramona said. "Those bears . . ."

"Yes, we have to stick together," the other sister added.

"If we stay here," Dogeye told her, "we're all going to be sucking bat fertilizer."

Loach looked down at the dynamite in his hand. He passed it on to his brother who gave it back to Juke.

"We're going back," Loach said. "We've got to blast on through."

"I can't," Gaby said, her voice fading out like a long-distance radio station.

"No choice," Juke said. "No choice."

"I just want to sleep," Gaby mumbled.

"Sleep will have to wait," Jocelyn told the girl.

"I'm gettin' a little sick of this goddamn tube," Dogeye said. He pulled a box of small black pebbles from his pack and counted the remaining carbides in his palm. "One for everyone," he said. "Hold your hands out."

He stepped around the group, dropping one pellet into each outstretched hand. "And enough left over for Juke's blasting device."

"I don't know if my knees will hold up another trip through that tunnel," Mona moaned as she reknotted the cold wet ties.

Ramona joined in, "Excuse me, Dr. Loach, dear, but do we have to go back through that dreadful tunnel?"

In reply, Rodney shot past them and scrambled into the tunnel like some nocturnal reptile, out of sight.

Dogeye stepped up to the tube quickly. "I'm afraid, ma'am, the worst thing we want to do in this cave is split up. We've already lost . . ." His voice entered the crawl, and the group followed with a plural reluctance. That reluctance was heaviest in the pit of Gaby's gut. She hesitated outside the tube opening. She tapped her foot, held her belly.

She was utterly disgusted. Bunch of lame-brained men. My knees are bleeding, my hands are scraped, fingernails shot to hell, sick as a dog. "Shit, piss, corruption, snot, nine dumb assholes tied in a knot," she said.

As if in answer, the pack on her back jerked softly as Juke unleashed the strappings. He pulled out some pieces of equipment and relaced the pack. Gaby could breathe easier now, the pack lightened. "Now if only there was air to breathe," she said.

Juke patted Gaby's pack. "Turn your head to the side to breathe in the crawl. It's easier."

"Just let me rest a minute, I'll catch up, just a minute's rest."

"Come on now," Juke said; he tugged Gaby's pack, "Come on." He crouched and entered the tube. Gaby followed, and the worm, disjointed and crippled, inched on again, for the third time.

Three times the cold, three times the wet, the aching, the scrapes and bumps and bruises. A wound can only be re-opened so many times before infection sets in, before something irreversible happens. The last thing anyone said came from Boyle, strangely full of optimism: "Third time's a charm, folks. Third time's always a charm." The third crawl seemed one of epic fatigue, minute motions. Cold water running over their battered hands and knees. Silence . . .

Finally Gaby had to rest, dire consequences or no. Her head rested easily on the rock behind her, her chest rose and fell, her face was calm. The lamp on her helmet cast both light and a steady hiss into the short, curved ceiling above her. She stared at the porous lava ceiling, dreamlike. But she wasn't dreaming. She was so exhausted that she was past that. Her headlamp changed its pitch and began to sputter, its beam flickered and Gaby stirred, the fuel ran lower, the flames strobed and sputtered until with a small resonating pop. It stopped.

Gaby's eyes snapped open to nothing. How long had she been sleeping? Complete darkness—total silence. She tried to blink in vision, but nothing changed.

"Goddamn," she whispered softly. "I'll just have a drink of water now, no need to panic." She spoke out loud to herself. The sound of her own voice made her feel less lonely. She was sorry, however, that she'd taken the water; her stomach churned.

"Well," she reasoned, "better get going if you're going to catch up with them." She crawled, accompanying the action with conversation. "Gaby, ol' girl, you're in sorry shape now." She laughed. There was no resonance, only stillness surrounding the sound, muffling it. It was the sound of her own laughter that scared her most.

"God, I really am in sorry shape." But it wasn't a joke this time. She wanted to be in bed, the covers pulled up over her head, she wanted to be held. Alone in this cave she could let herself feel, and what she felt was tired and cold and sick and alone. Like a child. She tried to hear herself laughing.

"Well, you're too scared to cry . . ." This sounded right. It was a simple statement. Slowly she thought about the direction she needed to go if she was going to find the others.

She crept forward, one hand extended in front of her, the other on the wall. "Is it day?" She thought of Paul. He's gone, wandered off. Perhaps they were both lost, together. She imagined the lava tube splitting and herself taking the wrong turn. Maybe I am like him . . . walking through the dark, feeling the way.

The only sound was her uneven breathing. She sucked in a huge gulp of air and held it for a few seconds.

This is what it's like to be dead, she thought.

"Hello," she said as she blew the air out. Her voice didn't echo; the sound was absorbed in the porous basalt around her.

"Loach," she said a little louder. Still her voice didn't carry past thirty or forty feet. "Loach!" she shouted, between cupped hands. Her voice was shrill and desperate. "Christ, I sound like that dumb parrot," she said.

Gaby felt the walls and floor, read the crawl like Braille, clung to hollows, juttings, knobs, anything. She noticed the huge implications of touch. But now the passageway seemed unremarkable. Almost smooth. Had she wandered down the wrong tunnel . . . a fork maybe? There was supposed to be

287

water sound in the tunnel, there wasn't any water here. Who knew how many twisting routes, unknown miles of passages lived down here. She felt tricked. Duped. Stupid. Scared.

She was reminded of all Loach's slimy manipulative tricks and the way he tricked them all, with Juke as the shill no doubt. "Well, where's my goddamn shill?" she said.

Her hands touched the basalt wall, she patted it with her palms. "Okay, wall, okay, you be my shill."

She started moving again, next to the encompassing curve, her hands sliding along its surface. She started thinking about water. How far back had she left it? How far had she gone before passing out? How long had she slept? She found a knot rising from her belly to her throat. "Oh, Christ," she thought, "you're not going to cry, are you? I thought you were through with all that." She stopped for a moment and wiped her eyes with the back of her sleeve. No crying. She could do that, at least.

She kept moving. Several times she ran into boulders, once a cluster of boulders that were so large she had to feel all the way around them to get back to the wall again. She figured the ceiling must have given way at that place. "Great, the ceiling gave way . . . boulders fell from above." Her heart pounded, she felt nauseous. This is alienation, I am a fragile human in the bowels of the earth . . . I am at the mercy of great natural forces and there's nothing I can do . . . the tunnel could collapse on me, I could be squashed like an ant. I'm a piece of helpless organic fluff!

"Gaby girl," she said aloud, "you have never, in your life, been a fragile, helpless piece of organic fluff. Just keep moving."

She took comfort in herself, having no other choice.

She snickered. "I can accept my fate as a helpless being in

288

the face of this callous, amoral, mechanized, messed-up universe, or I can break down and weep like a woman." "Woman" echoed. Sound. An echo? She moved forward more quickly. Her heart knocked in her chest, pulsed in her roving fingers and knees. Her mind flipped. Crawling. The carnival. Her mother. Her belly. Crawling faster, breathing harder.

The fingertips of her right hand were scraped raw with feeling, her feet throbbing. She called every few hundred steps and listened. Now, heart racing, hands racing, crawling toward anything different . . . and then a blast of enormous cool air, the wall disappearing from under her palm. She didn't hear anything, she couldn't see anything, but being in an open space was sure as hell better than being in a goddamn tube. No reason at all to feel relieved, but she did. Only one thing to do at this point. She stretched out flat on the ground. She took the next to the last cigarette out and groped for the next to the last match. She had to use the last match to get a light. She made the match burn as long as she could and then she lit the matchbox; when it burned her fingers she dropped it to the ground. She took the last cigarette in her hand and placed the empty pack on the little fire.

289

What next? When the Chesterfield was scorching its filter tip she lit the other one. She made it last. She knew a girl who smuggled a cig into school every night in her panties . . . an Old Gold. She claimed she could keep it going for twenty-five minutes. A Chesterfield is longer than an Old Gold . . . sure, if you smoke the cork. She laughed. In the middle of her laugh she felt her voice move closer to her . . . surround her. Smoke froze in her throat for a long minute before she could draw another breath. She remembered not to laugh anymore. It didn't do any good.

As she watched the last tiny red glow fade, the darkness became a wall in front of her again. She could have reached out with the tip of her last cigarette like a piece of chalk and written on it, if there'd been something that she wanted to say. What was to say? When you got right down to it, what? That it was dark? That she was alone? Or that she was alone in the dark? Or that in the darkness she found herself alone? Should've been a goddamn philosopher.

If she could not find herself in a world full of people . . . in the hard glare of noon . . . how could she expect to find herself alone in the dark? Besides, who gives a wrinkled rat's ass? You come into this shit hole lost and alone and that's how you get out. No one cares. Maybe no man is an island, but, she thought, *wo*-man sure the hell is. "Woman" again echoed and came back to her, around and back, mocking.

290

And the knot returned, tugged from the center. Without warning, she felt an ocean of tears burst from her eyes and rush hot down her cheeks. "Shit," she cursed in a sudden rage, disgusted with herself. She tried to suck them back into her brain. Here she was, supposed to be such a tough tootsie, bawling like a scared baby. "Shit," she cursed aloud again in the swaddled darkness, between sobs and heaves.

And then a curious thing happened to her rage. The tears continued, but she wasn't a scared baby crying at all. She was something else, and she imagined a tiny being even more alone and helpless in the dark than she was. Everybody wants out at least once. Everybody deserves their time in the moon glare. So she crooned in useless sympathy, "There, there. There, there"—and wept, and understood.

In her understanding she felt her body alive again, hungry, cold, weak. She stood and for the first time in a long while she saw colors. Strange glows unnatural, swirling. She squinted.

Then she swayed, realizing the colored flashes were indications of a weakened woman about to faint dead away. She dropped down to her knees. She felt nauseous again, and what's more, she was hearing things. A kind of ticking or tapping above her. She felt caught in a kind of whirling black funnel, wasn't sure she could stay conscious. The ticking, louder. "What?" she barely said, "who?" she whispered, and just before she fell over sideways, something dropped from the ceiling, crashing down less than four feet away from her. Pieces of small rock landed on her body. Something coughed. It was then that she saw a spark of light in her delirium, minute, dim, barely there at all, blurry, bobbing along, above what could be a face.

"Glad to see you, Kiddo," he said. Her cheek was against his chest, tears soaking the khaki. She could feel his big hand stroking at her matted hair.

291

"Glad to see you, too, Uncle Chuck," she said.

"Call me Grandpa," he said.

"Call you *Grand*pa?" she started. "But how—?"

"Easy," he explained. "It was that lavender toilet water. I won it for you at the baseball throw in Omaha, spring of '22, remember? You were twelve."

"Sure I remember," she lied, sobbing.

15

An attempt at survival . . .

Before Loach and Gaby reached the end of the crawlway they could see the others collected in a tight huddle, their lamps focused on Juke. Loach knew Juke and Dogeye were already preparing the blast, better than he could manage. He took his time, slowly unfolding his aching body and waiting for Gaby to catch up. The light from her headlamp barely glowed; he had divided the last of his carbide with her and, together, they scarcely flickered.

He straightened and drew a deep breath, holding his arms gingerly from his sides. He didn't want to touch the stinging skin of his torso. He'd given Gaby his canvas jacket and the front of his body was a mass of cuts, scrapes and tattered cloth. It felt like shaved meat.

More than anything he was aware of the minute residue of strength that still flickered in him, as delicate as carbide flame. He tried to let his mind choose the next move on its own, fearing that if he forced himself to think his brain would turn to stone and crumble apart.

He felt the immensity of the room press down on him, more than the cramped crawlway ever could. Some of the bats were still moving above him. He could hear their bony wings husking the cold air. They must have noticed the change in the water level. He fought the feeling that was rising darkly in him like the water, forcing himself to stand erect. He had his troops to see to.

His little light hissed like a leaky tire in the gloom, offering only occasional glimpses of the bats as they squeaked past overhead. They seemed crazed by the change in their habitat, enraged, working up to some kind of actual attack.

Outer reflects inner, he reminded himself. Don't give it a foothold in your mind. Keep control. Will your own world. If there was any one skill he had drilled into himself in jail, it was willpower. Boyle could quote Nietzsche all he wanted, but Loach knew Nietzsche in a different way. From the inside. He'd lived locked up with Nietzsche for six years; that cranky old Kraut's tortured sentences would circle in his head the rest of his life, like these bats. There was nothing to separate the inner from the outer, not steel bars not even stone walls. It was all either a chamber of horrors or a fun house. Mirrors waited at the end of every hallway, twisting every thought back on itself, intending to make you crack or make you laugh. It depended on your point of view. It was best to concentrate on actual, physical tasks—grasping the next rock, offering a hand, fighting fatigue. His battle instincts were still sharp. He could still fight. But the mirrors baited his spirit. He must not let them set the hook.

Finally he conjured a quote that held his attention. It was the old German's phrase from Zarathustra: "Man is a rope stretched between the animal and the abyss." Loach knew it was possible to climb that rope, hand over bleeding hand. Men had done it before him, and from deeper abysses than this. He had told himself this same thing in the prison cell, over and over. And read the words over and over to back it up. It had seemed to him that the words he read were battling with the words that judge had flown at him, right in his face, *worse* than these bats. A bilko artist, perhaps, yes; but no murderer. Never that! If there was ever one rule on the midway, it was that—never kill anybody. It's bad for business.

He had not wanted to injure Beamann at all, much less kill him. But it had all happened so fast. "Thrall of rage" was actually an apt description. The twisted little man had surprised him with that ultimatum slapped in his face—"More money, Loach, or I go to the papers!" He had hinted at it before, but Loach had been able to reason with him: wait a few more months; it would all begin to bear fruit. But for Beamann to come at him out of the dark like that, and in the *Temple* . . . Loach had not been able to stop himself. He grabbed him by the shoulders, like a little boy. "No! It's become too important, to too many people!" One shake was all it took and Beamann hung like a puppet with the strings cut. One shake. None of the broken skull and crushed ribs like the papers claimed. And that dog stuff—Loach didn't know why he had said that. That hadn't helped him or the Society, either. It was just that the man was smaller than he expected when he grabbed him. So slight, so fragile.

He and Gaby had reached the end of the crawlway and could stand again. Loach brushed the dark memories from the cracks, concentrating instead on those he cared for. He would get this deal straight with Beamann at another time, on another table. He had other cards to play, this hand around.

"Here she is," he called to the cluster of lights ahead of

them in the cavern. "She's fine. How's it going at this end, Dog?"

Dogeye chose not to mention Gaby's vanishing act. Instead, he gestured at the thing Juke was cradling against his chest. "Juke thinks he's got us a way to leastways blow that plug."

"For whatever good that'll do," Boyle grumbled. "Chances of us being able to follow this stream on to an outlet are bad and worse."

Nobody paid any attention to him. Loach stepped into the circle of light to see what Juke held.

"Okay, Juke, what we got?"

"Bomb," said Juke. He held out a complicated jumble of objects.

The four sticks of dynamite were still bound with Boyle's belt, like the staffs in a Roman fascis. But the lengthy excess of white leather that still protruded from the buckle was now wrapped twice around the two cactus brandy jars. Their wide mouths were still unlidded. One of the jars was empty, one full of all the carbide pebbles that Dogeye had been able to retrieve. He had taken everything that wasn't already percolating in the lamps.

Tied around the whole of Juke's apparatus was Loach's sock, the crystal ball swinging heavily in the toe.

"As an anchor," Ramona explained in a wistful voice. "It's cracked anyway . . ."

"O-kay," said Juke. "This one with the carbide is the detonator. We pour in warm water, then screw on the lid, tight and fast. Very fast. The pressure of the acetylene gas will build up until it breaks the jar." He looked up at Loach. "Now I ain't sure if this will be enough to set off the TNT. This other jar's tied next to it just in case. It's got the spark."

"Ah," said Loach. "What's going to be the spark?"

"Cigarette," Juke said.

"That's why we were waiting for you, dear," Mona said to Gaby. "We shall have to borrow one of your cigarettes."

"Good luck," Gaby said. "Because I'm fresh out."

"They were dribbling out of everywhere back in Moab," Dr. Jo said. "Check. You're bound to have a butt hidden someplace."

"Now that you *men*tion it—" She ducked demurely away from the group for a moment. When she turned back, she held a bent Chesterfield. "I had a friend in school that taught me always to stash a spare. Her name was Rita. Or was it Darla?"

"Never mind," Dogeye said. "Fire it up and fork it over."

Gaby intended to take a last long lungful, but the smoke no longer seemed to hold its allure. She handed the cigarette to Dogeye. He dropped it into the empty jar, butt-down and smoking.

"Okay," said Juke. "We'll need one big mouthful of water."

"That's me," said Boyle. He bent to the rising water at their feet. He stood over the jar, his cheeks swollen.

"Okay," said Juke. "Who has the lid for the carbide?"

"Right here," Dogeye held it up.

"Okay. Who has the lid for the spark?"

"Here," said Dr. Jo.

"Maybe we better turn on that spotting light, Charles."

"Right," Loach said. "I want to see this."

He dragged the big battery out of Dogeye's pack and flipped the switch. A triangle cut through the darkness, like a wedge from a blackened pie. The bats were dipping in and out of it, their fleshy pink snouts squeaking.

"Ready, Mr. Boyle?" said Juke.

"Mmm-hmm!" Boyle nodded.

"Ladies?"

"Yes, Emmett," the sisters said. They seemed actually fresher than any of the others; years of bickering had prepared them for this ordeal.

"Mr. Makai?"

Rodney's voice was a wood rasp in bad wood. "You left me for the bears."

"He seems to have done some damage to his lower chakra," said Ramona. "He says he squashed one of his orbs. Mr. Boyle had to practically carry him the whole way."

"Mmm," said Boyle.

"Ready, Charles?"

"Looks to me like you got it handled, buddy."

"Somebody's got to throw it. You was always good at that baseball toss. Get ready . . ."

"Yessir," Loach said, stepping into position.

"Okay?" Juke said. Everybody nodded. Juke turned to Dr. Jo. "Lid," he said. She twisted the rubber-ringed top on the jar that held Gaby's smoking Chesterfield. Juke looked up at Boyle. "Spit!"

Boyle squirted his mouthful into the second jar. The pile of gray rocks commenced to fume and fuzz. "Lid!" Juke said. Dogeye was already twisting it on, his hands shaking. When it was snug, Juke handed the whole business over to Loach.

"Throw," he said. "Throw, throw, throw!"

Loach threw. The bomb sparkled through the spot's light, parting a path through the swinging array of bats, the ball providing an ascentric orbit around its momentum. It splashed into the flotsam of scum where Ferrell had vanished, towing a trail of bubbles behind it.

Everyone withdrew to the obsidian foyer where the stream

spread out of the crawlspace. They crouched in anticipation. The big room was silent except for the fizz of water over the obsidian ledge and the whirring of wings. The onlookers leaned toward the big spotlight, still burning where they had left it. They waited for the blast that would liberate or obliterate them. They listened, their eyes widening as though to improve their hearing.

No sound came. There was nothing but the mindless fizzing of the steam, filling the pool.

The spot began to dim. At last Boyle snorted, the sound bubbling up. He snorted again, a prelude to one of his long laughing spells. The round was stopped cold in his chest by a bright flash of phosphorous orange, deep beneath the surface of the pool. This flash rose to the surface, expanding into a flat blister of light, then a knoll, then a hill of water.

298

It exploded, not with the ear-splitting blast they'd been expecting, but with an enormous blat, a blubbery flatulence. Steam spewed up in a geysering column, all the way to the ceiling, then fell back in a flat doughnut of watery ruin. A wave rolled out to the sides of the room, drenching the explorers.

The bats went berserk. The explosion had ruptured their echo-location mechanisms, leaving them completely in the dark. They began rocketing in all directions, bouncing off walls, smashing against limestone curtains and flittering into the water like downed Fokkers.

Slowly the activity subsided. The bats found a place to hang or dropped drowning in the pool. The Society stepped forward, dazed by their fatigue and their situation; here they still were—debris on a black beach. The water hadn't receded an inch.

Loach adjusted the fading lamp toward the shelf behind

him to assess the company's morale. Nobody looked that much different. Gaby clung to his arm, but it wasn't a grip of panic.

"It didn't work," she said.

"O, Great Spirit, King Invisible, Lord of roots and rocks—hear us in our darkest hour!" wailed Mona.

"O, Ye Fates," her sister joined, not to be outdone, "Deliver us in our desperation. We beg for Your Divine Intervention."

None was forthcoming. But Dogeye saw something happening in the shadows overhead.

"Look!" he said. "The damn bats are stirred up again. I wonder if they're like dogs before an earthquake."

Sure enough, the randomness began to give way to a swirling order—a twister about to touch down. The water began coagulating into a huge circular flow.

299

Jocelyn felt she'd seen enough spectacular sights for one speleological tour, but she had to admit that this one was truly awesome—the power of the water, the swinging of the entranced bats. Her spine itself felt as if it were spinning, away, away, as fragmented as the cold corpse of the drowned reporter.

The circle went faster and it began to slurp. The slurping grew louder and louder until suddenly there was a blast of cold air, coming out of the tube at their backs, fresh and clean and stiff, scouring out the whole nasty mess, from soup to bats, from smoke to steam.

The lake began to drain. They watched the water level drawing down, like an inverted theater curtain, revealing snatches of shapes and lines as it raised. Or lowered.

They began to see the wall.

It seemed to be both developing and decomposing in front of Jocelyn's eyes. She walked down the receding shore. The

first thing she was able to make out for certain was the eye—
a stylized, almond-shaped glyph, shadowed in lapis and out-
lined heavily in cracked black against the smooth limestone.
She stared slack-jawed. She knew this form—the Eye of
Horus—but she refused to accept it. Her mind refused to go,
as though its gears had been stripped. She scanned the wall
from side to side, allowing the images to flood into her. She'd
seen something resembling this strange vision before, many,
many times. But not in her dreams, nor in her work. Where?
Then the realization struck her, like a brick hurled by Krazy
Kat.

The Sunday funnies.

That dancing bear with the antlers and the drooping penis?
He was supposed to be the Sorcerer of Les Trois Frères. Why
was Betty Boop riding on his back? The stickman hunter
shooting an arrow? She'd seen him herself, in the Gasulla
Gorge in Spain. Why was his arrow sticking out of the Miche-
lin Man? It was as if someone had simply shuffled an
archeology textbook in with the funny papers. The wall was
some kind of cosmic joke, short-circuiting, one age across
another, a vomit of our collective unconscious, all of the
images potent and familiar and crazed.

All except for the huge blue shape that dominated the
center of the wall. It appeared to be a great bird of prey, its
wings outstretched as though to protect all the rest of the
mad nest beneath. An eagle? She thought of the old hymn
from her Four Square church: "Just as the eagle stirs her nest,
God stirs his people from their rest." She tried to recall an
eagle cult. Her mind was a blank. She could not think of one.
Maybe I'm not seeing this, she thought. That blast, and all
that stuff in the air. Maybe I'm delirious. No, that isn't it. I'm
all right. It's *this* that's making me dizzy—the whole naked,

gaudy, ridiculous fraud of it. Not even a hoax, really. Because who on earth could have ever imagined that they could get away with this? She turned to glare at Loach. He looked like he was as dumbfounded as she had been. Even more so. Then both of them sought another face. They located it behind a guilty whistle.

"Like the feller says," Dogeye shrugged. "Yer pays yer money and yer takes yer chances."

She turned back to the wall. There were three big glyphs at the top—a big R-shaped letter in the middle of two others. The big bird was now fully revealed, the scum peeling away from it in a graceful striptease. She saw now that the creature held a cache of thunderbolts in one claw and a cross in the other, and beneath it, almost totally obscured by reddish crust and its own deterioration, were the peeling remnants of mysterious letters.

Boyle's laughter started in earnest now. "Didn't no redskins paint this wall at all!" he roared.

The blue shape continued to dominate Jocelyn's attention, *who*ever painted it. Other letters were being revealed as the water went down. Jo squinted at the flaking letters, trying to make words out of the fragmented characters. "WE . . . DO . . . OUR . . ." she read slowly, like a child learning to recite. "Our *what?*"

"We do our *part*, you daffy dame," laughed Boyle. "You been tracking around in the wilderness too long. You don't even recognize that vulture Roosevelt's NRA eagle when you see it!"

Jocelyn began to laugh along. It was the same picture she had seen made of blue aquamarines in Dogeye's yard, the same New Deal picture-and-slogan one could see floating in any shop window.

301

"Some day this could be the eighth wonder of the world, Douglas," she said. "Who's to say?"

Boyle answered for Dogeye: "Good waste of dynamite, what I'd say. Whoops! *Look* out!"

The elaborate stone vision began evaporating before their eyes, from the drainhole up, eating itself away, rolling dead bats and debris, old paint buckets and stone daggers, into its growing maw. A bright string of topaz suddenly strung out through the batless air.

Gaby saw it as the thread of life and it was to this slender strand that her attention attached. Though she might expire herself, easily, and with some relief, she could not allow this thread to break. It would be more than the soul could bear. It was too brilliant. Eyes open or eyes closed, she saw the fragile strand clearly, pulsing, personal. We will never be apart, she said to it. If we have to go where dead things go, we'll go there together. I promise. She felt peaceful. She rocked, humming, as the shifting tons of earth rumbled louder.

What wasn't there at the focal point of their projected lights was bigger than any of them could have imagined. Void is too small a word to wrap it in. Each vision ricocheted off the collapsing arch into their own versions of hope—freedom, eternity, peace, transcendence; a moneymaking miniature golf course in Pasadena . . . all were there, wrapped in cellophane wrappers, revealing the raptures within. It was all vast and enticing and possible and melting, like a Baby Ruth in a hot matinee movie.

The chiseled darkness of centuries was cracking, giving way to blue-yellow warmth. Gaby's curiosity pulled her eyes open. Through the downpour of shadows she began to make out the Face of God, smiling down on them from His sunny

302

front porch. His car was parked in the drive—a white DeSoto. An attending angel robed in green called from his shoulder.

"Into the Valley, Kipling!" the green angel squawked.

"Tennyson!" Ramona corrected in an exasperated voice. "Alfred Lord Tennyson!"

The thing that thinks, thought Gaby, has stopped thinking.

"You-all's right on time, Chief."

It wasn't the voice of God. It was the voice of Ned.

Chapter last . . . in the key of light . . .

They were emerging from a marvel of coinciding geological phenomena, the intersection of a lava tube, a limestone cave, and geothermal activity.

The latter had been created first, by several conditions necessary for the formations of fumaroles. For these steam vents to manifest, there must first exist sufficient molten magma beneath layers of surface rock. Then there must be an underground supply of water that reaches the magma in such a way that it is heated and forced upward. Finally, there must be channels leading from the molten subterranean rock to the surface, and these channels must have walls strong enough to withstand the explosive geyser force—tens of thousands of pounds per square inch.

The underground water supply was furnished by melting glaciers, thus it was laced with various minerals scraped from the rocky eons. This mixture percolated down through faulted fissures of porous limestone, that calcium graveyard of biological buildup on a long gone ocean's bed.

This bed had gone dry and the bony deposit of limestone had been heaved upward during a night of the earth's restless snoring. Joints and cracks created in the dense calcium deposits gave them the needed porosity. The same melting ice worked its way through the cracks and excavated a network of cavities through varying layers of limestone and dolomite.

Little by little, the water enlarged the fissures into corridors and galleries. The shaping of these grottos was both mechanical and chemical, perfect examples of erosion and corrosion. The calcium carbonate of limestone was only slightly soluble in pure snow water, but when the water broke through from below it contained, among other things, carbon dioxide, which created carbonic acid. The resultant calcium bicarbonate was easily dissolved, leaving great caverns as it washed away. Some of it found its way to magma below and percolated up again, bringing with it additions of sulphur, argonite, barium sulfate, and pyrite.

305

This nectar of the netherworlds steamed up to the ceiling of the cavern and condensed there, then dripped back into the black pools below. Each drop left its contribution, creating the stone icicle.

The word "stalactite" has a Greek derivation meaning "drop by drop."

As the icicles lengthened through time, the pyrite crystallized together into Cubist sculptures of fool's gold, and the barium sulfate bloomed into a configuration called "red American roses." On the floors, among the building stalagmites, occasional upwells of magma left acidic solutions of minerals. As these solutions cooled, the dissolved minerals precipitated as pegmatites. The pegmatites produced giant crystals of quartz, tourmaline, and gemstone. Oxygen and aluminum welded this brilliant combination together and tinted it with impurities—chrominium atoms turning it a rich ruby red; silicone and beryllium mixing to make sapphire blue.

Sulphur spread here and there over everything like Beelzebub's butter.

It was the sulphur and the silicon that combined with the floating pumice particles of lava foam and the phosphate and urea of the bats' huckleberry-laden manure to create the vermilion aggregate that plastered the rocks and scummed the waters and finally plugged the syphon hole that drained the pool—a guano gunnite.

This speleogenesis had been going on a long, long time before the introduction of the lava tube (not to mention the bats). The little volcano, which had lain inactive since before the coming and receding of the second ice age, was suddenly awakened one night, nine thousand years ago, by the furor some of its kinfolk were kicking up to the west and northwest. Mt. Lassen was unleashing a load of flaming basalt, chunks of which were landing thousands of miles away. Mt. St. Helens was blistering buffalo and incinerating Indians. Mt. Mazama was destroying itself utterly in a Saturday night blast so splendid that it darkened the planet with a hangover of dust and smoke for days afterward. The pit it left became Crater Lake.

Our little volcano tried to join the party, but the best it could manage was one measly pop, like the cork out of a champagne bottle. Still, this was enough to knock down the southeastern rim of the old crater and slosh out a fair serving of lava. The blast cooled but a little trickle of lava continued to leak down the gentle slope, seeking a meandering filigree of channels. The main of these channels found its way to the collapsed entrance of the limestone cavern and fell away

306

there beneath the faulted wall, back toward the core from which it rose.

The subsequent sear of rising chemical steam added the diamond glaze to the underground garden of crystals and chemical buildup. The top of this river of hot rock cooled and hardened while the lava continued to flow within. When it had all flowed away, it left behind a long igneous tube. The workings of surface action covered the top of the tube with blowing loess and snow-cracked boulders and storm-sluiced skree. Lichens and moss found footing in this rubble, then buffalo grasses and burrs.

Finally a few hardy cedars and scrub pines were able to eke out a meager living among the boulders. The yearly fall of their needles leveled over the crack that had been the lava's channel, concealing all evidence of the tube beneath. Fungus and moisture broke the pine needles down, mixing it with dust and ash, creating humus. Now arctic heather blooms where burning rock once ran, and Scenic Highway 298 rambles right across it. Or did, before the cave-in.

307

The huge brightness that filled the eyes, ears, and minds of the spelunkers was all they wanted to think about for a while. Nothing else mattered; the cave had opened to sky. They gorged themselves from the platter of light above them. Finally a hoarse voice broke the silence:

"Bears, Father . . . watch out for bears."

"Yes sir, I sure will," Ned assured him.

"Hell-o, Sailor!" Boyle stepped into the light and gave Ned a sharp salute. "Are you a sight for sore eyes. You piloting my boat these days?"

Ned grinned at the DeSoto, parked not three feet back from the edge of the cave-in. "*Used* to be your boat, Mr. Boyle," he said. "There's been a kind of trade."

"Is everybody all right?" Loach called around him. He stretched to his full height and surveyed the faces. "Gaby, how do you feel?"

"Just dandy," she said, sounding as though she really did.

"Mona? Ramona?" said Loach.

"I've hurt my knee somehow," said Mona.

"Let me take a look," said Dogeye. "Look out, Makai." Rodney was still clinging to the old lady's legs. Dogeye had to pry him loose. He unwrapped the strips of blanket and examined the swollen joint. "Just scraped from crawling," he told the old lady. "As soon as we're up out of here we'll pack it in snow."

"Dr. Caine?" said Loach. "How are you? Are you all right?"

"Oh, some nicks and cuts, but nothing serious."

"Boyle?"

"Need you ask?" said the fat man. "I'm fit as a fiddle."

"That's a *bull* fiddle," cut in Gaby.

"How's Rodney doing?" Loach said to Ramona, whose sisterly burden had just been relieved by Dogeye.

"I think he's plumb lost his senses," the old lady said. "Other than that he seems to be in one piece."

Everyone stared at the pudgy little man. He responded by saying "Bears" again, three times.

"He's beginning to be a little like Mr. Juke was," said Mona.

"He's welcome to it," said Juke.

"If all are present and accounted for, then let's figure out a way to climb out. Ned, if you can locate our old campsite there should be some rope—"

"Locate it? You're practically sittin' in its front yard. I'll be back in a flash." He poked the parrot in the back seat of the DeSoto and dashed out of sight.

Loach took a seat on a boulder next to Dogeye. The prospector was unwrapping Mona's other knee.

"Dog, these caves must be like a mess of damned intestines. Here we've been walking and climbing and crawling for days, but we've hardly gone anywhere."

"It has been my experience," Dogeye said philosophically as he examined the old lady's knee, "that no matter which way you turn, there you are."

Mona gave a thin smile, despite her discomfort. "Oh, I hope so, Dogeye. I *do* hope so."

The trip up the rope lift was slow going for Mona Makai. When she finally reached the top, a pair of black arms came snaking out to grip her under the arms and help her up to safety. Boyle was close behind her. His big body flopped over the rim and his kicking feet disappeared.

"Phew!" said Ned. "Wasn't sure that rope would haul that much ballast."

Dogeye was the last one in the gorge. He patted his belt to make sure that the cluster of stone he had managed to rescue from the crumbling columns was secure. It was deep scarlet and shaped like a Valentine. The Crystal Heart of the Universe! What a great new attraction at the Moab Museum of Natural Curiosities.

Damn if the angels haven't pulled me through another one, he thought. The bright light was bringing his senses back to life. He was still seeing the fantastic swirls of the shattering formations everywhere he looked, and the shards seemed to sugar-coat everything he saw. He looked up. Jocelyn was just being dragged over the rim out of sight. She was dripping wet, and her dangling legs were covered with tendrils of the bat-guano aggregate. His kind of woman, he decided anew. It suddenly occurred to him that he was hungry. The thought of food filled him with glee.

"Hey, Jo!" he whooped. "When we get to Moab, I'm gonna check my cottontail snares and cook you up a *hasen pfeffer* that'll make you forget you ever saw this old hole!"

When Dogeye had been hauled up, the questions began.

"First thing, Ned," Boyle asked, "is I want to hear how you ditched my Whiteshirts."

"Mr. Boyle, them boys weren't at all difficult to fool. I just parked in the first nice bushy dark spot I come to and locked myself inside. When they were all baying and slavering around the doors and windows, I just slipped out through that there one-holer Mr. Dogeye welded on the bottom. I don't think they even noticed me drive off."

He turned to Loach. "Sorry I had to scuttle the ship, Chief. But you know? I'm getting the wearies over this old job anyway."

"I think it's about finished, Ned," said Loach.

Ned looked around the ragged circle, counting silently. "Who's missing?"

"We've suffered one casualty, Ned," Loach replied. "Perhaps two. We lost Mr. Ferrell and Father Paul."

"FAW-THER!" Rodney bawled, suddenly reminded.

"Strikes me as we perhaps have suffered two and three-quarters casualties," Dogeye said.

"Ferrell's down there," Loach continued, nodding toward the collapsed pit. "He did good, Ned. You'd have been proud. Father Paul . . . I don't know. He's somewhere up there."

As Loach raised his eyes to the peaks, so did Dogeye.

"Look!" Dogeye called out. He was pointing off toward the

mountainous skyline. "That peak, beyond our crater . . . I thought I saw something."

Everybody looked. "I don't see anything but rocks and trees," Gaby said.

"There it is again," said Dogeye. "Something pink—"

"Come on, Dogeye," Loach said. "Even you can't see that far. It's ten miles away."

"Well, I saw somethin'," said Dogeye.

"Could have been a dahl sheep," Boyle said.

"Coulda been," Dogeye agreed. "This is mountain sheep terrain . . ."

"It's bears," said Rodney Makai, in a reflective, almost affectionate, wonder. "Bears."

311

On the sunlit eastern slope, Father Paul ascended slowly through the scree. Small ripples of avalanche spread from each step. He was almost to the top. A hundred feet ahead of him the vegetation stopped. Just beyond that, the rock wall of the peak vaulted out of the rubble and leveled into a grassy mountaintop. Paul stopped. He was naked to the waist now. His shoes were gone, too. He turned to view the route he had taken, a tiny meandering of tracks back through the broken pumice.

A gnarled old juniper leaned over the cliff's edge, and Paul used its cablelike roots to pull himself up to the top. He hung in the tree and looked out over the mountains. The rocky peaks broke like waves into the distance. He seemed to hear a distant tinkling.

His crucifix flashed again. Paul pulled it over his head and hung it in the old tree's branches.

Again, he climbed, walking up to the highest angle of the ridge. When he reached the grassy slope at the top, he stood still a moment. The wind pushed his blond hair straight back from his forehead. He ran his thumbs behind the waistband of his shorts and slipped them down to his ankles. He stepped out of them and threw them into the breeze. The sailed in spirals to a green valley beyond.

He heard the ringing for certain now, myriad tiny bells approaching, leading a little flock of three-month lambs and grazing ewes. A black shine of long hair was lifted above the flock, singing. The language sounded to Paul like old Castilian Spanish—a love song.

312

Epilogue . . . happy trails . . .

Winter had stayed its sword as long as was seemly. This was, after all, the first of November. Time for the big push. A legion of seasoned Arctic air was dispatched. It swooped down off the Aleutians and rendezvoused with a Baja jet-stream that was foraging up the coast. The two joined forces, the Arctic Airborne taking command by virtue of its seniority and volume. They parlayed a few hours off the Farallons, exchanging data, gaining moisture and inertia, then, without warning, launched their assault on the dozing continent. The assault devastated northern California with forty-foot breakers, slashed Reno with a bayonet charge of ice. Colorado, Utah, and southern Idaho suffered beneath a blitzkrieg that dropped thirty inches of snow in three hours. The storm marched on across the great plains, setting wind-speed records still unbroken—up to 110 mph! The onslaught was eventually weakened by the warming effect of Chicago.

It paused in Chicago, regrouped, then dropped twenty more inches of snow before being driven out by a rogue high-pressure system from St. Louis. This roving high forced it on across Indiana, through Ohio and Pennsylvania, and finally into New York. Buffalo received the last bitter bombardment of the campaign; smallfire flurries of sleet and temperatures in the teens.

This was the big winter storm of the thirties.

The Society were paradoxically far enough north that they missed the big push. Only the storm's perimeter brushed them as they emerged from the steamy bunker of the cavern, and such little quills of ice as they suffered were generally regarded as an improvement of conditions by the cavern members. All in all, they were lucky—they had enjoyed a long fall and missed a bad freeze.

314

The large family of Basque shepherds from the down-country had been lucky as well. They had been working their herds in the high graze more than a month longer than normally. Usually they had long since driven the sheep down to protected pastures. One might think this Indian Summer was going to stretch on forever. But last night they had smelled the change—in the pines, on the wind. It would come today. All the family was spread out in all directions to bring the wayward to flock.

Nela, the second eldest daughter of the eldest son, had seen the flashing that was Father Paul. She was perplexed. This was an unusual thing to see, this high, this late—this far from normal human beings. She was even more perplexed when she saw a flutter of cloth, like a white bird flushed out of a naked tree.

Nela gave him her hooded goatskin to shield him from the thorny rain. Later, she would alter it in the shoulders.

He never uttered a word, though they found that he seemed to understand Latin. They named him *Le Retrouvé*—

"Found-Again One." The following spring, Nela gave birth to their first child, a son. He had his father's eyes and they named him Jack.

In the spring, Gaby gave birth to a daughter. Sometimes she called the little girl Eva; sometimes Jean. To support her hungry offspring Gaby got work as an assistant to one of Jocelyn Caine's old students in a Fresno biological supply house. Gaby lived in a room above the lab and saved her money. Eva Jean graduated from the University of California Medical School in 1959, a pediatrician.

With Rodney's influence, Juke became a recording engineer in Culver City. He won three Oscars for sound.

Rodney Makai moved into the vacated Makai mansion. For years he was reported to be writing a book. He was seen less and less in public. He disappeared in 1941 on a trip abroad, reputedly seeking his aunts for money. The lorry he was riding plunged into a lake in the Black Forest. However, in 1964, on the day of the death of Doctor Loach in Moab, a shrouded man appeared in the basement doorway of the old, old Temple—at the time the practice room of a group of hirsute musicians. He hovered there for more than a week. When the band vacated the premises this specter moved in. Temple of the Cavern tours are conducted from noon to five, Thursdays and Fridays, 9:00 p.m. till midnight. The cost of a tour is $3.00 per person, nuns free.

The ensuing years revealed that the Makai sisters had manifested their famous spirit knock with their respective kneecap and toebone. Mona's damaged knee prevented her from further plying her spiritualist trade effectively and her clientele diminished. In her subsequent frustration and bitterness, she lashed out against Ramona, exposing her sister's knockings as "hideously fraudulent—all done with a popping of the toe joint, just like cracking your knuckles!" Ramona in her turn exposed Mona: "The knee! She did it with her knee! And that she can't *do* it anymore after crawling around in that unholy cave of hers is *exactly* why she's spreading these perverications about me!"

Seeking new crannies, the sisters left America and shipped to Europe on separate liners. They traveled the rest of their years about the Continent, always to settle in a nation not inhabited by the other. All communication between the pair ceased.

The two old women died on Arbor Day, 1956, at sunset, two nations apart yet within ten minutes of each other.

After his experience in the cavern, Boyle disbanded the Whiteshirts and converted back to his Baptist upbringing. He moved his family to Seattle and clipped a coupon from the back of an issue of *Fate*—YOU CAN BE A BROADCASTER. During the Second World War he became a well-known radio evangelist. He made several million dollars before he was photographed outside the Seelbach Hotel in Louisville with a black prostitute.

Jocelyn Caine died on October 15, 1984, at the age of ninety. In 1955, as professor emeritus of the Department of Archeology at Stanford, she won the Hoffmann Research Science Award for her work on the Chaco Canyon Anasazi cliff dwellings.

Douglas Loach continued to expand the Secret Cave Wing of the Moab Museum of Natural Curiosities, creating the Crystal Heart of the Universe Exhibition and the Tube of Death. The Museum later added antique carnival rides, becoming an internationally known attraction due to an ad campaign of thousands of rhyming roadside signs. "Dogeye's Barbecue Juice" is still marketed in East Coast delis.

316

Ned Blue developed an interest in ornithology. Back in Vallejo, he opened an exotic bird shop called "Birds of a Feather." The elite and the aristocratic of the ornithological set came from all parts of the world to trade lore at Ned's shop. Ned himself became somewhat of a welcome rarity, occasionally glimpsed driving around San Francisco in the back of a long black limousine, a parrot perched regally on his shoulder.

There is no conclusive evidence as to what happened to Chick Ferrell. Perhaps he was offered by the whirlpool—a poached repast for the coyotes where the stream emerged down the slope. Perhaps he rotted in big old pieces of meat underground. Perhaps he is trapped in some mineralized crevice, on his back, his eyes wide open at the stars, asking, "What day is this?"

317

About the Authors

ROBERT BLUCHER grew up in Redmond, Oregon, and now lives in Eugene with his wife, Suzi, and Ivan the Terrible, a blue Persian cat. Blucher played trumpet with a San Francisco rock band called Peter Cosmos and the Universal Quantifiers and has taught computer science, philosophy, and playwrighting. He is currently writing a screenplay about a small-time psychobabble con man which examines the question: "If the wise man plays the fool and the fool pretends to be wise, what then of the drama critic?"

Walt's Photography

About the Authors

BEN BOCHNER is a writer and singer. In 1987 he released an album of original songs called *The Broken Place.* He is now working on a book about tree climbing in the Pacific Northwest, tentatively entitled "Last Stands."

JAMES FINLEY grew up in Spokane, Washington. After earning his M.F.A. in Creative Writing at the University of Oregon and sojourning briefly in Europe and New England, he has returned to his beloved hometown to finish up work on his first novel— a tale of "love and suffering" set in a small north Idaho community.

JEFF FORESTER studied rhetoric at the University of Illinois, then drove around the country in a van, following the Dead and selling sandwiches to get by. He worked on a schooner out of Martha's Vineyard, on a farm in West Virginia, at a ski resort in Montana, and cut wood on the Masabe Iron Range, all the while writing on an old Royal manual bolted down in the van. After a Chicago interlude, during which time he wrote corporate newsletters, résumés, and scripts for murder mystery parties, he moved to Eugene, Oregon, arriving on April Fools' Day.

About the Authors

BENNETT TRACY HUFFMAN was born in Pomona, California, in 1963. He received his B.A. from the University of Redlands, then traveled through Japan (where he lived for a year), Siberia, Europe, and North America. He earned his M.F.A. in fiction from the University of Oregon in 1989. He is currently working on a speculative-fiction novel, a post-Apocalyptic tale of the emergence of new tribes among the survivors.

LYNN JEFFRESS grew up on the Oregon coast in Waldport and attended Gonzaga University. From there she went to Paris. In 1981 she received a Ph.D. from the University of Oregon in Romance Languages, and in 1988 an M.F.A. in Creative Writing. She has completed a collection of short stories, "I Want to Go Home with the Armadillo." Now living in her hometown, she is teaching a group screenplay writing and video production course she developed for Oregon Coast Community College, modeled on her experiences in the Kesey group novel class. She is a fiction editor for *Northwest Review,* and codirector for Moon Fish, the first annual Summer Program in the Arts in Yachats, Oregon. She is currently coauthoring a screenplay.

About the Authors

KEN KESEY was born in Oregon, where he still lives. He graduated from the University of Oregon and later studied at Stanford with Wallace Stegner, Malcolm Cowley, Richard Scowcroft, and Frank O'Connor. *One Flew Over the Cuckoo's Nest,* his first novel, was published in 1962. His second novel, *Sometimes a Great Notion,* followed in 1964. *Kesey's Garage Sale* provided a highly personal portrait of the author and his friends, with whom he shared many extraordinary experiences in the 1960s. His third novel, *Demon Box,* was published in 1987.

NEIL LIDSTROM grew up on a farm outside Prineville, in the Crooked River valley of central Oregon. His family raised wheat, potatoes, and alfalfa on four hundred irrigated acres. After attending the University of Oregon for his freshman year, he moved to Oregon State for engineering, then moved to physics, and finally got his degree in math. He was in the graduate program in writing at the University of Houston for a year, then came home to get married. Neil, his wife, Beth, and her father, Norville, live in a red house on a hill in Summit, Oregon, with Starker forest for a backyard. They have two

goats, a fourteen-year-old dog, Lou, and a hell of a lot of cats.

H. HIGHWATER POWERS grew up in a crumbling textile town in upstate New York. After high school he took a Greyhound to Kentucky, intending to become a preacher. Somewhere between Kentucky Wesleyan College and Vietnam he instead became a reporter/photographer, with an M.A. in Journalism from Southern Illinois University. Working in the flatland towns of Kentucky, Indiana, and Illinois, writing stories about coal, corn, and soybeans, he won several national awards for news reporting—but wanted to write fiction. He borrowed a friend's hat, packed his typewriter and a few books, and moved to Eugene, Oregon. He has published many short stories in little magazines, and now teaches composition at Central Oregon Community College at Bend.

323

JANE SATHER was born in Torrance, California, in 1962. She began writing at the age of ten and graduated from California State University, Long Beach, in 1985 with a B.A. in English and Creative Writing. In 1989 she received an M.F.A. in Creative Writing from the University of Oregon. She

About the Authors

About the Authors

and her husband, the composer Blake Hodgetts, have one daughter, Angelica, "conceived during *Caverns*."

CHARLES VARANI was born of peasant stock in Detroit in 1955 and graduated from Wayne State University in 1977. His work history includes six years as a police officer, as well as time spent in drug sales (legal), delivery work, bookselling, teaching, and, most recently, bug trapping. In 1989 he took his M.F.A. from the University of Oregon and is currently living somewhere in America with his wife, Sue, and daughter, Kira. He is at work on a novel, a maximalist comedy about the collapse of Western Civilization.

324

MEREDITH WADLEY, a displaced fifth-generation Texan, was reared in a career military family. She's lived in Oregon since 1974 and has worked picking strawberries, filing and typing, training horses and young riders, teaching writing to children and college students, and trapping gypsy moths. After discovering that the university campus life was a perfect, and much healthier, surrogate for life on military bases, she completed her bachelor's degree in History and finished an M.F.A. in Creative

Joel Morton

About the Authors

Writing at the University of Oregon. She is now working on a novel, as well as a collection of short stories centering on military family life during the Vietnam era.

LIDIA YUKMAN lives among wolves. A resident of Florida, Texas, Boston, and Washington before coming to Oregon, she says of her life, "It would make a good story." Perhaps someday it will.

KEN ZIMMERMAN was raised in several foreign countries, including Alabama, Texas, Thailand, Turkey, and San Francisco. Despite the fact that his poetry has been published in many literary magazines, he still dreams of becoming a writer.

FOR THE BEST IN PAPERBACKS, LOOK FOR THE

In every corner of the world, on every subject under the sun, Penguin represents quality and variety—the very best in publishing today.

For complete information about books available from Penguin—including Pelicans, Puffins, Peregrines, and Penguin Classics—and how to order them, write to us at the appropriate address below. Please note that for copyright reasons the selection of books varies from country to country.

In the United Kingdom: For a complete list of books available from Penguin in the U.K., please write to *Dept E.P., Penguin Books Ltd, Harmondsworth, Middlesex, UB7 0DA*.

In the United States: For a complete list of books available from Penguin in the U.S., please write to *Dept BA, Penguin*, Box 120, Bergenfield, New Jersey 07621-0120.

In Canada: For a complete list of books available from Penguin in Canada, please write to *Penguin Books Ltd, 2801 John Street, Markham, Ontario L3R 1B4*.

In Australia: For a complete list of books available from Penguin in Australia, please write to the *Marketing Department, Penguin Books Ltd, P.O. Box 257, Ringwood, Victoria 3134*.

In New Zealand: For a complete list of books available from Penguin in New Zealand, please write to the *Marketing Department, Penguin Books (NZ) Ltd, Private Bag, Takapuna, Auckland 9*.

In India: For a complete list of books available from Penguin, please write to *Penguin Overseas Ltd, 706 Eros Apartments, 56 Nehru Place, New Delhi, 110019*.

In Holland: For a complete list of books available from Penguin in Holland, please write to *Penguin Books Nederland B.V., Postbus 195, NL-1380AD Weesp, Netherlands*.

In Germany: For a complete list of books available from Penguin, please write to *Penguin Books Ltd, Friedrichstrasse 10-12, D-6000 Frankfurt Main I, Federal Republic of Germany*.

In Spain: For a complete list of books available from Penguin in Spain, please write to *Longman, Penguin España, Calle San Nicolas 15, E-28013 Madrid, Spain*.

In Japan: For a complete list of books available from Penguin in Japan, please write to *Longman Penguin Japan Co Ltd, Yamaguchi Building, 2-12-9 Kanda Jimbocho, Chiyoda-Ku, Tokyo 101, Japan*.